Silent
echo

MW00914507

Silent Echo

Elisa Freilich

DIVERSIONBOOKS

For all my family, past and present.
I carry you with me always.

Diversion Books
A Division of Diversion Publishing Corp.
443 Park Avenue South, Suite 1008
New York, New York 10016
www.DiversionBooks.com

For more information, email info@diversionbooks.com

First Diversion Books edition September 2013.

Print ISBN: 978-1-62681-134-8
eBook ISBN: 978-1-626810-76-1

"So spoke they, sending forth their glorious song, and my heart longed to listen…"

—Homer, *The Odyssey*

Prologue

The fluttering of the birds' wings against the windshield produced a steady noise not unlike the whirring of a fan.

He looked over at the pained face of his wife. She was at the peak of labor, her contractions only two minutes apart. Her water had broken several hours ago, and despite his demands to leave immediately for the hospital, Helena had insisted on waiting it out, determined to relish the birth of their first child in the comfort of their own home.

Joshua had only conceded knowing that in Ridgewood there wasn't likely to be much traffic. Their worst delay might be having to wave to a familiar pedestrian.

But this roadblock could never have been foreseen. They were everywhere—the feathers, the flapping wings. When the first one had landed, a snowy white creature with clouded jade eyes, he had thought nothing of it. Swerving gently, Joshua was surprised that the bird held its ground, welcoming its identical twin, who swooped down and landed firmly on the hood of the car.

And then an avalanche.

Identical white birds streaming down in droves, their verdigris eyes boring curiously beyond the windshield.

She cried out in pain.

"Please," she pleaded with her husband, her voice barely above a whisper. "Please get me some help."

Joshua looked over at his wife. Her milky complexion, now blue as a flame, had taken on an unnatural translucence, revealing the frenetic pumping of blood through her veins.

But trapped inside the chrysalis of feathers and beak, there was no way to maneuver the car forward. Or in any direction, for that matter.

"I'm so sorry, baby, I can't see a thing…"

He tried prompting the flock to leave with a few angry bursts of the horn. But the sound only propelled the beating of their wings. And with each new unwelcome visitor, a sterile labor and delivery room became a fantasy reserved for another universe.

Dialing 911, Joshua tried maintaining his composure. He could sense the operator's skepticism until Helena let out a fortuitous moan, lending an undeniable truth to his tale. He tried pinpointing their location. Where *were* they anyway?

While he attempted to gain his bearings, Helena became entranced by the thumping of the giant wings. The percussion was a sponge, soaking up her anxiety at being trapped. The vibration of the wings made its way down her spine, relieving the immense pressure in her belly.

With a burst of sudden clarity Helena knew that this was going to be the birthplace of her child. Right here, on Thornton Road. There would be no hospital and no Dr. Schein. Joshua would have to deliver this baby and she felt it coming. Fast.

The birds continued to flock to the car, forming a layer three deep. Nestling their heads into one another, they hastened the rhythm of their wings, their movements in perfect unison. She stared them down and, as they returned her gaze, the balloon that was her swollen body was untied, her pain released in a slow and steady stream, replaced by an utter sense of calm.

There were only the birds now.

Never mind the fruitless attempts of her husband to open the car door against the impenetrable suction. No recognition of his own panic, his own understanding that if she didn't make it through this, there would be no tomorrow for either one of them.

And still, the birds remained.

The creatures lifted their heads up, one by one, revealing their aged green eyes. Helena basked in the comfort of the winged voyeurs, grateful for the way they had reversed the current of her pain.

"It's coming," she whispered to Joshua.

Joshua surrendered any vestiges of calm to which he had been clinging, his face a mosaic of horror and shock.

"What? You mean now?"

And before Helena could even answer, the child emerged. Joshua caught the tiny creature in the bath towel they had grabbed as an afterthought just before leaving the house.

"Oh my God, Helena, it's a girl!" His voice trembled, unable to find solid ground. "She seems perfect! Oh my God—"

Helena looked down at the child. She was perfect. A small silken tuft of brown hair sat like a crown atop her delicate skull. Her fingers were long and graceful, tiny papery nails topping each one. Her lips were full, forming a perfect ruby heart.

Joshua started wiping the child clean, offering his wife words of endearment and praying that the paramedics would arrive soon. But his words floated away like particles of dust. There was no room for them in the air, which had become filled with the cries of the newborn.

The thumping of the birds' wings began to fade, offering center stage to the cries of the baby. Gradually, one by one, they flew away, forming a perfect arrow as they soared into the dusky sky.

When the last one was gone, the baby's cries became a tornado, sucking away all other sounds and sights. The storm of the infant's tears held within it a somnolent melody, every sob the next movement in the tearful symphony.

Joshua and Helena struggled to keep their eyes open; deep sleep was suddenly beckoning them. The sounds of the child were a quicksand. And they were being pulled under.

Just as they were about to be submerged completely, the arrival of the paramedics jolted Helena, awakening her maternal instincts. She drew her new daughter to her breast, amazed at her ability to nourish the child from her own body. The baby fell silent as she began to suckle, breaking the dreamy spell that had been wielded by her tears.

Helena ran a gentle fingertip over the velvety cheeks of her new daughter. They would call her Portia, just like they had talked about.

"I will never grow tired of hearing your voice, little Portia," whispered the proud mother to her new daughter.

She could never have known then that for the next sixteen years the child would not make another sound.

Part One

Sixteen Years Later

Portia

Chapter 1

Portia turned the volume up on her iPod as the bus pulled up in front of Charlotte's house. Jeff Buckley's anguished voice coursed through her as he alluded to that magical secret chord that David once played for the Lord.

Not the most upbeat of the more than 7,000 songs she had accumulated over the years, but there was something about the lyrics to "Hallelujah" that always calmed her. And this morning she really needed an extra dose of calm.

How could Helena have stressed me out like this on the first day of school?

She had recently taken to referring to her mother by name—of course, to Helena's face, she still signed out "Mom," though this morning a few other words had come to mind.

A fresh wave of anger washed over her as she recounted the morning's events.

Things had actually started off well. Portia had allowed herself a few extra moments in front of her mirror, admiring her finally wireless grin. Figuring that she was now a sophomore and should therefore look the part, she had even applied a smattering of blush and lip gloss before heading downstairs.

She knew that Helena would comment on the length of her skirt, and her mother did not disappoint. Before she even took the last stair, her mother charged her, giving the plaid skirt an ineffectual tug.

"I can't believe those new uniforms I ordered didn't come yet. You're lucky your father had an early meeting. He'd never let you out of the house like this, Portia. When did your legs get to be so, so…" Portia watched her mother struggle for the right word—knobby and gangly were suddenly no longer in the running. "Umm…sultry?"

OK, so that wasn't necessarily a compliment one wanted to receive from one's mother, but Portia took it in stride and had even affected a mock pose, hip jutted, one arm raised gracefully in the air.

"Oh, sweetie, you look beautiful." Helena stroked her daughter's cheek with the back of her hand.

And that's when it happened. The gesture that had landed Portia a million deadly blows over the last sixteen years. Was Helena even remotely aware of the pain she inflicted every time she passed the pad of her thumb over her daughter's useless lips? Always with that *almost* imperceptible flash of disappointment in her eyes.

Almost—but not quite.

Portia's mental recap of the morning was interrupted when Charlotte Trotter boarded the bus, her expression as sullen as ever. She tried waving to her neighbor and was, as had become the case over the past five years, ignored. Oh well. She wasn't in the mood to deal. She had her own wars to wage as she braced herself for the one line in Leonard Cohen's lyrical masterpiece that had always cut her to the quick. The one where, against her victim's will, the seductress draws a hallelujah from her broken lover's lips.

Is that what Helena was expecting? That the mere touch of her fingertip would draw words, a single word, even a sound from Portia's silent lips? Portia had spent years trying to accept her voiceless self. All those doctor appointments, each diagnosis more inconclusive than the next. One time she was sure that they had finally cracked the code. A small mass detected at the base of her larynx would no doubt be what was causing the problem. But further testing showed the growth to be benign, not even worth removing. After this final letdown, Portia swore she would never allow another doctor to take a light to her useless throat.

She had hoped by now that her parents' expectations would have dwindled just like her own. After all, it's not like they had any lack of communication. Between signing, texting, and e-mailing, Portia felt like she was always mid-conversation with her parents.

When she was little, she used to indulge in lofty fantasies that would have her telling her parents over and over again just how much she loved them. She imagined thanking her father aloud for every time he kicked a soccer ball around with her or her mother for always alphabetizing her spelling words—an assignment she dreaded above all others.

But the years of silence wore on and, as Portia grew up, so did her fantasies. Reciting a Shakespearean soliloquy or def jamming a Nicki Minaj track were more probable goals these days.

Most recently, though, Portia had decided that fantasizing was a total waste of her time. Well, with one exception that is.

The birds.

The birds were the one thing she couldn't resist. Not just the reality of them—their colors, their wingspans, each one's unique flying pattern. But Portia also felt a constant need to eavesdrop on their calls, to be enveloped by their chorus. She loved nothing more than to spend hours getting lost in the aerial conversations of her favorite creatures, superimposing her own thoughts and feelings into their beautiful cries. All the things that she herself could never say. Could never sing.

Her favorite was the Red-winged Blackbird, whose male would sing out fervently to attract a female mate while the female would chatter back at him like a fishwife. Portia spent many hours projecting her own inane conversations onto these creatures.

"Yo, Blackie, I saw you at the bird bath today wooing that Blue Jay, Azure. What gives?"

"Come on, Robin, meet me in my crib. You know my nest only has room for two…"

But that was her only fantastical indulgence these days. Mostly she tried to stay grounded in reality and to focus on the positive things in her life. She had a family who loved her and friends who made her feel almost completely comfortable in her own skin.

And then, of course, she had Felix.

As the bus approached the tree-lined RPA campus, Portia decided to bury the wounds that her mother had inflicted that morning. She was only minutes away from seeing Felix.

And one thing she knew for sure was that voice or no voice, she was always the same to him.

Breathing a sigh of relief, Portia found that, true to his text last night, her locker was right next to Felix's. He must have called in a favor with the principal—a perk of calling the head of the school "Dad."

Where was Felix anyway?

She scanned the crowded hallways and spotted Kate, one of Felix's three sisters, talking to an impressively tall and broad guy.

Must be someone on the football team.

Portia liked Kate and thought of weaving her way over, but she preferred the comfort of the social sidelines and began setting up her locker instead. Looking around, she couldn't help but note that her locker décor was minimalist, to say the least. She spotted her friend Jacqueline Rainer across the hall, placing an obscenely large magnetic mirror in the center of a collage of pictures. She often teased her friend about her vanity, though secretly wished she could soak up some of her self-confidence.

Yeah, well, if I looked like Jacqueline, I'd also be hanging a mirror front and center.

And the locker to the left of hers was a virtual Teen Beat shrine, pictures of pop stars cut and plastered about in a free-form collage, outrightly accusing her own locker of being completely lackluster.

Hanging a magnetic message board on the outside of the door, she thought for a minute of what else she could add to spruce things up. A picture of J.K. Rowling? Steve Jobs? These were the true idols of her life.

As she unpacked her last notebook, she remembered a picture she kept in her wallet of her and Felix—a snapshot from when they were little and had fallen asleep together in the hammock, contentedly nestled into one another. It was one of her favorites. She was taping the picture to the inside of her locker door when suddenly a grip on her shoulders startled her.

Turning around, Portia expected to look right into the familiar black eyes of her best friend, but instead found that she was now barely eye level with Felix's jawline. And what was this? Was there actually a five o'clock shadow on that jawline?

Taking in the full view of her evolved Felix, suddenly she realized that *he* had been the giant she had spotted with Kate before. He must have grown a foot in height and breadth while he was away!

Feeling tiny beside him, she craned her neck to assess him. What were once features too bold for his childish face—a nose too long, onyx eyes burrowed deep inside his brow—had now settled comfortably onto this more mature countenance. And it wasn't lost on her that his expanded physique really knew how to exploit the slim cut shirt of the school uniform.

His mess of black hair had also grown over the last three months and was the perfect finishing touch to his evolution. Resisting her inclination to reach out and tousle it, she allowed a huge smile to erupt as she wholeheartedly approved of the boy-turned-man who stood before her. She wouldn't have classified Felix as conventionally good-looking, but in terms of exoticism, her best friend was deserving of high marks. Besides, conventional was boring.

"You got your braces off! Why didn't you text me?!" His voice was deeper than she had remembered, but the clarity of his speech was as impressive as ever. Ever since he had lost his hearing, Felix prided himself on honing whatever verbal skills he had already acquired in the first seven years of his life.

Portia signed her reply.

"I wanted to surprise you."

"Well, you did—you look awesome! Maybe now you'll even smile once in a while." He pulled her in for a bear hug.

She could feel the definition of his biceps through the cotton of his shirt. Quick to pull away, she signed, "You must have grown a foot!"

He smiled. "I know—my grandmother couldn't stop feeding me! It was unbelievable! You should have seen the feast she laid out for mine and Dean's big birthday bash!"

"Yeah, well, you can't blame her—not every grandmother gets to celebrate her favorite grandsons' birthdays on the same day," she signed enthusiastically. "My summer was also a total food fest—Helena had the Food Network going 24/7. My dad and I felt like Hansel and Gretel the way she was stuffing us!" Portia squeezed an imaginary inch at her belly.

"Trust me," assured Felix, "you don't look like a Gretel."

"And you don't look like a Felix. At least not my Felix. Were you working with a personal trainer out there in the boonies of Quebec? You're busting out of your shirt!"

He shrugged and ran his hands carelessly through his mess of hair, revealing a giant scab, shaped a bit like the boot of Italy, looming high on his forehead.

"What happened to you?"

His face hinted at mischief as he touched the wound. "Oh, this? That was how my grandfather celebrated the Felix–Dean birthday this year. He bought us ATVs! I guess we got a little carried away—no big deal."

"Yeah, well, you always get carried away when you're with your cousin—"

"You mean my brother from another mother—"

"Yes, your brother from another mother. And your grandfather's not exactly helping things by buying you guys ATVs—"

As their banter continued, Portia was momentarily distracted by a sudden warmth radiating throughout her body.

"Are they running the AC in here today?"

"Not sure," Felix said offhandedly.

The heat persisted, prickling her skin, and was quickly followed by a mild tickle in her throat.

Ignoring what was probably just a case of first day jitters, Portia realized that Felix was taking in her full person just as she had done with him.

"Anyway, wow," he said, "where's the string bean I left here before break?"

She wasn't sure how to address his reference to her recently formed figure.

"Guess I'm a bit of a late bloomer," she signed, avoiding his eyes.

"Guess so," he answered approvingly. An awkwardness ensued. "I don't think I've ever seen you so, umm, tan…"

"Yeah, well, I think my bird-watching bordered on obsessive this summer."

"I'm sure it did. You're such a freak, Portia," he said playfully.

Portia would have ordinarily come back with a witty retort, undoubtedly aimed at Felix's own obsessions with hockey or football, but the tickle in her throat was worsening, segueing into an unwelcome constriction. She tried swallowing away the clog in her windpipe, her eyes tearing at the effort.

Bent over his locker, Felix failed to notice her malaise.

"So yeah, anyway," he stood back up, looking like the cat who swallowed the canary, "I have something for you." He revealed a wrapped gift from behind his back and placed it into Portia's hands.

"What's this?!" she mouthed silently. Gift exchanging was not usually part of their repertoire.

"It's just something I saw that I wanted you to have."

Portia looked up into Felix's eyes. Sometimes it was hard to see beyond the thick black fringe of his lashes. But once she got past, she could still see the spark. That same spark that she saw in that little boy who had saved her all those years ago.

How long had it been since that fateful day? The day she secured what Felix adoringly called the "Ridgewood Prep World Cup." A bit dramatic for a third grade soccer match, but it had been a pivotal event for both of them.

Lifting her tiny self into the air, Portia had pulled off a mind-blowing, goal-scoring bicycle kick. It was one of those perfect moments until, out of nowhere, Zachary Wilson knocked her down to the ground, his anger fueled at being upstaged by a girl with pigtails and tiny cleats.

She had landed with tremendous force on her right knee,

and the whole class had braced themselves for the ear-piercing cries that would surely follow such an attack. When none came, they had assumed that Portia was fine and immediately turned their attention back to Zachary, who was being carded by the coach.

Except Felix.

"Are you OK?" he had approached her. She wondered at the uniqueness of his speech and looked up at him, her eyes misted with tears, revealing the answer to his question.

She shook her head and pointed to her throat, indicating its uselessness. He shook his head back and, to her amazement, pointed to his ears, indicating their equal measure of uselessness.

He had propped her up against his shoulder and supported her weight all the way to Nurse Leucosia's office. And from that moment on, they were inseparable.

An unlikely pair of best friends, together Felix and Portia navigated their way through the winding roads of middle school and high school, communicating with what to them was a natural combination of signing, mouthing, talking, and lip-reading.

Felix had taken some razzing for having a girl as his best friend, but growing up in a house full of women, he was up to the task. So while other kids were busy giving each other cooties vaccines in the playground—a foolproof procedure involving the tracing of two circles and three dots onto the back of a friend's hand—Felix and Portia were off in their own world of childhood wonder.

Her stroll down memory lane was interrupted by the nagging sensation that her body's thermostat was completely freaking out.

"Open it already—oh, never mind, I'll open it." Felix grabbed the gift and carefully removed the thick paper wrapping. She didn't argue with him as the heat traveled into her limbs, weakening them and sparking a steady tremor. Nonetheless she was delighted when into her trembling hands he placed an ancient oversized volume of Audubon bird illustrations.

The gift was perfect, and she hoped that he sensed her gratitude despite her being distracted by the growing constriction in her throat.

"I found it lying around a secondhand bookshop when I was out with my grandfather one day. Wait until you see some of these drawings. The detail is amazing!"

"This must have cost you a fortune," she managed to sign.

"Do I look worried?" Felix responded. "Just enjoy it."

Portia cautiously fingered the leaves of the book. The illustrations were breathtaking, drawn with meticulous perspective. Flipping through the pages, she stopped at one breed that was unfamiliar to her. A white bird with snowy feathers, its wings disproportionately large for its body, its green eyes clouded and muddied. A plumed Mona Lisa, those eyes followed her no matter which way she angled her head. Something about it was unnerving.

She looked up at Felix, who had been sidetracked by the arrival of Luke and Lance O'Reilly. The twins were ribbing their friend about Ellen Chadwicke.

"Hey, if I knew the sign language interpreter would be so hot, I think I might consider going deaf, too." Lance was speaking and signing at the same time. When their friendship with Felix had sprouted, the twins had challenged each other to see who could learn to sign better. Lance was definitely in the lead.

Felix good-naturedly pointed out to the brothers that he had become something of a giant over the summer and could probably take them both with his eyes closed.

"Yeah, well, don't keep 'em closed too long," shot Luke, "Lance is right—Ms. Chadwicke is looking f-i-n-e." He challenged his brother by signing out the letters to the word with great flair.

Portia ignored their conversation and looked back at the book. Reaching her hand out to stroke the lifelike drawing, her fingers recoiled as they met the true texture of silken feathers. And she could have sworn that a moment ago the bird's head was facing left.

Now it stared at her full on.

And then it blinked its muddied eyes.

She snapped the book shut and steadied herself against her locker.

What the hell is wrong with me this morning?

She knew her mind was playing tricks on her and wondered if this unprecedented dementia was somehow related to the hot flash and throat constriction that had not yet eased up entirely.

Before heading off, the O'Reillys offered Portia a quick hello, which she barely acknowledged.

"What's the matter, Portia? You look hot, too, it's just, well, you know, Ms. Chadwicke is a woman. Although, I gotta say, you're looking pretty womanly yourself. You're really working that whole olive-skinned, blue-eyed—"

"Brown-haired, full-mouthed—is 'full-mouthed' an expression?" Luke had picked up where Lance had left off.

"OK, that's enough. Move along, boys. Nuthin' to see here." Felix ushered the brothers along and then returned his attention to Portia.

"So, do you like it?"

If I weren't coming down with some kind of hallucination-inducing flu, I'd be jumping for joy.

Instead she looked up at him and crossed her hands over her heart.

"I know, I know. I'm a lovable guy. What can I say?"

Looping her arm through his, Portia forced a grin, hoping Felix wouldn't notice her firm grip, the way she was allowing him to help support her weight. She felt unsteady, completely shaken by the bird's movement and the silkiness of its feathers that should have felt like nothing more than the parchment upon which they were printed. Luckily, at least her limbs had started to regain their strength, and the hot flash was ebbing away.

But as they walked together to first period, she couldn't help but notice the look of sheer delight on Felix's face.

"What?" she mouthed the word silently.

"Nothing—I'm just happy that Zachary Wilson pummeled you that day, you know?"

"Me too, Felix." Though her words were silent, she hoped that they resonated in the deaf ears of her best friend.

Chapter 2

The dining hall at Ridgewood Preparatory Academy was the favored hangout on any given school day. Glowing with the light of giant leaded glass windows, the dark maple wood tables, laid out in perfect symmetry, offered each grade its own area to eat. With a student body of only 427 students, lunchtimes were rarely staggered, offering a unique sense of camaraderie between upper and lower classmen. The hall was especially loud on the first day of school while everyone caught each other up on their summers.

"Hey there, care to dine with a hearing-impaired sophomore?" Portia was comforted to hear Felix's familiar voice in the sea of noise.

"I don't know," she signed back, "the whole 'handicapped' thing doesn't really do much for me." She smiled at her own joke. She was feeling a lot better and had convinced herself that the morning's hallucination was just first-day nerves. OK, maybe there was also some intimidation fueling the morning's episode. Seeing the way Felix had ripened over the summer had been totally unexpected for her.

"I'm gonna have to get used to that thing," Felix said as he pulled two trays and ushered her forward in the lunch line.

"What *thing*?" she mouthed silently.

"You know—the smile. The thing you've barely done for like the last gazillion years."

Portia instinctively brought her hand up to hide her mouth.

"Don't." He eased her fingers away.

They ambled along the lunch line, Felix filling his tray with anything that was being offered. Blessed with a speedy metabolism, Portia loaded up on her favorite—carbs. Spotting

Jacqueline Rainier across the room, they made their way over to her table. Portia set her tray down next to Jacqueline's, shamed at her heap of potatoes and rolls next to Jacqueline's iceberg wedge, its dressing notably on the side.

"Aren't you Frenchwomen supposed to gorge yourselves on Brie and baguettes?" Portia typed the message out on her phone with lightning-fast thumbs.

"Ahh, cherie, you Americans will never really understand us. We are all about le mystere, you see?"

"You should pitch that as a slogan to your dad," Portia typed out. Jacqueline's family had moved to the States two years ago when her father had been promoted to the US division of *Bourgeois*, a cutting-edge cosmetic company. Jacqueline had taken an instant liking to Portia, delighted by the fact that she wouldn't have to suffer another American accent—'Quel horrible!' Portia welcomed the exotic newcomer into her life, especially since Jacqueline loved nothing better than to dominate a conversation.

Portia smiled as she sat down next to Jacqueline, eliciting a torrent of compliments from her friend about her brace-free mouth.

While the gushing continued, the O'Reillys made themselves comfortable next to Felix. Portia had only just come to tell the twins apart, as they really were identical in every way. Luckily she had spotted a tiny freckle on Lance's left thumb last year and now she never mistook one for the other. She used to resist the twins, finding their brusque maleness a bit overwhelming, until she saw what loyal friends they had become to Felix. And if Felix was willing to put up with Jacqueline's constant references to fashion and shopping, then the least she could do was loosen up around the twins.

She was feeling quite content, sitting together in the dining hall and buttering her second crusty roll, when suddenly the heat came back with a vengeance. An intense ache between her shoulder blades also popped up out of nowhere and had her wondering if maybe she was developing some kind of flu.

I sound like my mother, she reprimanded herself. *Stop worrying.*

She stretched her neck from side to side to try to relieve the tension in her back and spotted Charlotte Trotter on the periphery. Her neighbor was snaking her way quietly past Portia's table.

"Charlotte might as well get homeschooled. I mean, if I lived in that mansion, I'd probably never want to leave, and it's not like she ever bothers talking to anyone anyway—"

Luke elbowed his brother and told him to shut up.

The stabbing pain in Portia's upper back worsened as she watched Charlotte find a quiet corner where she settled herself down to a paltry-looking pear and a bottle of water. As always, the shirt of the skeletal girl's uniform was buttoned all the way up to her collarbone and her legs were encased in thick opaque tights despite the heat wave.

Portia struggled to remember when it had all gone so sour with Charlotte. When they were little, she and Charlotte used to have playdates all the time. Portia could remember toddling over with her mom or dad to her next-door neighbor's house, which was then a charming stone farmhouse with a multitude of nooks and crannies, perfect for hide and seek. Back then, Charlotte was still Charlotte Avery. Her father had been such a nice man, always helping the girls devise new games that would not oblige Portia to speak—silent tea parties, exotic scavenger hunts.

And then Michael Avery went to sleep one night and never woke up. He was thirty-four.

Portia had tried being there for her friend when her father died, but her four-and-a-half-year-old arms were simply too small to wrap around such a senseless tragedy. The girls began to slowly drift and then six months later Janie Avery announced that she was remarrying.

"...that famous architect, Harold Trotter," Portia remembered her parents discussing. "It's so soon, but maybe she's just terrified of being alone…"

Over the years the once-charming farmhouse transformed into a cavernous mansion. With each new wing added, Charlotte retreated further and further away from her friends, from Portia. And then one day Portia was forced to admit that Charlotte had become unrecognizable—hair cut to the quick, dyed jet black, heavy streaks of eyeliner angrily applied. She had even abandoned her own father's last name, legally changing it to Trotter.

The only thing that remained from the house of her youth was the old stone well at the edge of the footpath. Portia had often spotted Charlotte standing outside, peering down into the stone well. She wondered what thoughts were going through the girl's mind while she glared down into the darkness. But after several attempts to break the ice, Charlotte had made it clear to Portia that whatever thoughts she had were for private consumption only.

Still, Portia felt an allegiance to her childhood playmate and hated when her friends made digs at her.

"Lance, perhaps you have a little crush, non?" Jacqueline teased.

"Yeah, Lance," shot Luke, "Me think thou doth protest too much."

"Yeah? Well me think you're an asshole…"

Portia was about to chime in and tell her friends to ease up on her neighbor, but the pain in her back began to intensify, radiating from between her shoulder blades all the way down her spine. Her chest felt tight and the pressure in her throat brought forth a coughing fit. Taking some sips of water, she attempted to calm the episode, wondering what would be causing such a strange combination of symptoms.

Jacqueline was busy applying a fresh coat of lip gloss to her plump lips and from the way Luke and Lance were hanging on Felix's every word, she suspected he was saying something about football.

"…the fumble…going crazy…when they lost…" Felix's voice traveled in and out of her reach. She tried latching onto it to bring herself back to the moment, but it was like trying to grab a moving wave. A ringing in her ears swelled, drowning out the din of the dining hall. Her throat grew tighter and an increasing pressure at the base of her neck made her feel like she was being strangled. As rivers of sweat ran down her face, a fleeting image of the mysterious white bird from the book clouded her mind, sending her heart rate into an altogether new stratosphere. Looking at her wrist, she could actually see the movement of her own pulse, a tiny balloon inflating and deflating at mind-boggling speed.

Portia had always been stoic about issues regarding her health, reluctant to call any extra attention to herself. That fear of an endless cycle of doctor visits always loomed in the back of her mind. She would have done anything to avoid involving her friends in whatever it was that was happening to her. But as her breathing grew more labored, she knew she didn't have a choice.

Grabbing Felix's sleeve, she tried interrupting him. He was so caught up in what he was saying, though, that he held up his hand without even looking her way.

She tugged at him with greater intention.

Finally he turned to look at her. "What? What is it—?" When he saw the strain in her face and the shade of crimson that had flushed her cheeks, Portia suddenly had his full attention. "Oh my God, Portia, what's the matter?"

Panic was snaking its way through every inch of her body. She was afraid of losing consciousness as the room spun faster and faster. The image of the white bird took on a sardonic smile, jolting her with an electric current. Before the attack overtook her entirely, she steadied her trembling hands long enough to sign out two desperate words to Felix.

"Help me…"

Portia could barely remember the walk to the nurse's office. She had a vague sense of déjà vu as she leaned against Felix for support while he escorted her to the small room on the lower level. By the time they got there, the episode had subsided a bit. Entering the sterile office, she collapsed onto the gurney, overwhelmed by an intense weariness.

A deep sleep beckoned her, adding a weight to her eyelids that she didn't even bother to fight off. She drifted off, welcoming the kind of slumber usually reserved for one's own bed. The last thing she remembered before surrendering was Ms. Leucosia thanking Felix and sending him back to class.

As she slept, Portia's dreams traveled into unfamiliar territory. As a person obsessed with the avian world, it wasn't so far-fetched for a winged creature to have a supporting role in one of her dreams. But the ones flying around this reverie were determined to play the lead. The birds were staggeringly white, almost blue in fact, the green of their eyes filmy and clouded.

The breadth of their wingspans seemed endless as they circled her, each one making an odd throaty noise, something like bubble wrap being popped. Portia couldn't place this birdcall, but she knew instinctively that they were beckoning a response from her. Signing feverishly, she tried explaining to them that she couldn't sing back. Even in her dreams she didn't have a voice.

The flock continued to call out more fervently, their collective voices growing louder and louder. The sound was dizzying as Portia spun around and around trying to address the ring of birds. As their speed increased, it became impossible to distinguish one from the next until suddenly, midflight, the birds converged into one giant creature.

The bird was hard to look at full on, its down whiter than freshly fallen snow emblazoned by the sun. The mutant creature must have stood upward of eight feet tall, its wings stretching for miles. The popping noise had evolved into something altogether explosive as the giant wings flapped back and forth, catching Portia in their breeze.

Portia could feel a looming sense of danger as the winged mutation picked up speed. She was terrified to look into its face, closing her eyes against the fluorescence of the wings. Much as she tried to avoid it, though, there was no escaping the explosive song of the bird, which had suddenly taken on the spoken word.

"Portia, you're all grown up. No more silence…"

"What do you mean?" she signed back, ignoring the fact that she was conducting a conversation with a giant freak of nature.

"You'll know." The creature started laughing, a loathsome sound that was both painful and beautiful.

Portia began floating up to the surface of the slumber, determined to escape the clutches of the unsettling dream.

"Open your eyes, Portia."

The menacing laughter of the bird grew more distant as Portia climbed further and further out of the grip of her sleep. Right before she broke through the surface, the creature drew her back in with one final song. The lyrics were weighty but secondary to the actual beauty of the vocals, which were unparalleled by anything she had ever heard before.

She was caught in the music, her entire person riding the tide of the melody. The oddest combination of euphoria and dread settled over her as part of her longed to remain in the song forever and part of her wanted nothing more than to run for her life.

"OPEN YOUR EYES, PORTIA!"

Her eyes flew open with a start and she found herself curled into a fetal position, Ms. Leucosia's slender hand stroking her forehead. The nurse's touch was a welcome tether back to the real world, her world, where giant winged creatures were reserved for fables and legends. Portia made the universal sign for "something to write with" and then remembered that Ms. Leucosia was fluent in signing.

"Have I been sleeping long?" her weary hands managed.

"About twenty minutes," the nurse said as she took Portia's wrist in her hand, feeling for a pulse.

Portia could not believe it had only been twenty minutes. She felt like she had been sleeping for hours. Her limbs were heavy and a dense headache had settled itself in for what she was certain was going to be a long visit. Mostly she longed for a toothbrush to rid herself of the thick pasty feeling that had developed in her mouth.

Once she awoke, only brief fragments of her dream were retrievable—the strange noises of the birds, their aged eyes, the enormity of the one giant winged creature. Something specific was gnawing at her, something the creature had said just before she woke up. What was it?

Jolted back to her present surroundings by a pungent, not

altogether unpleasant odor, Portia noticed Ms. Leucosia closing the lid on a glass jelly jar.

"What's that smell?" she signed. She detected lavender and citrus.

"It's just a little homemade remedy I keep on hand. I applied some to your shoulders and back to relieve your pain."

"Thanks," Portia signed, "It feels much better." Indeed the pain had actually subsided and Portia offered Ms. Leucosia a grateful smile.

The nurse smiled back and Portia noticed, not for the first time, what an attractive woman Ms. Leucosia was. Her ivory complexion was the perfect canvas for her scattered freckles and glossy red curls, which she always wore with two braids pinned back on either side. The style really highlighted her eyes, which were a green that was caught somewhere between a Granny Smith apple and the needles of a spruce tree.

"Felix explained what he could to me, but can you tell me what exactly you were feeling?"

Eager to get back to class, Portia tried to minimize the attack.

"I was feeling a little off this morning, and then at lunch I just suddenly felt so tired—"

"Tired would not cause throat constriction, my dear. Is it possible you were, um, nervous about something? Panic attacks in girls your age are actually more common than you would think."

Portia began to rise up off the gurney. If she hurried, she could still make it to her Lyrical Poetry elective on time. Besides, Ms. Leucosia was right. It was probably just a panic attack. After the solitude of summer break, she was probably more nervous than she realized to get back into the swing of things.

"Yes, panic sounds right," she offered the nurse.

Ms. Leucosia flashed her a brilliant smile.

"OK, dear. You may go." She handed over the admission slip and Portia opened the door to make a quick exit.

"Oh, and Portia," the nurse said, her voice smooth as melted butter.

Portia turned back and was once again startled by the

intensity in Ms. Leucosia's grassy eyes, the way her thick lashes grazed at her cheekbones.

"I'll always be here for *you*..."

The door to the office closed just in time for the bell to signal the beginning of the next period.

Chapter 3

When Portia left the nurse's office, Ms. Leucosia's strange parting words had her feeling agitated.

It wasn't as if she made a habit of frequently visiting the nurse. She knew that some girls were regulars, always looking to be excused from gym or a pop quiz, relying on their "monthly visitors" as the perfect scapegoat. But Portia actually enjoyed most of her classes. Even gym.

Was Ms. Leucosia implying that Portia's handicap would necessitate more visits? Portia had never once taken advantage of her condition, and she was angered by the insinuation.

It was more, though, than what the nurse had said that had her feeling unnerved. She couldn't remember telling Ms. Leucosia that she was having pains in her back. Had she rubbed at it in her sleep? And the dream? That twisted dream that still had her skin crawling? It had been so ludicrous, yet had felt so real.

The last one to enter the classroom, Portia stopped dead in her tracks when suddenly the words of the giant bird's song came back to her with perfect clarity.

> *"Beside the bones upon the hill,*
> *We sat to view our latest kill.*
> *And soon you, too, will know the thrill,*
> *The evil from your mouth shall spill…"*

The words were chilling, nonsensical. She tried to put them out of her aching head so that she could focus on the Lyrical Poetry elective in which she had been lucky enough to land a spot. But, much as she tried to forget, the twisted poetry of her dream hovered like a ghost in the attic of Portia's confused mind.

Mr. Rathi was that one teacher that every student hoped to have. Well, at least Portia thought so. Felix had actually made fun of how worked up she was about getting into his class, but Rathi was known to be an amazing lecturer, and considering her unconditional love of music, Portia would have been incredibly disappointed if she didn't get in. Since she placed, she had been looking forward to this class and was determined to shake free the stress of her day.

Passing around a paper to each of the students, the teacher called the class to attention. When she looked at the handout, Portia was surprised to see the lyrics to a song she had never heard of. "Every Note Played" by Derek Delacroix. She scanned her mental musical library, knowing that she had definitely heard of the artist but wasn't actually familiar with his work. Psyched that she had a few iTunes gift cards stored up, she decided she'd download all of his albums when she got home. If Rathi felt the guy was worth opening up his class with, then he must really be good.

"And so, my friends," the teacher began, "as we embark on our journey into the land of lyrical poetry, I thought we would begin with a premiere musical poet, Mr. Derek Delacroix. Some of you might not be familiar with Delacroix's work, but I trust that you will come to admire his genius, as I do. Please listen closely as I play this song in its entirety for you. When it's over I'd like to hear your initial thoughts, and then we will analyze the verses more closely. Why don't you all close your eyes…"

Portia closed her eyes as Delacroix's croaky voice filled the room, exuding confidence though many of the notes stretched slightly beyond his vocal reach.

> *In every note played,*
> *Beds by lovers unmade,*
> *Flowers growing from graves,*
> *It all leaves us dismayed…*

> *We end with a curve,*
> *The question mark is preserved,*
> *So ask as you might,*
> *But it ain't worth the fight…*

The song journeyed on until its final refrain:

> *It's all in the notes, friend,*
> *Each question, each end.*
> *And that's why we play,*
> *So the notes float away…*

She reluctantly opened her eyes when the song ended and quickly typed out a few knee-jerk reactions on her laptop, raising her hand enthusiastically.

"Ah, Miss Griffin. Let's have a look." Mr. Rathi took the computer and perched himself on her desk.

"The language is so simple—which I think must be why the song is able to really have its own voice. But even though it's simple, it still makes you want to go back and read the verses again. It's like you know that the lyrics are layered and that even though this guy's voice isn't exactly beautiful, his singing is."

Mr. Rathi handed the laptop back to her.

"Excellent, Miss Griffin. Indeed that is the beauty of Delacroix. His ability to take simple language and imagery and infuse it with emotion and rhetoric…"

A few more hands shot up in the air.

"…It's cool that the singer doesn't talk only about himself. So many of today's lyrics are in the first person. You know, like 'me and shorty on the dance floor' kind of stuff…"

A few more thoughts flew around the room, drawing the class further into the discussion.

"OK, now let's start to examine some of the verses more closely…"

> "…*And every note played,*
> *Fires like a grenade,*
> *Shards all around,*
> *Questions profound…*"

"…There are questions everywhere. Everything holds its own mystery. It's all around us. We just have to seek out the questions and then decide whether or not they are worth answering."

Portia heard a snicker from behind. She glanced behind her and was caught off guard by the oaky eyes of a boy she'd never seen before.

She held his gaze for an uncomfortable moment and then turned her attention back to the classroom discussion.

She could sense that he was still staring at her and it was very unsettling. Something about his gaze had been accusing, dismissive. His look held an arrogance that made her feel like the class's thoughts on the Delacroix song were banal and trite.

Who the hell made him the authority on Derek Delacroix?

> *"Questions all the same*
> *In this musical game…"*

"…We are all faced with the same questions all the time. Even if we like different music or come from different backgrounds, we all have to face the same questions about our humanity…"

Portia wanted to turn back around and take in his face once again, but she resisted.

> *"…But the melody speaks true,*
> *Holds answers for me and for you…"*

"…But if you listen to the music and just kind of get lost in it, then you can find all of the answers. All the answers we need are right at our fingertips—you know, all around us in music and in everything…"

"You think so? Do you really think that all of the answers to our questions are at our bloody fingertips?!" A silence fell over the classroom as everybody, including Portia, turned back to look at the new student. "I can assure you—they're not. There are no answers. Only more questions, no matter what kind of notes you're playing or music you're listening to. The only song is one that keeps asking questions." He lowered his voice a bit, but it didn't detract from the impact of his words.

Mr. Rathi cleared his throat uncomfortably. "Yes, um, students, let us welcome a new pupil at RPA, Mr. Maxwell Hunter—"

"Just Max will do fine, thanks." His tone was already softening. In fact, Portia noticed, his voice was actually quite lovely—a block of milk chocolate wrapped in sandpaper. Was she imagining that it held traces of a British accent?

"I think what Mr. Hunter is trying to say, albeit somewhat overzealously, is that the answers are always *just beyond* our grip. Perhaps that is why Delacroix ends by saying that that's why he plays—to make the notes float away. Perhaps he knows that some answers to life's mysteries are beyond our grasp, so we're better off not agonizing over them. The only constant we can ever count on in the melody of life is that there will always be questions…"

The teacher's words drifted off as Portia held Max's gaze. His glare drove straight into her, bypassing the guards who usually stood sentry to her vulnerability.

She turned back around and nervously typed out a new message. When he saw her hand raised, Mr. Rathi navigated his way back over to her desk, accepting the laptop once again.

"I don't think Delacroix was saying that the answers are always beyond our reach. I think it's that he's talking about a specific kind of question. You know, the questions that make us examine who we are as people—moral questions. I mean, I'm sure even Delacroix would agree, we all would agree, that there are questions out there with obvious answers. Maybe we try to make them float away because they are just too painful to ask. You know, because we live in such an imperfect world…"

While Mr. Rathi was reading Portia's words, she turned back to give Max a pointed look. His eyes, which held the same amber fluidity as the single malt scotch her father often enjoyed, remained stormy.

They were an odd accessory to the unexpected grin that erupted on his face.

Portia couldn't focus on anything else for the rest of the class.

Something about Max Hunter was so disconcerting. His comments had been well stated and certainly proved his confidence, not to mention his blatant disregard for what anyone might think of him. But while solid oratorical skills were always a major draw for her, she had to admit that his extreme good looks also had her a bit hot and bothered. She wanted to turn around again but instead had to rely on her memory to conjure his image. Not a problem. In fact, she was certain that if she never saw him again, she would still remember that face, the eyes, the cowlick that fell stubbornly onto his forehead. Still, there were things she had not had enough time to glean. Did his cheeks share the same dimples as his chin? What about his hands? Were they sturdy? Graceful?

A warmth began to flow through her body. It wasn't the same as the heat that had assaulted her earlier in the day. More like the radiating comfort of a crackling fire on a cold, wet day.

She couldn't handle the tension that was assaulting her from the back of the room and kept checking the time on her laptop, waiting for the bell to ring. When Mr. Rathi finally dismissed the class, she gathered her stuff and bolted for the door, finding Felix waiting for her right outside.

"How are you feeling? What did Ms. Leucosia say?" he asked her before she even made it out into the hall.

She glanced back into the classroom and saw Mr. Rathi pulling Max Hunter aside. The teacher placed a sympathetic hand on the boy's shoulder. Max responded with a sheepish grin.

It appeared that his cheeks were in fact dimpled.

"Better…definitely better," she signed distractedly to Felix.

Max exited the classroom, walking past Felix and Portia, nodding a quick acknowledgement her way.

As he walked out of sight, Portia saw him secure a pair of ear buds into his ears and adjust his iPod. She wondered what he was listening to.

Something told her it was definitely not Derek Delacroix.

As the day wore on, Portia tried to focus on all of her new classes, but her mind kept flashing its official new screensaver—the magnificent face of Max Hunter.

At the beginning of each class, she surveyed the room to see if he was there. A part of her was relieved when he wasn't, but another part of her felt an unabashed desire to see him again.

She was about to accept that she would have to wait until Mr. Rathi's next class when suddenly he walked into AP French. Something about his gait was noncommittal—as if he was present, but a part of him was elsewhere. Once again he had Portia's full attention as he offered the teacher a flawless, "Bonjour, Je suis Max Hunter…"

Seated in the back row, a spot she always reserved for foreign language classes in an effort to divert attention from her inability to execute the spoken word, Portia squirmed in her seat. Max caught her eye and motioned to the empty seat beside her. Her heart pounded as she indicated that it was as yet unoccupied.

"Hey," he offered as he stuffed his long legs into the cramped space under the desk.

Portia nodded in response, strategizing in her head what the best approach would be to explain her handicap to him.

"Portia, right? Griffin, I think I heard someone say? I really enjoyed your comments in Rathi's class today. I'm sorry if I came off a little harsh. You know—cross to bear and all that…"

There was that disarming smile again.

Portia always hated this part. The explaining. In her iPhone notes she had a typed explanation of her handicap and was about to pull it up when he handed her his own phone, setting it to text mode.

How did he know? Had he been asking about her?

No, stupid, he saw you use your laptop in Rathi's class. That was pretty much a dead giveaway. Pull yourself together!

She couldn't believe that this guy had reduced her to such silly schoolgirl mode after only one encounter.

"Nice to meet you, Max," she typed and then, before she could stop herself, added, "I think." She handed the phone to him with a smile that she hoped he would read as flirtatious.

Reign it in, Portia! You've known the guy for like less than five minutes!
But since their earlier meeting, she felt like she had been perched at the top of a roller coaster, knowing that the thrill of the ride was only a moment away. And now that he was here again, she felt that speedy downhill rush. And it didn't disappoint.

His lips curled toward a smile, a hint of mischief in his eyes. She noticed that he had the ability to flex just one of his dimples while the other remained dormant.

"Oh, come on, I'm not so bad. I actually felt like we had a connection in class earlier today."

"Is that what you would call it?" she typed out. "I would have gone with 'intellectual ambush.' "

Max read her response. A darkness veiled his face, adding another dimension to his beauty.

"I'm sorry, Portia Griffin. I guess some things still set me off."

"Like Derek Delacroix?" she wrote.

"Yeah, like Delacroix…" he offered. He parted his lips as if to say something else but then thought the better of it. Instead he ran his hands through his mess of hair, a mild look of frustration settling upon his flawless face while he opened his notebook.

Class began before Portia could eke out another written message. She was grateful for the distraction—she wasn't sure what she would say next to this mystery guy who had invaded her thoughts in a way that could only be described as viral.

Halfway through class, though, he tapped her subtly and motioned to his own notebook. His handwriting was a bit erratic, a reflection of his mood swings, perhaps? Nonetheless she read through his words three times before daring to meet his eyes.

> *If Delacroix were the only thing*
> *That caused in me that need to sing,*
> *My songs, I swear, they would remain*
> *Lost in pleasure—no more pain.*
>
> *And I think my solo act's run dry,*
> *Alone can stifle, too.*

Maybe sometime I'll ask you "why?"
And find the truth in you…

Portia's heart was pounding as she managed to level her eyes with his. There was no point in trying to mask her reaction—it would be impossible to be feeling something so intensely and not have it reflected in her face. And what she was feeling was an absolute, unmitigated desire to spend the rest of her life dissecting every provocative word that he had written.

"I was thinking something in B minor—I can kind of already hear it in my head," he scribbled underneath the lyrics.

Portia didn't know what to say, what to do. A storm of questions and unspoken words rained down on her mind, but she couldn't grab hold of any one in particular. She was overwhelmed by his honesty and began to write something in her own notebook but found that her hand was shaking, and she couldn't control her pen.

Suddenly his hand was over hers, stilling it.

"I'm sorry," he murmured. "Please don't think I'm a freak or anything—"

"Monsieur Hunter, was there something you wanted to share with the class?"

He allowed his hand to linger on hers for a moment, their eyes caught in a deadlock, before addressing the teacher.

"Pardon, Madame…"

Portia didn't hear anything else he said. She focused instead on steadying her breath, which was coming in heady spurts.

When the bell rang, he stood up and finally looked at her again. Or through her. She wasn't sure how to classify what exactly it was that Max Hunter's eyes had the ability to do.

After a moment or two, he ripped the page from his notebook and handed it to her.

"Pour vous, mademoiselle," he said with a bit of a flourish.

And then he walked away.

She looked down at the paper. He had given the song a title. It was called simply "Portia."

On the bus ride going home, Portia listened to Enya. She never understood a word the Irish singer was saying, which made for perfect background music when she needed to think.

She was exhausted from the day's events. First the choking fit that had landed her in the nurse's office, followed by the disturbing dream and then the encounters with Max Hunter.

Max. Hunter.

She took out the sheet of paper that she had carefully folded and stowed in her pocket. Looking at it again for the first time since French class, she was amazed to see that he had added another verse before giving it to her.

> *You have a way, you charge the air,*
> *With cobalt eyes and chestnut hair.*
> *And though your lips don't make a sound,*
> *They speak of being pleasure bound.*
>
> *Can one moment produce this draw?*
> *And do you feel it, too?*
> *A current filled with shock and awe.*
> *I'll search for truth in you…*

Portia read and reread the lyrics over and over again, the paper itself becoming a magnet from which she could not pry her quivering fingertips.

He's wondering if I felt it? I feel like I've been hit by a bus.

She smoothed out the creases in the paper and placed it carefully inside the oversized bird book that was weighing down her backpack. The book happened to open to the white bird, and she was relieved to cover the image with Max's beautiful words.

What was it about this boy that was so damned magnetic? The fact was that before he had even dashed off a love song about her while he should have been busy with verb conjugation, she had already been smitten. Was it his looks? They were extraordinary, no question. But there were lots of good-looking boys in school. Was it the voice? Deprived of one herself, Portia always measured people's voices carefully, the inflection of their words, the ease with which they turned a phrase. Max's had been throaty and smooth at the same time. His words poured out like warm caramel sprinkled with coarse sea salt—a recent favorite delicacy of Helena's.

After Portia's second exchange with him, she was also certain that, as she had suspected, his speech did hold vestiges of a British accent. That would explain why he was new to the school. But what was his story? What had landed Max Hunter on the shores of Ridgewood of all places?

Her thoughts were interrupted by Charlotte Trotter, who came slumping down the center aisle to get off the bus. She was angrily swiping away tears that were clearly freshly shed. Portia's heart went out to her, to her sunken cheeks streaked black from tear-laden mascara. She reached out and tapped her from behind.

Charlotte snapped her head around—there was fire in her eyes, but her voice was meek. "Portia, just leave me alone, OK? We're not four years old anymore…"

Portia didn't know what to say. She took her phone out, but before she could type anything, Charlotte was gone. All that remained was the sight of Mr. Trotter opening the door and ushering his stepdaughter inside.

The pain between her shoulder blades reemerged at the sight of Harold Trotter's cold face. She reached a hand to her neck to massage her sore muscles.

I better not let Helena see me like this…

She closed her eyes and once more conjured a detailed image of Max Hunter's face. The throbbing receded, replaced by the delicious warmth, just in time for her to hop off the bus in front of her own house.

$$\oint$$

Helena was home, as always, when Portia walked in. She was chopping up some fresh herbs from the garden and stuffing a butterflied trout with thin lemon slices and roasted garlic. Portia loved watching her mother cook. The kitchen was Helena's studio, every dish a blank canvas upon which she painted exquisite combinations of ingredients. Sometimes Portia had the privilege of being her mother's sous chef, but after a long school day, she was happy to just sample the fare that was being offered.

Dousing the trout with some Greek olive oil, Helena deftly placed the stuffed fish into a grilling basket. It was the kind of dish that could have been featured on the cover of *Gourmet* magazine, a meal reserved for a special occasion. But at the Griffin house, every meal was a special occasion.

Closing the door behind her, Portia walked into the kitchen and dropped her bag, startling her mother, who then, without hesitation, charged her daughter for a hug that was instantly thwarted.

"Your hands smell like trout," Portia signed.

"Oh, for God's sake," grumbled her jilted mother. She hurriedly washed her hands off and pulled her daughter in, planting several kisses on Portia's forehead.

"How was the first day? I want to know every detail."

Portia popped a piece of roasted cauliflower in her mouth. "It was interesting," she signed as she chewed. She had already decided that she would keep the day's health scare under the parental radar and was relieved and a little surprised that Helena had seemingly not been contacted by Ms. Leucosia. "Mr. Rathi is just as good as everybody says. And then there was this new kid in class…a boy, actually—" Her hands stopped abruptly when she realized Helena was gaping at her.

"Yeah, go on!" her mother urged.

But Portia knew that if she mentioned Max's name, she'd never hear the end of it. For years she had begged her parents to have more kids, desperate for the company, but more importantly so that she wouldn't be the sole source of familial gossip. But her parents insisted that Portia was the perfect finishing touch to their little family. (Though secretly she suspected that her handicap was challenging enough without her parents having to deal with more children.)

And so she resorted to her most oft used method of distraction before she got roped into any Max discussion.

"I will tell you everything, Mom," she signed, "but right now I'm starving. What are you whipping up here?"

Helena immediately took the bait.

"Oh, well, the fish at Whole Foods this morning was irresistible and I felt like grilling…"

Her mother's voice trailed off into a land of epicurean adventures while Portia reminded her that the grill was going to overheat. When Helena hurried for the terrace, Portia made a hasty retreat toward her own room. Kicking her shoes off, she flopped down on her bed and nestled into her quilt, inhaling its familiar fragrance.

Instinctively she opened her laptop, logging in her password, "stevejobs." Her iChat icon was already flashing. A couple of quick clicks revealed Felix's face on the screen.

"Hey, how are you feeling?"

Before she could type out a response he continued:

"Get this—my parents are flipping out! Wendy just told them that she is deferring college so that she can waitress at Café on the Ridge. My dad was freaking! She swore that it would only be for one year—she thinks that should be long enough to launch her musical career, not that my parents found that at all comforting.

"Anyway, I, of course, was looking for the selfish angle in all of this, and Wendy told me she would hook us up with free food and drinks whenever we want. She told me she'd secure me a VIP spot for Open Mic Night and I told her that she better make it a spot for two. What do you think?"

Portia loved being drawn into the drama of Felix's home life. She knew it wasn't easy for him to be surrounded by women all the time, but she envied the constant bustle that came along with having a big family.

"Why would you care about Open Mic Night?" she chided him. "You can't even hear anything!"

His reply caught her off guard.

"True, Portia, but I might get to dance with you again."

Portia looked away from the webcam. She had deliberately avoided discussing the events of the last time they had been at Café on the Ridge. But now that he had brought it up, she remembered every detail of that night.

In high def.

Right before Felix left for his annual summer with Dean and his grandparents, he had convinced Portia to go out on the town with him. Of course, "out on the town" in Ridgewood did not offer many choices. They decided on Café on the Ridge, a comfortable café that transformed itself into something of a nightclub when dining hours were over.

It was noisy when they got there. The lights had been dimmed and Justin Timberlake's falsetto filled the room. They greeted some familiar faces from school and Portia was suddenly happy that they had decided to come. The music wound its way through her body, relaxing her, prompting her stride to keep time with the beat. She looked over at Felix, eager to share the moment.

He looked lost.

"Explain it to me." He signed in earnest, a rare admission of his desire to experience the sound, to know the music.

Portia brought him over to one of the many speakers in the café and placed one of his hands on the black mesh fabric, his other on her hip. His hand was so big, her hip so slender, that she could feel the press of his thumb and fingertips at the front and back pockets of her jeans.

The music thrummed to that rhythm that only Timbaland seemed able to fully master as she began to move her hips to the music. Felix's grip tightened, an earnest plea for her to stay with him, to not get carried away by the music without him. His other hand was tapping on the speaker, picking up on the vibrations that met his fingertips.

Felix held Portia's gaze as he kept one hand on the speaker and allowed his other hand to travel up her back and rest on her shoulder. He held her an arm's length away, taking in the full measure of her movements. Her gestures gained momentum, intensifying to the beat of the music.

She wondered if he could detect the range in Timberlake's vocals, if a vibration at his fingertips could relay the sultriness of the music.

He moved in a little closer and she could feel his breath on her neck. A delicious chill traveled up and down her spine as she boldly took his hands in her own. Their fingers interlaced instinctively, and she pulled him in even closer. As always, the warmth of his frame made her feel safe. But suddenly also not so safe. The air around them had become thick. Balmy with a mist of unfamiliar sensations, foreign emotions.

The music segued into something or other by Sean Paul. She wasn't sure what—all of his songs sounded the same anyway. It didn't matter to them, though. Felix and Portia had created an invisible force field around themselves, caught in a moment where nothing and no one existed besides them. Portia, daring to look up at Felix, searched for that assurance that whatever it was she was feeling was mutual.

He was hard to read.

Over the years Felix had perfected what Portia nicknamed his "Zorro Mask"—a blank face that combined bravado and indifference. This was definitely one of those Zorro moments. And she couldn't help but wonder: was he enjoying dancing or was he enjoying dancing *with her*?

Her insecurities got the best of her, and abruptly she begged off the dance floor. She signed to Felix that she was starving and made a dash for the coffee counter, trying, without much success, to slow her racing heart. He tried following her but was hindered by Wendy, who insisted that her brother give her a turn on the dance floor.

As they walked home later that night, the tension hung heavily around them. When Felix suddenly grabbed her hand and held it all the way home, Portia tried acting as though this was completely normal for them, walking hand in hand together. When they reached her house, though, he drew her hand up to his lips, kissing her fingertips.

She was about to sign something to lighten the mood when Felix said abruptly, "Have a great summer, Portia." He then turned on his heel, leaving her alone to sort out the sudden volcano of emotions that had erupted between them.

They had video chatted and texted steadily while he was in Canada, but they always skirted the topic of their encounter at the café. A part of Portia wished that they both had the courage to just clear the air about what had happened that night, but the other part of her was flooded with relief at avoiding the confrontation.

Now, two months later, Felix wanted to revisit the scene of the crime. She wondered at his nonchalance. Maybe she had imagined the whole thing.

Exhausted from the day, she just wasn't ready to commit to the date with Felix, platonic though the offer might have been.

"Why don't we play it by ear?" she typed back.

"That's a crazy thing to say to a deaf guy," he wrote in response. She could see him smiling in the image coming across the webcam.

"Well, in case you didn't notice," she shot back without missing a beat, "I didn't actually *say* anything."

"Touché," he conceded.

Her emotions running high, she ended the conversation, opening up iTunes to begin her Delacroix downloads. As she headed back downstairs for dinner, she couldn't help noticing the return of a disruptive tickle in her throat.

Chapter 4

The spindled terrace of the Griffins' Queen Anne Victorian had been a late architectural addition, which the family used to its fullest. Overlooking the vegetable garden, the air was perfumed with the smell of fresh basil and rosemary, Helena's current herbal obsessions. Inhaling the fragrance, Portia did a quick check of her bird feeders and then sat down to dinner with her parents.

She offered up selective information about her day, sharing Mr. Rathi's insights into "Every Note Played." Back from his trip, her father, just as musically obsessed as his voiceless daughter, was intimately familiar with the song that she had heard for the first time that day. After a few of glasses of Chardonnay, Joshua and Helena began a Delacroix sing-off, delighting in each other's voices and laughing at their own screechy efforts. Portia shook her head in mock disgust but couldn't help smiling. Her parents' affection for each other was infectious. Even if they were acting like total dorks.

Portia made a quick exit and bolted for her room. She thought about taking a hot bath but opted for a quick shower instead, unable to shed the same fatigue that had blitzed her in Ms. Leucosia's office. Throwing on an old ribbed tank and boxers, she began surveying her room for the perfect spot to showcase Felix's gift.

A few years ago, when she had gotten hold of the first *Harry Potter* book, Portia had caught the reading bug. And caught it good. She tore through the series and after that was seldom found without a book in hand or somewhere on her person.

And now her overstuffed shelves did not have an inch to spare. Too tired to face the task of reorganizing, she cleared off a spot on her nightstand instead. Happy knowing that Felix's gift was within arm's reach, she climbed under the covers. She was about to start perusing the lovely illustrations again and reread Max's song once more, but sleep proved too delicious to resist. Her eyes were already closed when she reached up to shut off her reading light.

Portia's sleep that night was fitful at best, her vivid dreams a disjointed myriad of images. The white birds were back, only now they were flying around the dance floor at Café on the Ridge, circling a dancing Felix and Portia. One of them landed on Portia's back, right in between her shoulder blades. The bird dug its claws into her skin, sending a searing pain throughout her body. She opened her mouth to scream but couldn't make a sound. Felix was spinning around to the music and when he faced Portia again, she realized it wasn't Felix at all. It was Max Hunter.

The music was pounding as Max tried wrestling the bird off of Portia's shoulders, but his efforts were obstructed by the rest of the flock, which descended between them like a stone wall. The piercing pain in her shoulders was agonizing as Portia tried desperately to call out for help.

Somewhere on the periphery, she glimpsed Ms. Leucosia weaving her way through the crowd, a glass jelly jar in her raised hand. Luke and Lance O'Reilly clumsily knocked into the nurse, causing her to drop the jar. When she leaned over to retrieve it, streams of blood started flowing through her shirt, thick droplets falling to the floor, forming a sanguine Rorschach image.

Portia opened her mouth as widely as she could and focused all of her energy into her throat. But still, she could not bring forth a single sound. The pain of the claws digging into her back had grown unbearable.

Suddenly Charlotte Trotter appeared. Her eyes were wet with tears, and she reached her arms out to her sides. The birds perched themselves on Charlotte's outstretched arms, digging their claws into her frail limbs, pecking at her extremities.

Tears spilled down Charlotte's cheeks as she told Portia not to worry about the pain.

She would cry aloud for the both of them…

The next morning when she got on the bus, Portia was cursing Helena's new policy of no caffeine in the house. She'd had a terrible night's sleep, but despite her weariness, her heart began to race at the thought of seeing Max again. Wishing she had applied some concealer over the black rings underneath her eyes, she hopped off the bus, registering a quick mental note that Charlotte was absent. Charlotte was never absent.

When she arrived at her locker, she was greeted by what had to be a practical joke.

"What are your thoughts on 'Headed for Earth'?" Max had scribbled down his cell phone number and signed the note simply, "M." Luckily she had made good on her decision to use up all of her iTunes credit and had downloaded Derek Delacroix's earlier works, too. "Headed for Earth" had struck her as especially heart-wrenching. Apparently Max thought so, too.

And actually wanted to discuss it.

With her.

She heard Felix approaching from behind with Luke and Lance and quickly erased the message with her cuff, having already committed the phone number to memory.

"What up, girlfriend?" Lance greeted her.

"Not a good color on you," Luke dug at his twin. "We're Irish, you idiot. Our ancestors were probably Catholic priests. 'What up, girlfriend?' was definitely not part of their lingo."

Lance grinned at his brother.

Portia begged off quickly, barely saying hello to any of them, signing something about "girl business" and heading for the nearest bathroom. She wasn't sure why she had erased her message so quickly, she just knew that she didn't want to share Max yet.

She had her phone out in a flash, her thoughts racing as she tried to think of a clever response to his note.

> *My heart the equator,*
> *I dare you to explore,*

Dive into the crater,
I promise, there's more…"

She regretted it as soon as she hit "send." Even if he got the reference, what kind of person would she be coming off as? Already asking him to dive into the crater of her heart? Still, this imagery had struck her so hard that it seemed instinctual to come back at him with it. So often had her silence made her feel that her own heart, though at the center of her world, was so distant to others.

She steadied her breath while an ellipsis on her iPhone indicated that he was texting her back.

"Ah—so you are a lyrical master, as I suspected. I've always loved those lines. Wanna have a lyrical showdown over lunch?" he wrote back. "I think I might be able to go head-to-head with you."

Portia would have loved to have lunch with Max, but the last thing she felt like doing was bringing him over to their table for Jacqueline's scrutiny and Luke and Lance's crass comments. Not to mention what Felix might make of it.

On the other hand, she didn't want to pass up an opportunity.

As if sensing her hesitation, he wrote, "Why don't we skip the 'lunching' altogether? I'll be in the music room at 11:45 a.m. Hope to see you then."

She was intrigued by the designated locale and texted him a quick "Kk."

Kk? What am I, twelve?

Prompted to class by the sound of the bell, Portia sat next to Felix in Chemistry and contemplated telling him about her sort-of-a-date.

Instead she passed him a note.

"Some freshman asked me if I would come help the new Lit Journal committee—soooo annoying! It will prob take up my whole lunch!"

Felix looked up at her and she detected a hint of skepticism in his eyes, but she was so excited about her covert meeting with Max that she decided to let it slide.

"Bummer," he wrote back.

The music room was Portia's favorite spot at RPA. The school had received an anonymous endowment that outfitted the studio with every manner of instrument. A beautiful Steinway Grand sat in the center, surrounded by a string section of elegantly carved cellos, violins, and violas. Guitars, both acoustic and electrical, lined the walls of the room and horns, ranging from the saxophone to the clarinet, crowded the drum sets in the corners.

Entry to this musical Camelot required a code, just in case someone decided to make off with a brand new Gibson or an inlaid Bergonzi. Luckily Felix had charmed his dad into giving him the code, and he and Portia sometimes took refuge among the instruments, which Felix always ogled with great curiosity. She felt a twinge of betrayal when she walked into the room without him. More importantly, though, she wondered how Max Hunter had managed to gain access to the studio.

"Mr. Woods gave me the code so I can come in and practice," he said when she entered the room. "It's not a bad setup considering what I left behind…"

She looked at him questioningly.

"Yeah, I guess I didn't have a chance to tell you yesterday that I transferred here from Performing Arts in New York."

He had been sitting in the far left corner, an acoustic guitar on his lap, absently strumming a couple of melancholy chords. He stood up, though, as soon as she walked in, a mark of chivalry in his favor. Portia made her way around the maze of instruments. Sitting down beside him, she looked up at him, her eyes asking him the questions that her mouth couldn't.

"I live here with my aunt and uncle—my mom's sister. My dad just couldn't take care of me anymore—couldn't take care of himself, either. Too many memories for him in The Big Apple, I guess…" his voice trailed off. He sat down again and adjusted the strings on the guitar.

Portia was afraid that her silence might be off-putting,

but Max didn't seem to mind. He used the quiet moment as an opportunity to study her face more closely.

"You're very pretty."

Somehow, it didn't sound like a line, just a simple observation. Nonetheless, Portia avoided his gaze, embarrassed by the compliment.

Max cleared his throat and changed the subject. "You know, my dad is actually tight with the guy who endowed this place, but he still won't tell me who it is. All I know is that it's some retired musician that he's done some legal work for in the past. He's in, or *was* in I guess, entertainment law."

Portia didn't know where to go first. Performing Arts? New York? Too many memories? You're very pretty?

She decided to tackle the personal stuff head on.

Behind her, a whiteboard hung around the perimeter of the room. "What kind of memories?" she scrawled out.

He stopped strumming and his face turned stony. She was fascinated to find that even veiled in ice, his looks were mesmerizing.

"My mom disappeared in New York. Vanished into thin air." He attempted a light smile, but the pain in his eyes couldn't be camouflaged. "My dad's from London and had met her when he was doing a law internship in the States. He's a romantic, to put it mildly. I think I inherited that gene from him," he flashed her a flirtatious smile, though his eyes remained somber. "They met through business and apparently for both of them, it was love at first sight. London was a tough sell for her, though— she hated the rain. But he wore her down—flowers, poems, you know. The whole bit. They were married within a year, moved back to London, and I was born about a year after that."

This was one of those moments when Portia's handicap was especially frustrating. A moment that called for a subtle verbal encouragement to continue on with the story. She would have felt like an idiot writing "go on" on the whiteboard and chose, instead, to place her hand encouragingly on Max's forearm.

He stopped strumming and looked at her full on. "Is it your eyes? I bet those eyes could get anyone talking, right? I mean,

I have never once told this stuff to anyone. It feels good." He glanced down at her hand resting on his arm.

Portia allowed her hand to linger. She could feel the veins in his arm tensing at her touch—it was exhilarating, too exhilarating. She stood up and began a slow pace, fingering some of the instruments.

"Yeah, so anyway, the rain drove my mom crazy but otherwise we were all really happy, you know? She traveled back and forth to do some consulting here and there. One day she went to New York on business, and we never saw or heard from her again. No phone call, no letter, no mysterious change in her behavior before she left. Nothing. The investigation went on for years, but they never turned anything up. Not even any leads. She was supposed to show up at Bonnie's house—that's my aunt—for dinner one night and just never did."

He ran his fingers through his hair, closing his eyes against the memory. Portia had once again inched closer to him and stood still as a statue, not knowing where to go with this information.

"It was so sunny in London for weeks after her disappearance. I thought for sure the sunshine would bring her back. But it didn't. After a while I just wanted it to rain again, for things to go back to normal. But there was no more normal. We stayed in London for a few more years. My dad flew back and forth constantly to check in on the investigation. Thank God for nannies, you know? Eventually he just moved us to New York. I think he thought that he'd be able to do what the police couldn't. You know, it's hard when there's no body to bury. Lack of closure and all that…"

"So you think she…died?" Portia wrote out. Her shaky scrawl on the whiteboard spoke of her hesitancy to ask the question.

"That's what the police think. Do you know how many people just disappear every year? People think that life is really like *Law & Order* or *CSI*. But it's not. Her case is still open, but I think she's pretty much presumed to be dead." He shook his head from side to side, a feeble attempt at blurring the thought.

"Anyway, one day I came home and my dad was asleep on

the couch. I couldn't wake him up, and then I saw an empty bottle of Xanax on the floor. I called 911, and somehow they got to us in time. A few days later, we checked him into Havenhurst and voilà! Here I am." He attempted another weak smile.

Portia sat down next to him. There were no right words to offer him after hearing his story and, for once, she didn't feel so self-conscious about her lack of voice. She looked up into his face and took Max's dimpled cheeks into her hands. He closed his eyes and she gently brushed her thumbs over his cheeks, trailing the angles of his jawline. She could feel the tension ease from his body at her touch. He placed his hands over hers, lowering his face further into the comfort of her grip.

As her emotions were fueled by the feel of his warm skin in her hands, she felt the tickle in her throat come back and tried desperately to hold back her cough for fear of interrupting the moment. But when she began to feel the constriction of her windpipe come back, she broke the pose, hoping to calm herself down and ward off another coughing fit.

What the hell is my problem? It's like I'm incapable of having an emotion without bringing on whooping cough…

As the symptoms relented, she decided to try to lighten things up a bit by diverting the topic.

"So are you exclusively a strummer?" she wrote on the whiteboard.

Max looked over at her. "No, not exclusively," he said while sounding off a chord or two. "I enjoy tickling the ivories as well as exercising my vocals." He offered a dramatic flourish with his hand and a mock post-performance bow. She could tell that he was trying to deflect attention from his mention of his voice.

It was too late, though. She was dying to hear him sing. In fact, since yesterday she had wanted nothing more than to hear him sing the song he had written for her.

"So how 'bout charming a voiceless girl with some crooning?" she wrote.

"Another time, maybe."

Accustomed to people feeling uncomfortable around her about vocal matters, Portia understood his hesitation.

"Come on," she wrote. "I wanna know what Performing Arts is missing out on."

Max assessed her sincerity, and she flashed him her most eager face.

"Well, I don't know what kind of music you're into. I mean, besides Derek Delacroix. And I haven't yet fully worked out the music to what I wrote for you yesterday…"

He started strumming the guitar, his reference to yesterday's romantic gesture floating around them.

"Surprise me," Portia challenged. She added a smiley face at the end of the words to try to keep the mood light.

He smiled back. "Well, I've actually been working on something new. You'd be the first to hear it. But you have to promise to be honest with me, OK? If it's bloody awful, you can't try to spare my feelings."

She nodded her consent and crossed her heart for extra measure.

"OK, so it goes something like:

> *Will I ever know another place?*
> *The comfort of a room,*
> *A tender woman's touch,*
> *The safety of the womb?"*

His singing voice was just as she'd imagined it would be—melodic and raspy. It was sweet cotton candy wrapping itself around a paper cone, building up layer by billowy layer.

> *"You see, the sun was shining bright*
> *The day I learned of pain.*
> *And now I swear when I wake up,*
> *I pray that it will rain.*
>
> *Oh God, just let it rain."*

Max closed his eyes, surrendering himself to the song.

> *"The images we found in clouds*
> *While the earth did slowly spin,*

Her voice so sweet and silky,
The perfume of her skin.

The sun would illustrate,
As morals she'd explain.
And now I see the sun shine bright
And pray to God for rain…"

He looked up at Portia to try to gauge her reaction, and she coaxed him on with a smile.

"One day I'd love another,
She'd say with an embrace.
I wondered at her words,
At her face that was my face…

But then the sun came out,
From life no more to gain.
Do you hear me, God? I'm screaming out
Please, just let it rain…

Oh, please, just let it rain…"

Max strummed the last chord and looked expectantly into Portia's eyes, which had welled up with tears.

"Was I that bad?" he tried breaking the awkward silence.

"Would it be too ironic for me to say that I'm speechless?" she texted out on her phone. A brief chuckle escaped his lips and then more silence.

"It was amazing," she added, though the compliment didn't begin to do justice to what she had just heard.

"Yeah, well, you probably think everybody's voice is amazing."

The words pierced her like arrows before they even finished stumbling out of his mouth, her face crumpling.

"Oh, God, no. I didn't mean it like that, Portia—" He dropped the guitar on the floor and stood up, nervously wringing his hands. "I just meant—well, I don't know what I—"

But she had begun texting at super-human speed.

"What, you think just cuz I don't have a voice, I go nuts for anyone who does? Anyone who's willing to show the handicapped girl some extra attention?"

"No, Portia, I swear. I was just trying to dodge your compliment, play the modesty card. I promise—"

But before he could finish, she was racing out of the room, the door slamming hard in her wake.

Portia's blood was boiling when she took her seat in History. How could she have been so stupid? She didn't need anyone's goddamned pity.

Why did she have to swoon like that over his singing? Could she have been more obvious about the impact he was having on her?!

An enormous sense of relief flooded through her when Felix walked into the room. When he sat next to her, it was like she shifted planes. His presence brought her back to the familiar, back to a world where Max Hunter and his insulting remarks didn't exist.

"How'd the Literary Journal meeting go?" he signed.

It took her a minute to figure out what he was talking about.

"Oh. Same old, same old," she signed back, avoiding his eyes.

She inched her desk a little closer to his, comforted by his proximity, the familiarity of the scent that was so uniquely his. Why hadn't she just been up-front with him about Max in the first place? His shoulder looked so inviting—she wished she could rest her head on it and have a good cry.

"You look upset," he quickly signed, though class had already begun. This below-the-radar mode of communication was a cherished perk of the Portia–Felix relationship.

"Just something someone said to me," she gestured back. "It's nothing."

Just then the door to the classroom swung open and Max Hunter walked in. Portia squirmed in her seat as Max feebly excused his tardiness and grabbed an empty desk at the front of the room.

Please don't look back at me. Please. Not now.

But the telepathic plea didn't work. Max turned around to look at her, to openly stare, in fact. She could feel her cheeks flushing red, and she tried ignoring Felix as he gently kicked her under the desk. Finally, she turned to him.

"What?" she signed impatiently.

"Is this Mr. 'Literary Journal'?" he signed back.

"Let it go, Felix," and then she added the special sign they had invented when they were kids to represent the exclamation point. After that she kept her eyes glued to her textbook, feigning an intense fascination with the Battle of Bunker Hill.

The bell rang after an eternity, and Portia hurriedly collected her books, hoping to execute a seamless exit. To her horror, though, as she looked up, Max was walking over to hers and Felix's desks.

Felix stepped directly to Portia's side, standing taut.

"Hi there. Felix Fein." He presented Max with an imposing hand. They shared a brief handshake, backed by some pretty intense eye contact. "I suspect you might already know Portia." He gestured back to Portia, whose eyes were shooting him daggers of warning.

"Yeah, we have a few other classes together. They put me in the wrong History class originally. So, um, here I am," Max said. Portia noticed that he was enunciating his words very deliberately.

"Yeah, here you are. Oh, and no need to speak like that, dude," Felix assured him. "I can read lips with my eyes closed."

"Oh—sorry. Didn't mean to offend."

An attempt at casual banter ensued. Felix had apparently noticed Max playing basketball in gym that morning and offered him a reluctant compliment on his hoop skills.

"I'm more of a hockey kind of a guy. Must be the Canadian roots, ay?"

"Must be," acknowledged Max. He was trying to make eye contact with Portia, who continued to avert his gaze. She just didn't want to get into it in front of Felix.

As the tension mounted, the now-familiar pain in her upper back returned. She absentmindedly reached her hand back to rub out the knots.

"Is your back starting to hurt again?" Felix asked. The look of concern on his face reminded her of yesterday's health episode, which had become something of a distant memory since her encounters with Max.

She gave him a subtle nod but was taken aback when Felix placed his hand over hers, easing hers aside and applying pressure onto her sore muscles.

Max abruptly excused himself and walked out of the room.

The instant he was out the door, Portia pried herself out from under Felix's hand. "What's with all the touchy-feely stuff?" she signed angrily.

"Just trying to help out," he replied. The innocence of his smile was betrayed by the look of mischief in his eyes.

"You don't own me, Felix." She mouthed out the harsh words deliberately, momentarily satisfied by the look of hurt on his face. She herself was surprised by her own malice, knowing that Felix was only trying to help her. But before she could retract the sting of her words, she turned and walked away.

Hurrying down the hall at breakneck speed, Portia finally indulged in the tears that had been welling up inside her since Max had so carelessly insulted her. She needed something to ease the pain of the blow. Something to assure her that she wouldn't be plagued by her "differentness" for the rest of her life.

She needed something that felt, well—that felt as natural as Felix's damned hand on her neck.

Chapter 5

As the day wore on, Portia's chills grew worse and her aches and pains became more pronounced. She had been coughing intermittently and was sure that by tomorrow she would have a full-blown flu.

When she went to her locker to pack up her bag at the end of the day, she was surprised to see a bunch of messages scrawled out on her whiteboard.

The top one was from Felix—she'd recognize his chicken scratch a mile away.

"Hey – sorry if I overstepped my bounds today. I'll I.M. you later…" No signature—none needed.

The next note was from Max. "It was performance anxiety. I promise it won't happen again." Despite herself, she half smiled at his wit.

The third note was written out in a bold calligraphic hand. "Portia – Please come and see me if you feel that your condition is worsening. – Ms. Leucosia."

She reread the message just to make sure she had it right. How did Ms. Leucosia know that her condition had worsened? Maybe something was going around school.

She slung her bag over her shoulder and headed out for the bus, taking a seat in the back and strategically plopping her backpack down next to her, hoping to ward off any unwanted company. As the usual kids made their way onto the bus, she pumped up her iPod.

She had recently downloaded an App of different birdcalls and often enjoyed challenging herself to identify which species was singing which song. But right now she was feeling so lousy that instead she just allowed herself to get lost in the harmonious chirping.

Hers being one of the last stops, Portia watched with relief as one by one the kids got off in front of their houses. She was counting the minutes, the seconds, until she could take refuge in the solitude of her room.

As the route continued, though, her symptoms worsened dramatically. The pain in her back became razor sharp and was emanating forward into her chest and throat. Her breathing had grown shallow and labored and when she looked out the window, she was overcome with panic when she realized that they were still a good few houses away from her own.

I need help.

The coughing started again but quickly segued into a desperate wheezing, followed by another terrifying constriction of her windpipe. She felt as though her head was spinning as thick beads of sweat fell into her eyes, clouding her vision.

Struggling to draw new breath, any breath, into her lungs, she tried massaging her throat, hoping to encourage her windpipe open, but there was no air to be had.

Desperately Portia looked out of the window, trying to gauge whose house was next on the route.

I've got to get off this bus.

There was no rationale to her thought. Just fear. She was sure she would suffocate to death on the bus if she didn't get off and find help.

In the recesses of her panicked mind, she registered that the bus was at the shared stop of the Nelsons and the Trotters. The Nelson house was perched at the top of a ridiculously steep driveway that there was no way she'd be able to climb in her current condition. Groping the seats, she half crawled up the aisle, pushing past Alexander Nelson, who was saying good-bye to his buddies.

"Hey, what gives, Griffin? This isn't even your stop…"

But Portia hardly heard the recrimination as she headed for the open door.

I'm going to die! Please, oh, please let me get to Charlotte's house without dying.

She repeated the mantra to herself with every desperate step she took toward the imposing oak door of the restored farmhouse. As she got closer, she suddenly felt a smooth relief spread through her windpipe. It was as if she had been choking on a block of ice, which had warmed suddenly, coating her throat with a cool trickle.

Gulping in gigantic breaths of air, Portia thought about turning around and heading home. She knew that she needed to fess up to Helena about these reoccurring health incidents, even if it did mean a visit to Dr. Loring. But a sudden barrier between her actions and logic had sprouted up out of nowhere, and so she continued toward the Trotter house, despite the easing of her symptoms. As she drew nearer, she began to feel like a trespasser in her own body. She was not so much walking as floating—her body following the instructions of a mind that belonged to someone else.

Portia couldn't decide what was scarier: the attack on the bus or her sudden inability to control her own movements. But before she could follow this thought through to its end, a thunderous voice penetrated the haze that had settled upon her.

"Do you see the goddamned ring you made on this wood, Janie?! Allow me to give you a closer view. Have you never heard of a little invention called a coaster?!"

"I'm sorry, Harold, I'll get it out –"

Janie Trotter's voice was shrill, and Portia heard a solid thud followed by a shriek of pain.

"YOU'RE GODDAMNED RIGHT YOU'LL GET IT OUT!"

Portia wanted to run. She had to run. Only her feet wouldn't move. Instead she watched in horror as her hand started rapping on the faceted glass of the front bay window.

Her inner voice kept screaming at her to get away as fast she could, but as she peered through the window, that voice became a whisper. She could hear a quiet sobbing coming from inside, and her hair stood on end at the chilling aura that seeped from every perfect architectural detail of the Trotters' home.

Suddenly Charlotte's face appeared in the window, her

lifeless black eyes meeting Portia's, silencing that inner voice completely. Charlotte shook her head and motioned for Portia to go away. But Portia was floating further and further away from any rational thought as the magnet of her neighbor's eyes drew her closer.

"Let me in, Charlotte. Let me help you." She mouthed the words, hoping that her eyes reinforced her plea, though she was still unsure what exactly she was going to do to get Harold Trotter to back the hell away from his wife and daughter.

Charlotte, her affect as flat as ever, shook her head and again motioned for Portia to go away. Portia responded with the most earnest gaze she could muster.

"Charlotte, get over here and clean your mother up. She's getting blood all over everything…"

Charlotte moved away from the window, and Portia was both terrified and relieved when suddenly she heard the door unlock. Her neighbor stood in the doorway trembling, her limbs exposed in her T-shirt and shorts and covered in a melee of bruises.

"What are you doing here?" asked the battered ghost of a child that Portia had once considered her close friend.

Portia pushed past Charlotte and entered the rambling foyer with its vaulted ceiling and knotted wooden beams. The house was beautiful, its decor the perfect blend of modern and traditional. If not for the red streak of blood on the dining table where Mr. Trotter had smashed in Mrs. Trotter's face, Portia would have thought the place had been prepped for a photo shoot.

"What the hell do you want?!" Mr. Trotter's hand was still gripping his sobbing wife's hair. "Oh, wait—you're that mute Griffin girl, right?" A twisted smile was the highlight to his callous use of the word 'mute.' "Well, I guess I won't have to warn you about saying anything. Now get the fuck out of my house…"

He let go of Mrs. Trotter, making a move toward Portia. But she stood her ground and glared at him with a fearlessness that could only be explained by her increasing detachment from reality. She was there, in the moment, this horrible tragic moment, but half of her was somewhere else. And in that other place, she was invincible.

Mr. Trotter was a few feet away from her when suddenly he stopped dead in his tracks, plagued by an inexplicable inertia.

"What the…?" His words sounded small as he tried to make sense of his sudden paralysis. "Janie, get her the hell out of here."

The ease with which he shot out this order to his wife only furthered Portia's fury. A tremor sparked in her throat, a steady vibration that was more soothing than painful.

"Portia, please go." Mrs. Trotter's voice was so detached it could have been computer generated.

Portia ignored her and looked at Charlotte. Her desperation to speak was painful, pitiable. She feared she would explode with questions.

Her hands began signing all the thoughts, the questions that were racing through her head.

"How long has he been doing this? Why didn't you ever tell anyone? Why didn't you ever tell me?"

The strain in Harold Trotter's face grew worse as he tried, to no avail, to charge the unwelcome visitor. But the most he was able to manage was a threatening gesticulation toward his wife. "Janie," his voice was calm and manipulative. "If you don't get this freak out of my house in the next ten seconds, I swear to God you will live to regret it."

Portia kept signing, the monster's threats slipping away into oblivion.

"Is this why you're always so covered up? To hide the bruises?"

Charlotte stared at her uncomprehendingly. "I don't sign, Portia."

Mrs. Trotter's voice came at her again. "Portia, you need to leave—"

The vibration in Portia's throat grew stronger, a steady drumbeat, a percussion that began snaking its way throughout her body. Her hands kept signing, running on autopilot.

There was no forethought to what she was asking, no fear of crossing the line.

"JANIE!"

Portia leveled her eyes with Charlotte. She could feel herself slipping further and further away. A bizarre vision of being nestled among a flock of birds, soaring away into the furthest depths of the sky, began to cloud her mind. Her hands were signing at a fevered pace. Even Felix would have had to tell her to slow down.

"I can't understand you, Portia. I can't…" Charlotte's face was crumbling.

"GET THE FUCK OUT OF THIS HOUSE!" The words boomed out of Janie Trotter's bruised lips and, just as suddenly, Portia's hands stopped moving. She looked down at them in wonder and watched as her two index fingers interlaced, offering Charlotte one final word.

Friend.

She looked back up at her suffering neighbor. Charlotte didn't have to know sign language to understand the connection that Portia was offering her. A slight nod of her head came. An acquiescence that meant that both of their lives were about to change.

Portia's whole body began to quake. She couldn't think or see straight, and the outside world had completely disappeared. The only thing that existed now was the pain endured by Charlotte and Janie Trotter.

She opened her mouth to scream, forgetting for a moment that the effort was wasted. The pain between her shoulders reemerged, and the vibration in her throat had grown so strong that she wondered if they could hear it, too, this jackhammer that was breaking through the asphalt that encased her larynx.

With an obscene sense of calm, she suddenly knew what would happen—that the abused forms of Charlotte and her mother had proven to be the elusive key to her locked-up voice box.

After a final glance into Charlotte's eyes, what emerged from Portia's lips was so blissful, so otherworldly, that anyone present would not have been surprised to see the face of God revealed in that very moment.

> *"On black wings secrets float into a blazing sky,*
> *No longer stumbling, living a lie.*
> *No choice but to soar higher and higher,*
> *Just pray not to be consumed by the fire…"*

It was the most mesmerizing sound that any of them, including Portia, had ever heard. Any shock they felt at this bizarre unfolding of events was instantly overshadowed by the sheer beauty of her voice.

> *"Can you know, my friend, that I feel as you do?*
> *Each blow landing upon both me and you?*
> *And no longer will fear and pain pave your path,*
> *Stopping at stop signs, containing your wrath…"*

Entranced by her own voice, Portia continued to run on autopilot, not knowing where the words or melody came from. Slowly, instinctively, she made her way over to the far corner of the room where Harold Trotter was standing, his mouth agape.

Holding Charlotte's gaze, Portia extended her hand toward Mr. Trotter, the strings of her voice guiding him like a puppet. He had no choice but to take it as she directed him toward the front door of the house.

Charlotte and Mrs. Trotter remained silent as they took in the actions of Portia the Puppeteer.

> *"For we are warriors, both you and I,*
> *White wings fly. White wings fly."*

Her voice was a curious combination of pain and pleasure. A fabric woven of silk and sisal.

> *"A skeleton melting inside of yourself,*
> *A winning ticket but never the wealth,*
> *A child who had to stop being a child,*
> *A spirit that could never dare to be wild."*

Portia's singing resonated off of every beam in the house, drenching every square inch of the cavernous room with the thick beauty of her voice.

Mr. Trotter continued to be led by her hand out onto the cobblestone path, entranced and terrified by Portia's voice.

Charlotte and Janie Trotter followed closely behind. The blood on Mrs. Trotter's face was starting to congeal, frozen lava trapped in the ridges of her swollen skin.

> *"I am here for you now—I feel the wind blowing.*
> *Can you feel it, my friend? Take joy in the knowing?"*

Propelled by a force beyond her control, Portia guided Mr. Trotter up the path in the direction of the old stone well. The sound of flapping wings all around her grew louder, fortifying her, feeding her.

She continued to stare hard into Charlotte's eyes as she and Mr. Trotter approached the well.

> *"The touch you now feel is my gentle hands,*
> *Your travels traverse you to glorious lands…"*

Her ethereal voice grew stronger as she placed his bloodied hands on the rim of the well. His eyes were terrified as he pivoted himself and slowly began to lower his body into the dark abyss. His voice trembled across desperate objections to unwittingly bringing on his own death.

> *"For we are warriors, both you and I.*
> *White wings fly, White wings fly…"*

"No, Portia. Don't do it. Please don't kill him—we'll get help. Please don't!!!"

Charlotte had started to scream, but Portia was lost in her own song.

> *"No more tears clouding young eyes,*
> *Floating up higher, flames blazing the skies."*

"Portia, no!"

Mr. Trotter's grip on the rough-hewn stone was starting to give. Thick tears of fear blended with beads of sweat on his reddened face.

"Forcing us both to brandish our armor,
Guiding the evil, as a snake charmer."

Charlotte and Mrs. Trotter grabbed hold of the petrified Harold Trotter, trying to pull him away from the sure death that awaited him at the bottom of the deep well.

"Portia, please stop!" Charlotte was pleading, tears running down her face, as she and her mother struggled to ease Mr. Trotter up out of the well. He couldn't hold on much longer as the stone cut new welts into his guilty fingertips.

"For we are warriors, both you and I.
White wings fly,
White wings fly…"

Chapter 6

Portia awoke to the distinct call of the male Red-eyed Vireo beckoning his mate. She was completely disoriented as she struggled to remember how she had ended up in her backyard hammock.

After the episode at the Trotters' house, which began coming back to her in bits and snippets, Portia had collapsed to the ground, crossing over into a clouded semi-conscious state. Her eyes had remained open just long enough to see Charlotte and her mother pull Mr. Trotter out of the well. The desperate man had been a babbling fool of apologies and meaningless clichés as he thanked them for saving his life.

After that, she could only hear their voices through the dense haze that sheathed her while she slipped into oblivion.

"...gotta get her out of here..." Charlotte spoke conspiratorially to her mother.

"...can't call any added attention to the situation..." Janie Trotter's voice trembled.

"...the hammock in their backyard..."

And now here she was.

What day is today? Wednesday. I think it's Wednesday.

At least Helena and Joshua weren't home. They rarely, if ever, missed their standing dinner date with the Feins.

A bee flew over her throbbing head, its buzzing reminding her of the vibration that had hammered away at her throat, had enabled her to speak. No, to sing.

Did I actually sing?

The hammock began to sway in time to her trembling body as she leaned over the side and started to retch.

What was she thinking, trying to take on a situation like that by herself?

Portia wasn't exactly a shrinking violet, but a warrior? Isn't that what she had sung out? That she and Charlotte were warriors?

The retching continued, bringing up nothing but bile.

Where the hell had those words come from? That melody? That voice?

She returned her head to the hammock, the movement bringing back threads of the excruciating pain in her back, which had now settled itself into a tangible memory.

I have to get inside. I need to get inside.

Much as she yearned for her room, though, Portia was still too unsteady to stand. She reached for her cell phone and saw a text from Helena.

"Where are you, Portia? We're out with the Feins—could you please text me to let me know you got home?"

It took Portia four tries to text back a legible message.

"I'm fine. Forgot to tell u I had to stay late for Lit Journal. Am home now. All good." Thank God for that literary journal.

What if they go to the police? What if they accuse me of trying to murder Mr. Trotter?

She tried dismissing the concern, realizing how preposterous the story would sound:

"Yeah, this mute girl in our neighborhood started singing all of a sudden and almost forced him down into the well with the sheer power of her voice!"

Even Portia, the protagonist of this bizarre tale, could hear how ridiculous it sounded.

Allowing one leg to fall to the ground, she tried to gain her footing. The swaying of the hammock brought on a fresh wave of dizziness. She was determined, though, to get upstairs to the sanctuary of her room. To smell her pillows and touch her books. Something, anything that would help bring her back to reality.

She swung her other leg over and slowly pushed herself up. Her steps were sluggish and deliberate as she finally reached the back door. Punching in the code on the keyless entry, Portia was comforted by the familiar smells of the house. Her energy continued to wane, however, and by the time she got to the staircase, she had to resort to all fours, her muscles exhausted, her ears ringing with the echo of her own shortened breath.

Finally, she crawled into the safety of her room, closing the door and slumping heavily against it, where once again she drifted off into unconsciousness.

She was sitting on her bed, Felix's beautiful bird book spread before her.

Joshua poked his head in to say goodnight.

"Goodnight," she signed.

He paused for a minute, "God, Portia, when did you go and grow up like this?"

She started to sign back again, but suddenly the book began to quake in her hands, its pages tearing themselves from the binding, flying around the room, whipping away her father's form until he vanished. The only page that remained intact was the one with the white bird.

With a sense of dread, Portia cautiously extended her hand to the drawing, but the bird's wings began to flap and flap until it flew off the page, circling her, laughing and squealing.

"Why did you sign to your father, young Portia? Why not show him your voice? That beautiful, murderous voice…"

The bird's wings stretched out to the walls, knocking everything down in their path. Portia cowered into her bed.

"How did you know? What are you?" She spoke the words aloud, her voice as resonant as it had been at the Trotters'.

The bird's wings broke through her bedroom walls, stretching and stretching through to the outside. She felt the cold rush of the night air and found herself chasing the creature, following it as it flew to Charlotte's house.

It landed on the well.

"Have a look, dear Portia. Have a look at what you are…"

"I didn't kill him! I didn't do it! I am not a murderer—they pulled him out, I know they did…"

She turned to run, but the creature swooped her up in its giant wings, holding her directly over the black orifice.

"Open your eyes, Portia. OPEN YOUR EYES!"

She opened her eyes and looked down into the abyss, expecting to be met with the cold dead eyes of Harold Trotter.

Instead, Max Hunter's lifeless face peered up at her from the darkness.

When Portia awoke, she was lying on the floor, the wooly threads of her shag rug tickling her nostrils. It was all a dream. It must have been a dream. All of it. She can't sing—she can't even talk. And yes, she was upset by what Max said to her, but she certainly didn't wish him dead. She sat up and took a moment to gain her bearings, unable to process the millions of bizarre thoughts that skipped through her mind.

A glance over at the clock told her that it was 9:30 p.m. Her parents would probably be home within the hour. She had to pull herself together. Testing her strength, she found she was able to rise steadily. The relief of regaining her footing flooded through her as she made her way into the bathroom, turned on the tub, and titrated the water to her favorite temperature— boiling. She poured some lavender salts into the water and allowed the fragrance to penetrate her tightly wound nerves.

Before settling into the tub, she went back to her bedroom and opened her laptop. Any hopes that the events of the past few hours had all been a dream vanished when she saw an e-mail from Charlotte. Filled with dread, she clicked it open.

> *Portia —*
>
> *I don't know what to say. I'm so ashamed. You must think I'm so weak. But you showed me strength tonight. You showed me something—something unbelievable.*
>
> *Secrets have been the story of my life. Sometimes the threats of what he'd do to us if we told were worse than the abuse itself. We were always so worked up about keeping up*

his perfect reputation. Do you know they once photographed us for a spread in Arch Digest? He had to hire a special makeup artist to cover up my mother's face…

I called the police after we brought you home. I'd rehearsed that call in my mind a million times—it felt so weird to actually be making it. When I hung up I felt almost giddy…

The police came and arrested him. They said that the road ahead is going to be bumpy. One of the cops was a woman—I could tell she was sincere. I wonder how often she sees this kind of thing. Anyway, I think we're finally ready for those bumps. They can't be any worse than what we've already been through, right?

I will never be able to thank you for what you did for us tonight, Portia.

Your friend (I hope I can call you that now),
Charlotte

Portia closed her laptop.

No, she had not dreamed any of it. It had all gone down just as she had remembered it. An obscene blend of euphoria and fear welled up inside her. Her mind scrambled to make sense of it all. She felt like she had won the Powerball lottery—excited about all the ways her life was about to change. Terrified of the ways her life was about to change.

The sound of the running bathwater was calling to her. She needed time to think. To sort it all out. But first she had to e-mail Charlotte back. To make sure that her winning ticket would remain under lock and key until she was ready to cash it in.

She reopened her MacBook.

Charlotte –

I don't know what exactly happened over at your house—how I suddenly managed to speak out—no, to sing out. But I can't really say that I'm sorry I interfered. What I am sorry for is that it has taken this long for someone to help you and your mom. I should have read the signs earlier. We all should have.

You deserve a life, Charlotte. You and your mother

deserve a life.

About the singing, though. I know you have so much to figure out right now, but I think I do, too. Could I ask, then, a favor? Could you maybe not tell anyone about my role in whatever played out tonight? I need some time to make sense of it all.

She had carried the laptop into her bathroom, and the steam from the bath was drawing her in. She needed to wrap it up. Besides what else could she possibly say?

Anyway, of course you can call me your friend. I will definitely be calling you one of mine again.
Take care of yourself and your mom,
Portia

She rested the laptop on the decking of the tub. Before climbing into the scalding water, she tilted the screen so that it was well within her view.

A slow descent into the water proved incredibly soothing, the silken bubbles caressing her skin and easing her muscles. The scent of the lavender reminded her of Ms. Leucosia's special ointment.

She glanced over at the laptop, surprised to find that she had one more e-mail from Charlotte:

Portia –

I already told him that if he ever so much as breathes your name, I will kill him. At first he started to laugh, but I stared him down. I can't remember the last time I leveled my eyes with his. Anyway, I can assure you that, until you are ready to share your voice with the world, your secret is safe with us.

By the way, have you ever heard those stories about people showing superhuman strength when they're in a crazy situation? Like a mother suddenly being able to lift up the weight of a car in order to free her child? Maybe that's what happened to you tonight. Maybe when you saw our situation you somehow found that superhuman power. I don't know—

just a theory…

*Anyway, I won't even say thank you again because those
words can't really express the gratitude I feel.*

*I will say, though, that your voice is the most beautiful
thing I have ever heard in my life, and I can't wait to hear it
again. Under better circumstances, of course.*

Charlotte

Submerging herself back down into the water, Portia
closed her eyes, allowing the words of Charlotte's e-mail to
float around her weary mind. Maybe her neighbor had a point.
Maybe the singing was just a superhuman reaction to a life-
threatening situation.

Her nerves tightened at the thought that perhaps the voice
was only a one shot deal, a fleeting gift of strength to help
halt the abuse. Maybe she only had enough of the Powerball
numbers to collect the $10,000 prize, while the $100 million
prize remained beyond her reach.

Portia swallowed hard at the thought that she might never
hear her voice again.

I can't go back now. How can I go back?

She was terrified to open her mouth and be faced with
silence. Her pulse raced at the thought, and she half expected
the water to rise up and down with the increasing intensity of
her heartbeat. But the waters remained still. She was surrounded
by silence.

She tried focusing on the sound of the popping bath
bubbles. This was the symphony of her life. Sound bytes floating
around her, bubbles bursting in her silent clutches.

I won't go back.

Downstairs, she heard Helena and Joshua enter the house,
laughing about something. If she was going to give it another
go, she needed to do it now before her parents came upstairs.

Her chest tightened as she readied herself for the ultimate
test. She could feel the blood pumping through her veins,
burning her from within.

I just need to know that it wasn't a one shot deal. Please…

She wasn't even sure who she was pleading with as she lowered the back of her head into the bath, allowing the water to cover her ears.

Closing her eyes, she drew in a deep breath, inhaling the noiselessness, the absence of sound a reminder of the world she hoped to now leave behind.

She opened her mouth and coaxed out one word before she would retreat back into the façade of her silence.

"PORTIA!" she screamed into the scented water.

The still bathwater rippled at the sound of her angelic voice.

Part Two

Odyssey

Chapter 7

In the days following Portia's near murder of Harold Trotter, Max Hunter was the farthest thing from her mind. OK, maybe not the farthest. With everything that had happened, she was astounded to find that thoughts of him had still managed to worm their way under her skin.

But things had changed.

She had a voice now.

A VOICE!

Whatever careless remark Max had made to her in the music room seemed a million miles away now. Clearly he still felt uncomfortable about it. For days, he seemed to be avoiding any real conversation with her, offering instead only slight apologetic smiles when they passed each other in the halls. Truth was, she was bursting at the seams with it all and thought about breaking the ice with him herself. But Portia was an old-fashioned girl at heart.

Let him make the first move.

Instead she focused on the voice. Every morning after her miraculous acquisition, Portia had mumbled a few words into her pillow, just to make sure that she had still hit the vocal jackpot. She said them, she sang them, whispered and screeched them, bending her new voice backward and forward. Every way she revisited the spoken word delighted her.

After hearing herself, she was absolutely buoyant—totally high on vocal adrenaline. As long as she put the more bizarre aspects of that fateful day at the Trotters' on the back burner, a luxury she would allow herself for a few days at least, her entire world had just gone from black and white to Technicolor.

Charlotte was notably absent for a bit, but for the first

time in years, Portia felt like she knew what to expect from her neighbor. She wondered how long Charlotte would need before trying to slip back into a normal routine and made a mental note to keep checking in with her.

But except for speaking to Charlotte, she would remain silent for now. She wasn't ready to reveal her new voice— couldn't imagine how she ever would be ready, especially when it came to Felix. Her pulse quickened at the thought of him. How the hell was she going to tell Felix? How the hell wasn't she going to tell him? She was bursting with it, foaming over with excitement. He would definitely notice—he usually noticed if she developed a new freckle, for God's sake.

She found herself avoiding him for the first few days, hiding out in her room all weekend. Between the awkwardness with Max and trying to sidestep Felix, she couldn't help but feel some rain pouring down on her evolutionary parade. And so she faced an inevitable truth—she had to try to tell Felix. She had to try to ease him into the idea that they might no longer stand on the same handicapped platform that had supported them all these years. After third period on Monday, she began to strategize about how she could do this, until she opened her locker and was greeted by a CD, boldly labeled "Portia—a Song." Suddenly all thoughts of Felix were erased.

Her heart stopped. And before she even played the CD or read the note that Max had scrawled out, she knew that peace between them would be restored.

> *"Hey –*
>
> *I was going to record this even before I made a total ass out of myself last week in the music room. This song was born the minute you turned around and glared at me in Rathi's class.*
>
> *The long and the short of it is, Portia Griffin, I have never told anyone the things I told you that day. And, considering how messed up my life is, I don't feel like I have time to play games. I don't want us to avoid each other anymore. If I'm feeling it, I want you to know I'm feeling*

*it. Even if you're not feeling it, too. (Which I hope to God
you are.)*

I'm so sorry if I hurt you. Forgive?

*With crossed fingers and a bleeding heart (what can I
say—I told you I inherited my father's romantic gene),*

Max Hunter"

Portia read and reread the message. She could barely
maintain her footing as she grabbed her laptop and raced for
the bathroom in the library stacks—the most remote place she
could possibly think of.

She slipped the disk into the computer and turned the
volume up as high as it would go. And then Max Hunter's voice
was singing the words that he had written for her.

*"...a current filled with shock and awe
I'll search for truth in you..."*

She conjured an image of his mouth forming these words,
of his knee bouncing in time to his own rhythm. His voice was
infectious—invading her pores, bringing a flush to her cheeks
and a cyclone of warmth to her belly.

And then a verse he must have added after the music
room debacle:

*And now my words have caused you pain,
But there's also pleasure to be gained.
I can murmur verses sweet,
Can take the cold—turn it to heat*

*And then when silence does descend,
Your touch for words in lieu,
I think that's when my heart will mend
I'll find my truth in you...*

Portia sunk to the floor, her breath coming hard.

Had she actually inspired this...this poetry? It
was unbelievable.

The bell rang and she knew that if she wanted to make it to
her *Odyssey* class on time, she was going to have to sprint across

the school. Whatever. Homer could wait. She had something to do first.

She took out her phone and steadied her hands.

"I'm so glad the romantic gene turns out to be hereditary."

She hit send but couldn't wait for him to respond before typing out, "BTW, did I mention that you're 100%, totally and completely forgiven?"

Satisfied that she had made her point, she sent the second message and raced off to class.

The sophomore elective on Homer's *Odyssey* would have started on the first day of school had Mr. Morrison not come down with a sudden case of food poisoning.

Portia had been delighted when Felix told her that they'd be in the class together—they both viewed the Homeric classic as the original *Harry Potter*. It wasn't until she ran into the classroom that morning, though, that she realized Max would also be exploring Odysseus's journey with them.

She flushed red at the sight of him as he offered her a grin that reached deep into his eyes. It was the first time in days that she smiled back at him fully, holding his eyes and offering him a conciliatory tip of her head. She was absolutely afloat with joy, with Max, with her voice.

"He was about to shut the door, Portia—you just made it," Felix signed, bringing her back to reality. She hoped he didn't pick up on the heat in her cheeks.

She started signing back some feeble excuse, but suddenly her hands felt sluggish. She tried lifting them up again, but for some reason they just weren't up to task. And then, Felix's form grew hazy. Fearing another odd health episode, she allowed her hands to drop to her lap, closing her eyes in an effort to regain herself. She blinked a few times to bring Felix back into focus, and when she looked back at him, he was already looking straight ahead at Ellen Chadwicke's dexterous signing. The interpreter's hands were moving at a frantic pace, though Mr.

Morrison's words poured out like slow maple syrup as an abrupt calm settled over the class.

"So let's get started, my friends. *The Odyssey*—real or imagined?" He didn't wait for a response. "Of course, logic would tell us that there was no such thing as a giant Cyclops or a Goddess named Circe who could turn man into beast. But how many of you have used the phrase 'between a rock and a hard place'?" Again, no pause for response. "The origin for this expression comes straight from *The Odyssey*. It refers to the proximity shared by the two evil sea Goddesses—Scylla, who was tethered to a rock, and Charybdis, who would suck sailors in like a whirlpool, making her 'a hard place' to cross. We wouldn't be adopting everyday expressions from a story that was entirely fictitious, would we?

"So for the purpose of this class, I want us to approach these lessons with the knowledge that there just very well may be a whole world of Gods out there, wielding their magic at every turn. Some can enter dreams, some can procure love, and some can sing. I think this will give us all a better grasp on the subject at hand…"

As the lesson drew to a close, the professor announced how the class would be graded.

"There will be a midterm paper and a final exam. For the paper, each of you is going to research a different obstacle that Odysseus was forced to overcome. The assignment list is as follows…"

Portia gave Felix a quick smile when he was assigned the Cyclops. Considering his recent growth spurt, she felt the shoe fit.

"Portia Griffin, The Sirens—"

An obnoxious snicker escaped Zachary Wilson's unfiltered mouth. "Talk about ironic," he muttered.

Portia shot him a blazing look, though she, too, wondered at Morrison's choice—a group of Goddesses whose sole strength lay in the one thing the professor knew her not to have.

"What? What happened?" Felix signed.

"Nothing, just Zachary Wilson being an asshole," she

signed back. "Not worth getting worked up about."

And then she remembered that it really wasn't. None of it mattered anymore.

Luckily Max's assignment was called out next. He had heard Zachary's snicker and looked ready to pounce. The Six-Headed Scylla would be his topic, which had Portia a bit jealous. Something about the evil sea Goddess snatching up sailors with each of her six heads had always fascinated her in a morose, grotesque kind of way. She worried, though, that Max might not be as excited about the prospect of studying the violent creature, considering his mom and all. But when she looked over, it was clear that he was more interested in ripping Zachary Wilson a new one than the topic of his research paper.

When class was over, he approached Zachary's desk in a flash.

"Hey, mate, you like laughing? How about I laugh while I beat that bloody smirk off your face?"

Portia didn't like where this was headed. Felix had moved in closer and was following the bogus apology Zachary was offering up. She tugged on his sleeve.

"Please, let it go. It's not worth it, Felix."

He signed back, "If he laughed at you, it's worth it to me, Portia."

"No, really, it's not important. Max is new—he shouldn't get in trouble because of me, shouldn't get into a fight. Just grab him and get us out of here before one of us ends up expelled. Please…"

At the mention of Max's name, Felix pulled back. "So it's not that your honor shouldn't be defended. It's just that you don't think *he* should be doing the defending, right? Don't wanna mess up that pretty face of his, right?"

Portia could not believe that was what he thought. "No, it's not like that at all."

She wanted to come clean with him. She wanted to explain that something—everything—had changed in an instant. That she could study Sirens from now until the end of time and it wouldn't bother her anymore because everything was different now.

But first she had to get them out of the classroom before a punch was thrown. Portia looked around the room, relieved to see that Ms. Chadwicke was still there. She motioned her over, signing quickly that she needed her to interpret.

"Hey, Zachary," the sign language interpreter orated for Portia, "too bad you didn't get Calypso as your topic. Closest you'd ever come to being held hostage for sex. Come to think of it, closest you'd probably ever come to sex at all…" Ms. Chadwicke inflected the words with the proper sting, despite the blush that had risen to her cheeks.

Portia thanked her, grabbed Felix and Max, and left a belittled Zachary Wilson to nurse his wounded ego.

As soon as they were out the door, Max got a text that instantly brought a grave look to his face. "Sorry—my dad…" he excused himself and hurried off toward the school office.

When he was gone, Portia pulled Felix into the auditorium, dragging him backstage to the sound and lighting booth.

"Sit down," she signed.

"What's this about, Portia? We haven't snuck in here since that time we spied on Jared Weber doing his secret rendition of 'Defying Gravity.' " His mood was already lightening since the almost-altercation.

"I forgot about that! You gotta admit, he does a mean Elphaba—"

"Well, I couldn't exactly hear him, but Weber definitely gives off that 'meant to be on the stage' vibe."

Portia agreed with a smile, her stomach flip-flopping all over the place as she tried to figure out the best way to break her big news to Felix. She decided to just say it. Literally say it.

"Felix, I've changed." She was so relieved to hear her voice again and wondered if she would ever take for granted that she was now able to speak. A quick double take around the small booth ensured her that no one else was around to hear her speak the words out loud.

"Yeah, I've noticed. I mean, you look completely different than before I left—"

"No," she repeated louder, "I've really changed, Felix. Something inside of me has changed."

"What do you mean? And why are you exaggerating your lips so much?"

Her heart broke at the question. He couldn't hear her, would never hear her, and the confusion on his face had her second-guessing her decision to reveal her secret in the first place.

"Felix," she attempted another approach, "if one day, I moved on, if I became like a famous actress or singer or something, would things with us have to be different? I mean, there would still be an 'us,' right?"

She knew she wasn't making any sense, but she just couldn't say the words. Though, ironically enough, this was the first time she was speaking aloud in public in her whole life.

"That's obviously a ridiculous goal, Portia. I'm not sure where you are heading with all of this." He looked at her hard, his eyes unwavering. If he was confused, angry, hurt, he was determined not to let her know.

"Never mind," she signed.

But the line had already been cast. "What is it? That Max guy? Is that what the big change is all about? Why should that matter to me? You've known the guy for like a day and already you feel like you've completely changed?!" His mask broke for an instant, and she could detect a hint of something in his eyes. Jealousy? Fear of losing her?

This conversation was going nowhere. If Felix was afraid of losing her to the new guy at school, she could only imagine how he'd react to knowing that the label of 'handicapped' was now exclusively his...

"Yeah, it's Max, I guess. He seems like a pretty cool guy. The whole accent thing is kind of charming—"

"I hadn't noticed." His tone was facetious. She couldn't believe how badly she was bungling this conversation.

"And you're right," she attempted to assuage him, "I've only known Max for like a millisecond…" She had stopped speaking out loud, allowing her hands to pick up where her voice left off.

The door to the darkened auditorium suddenly swung open, and the darting figure of Jared Weber crept into the auditorium as if he was on a black ops mission. Portia and Felix sunk down at the sight of him. They looked at each other and laughed, a cautious laughter that reflected a vague awkwardness between them.

As Jared started warming up to a medley of show tunes, Portia wondered how things with Felix could ever go back to the way it was before the voice.

Or, for that matter, before Max Hunter.

That night Portia took her laptop into her bathroom and turned on both the sink and bath faucets. Certain that her voice would be fully camouflaged by the running water, she invited Charlotte Trotter to a video chat. Charlotte's hollow face appeared on the screen, offering Portia a pitiable smile as the dark rings around her eyes revealed what must have been another sleepless night.

"Hi." And there it was again. That one syllable, spoken out loud, assuring her that she was still released from the shackles of silence.

"Hey. You sound like you're under a waterfall."

"Yeah, I still don't want my parents to hear me yet. Just not ready. Um, how'd it go today with your mom, Charlotte?"

Charlotte's bed was so tightly made that Portia half expected her neighbor to be bouncing a quarter off of it. "It was rough." She picked at an imaginary piece of lint. "My mom, like, wavered between hating me and thanking me for making that call, you know?" Her voice broke a bit and she batted away the dew at her eyes. "Jesus Christ, I haven't stopped crying. What the hell is wrong with me? I don't know, Portia. I don't know if I did the right thing—"

"You did, Charlotte. You'll see in time. You'll see. It just hurts so much now—"

"Will it ever not hurt?" she sounded so desperate.

"I don't know. I wish I did. But people learn to live with all kinds of pain, right? And you're not alone now. I promise you."

Charlotte's face softened at the reference to their new friendship.

Portia tried to lighten things up a bit. "Hey, why don't you kick off your new life by untucking your blankets a little bit? Nobody's bed should look like that," she teased.

Charlotte scanned her bed. "You're right," and she started ripping her blankets up, deliberately tossing her pillows all over her pristine room, causing the laptop to crash to the floor.

"Portia, you still there?" Portia could hear the laughter in Charlotte's voice, though she was now eye level with the casters of a desk chair. When Charlotte brought the webcam back into focus, Portia was delighted to see that the bed had become a mess of billowy clouds.

"God, that felt good." Charlotte plopped down on her stomach, clearly enjoying the feel of the mess beneath her. "So tell me something juicy, Portia. How's that new hot guy in school?"

"Which guy?"

"Oh, come on. You just turned like ten shades of red. You know, the tall one with all the dimples."

At the mention of Max's dimples, Portia spilled it. The whole thing. The Lyrical Poetry encounter, the music room, the song. The only thing she left out was the situation with Max's parents. She felt bound by some unspoken 'music room confidentiality agreement.' "I think he just needed some time away from the big city," she offered as a reason for Max's resettlement.

She had downloaded Max's song to her music library and was excited to play it for Charlotte.

"Holy shit, Portia! That was ridic! Does Felix know?" And just as quickly, the balloon of Portia's euphoria was popped.

"Know what? About Max? I think so. I mean, today I tried telling him about the voice—I just don't think I can keep something so major a secret from him. I mean, he's always noticing my moods and if I'm, like, floating on cloud nine, he's gonna pick up on it. But then I just couldn't. I can't leave him behind. So I kind of used Max as an excuse for my newfound happiness. He was weird about it. I don't know why—I mean, Felix and I are just friends. It's complicated, I guess—"

As she chatted with Charlotte, Portia scrolled through her e-mails.

"Speak of the devil, I think Max just gifted me another song on iTunes."

"He did? What song?"

"It doesn't say. It's just an e-mail from iTunes with a gift card saying, 'Hope this gets the ball rolling.' It's signed just 'M,' but who else could it be?"

"Well, why don't you go find out?"

"Yeah, OK. I'll see you tomorrow, Charlotte."

The girls signed off and Portia opened the e-mail, her heart pounding with excitement. She couldn't imagine what Max thought might top his own song, but she was thrilled that he was thinking of her at all.

The song began downloading, something called "Music We Once Made" by Marsyas. She had never heard of the singer but was always up for something new. What she got, though, was not what she was expecting.

The album cover that appeared on her screen featured a faded illustration of a gaunt man in tattered robes, some ancient wind instrument in his hands. When the song started playing, the image became something of a music video, the man blowing into the instrument with the ease of a great flautist, bringing forth a melody drenched in sadness. The music rose up, higher and higher, until finally the instrument sailed out of the withered man's hands, soaring up into the sky, all the while sustaining the melody. When he began singing, or more like chanting, his voice was old and tired.

> *Once I knew the sisters' song,*
> *When it was good and true.*
> *"Marsyas, come play along,*
> *And we will sing for you."*
>
> *And the glory of their voices,*
> *Never did I doubt.*

Their mother, Terpsichore,
A Goddess who danced about.

Their father, Achelous,
The God of Rivers flowing,
To his daughters gave the gift
Of rhythm ever-knowing.

And so three Sirens came to be,
Sisters of flaming hair.
With eyes of jade and ivory skin
And voices to ensnare.

And then the voice of Marsyas mimicked that of a teasing girl:

"Marsyas, Marsyas,
Ever is he smart with us,
Thinks he'll play the harp for us,
But now he'll play apart from us…"

Portia hit pause. Why the hell would Max have sent her this song? She wondered if he still felt bad about the Zachary Wilson incident and was trying to help her out with her Siren research. Though how this song was supposed to help, she wasn't exactly sure.

She decided to text him.

"Hi, Max—it's Portia. Where'd you find this Siren song?"

While she waited for a response, she powered down her laptop. She wasn't ready to tackle her *Odyssey* assignment yet.

"Huh?" came his reply.

"The song you sent me on iTunes, to 'get the ball rolling.' "

"I'm not sure what you're talking about, Portia. And, btw, I knew it was you. You're like the only person in my contact list…"

As she read his words, she could have sworn she saw the light on her laptop reignite, despite not having pressed a single button. Portia tried to convince herself that maybe she had never fully powered the machine off, though she was never careless with her laptop—it was, by far, her most prized possession. A familiar fear that she was losing her mind crept up her spine as the screen came back to life, picking up right where it had left off.

> *"You cannot escape this song of truth,*
> *A story fierce and sad,*
> *To make a God or mortal weep,*
> *Of Sirens going mad.*
>
> *One indeed remained pure,*
> *Her heart never straying,*
> *But her older sisters' joy,*
> *Came from mortals slaying.*
>
> *And the purpose of my song?*
> *Portia, you will see,*
> *Is to etch into your mind these names:*
> *Ligeia, Parthenope.*

At the sound of her own name in the song, her heart crashed hard into the wall of her chest.

She held her finger on the power button of the MacBook. She held it and held it. But the voice kept sounding off the chorus of the bizarre chant:

> *"Marsyas, Marsyas,*
> *Ever is he smart with us,*
> *Thinks he'll play the harp for us,*
> *But now he'll play apart from us…"*

"Portia? Are you there?" Max texted a couple of times.

Was he playing a joke on her? This song was clearly written *for* her and who else would write a song for her?

"Marsyas, Marsyas…"

"To get the ball rolling…"

"I'm not sure what you're talking about…"

She was drowning in confusion as her heart rate soared, her panic intensifying.

What the hell is going on?

She gave her laptop one last desperate glance.

On the screen, Marsyas straightened up his bent posture.

"Sleep now, Portia."

And thankfully she slept.

Chapter 8

"So has your mom been up at all?" Portia asked Charlotte the next day.

She had gotten off at Charlotte's bus stop, and they were sitting on the Trotters' patio, inches from the infinity pool that Portia never even knew her neighbors had built. The rendezvous was unexpected, and Portia tried telling herself that Charlotte really needed a friend right now, but the truth was she herself was feeling pretty needy. Throughout the day, she had exhausted all of her mental and emotional resources to try to make sense out of the bizarre iTunes gift.

When she saw Max at school he had confirmed for her once again that he had nothing to do with the iTunes song, and Portia didn't press the matter. She certainly didn't need him thinking she was some kind of paranoid lunatic.

Mr. Morrison and Felix also proclaimed innocence, and Portia believed them to be sincere. She thought of who else might have pulled such a weird prank on her but came up empty. Luke and Lance probably didn't even know she was taking *Odyssey*, and Jacqueline prided herself on her lack of virtual interaction—she never even bothered to check her e-mails. In a last-ditch effort to gain some understanding, Portia decided to see if Charlotte could shed some wisdom on the situation.

Charlotte kept her voice down as she addressed Portia's question. "Not much, and I've been trying not to wake her. I keep turning the ringer off on her cell, you know, just in case he tries to contact her…"

When Charlotte referenced her father, she looked like someone who had just been forced to swallow something rancid. Yet every day since she took her own life back, her head tilted another degree higher and her posture was a bit more proud, though still she remained encased from head to toe in thick clothing, preserving that final barrier between her and the rest of the world.

"…Anyway, I figure I'll give her another couple of weeks to wallow in her depression before trying the tough love thing, you know?"

"Yeah, that sounds about right," Portia offered, following Charlotte's lead of a hushed tone. She marveled at her ability not only to speak, but to manipulate her voice, its volume and tone.

"Anyway," Charlotte said, "Let's change the subject. Tell me about the song Max sent you last night. Was it as awesome as the other one?"

Portia reached into her backpack to retrieve her laptop. "Well, you see, that's the thing. It actually wasn't from Max. It was from some guy named Marsyas. But, well, Marsyas seems to be like a gazillion years old."

As she spoke, she pulled up her iTunes library. Scrolling down her list of artists, she found that Marsyas's name was no longer there.

"Wait, let me look under tracks—"

"Portia, if there's, like, some old pedophile stalking you online, you better tell someone."

Music We Once Made was no longer listed in her songs. She opened her e-mail, searching for the notice from iTunes and suspecting, correctly, that her efforts were wasted.

Had she imagined the whole thing?

"I'm not gonna start a relationship with some lunatic on the Internet, Charlotte," she offered offhandedly, though the mercury of her fear was steadily rising as she failed to recover even a trace of the mysterious gift. "Anyway, I must have deleted it by accident." She tried sounding blasé, though her mind couldn't find a comfortable resting spot that would explain the iTunes gift. She just couldn't rid herself of that nagging sensation that someone had hacked into her screen name. Hacked into her life.

"Maybe it was a mistake," Charlotte said dismissively. "So, hey, are you planning a big reveal any time soon?"

But Portia was lost in thought, her eyes fixated on a manicured wall of purple flowers, swarming with butterflies.

"Hello, Portia? Are you listening?"

"Why do they all fly to that one bush?" she asked Charlotte distractedly.

"What are you talking about?" Charlotte followed Portia's gaze to the butterfly bush, which had always been her favorite. "Oh—it's a butterfly bush. It's meant to attract butterflies." Charlotte got up and approached the bush, extending her hand until one of the spotted creatures landed gently on her palm. "When I was younger, this was actually one of my, like, 'focal points,' you know. While stuff was going on inside, I would stare out the window at the butterflies, wishing I was one of them and that I could just fly away…"

"What attracts them to it?"

"They say it's the flowers," Charlotte said as the butterfly flew off her palm. "Hummingbirds come by, too."

Portia welcomed this bit of unknown bird trivia.

"One morning," Charlotte continued, her eyes a bit glazed, "after a pretty bad night, I found my mom out here, staring at the hedge—can you imagine that he planted a whole hedge of something so beautiful? Anyway, she told me that she thinks that all the butterflies are really souls in pain and that they have found this one spot, filled with beauty, where they can all come to be together. Help each other." She unbuttoned her collar and leaned over suddenly. "God, it's hot out here, isn't it?" She peeled off her tights in one fell swoop.

It really wasn't. If anything, there was a bit of a chill in the air. But Portia understood Charlotte's need to start breaking down some more walls and offered her a supportive smile, trying to ignore the healing bruises on Charlotte's bare legs.

Suddenly her iPhone sounded off—a ringtone which she wasn't familiar with. The screen flashed an iCal reminder that said "Siren Research."

As avid an iPhone fan as she was, Portia had never once used her iCal.

Ever.

"Hey, do you think it's possible that Morrison figured out how to get into our iCals?" she asked Charlotte, who was looking much more comfortable, stretching her bare legs and curling them comfortably beneath her.

"I guess it's possible. I don't know," Charlotte said dismissively. "So, like I was saying, are you thinking yet about how you're gonna tell everyone about your new voice?"

Portia thought it over for a minute, stuffing her iPhone into the bottom of her bag.

"I don't know…I don't think I can do it, Charlotte. Seriously, what are people going to say about me? Half of them will think I've been faking all my life, and the other half will just think I'm a freak."

Charlotte grabbed them a couple of sodas from the built-in beverage fridge near the pool.

"I don't think you're being honest with yourself, Portia. I think the only two halves that really matter to you right now are the Felix half and the Max half."

Portia looked back at her friend, visibly impressed.

"What?" Charlotte asked, swigging her Diet Coke. "Do I sound like a therapist? Oh God—I sound like a therapist."

"You don't sound like a therapist. You're right. It's just hearing my predicament said out loud just makes it more, I don't know, real, I guess." She cracked open her soda. "I can't even begin to explain to you the bond I have with Felix."

"Try," Charlotte challenged.

Portia closed her eyes, conjuring an image of her best friend. "You see, Felix has this theory—well, actually it's something his grandmother once told him. She told him that you only have a certain number of words to say in your lifetime, and so you shouldn't waste your words on anything stupid or mean. When he told me this theory, me who couldn't utter a single word, he said, 'so, Portia, you're invincible, you see? You are my forever.' And now I'm not invincible anymore. I'm going to be just like everybody else to him. I don't think things will ever be the same. And now with Max in the picture… I mean, Charlotte, the minute I saw Max, I don't know—it was like…it was like all this silence didn't matter. He's so full of music and sound. I don't feel like an incomplete fraction when I'm around him." She smiled. "Oh God, did I just use an algebraic metaphor?"

"You did, but I won't tell anyone," Charlotte offered. And then, more seriously, "Really, Portia. I won't tell anyone. You'll know when the time is right."

Portia suddenly realized how selfish she was being—spending so much time talking about her own problems, which paled in comparison to Charlotte's.

"Anyway, let's change the subject," she offered up. "Will you please promise to sit with us at lunch tomorrow, Charlotte? How many times am I going to have to ask you?"

Charlotte ran her graceful fingers over the pale flesh of her legs. "I'm getting there, Portia. Any day now…I'm getting there."

As the days wore on, despite the constant unsolicited alerts from her iCal reminding her about her *Odyssey* assignment, Portia couldn't bring herself to start the work. Sleeping had become an overwhelming challenge for her, her nightly dreams a boxing match between the menacing white bird creature and the withered Marsyas, each with their own demands. For some reason Marsyas was fixated on getting her to do more *Odyssey* research and the bird was hell-bent on getting her to reveal her voice to the world.

Portia hoped it was this lack of sleep that was causing her erratic mood swings. She found herself snapping at her parents at the slightest provocation. On more than one occasion, she even started forming angry words in her throat before regaining control. She certainly didn't want to debut her voice to her parents in a fit of fury.

And then there was the elation, the ecstasy. Maybe it was Max. She was finding it more and more difficult to spend time apart from him. Luckily he had decided to join their lunchtime gathering, which had also come to include Charlotte, an addition that her friends had welcomed with a remarkable measure of tact.

Max's reception was not as welcoming. Though Jacqueline had been instantly charmed by him, Luke and Lance were more than a little cold the first time he set his tray down at their table. Their unspoken allegiance to Felix was like a stone wall.

This is not going to be pretty.

Portia had tried easing the tension with valiant conversational efforts with Felix and the twins, which were inevitably lost on Max, who didn't know how to sign.

No, not pretty at all.

Felix seemed to enjoy watching her struggle to bridge the gap until finally he must have taken pity on her and told Luke and Lance to ease up on the new guy.

"No need for turf fights, right? It's not *West Side Story* here, guys…" he had signed to them.

Portia shot him a look of thanks, and he tipped his head toward her. The twins loosened up, immediately segueing into a conversation with Max about how hot Kate Middleton is.

"Yes, I'd have to agree, though I had already moved to the States before they got hitched…"

Ok, this is a little better—not that I need to hear Max acknowledge that another woman is hot…

"Hey, while we're on the topic of dating—" Felix came out with suddenly.

Were we?

"Gabrielle said yes to a second date."

Portia assumed that he must be talking about Gabrielle Parker, a freshman akin to the Heisman Trophy.

When had they had a first date?

Luke and Lance high-fived their friend with great machismo, and Portia unconsciously inched her way closer to Max.

The rest of the lunch was filled with offhand banter. Charlotte even chimed in once when the boys got onto football. Her real father used to be obsessed, and it was the one thing she had always kept up with. But though the table talk might have been simple, the seesaw of glances between Portia and Felix were full of unspoken innuendo.

Later that afternoon, Max threw another ball into the volley of Portia's emotional struggles.

They were standing in front of his locker when suddenly he moved in close to her, gently forcing her up against the metal door. They had not yet shared a kiss and were running out of excuses to touch each other in ways like this. The other day his biceps had looked so inviting that she had purposely stained his sleeve with a chocolate pudding fingertip, just so she could have the pleasure of spot cleaning it for the rest of lunch.

"So, I've got this thing in about a week…"

God, he smelled good.

She waited for him to elaborate.

"It's kind of like a gig—at The Ridge Café…"

Portia took out her phone.

"You mean Café on the Ridge?"

He smiled and moved in even closer. She doubted that a sheet of tissue paper would fit between them.

"Yeah—that's the place. Anyway, there's this girl who I think about, like, all the time when I sing now. I mean, I can't get her out of my head, you know?"

Portia brought her hand to her chin in mock wonder.

"It's bloody hell."

She loved when he regressed into his British dialect.

"Anyway, I was thinking of asking this girl to come see me perform. Do you think she might agree?"

"I think she wouldn't miss it for the world." She held up the phone to Max and then took a chance by gently brushing her lips against his cheek, coming dangerously close to the corner of his mouth.

It wasn't until she saw Felix in her next class that she realized the double booking.

"Hey," she signed to him, "is Wendy still performing Wednesday night?"

"Why? Do you have other plans?" he shot back. Why the

hell was he so angry with her lately?

"No—I mean, um, I'll be there, Felix."

He continued to look at her while she took out her notebook and set up for class.

"What?" she signed, darting her hands angrily into the air. "I said I'd be there."

Finally he looked away.

I'm just not sure who with…

If Portia had any misgivings about accepting his invitation for fear that Felix might be hurt, Max totally sealed the deal that night when they chatted online for an eternity. They seemed to never run out of things to discuss. He had traveled throughout Europe and had a passion for Gothic cathedrals, which Portia found to be endearing.

She, in turn, revealed her own passions for reading and ornithology.

"Omi-what?"

"Omithology—also called ornithology—weird, huh? It's the study of birds," she wrote back, taking in Max's perplexed expression. "It's something I've been drawn to since I was little. I like the way the birds sing to each other. You know, their mating calls…"

She noted the now-familiar spark in Max's eyes when she referenced the mating.

"I'm also a huge Ella Fitzgerald fan." She offered up the non sequitur to change the subject. Music especially was a topic they seemed to never exhaust.

"Really? You've got to be the only sixteen-year-old alive who even knows who Ella is."

"Not true! Besides, since you seem to be on a first-name basis with Ms. Fitzgerald, I'd venture to say that you're not unfamiliar with her yourself."

An annoying pop-up window flashed on her screen with a link to a '.god' address. She X'd it out immediately. She hated pop-ups.

"OK, busted. But I think I prefer Billie Holiday." He smiled into the webcam.

"Well, while we are admitting things," Portia typed out hesitantly, X'ing out the pop-up again when it reappeared, "I think I might also have Bieber Fever."

"NO WAY! You do not."

"I'm telling you," she wrote out hurriedly, "the kid can sing."

"Oh baby, baby, baby, no," Max gave his hair the signature Bieber shake.

Portia smiled. "That was pretty dead-on for a hater," she wrote.

"Yeah? Well, I can also do a mean Dave Matthews," he said, speaking out of the side of his mouth just as Matthews was known to do. "You know, my dad and I went to see him in concert right before his, um, breakdown. It was awesome— we had backstage passes cuz my dad had done some copyright work for the band once. I got to meet all of them—even Tim Reynolds was there. It was amazing, Portia!" she loved hearing him say her name. "I acted like a total groupie, though—asking them to sign my iPod," he held up the device, showing off the bold autograph of Dave Matthews.

"That must have been awesome," she wrote back. "I love Dave Matthews." She glanced at her own iPhone, the screen filled with a barrage of unsolicited reminders to start her *Odyssey* research.

I think I'm going to switch to a Blackberry...

"That's a relief coming from the Fitzgerald–Bieber fanatic," Max chided her.

The pop-up on her laptop came back, this time in bold red letters, which inadvertently made Portia's hair stand on end. Who the hell ever heard of a .god address anyway?

"Hey, Max—can you check out this link I keep getting? I'm totally paranoid about viruses and since you're so chivalrous and all…" she batted her eyelashes into the camera as she typed out the words.

"Anything for you, m'lady," he obliged.

Portia copied the link and zoomed it across cyberspace to her knight in shining armor.

"Send it over, Portia."

"I just did…here, wait, I'll do it again," she wrote. Copying and pasting again, she looked for a sign in Max's face that he had received the link. After her tenth attempt, he was still coming up with nothing.

"Never mind," she wrote, determined to get back to the flirting at hand.

"You sure? That's weird that you couldn't send me the link. Did you try to type it out manually?"

She had, actually, but every time she tried sending the link to Max, her screen went blank for a millisecond before bringing him back into focus.

"Yeah, whatever." She wrote. She was exhausted—it was almost 2:30 a.m., and they had been chatting for hours.

"You look tired," he said. He seemed to have a knack for reading her thoughts. "Should we call it a night?"

"I would normally say yes," came her response, "but I've been having such bad dreams lately. I feel like falling asleep is just an open invitation for the creepies to come get me."

"Really, what have you been dreaming about?" Max asked.

Portia was embarrassed to tell him about the strange cast of characters that had occupied her dreams recently. She didn't want to describe to him the monstrous flock of white birds, who kept beckoning her to "wield her powers," or the ancient withered man, who was obsessed with her getting an A in her *Odyssey* elective. Clearly all the pressure was really getting to her.

"Too personal," she wrote back. She knew she sounded vague, but what was it Helena always said?—"Always keep them guessing…"

"Oh, is that how you're gonna play it?" Max smiled. She could have sworn she heard his dimples crunch.

"Well, how 'bout I sing you to sleep then, Portia Griffin?"

I gotta get me some of that confidence.

"Whaddya mean?" she typed with an equal measure of

eagerness and anxiety.

"You know," Max responded, "like a lullaby." His easy affect gave off the impression that he was like some kind of angel who spent his nights flying from room to room, easing girls into the delicious and undemanding throes of slumber.

"We can try that, I guess." There was an anxious twitch in her fingers as she typed out the words that welcomed this next level of intimacy between them.

She looked into the webcam, wondering if he realized that she was a bundle of nerves.

"Hold on a sec," he said. He disappeared for a minute and then came back into view with his guitar. During his absence, Portia was able to see that his room looked like a tornado had hit it, piles and papers covering every surface.

She X'd out the determined .god pop-up again. Nothing was going to force her away from this moment.

"Let's see," he made a great show of cracking all his knuckles at once. She smiled at the gesture.

He started strumming his guitar. "Relax, Portia," he said. "It's not like I'm going to show up in your bedroom or something."

When he said it, she realized that a part of her was actually hoping he would.

I have got to stop comparing myself to Bella Swan.

"It's just a lullaby," Max was saying. "Why don't you lie back and try to relax?"

She took his advice, crawling under her heavy quilt, resting her head on the soft cotton of her pillowcase. When she had the laptop comfortably perched on her belly, she gave him the thumbs-up sign.

"So, have I mentioned that I'm a bit of a car fanatic?" Max asked as he adjusted the tension of the strings.

"No, but I thought I spotted a pile of *Car and Driver* magazines on your night table," she typed.

"Yeah, well, I'm a bit of a slob, too. Comes with the territory of creative genius. At least that's what my aunt always says." He smiled widely.

"I'm sure you've said it a few times yourself, Max,"

Portia shot back.

"Maybe. Maybe. Anyway, let's see what you think of this one:

> *You won't share your dreams,*
> *But I'll tell you mine.*
> *They ease with extended release.*
>
> *They don't stray from the theme,*
> *And I'm lost in time*
> *As I dream every crevice, each crease.*
>
> *There's a way your hip curves—*
> *It invites, then recedes,*
> *And it makes a man wish for the road.*
>
> *It sways and it swerves,*
> *No limits to speed.*
> *Ease the clutch, man, before overload.*
>
> *You're the Moyenne Corniche,*
> *the Autobahn,*
> *Just stop and admire the view.*
> *And my dreams they do teach*
> *That I could drive on,*
> *But I'll always just come back to you.*

Max closed his eyes, folding himself around his music. Portia noticed the beginning of a kneehole in the faded denim of his jeans. She wondered if he realized just how loaded his lyrics were and then berated herself for her naiveté.

He probably patted himself on the back with every double entendre he wrote.

He switched octaves and continued.

> *Road maps don't reveal,*
> *No warnings to heed,*
> *Be aware there are sharp turns below.*

Behind this wily wheel,
Shoulders just increase speed,
And bumps also can't get you to slow.

And the rearview so appealing–
God, where's the U-turn?
I've gotta see it again.

My tires are squealing,
Almost crash and burn,
But this time I'll take it at ten.

Cuz you're the Moyenne Corniche…

She was melting in her bed. One minute his sounds were rich and multilayered, the next his vocals were absolutely weightless as they traveled into falsetto. She imagined him whispering the suggestive lyrics into her ear, breathing them into her neck. He opened his eyes momentarily to assess her reaction, further electrifying her, mirroring her own desire and longing.

Our bodies now sweaty,
The wipers full force,
But still it is so hard to see.

I'm Mario Andretti,
I'm stuck on the course,
And you, baby, are the Grand Prix.

And then the dream starts to slip,
It's time to look for a spot,
The end of this driving mission.

But that clutch I still grip,
Idling not,
My key always in the ignition.

Max looked directly into her eyes and sang the refrain once again. At this, Portia couldn't take it anymore. Rubbernecking deeper into her pillow, she pretended to sleep. It was the only way she could think of to quiet the storm that was brewing between them.

"Baby, I come back to you…"

He hummed a few last bars until eventually his voice trailed off, leaving swirls of steam in its wake.

Chapter 9

Though she had pretended to fall asleep quickly, the fact was that Portia couldn't fall asleep that night. How could she have after being serenaded like that? Were people even still serenading each other these days? She felt like she had been thrust back in time to an era where romantic inclinations were a thing men wore proudly on their sleeves.

No—sleep would definitely not be happening.

Recalling that Charlotte was a die-hard insomniac, she decided to scroll through her buddy list on the off chance that Charlotte was online. Scrolling down to Trotter, her hand stopped dead on the track pad when she saw Marsyas's name front and center on her buddy list.

He was inviting her to chat.

Her hair did the standing on end thing again as her mind urged her hand away from accepting the chat. How many lectures had she heard about cyber-bullying from her parents? How many RPA assemblies had been devoted to this exact scenario?

But logic had no voice tonight and she ushered Marsyas into the sanctuary of her bedroom with a single click. The craggy caves of his cheeks appeared on her screen, his thin lips hanging like tattered curtains over the run-down stage of his mouth. It was hard to make out where he was, the background behind his image fuzzy and dark.

Portia stared at the screen. The time travel thoughts she had had about Max just a few moments earlier came swarming back to her. Only this time she was venturing way before the era of Victorian gentlemen or medieval knights. Marsyas looked like he was born at around the same time as the world itself.

"What do you want from me?" The words were rising up

in her throat, but she forced them back down, touch-typing the question instead as she stared at him over the webcam. If she couldn't reveal her voice to her family and friends, she certainly wasn't going to reveal it to this anachronistic cyberstalker.

The .god link popped up again and she was about to X it out when Marsyas suddenly spoke:

"Hit the link, Portia."

How did he know?

"Portia, hit the link," he repeated.

And so, against her better judgment, she clicked on the link.

The link, laboriously titled "www.daughtersofachelous-andterpsichore.god," brought Portia to a digital storytelling site, where the lines of reality and fantasy were blurred and blended so skillfully that by the time she brushed her teeth in the morning, she was certain that if she lived until the end of time, she would never forget the story of the sisters that was revealed to her that night...

More than three thousand years ago, when Gods lived among mortals and cast their magical spells at every turn, there lived three sisters. The sisters dwelt on an island just beside the evil Six-Headed Scylla, who with each of her long-necked heads plucked sailors from the hulls of their ships and feasted upon their flesh and bones. The island was lush, blanketed in flowers and rich with olives. The grass grew green and the trees provided cool shade from the ever-shining sun.

The three sisters, Parthenope, Ligeia, and Leto, were of hauntingly beautiful face. They had inherited the milky skin of their mother, Terpsichore, Goddess of the Dance. From their father, Achelous, God of the Rivers, the young maidens were gifted with eyes so green they made the purest emerald appear lackluster. A bounty of fiery locks crowned their delicate heads like silk woven of the finest threads.

The extraordinary beauty of the maidens was contained in their voices as well. For they could sing more sweetly than a lyre cast of solid gold.

And so the sisters enjoyed goodness, faring well on the island that was their home.

As children, often were the sisters visited by Marsyas, an immortal with music running through his very veins. Marsyas played all manner of instrument with blessed skill and passed many days with the sisters, playing the double-piped reed or the ivory harp while they sang their glorious songs.

But as the years of their childhood passed, Parthenope and Ligeia thought to challenge Marsyas, though he had become but a brother to them. They tricked him by singing ever slowly and then suddenly speeding up their song. They sang melodies with which Marsyas was not familiar. Then they teased him with cruel words:

> "Marsyas, Marsyas,
> Ever is he smart with us,
> Thinks he'll play the harp for us,
> But now he'll play apart from us…"

The sisters taunted Marsyas, wounding him in his heart for he had thought of the young Sirens as no less than his own kin.

"Parthenope, Ligeia, why do you wound me so?" he asked the Goddesses.

The sisters then laughed and responded, "Marsyas, it humors us that ever you thought your skills could match those of the Sirens."

Leto pitied the young God and tried to soothe him with her own song. But Marsyas was forever changed by the betrayal of Parthenope and Ligeia. For the rest of his days, he questioned his skills as a maker of music.

Terpsichore, the mother of the Sirens, feared the scorn that her daughters showed Marsyas. One day she lamented her daughters' ways unto Themis, a Goddess who could see the future.

"Terpsichore," said Themis, "It saddens me to tell you that the souls of Parthenope and Ligeia are doomed, for their evil ways will only grow stronger with the passing of time. Yet Leto will ever retain a soul that is pure and true. But hear this, Terpsichore, if Leto dares to defy her sisters, they will surely kill her. I have seen a vision of your daughters tearing your youngest limb from limb at her refusal to partake in their evil. But a Goddess such as you, dear Terpsichore, can surely see to it that this vision is never realized…"

The words fell heavily upon the heart of Terpsichore and filled her with great dread. Alas, she did love her Leto best of all her daughters, knowing that she would ever be kind.

As word of Leto's gentle heart spread among the Gods, Parthenope and Ligeia felt the winds of envy stir within them. They watched as their youngest sister was often invited by the Gods to sing for their pleasure, though they, too, possessed voices of glory. All manner of immortal spoke of the great Leto, whose voice soothed their nerves like a sweet tonic.

One fine day Terpsichore was dancing for the eyes of Poseidon, the great earth shaker. Poseidon's son, an evil Cyclops called Polyphemus, was moved by the seductive dance of the Goddess. He drew near to Terpsichore, begging her to come dwell with him in his own land, where she could dance for him the many days of his life. Terpsichore said then to the giant Cyclops Polyphemus:

"Surely you must see, Polyphemus, though you stand so tall with your head lost in the skies, that I am bound to another. Achelous, the great God of the rivers, shall forever hold my precious heart."

So stung was the evil Polyphemus by these words that with his giant hand he thrashed Terpsichore to the ground, impaling her head on the jagged edge of a stone.

The dancing Goddess cried out in her pain, knowing that soon death would be upon her.

"I beseech you, Poseidon, great God of wind and thunder," she said, "bring unto me my most cherished and youngest daughter, Leto. For upon her glorious face I wish to set my eyes once more before death takes me away. Beg her, make haste, for even now I do feel my last breaths upon me."

Poseidon beckoned Leto, who then traveled to the side of her dying mother, uttering not a word to her sisters, for she did not dare ignite their fiery envy.

But, alas, Ligeia had been bathing at the edge of the meadow when the great Poseidon came to call upon Leto. Her ears burned with the news of her mother's imminent death. An arrow of envy pierced her heart with the knowledge that her mother had beckoned only Leto to her side as she made ready to leave this earth.

When the fair Leto reached the side of her dying mother, she wept giant tears of silver. Her mother beseeched her, "Leto, draw near for there are things I must say to you before I am to join the spirits in Hades."

Leto drew near to the face of her beloved mother, which even now trickled with blood.

"Leto, widely known among the Gods is it that the goodness which *grows within you will not as such grow within your sisters. For in them there lies an evil that cannot be destroyed.*

"One day it shall pass that Parthenope and Ligeia will beckon you to partake with them in their evil ways. Themis has assured me that if you resist them, they will surely kill you. I beg of you, do not resist the demands of your sisters. For I cannot go in peace to my death without the certain knowledge that you will remain safe."

Leto swore all that her mother begged as thick silver tears marred her lovely face. She sang sweetly and placed a gentle hand on her mother's supple cheek, soothing Terpsichore's nerves. Her song was one of peace and harmony—the magnificence of her voice infusing beauty into the dying moments of the Goddess who once had danced like no other.

And so, after many years, the ageless maidens began to feel the ennui of living only with each other's company. They gazed longingly at the ships that passed their island, thoughts of evil and mischief clouding the minds of Parthenope and Ligeia.

"Sisters," beckoned Parthenope one day, "fair maidens such as we should not to all the world go unnoticed. Let us call upon our glorious voices to lure in the sailors who pass us by in their wooden ships."

Ligeia found favor in the words of her oldest sister and said:

"Dearest Parthenope, long have I waited for the words you have just spoken. What say you, Leto? Shall you join us in wielding our powers of seduction?"

Leto then remembered the oath that she had taken moments before her mother's death.

"Dearest sisters, I have known only great love for you these many years and will surely be among you in whatever journeys you will take."

Thus the Goddesses conjured up the giant white wings, which at their behest could emerge from their delicate backs. They flew to the edge of the island and began to sing their sweet song. Their voices carried strong along the waters, rippling in the foamy waves.

As a new ship appeared, they beckoned the sailors and watched as the ship's mast turned and began rushing toward the island, delighting the sisters and assuring them of their great powers. Their voices thus grew stronger, hastening the current of the waters.

The young Sirens grew more frenzied as the ship neared the island. Their beauty became even greater, their voices more ethereal as they could make out the forms of the mortals. So consumed were Parthenope and Ligeia by their own seductive powers that they failed to notice the great sadness that veiled the face of their sister, Leto.

The sisters floated ever higher and joined hands. The crashing of the waves beat in time to their glorious song as the ship grew nearer to the island.

The sailors were powerless to resist them and called out in earnest:

"Come to us, Goddess of the sea, so that you may make yourselves known!"

Parthenope and Ligeia laughed at the beckoning of the mortal men, thoughts of evil consuming them. They sang louder and flew faster, creating dizzying rings above the sailors, who were mesmerized by this vision of the deities.

"My fair sisters," said Parthenope, "join me now in the destruction of these mere mortals for they are not worthy to know us. So weak are these men who cannot but for an instant resist the powers of a beautiful woman."

Leto turned her glorious face from her sisters for fear that they would see her tears. She thought of her beloved mother as she yielded to their demands. The three Sirens then merged their beauty and powers into one great creature. They revealed themselves anew to the sailors with the supple body of one woman, whose form was suspended by giant wings that reached as far as the edges of the sea.

"Oh, beautiful creature surely sent to us from the great Zeus himself, deny us no longer. Come to us so that we may quench our desires for one as fair as you." The sailors were on bended knee, pleading for the attentions of the Sirens.

But as the thoughts of Parthenope and Ligeia continued toward evil, so distorted did the face of the creature suddenly become that a deep fear and disgust came into the hearts of the sailors. The mortals then knew that danger was upon them.

"Spare us, oh creature of the sea!" cried the men. "For we are but mere mortals, powerless to the beauty of your voice. Now we see that we have been greatly fooled, for your face does reveal to us the evil that lives within you."

But there was no halting the evil that was growing inside Parthenope *and Ligeia. The giant winged creature sang ever louder and swooped down into the hull of the wooden vessel.*

Loud were the screams of the sailors, the sounds of their bones crunching as the sisters destroyed and consumed them. The Sirens sang throughout the entire murderous frenzy. They sang of the beauty of women and the foolishness of men, of appetites for passion that could never be sated, of the infinite powers of the Gods.

When the maidens had their fill, they pried their forms apart and were once again three beautiful sisters. They gathered the bones of the men, so light within their immortal hands, and brought them to the edge of the meadow, where they laid the foundation for what would grow to be a great mountain.

That night Leto sought out a veiled crevice of the island on which to lay her weary self. Streaks of silver stained her silken cheeks as finally she drifted off to sleep.

As word of the attack made its way to the many Gods of earth and sea, Morpheus, the great God of Dreams, granted Leto a dream to soothe her aching heart.

Terpsichore once again appeared to her daughter, bearing no traces of the injury which did claim her life.

"Do not be sad, Leto. You have done well to follow the promise you made me. One day you will know another, and she will share your goodness. She will have skin the color of olives and eyes of lapis. She, too, will sing like no other…"

As Portia pulled herself together the next morning, she tried, in vain, to reorient herself. She felt trapped in a vortex of fantasy, so unsure about what was real and what was imagined that she wondered if she had even dreamt Max's seductive song.

Looking in the mirror, she was overwhelmed by the black rings under her eyes. Taking special care to camouflage her fatigue, she decided to run the straightener through her hair that day. Why not opt for some pin-straight sophistication over the rambling waves that usually comprised her mess of hair? But no matter how high she set the heat on the iron, she couldn't calm her hair, which seemed to have thickened overnight.

Deciding not to argue with Mother Nature's rebellious streak, Portia gave her head one final tousle and headed downstairs.

"Whoa," Joshua stopped her in the kitchen. "That's quite a hairdo, Portia. Wait, do people actually still say hairdo?"

"I don't think so, Dad," she signed.

"Is there something special happening at school today? Someone special, maybe?"

Portia glared at her father with fire in her eyes. How dare he presume to know what was going on in her love life? In her life at all? When he sensed her wrath, she watched with a modicum of pleasure as the blood drained out of his face.

"What? What did I say?"

And then it passed. Just like that, the anger was gone.

"Nothing," she signed, "Sorry—I didn't get much sleep last night."

He walked over to her, arms outstretched, but for some reason she recoiled from his touch, grabbing her bag and heading out without turning back to take in the hurt on Joshua's face.

Seated in comfortable silence next to Charlotte on the bus a few minutes later, Portia replayed the run-in with her father.

What the hell was that about?

She never got that angry with her dad—or with anyone— and was typically pretty open with her folks about what was going on in her life. But this burst of rage was utterly indescribable. And what for? He hadn't even really said anything wrong.

Maybe I just don't have room right now for a third man in my life, she thought with a stab of guilt.

At the thought of her men, she remembered Felix and wondered if he would be carrying a grudge about last night. She had refused a number of invitations from him to video chat, not wanting to interrupt her time with Max.

Charlotte was busy texting her mom, so she decided to give Felix a shout-out.

"Hey there," she texted him, invoking a casualness she did not really feel.

"Oh, look who decided to crawl out of the woodwork," he wrote back. "What's with u declining me last night?"

"Three times…" he added just as she began typing back.

"Sorry—Charlotte and I were reviewing chem."

"For three hours?"

Portia waited, letting the comment slide. What could she say?

"Whatever—did u ask Char if she's coming to open mic nt?"

Here was her chance to throw out a blasé warning to Felix about Max's scheduled performance at the café. There was a slight tremor in her thumbs as she texted, "Not yet—will today…"

And then the bomb.

"U know, Max is gonna be performing that nt—cool, right?"

Was that blasé enough?

"No, actually I didn't know that," came Felix's response, "Like I said before—whatever."

Guess not.

The rage she had felt earlier returned without warning.

"Felix, I already told you. You don't own me. And you never will," she added.

Her fury propelled her fingers to type at a speed that matched her pulse.

There was no response from him as the bus pulled up to campus, and Portia tried to calm herself before heading into school. She cleared her mind of everything—Felix's pettiness, the random story of the three sisters, and Marsyas, the newest addition to her buddy list, though she had never invited or accepted him.

She just wanted to feel ordinary. Wanted to mentally replay Max's "lullaby" in her head without interruption. She had never thought of herself as a vehicular metaphor, but after last night, she knew that her relationship with him had permanently shifted out of neutral.

With these thoughts, the spring returned to her step as she

bounded off the bus. She was just moments away from hearing his voice again.

When she walked into *Odyssey* class that morning, though, she saw only Felix. She wondered where Max was, but Mr. Morrison wasted no time beginning the class, so she settled herself next to Felix, exchanging only a brief awkward greeting with him.

Morrison's lecture that day turned out to be something of an Odysseus pity party. "So, show of hands—is there anyone among you who has *not* had to overcome obstacles in your lifetime?"

She looked over at Felix, whose eyes were glued to Ellen Chadwicke's hands, and a wave of guilt washed over her when she thought about his obstacles, their obstacles. The ones they had had to face together. The ones that *she* had finally overcome, leaving him to go it alone. And he didn't even know it yet.

When the bell rang, there was still no sign of Max. She took out her cell phone to see if he had texted her but came up with nothing.

"What, no word from him?" Felix asked.

Portia shoved the phone back into her backpack and started storming away when he suddenly gripped her arm.

"Wait. I'm sorry. I know I'm acting like a baby. I'm just trying to figure some stuff out. I'm sorry. Let's forget it for now, OK? Please?"

She had to strain her neck upward to follow his hands.

What was the sense in worsening the situation right now? Better to let it go for the moment.

"Did you grow like a foot since yesterday?" She allowed a smile, breaking the tension.

"Definitely not since last night," his posture relaxed visibly. "I don't think I slept for a straight hour last night. Dean kept iChatting me to talk about dirt bikes. He's more of an adrenaline junkie than I am, I swear. It all comes from my grandfather, though. I mean, he probably shouldn't be buying Dean a bike—

my grandmother is freaking out about it."

"I don't blame her. Just because he's got a fat wallet doesn't mean your grandfather has to indulge your every whim," she held her smile, relieved to be having a normal exchange with him. "Just tell him that he better not buy you a bike. I couldn't handle if anything ever happened to you, Felix."

He put his arm around her, pulling her in close. "I'm not going anywhere, Portia. Don't worry…"

It felt good to have his arm around her, and she wished for a moment that some kind of tornado would come swooping down the hall, carrying them away to an easier place.

But the only thing that did come swooping down the hall was Gabrielle Parker. And when Felix spotted her, he broke their pose and followed the freshman to her locker like a horse with a carrot dangling before him.

It wasn't hard to understand what Felix saw in her. Gabrielle was pretty, in an unchallenging way, with her blonde hair in its perfect ponytail. And there was a kindness to her face, a contagious laughter as she tried following Felix's lead for the sign for "math class."

So why was it that at the sight of Felix's new love interest, the rage that had been sweeping over her in violent spurts returned so fiercely that she all she could do was turn around? If not, the words that were creeping up in her throat would surely have broken the surface:

"Hey Parker—stay the hell away from him…"

Max didn't show up at all that day. Portia couldn't imagine why he wasn't at school. He had seemed fine last night. Better than fine, actually. Finally, right before the last class of the day, he texted her:

"Hey—had to go see my dad—big setback, will give you the deets when I get back. Hope to catch a train tomorrow…"

Portia read the text and resisted the urge to write back a million questions. She figured that he had probably already had a draining day.

"K—hope everything works out," she wrote back, unable to imagine what it must be like for Max to see his father this way. "I'll c u when u get back."

"U know it," he wrote. Something about when he tried to talk street always made her laugh.

"Peace out, brother," she offered and then slipped her cell phone into her backpack. Images of Max floated through her like a healing vapor. She loved that he maintained his humor even when his life was falling apart. Carried by these meanderings through the RPA hallways, Portia perused the bulletin boards and stopped at the one that invited students to audition for the RPA musical revue, *The Whole Cole—A Tribute to the Genius of Cole Porter*.

"Thinking about trying out?"

Any thoughts of humor instantly drained from Portia, replaced by a boiling anger. She turned around to tell off whoever it was that had asked her such an obviously mocking question and was surprised to find Ms. Leucosia standing behind her, her red hair as fiery as ever. She expected to see sarcasm in the nurse's eyes, a facetious look that would support the nastiness of her question. But her eyes held only a look of unnerving understanding.

Portia returned Ms. Leucosia's gaze uncomfortably until finally her cell phone interrupted them. It was the twelfth time that day that her iCal was reminding her to start her *Odyssey* assignment.

Chapter 10

For many years the sisters lured in the sailors with the beauty of their voices. The evil in their hearts grew ever greater as they destroyed the foolish mortals. The mountain of bones swelled at the edge of the lush meadow and Parthenope and Ligeia often flew above the great pile, their laughter smooth as silk, never noticing the puddle of silver that seeped from below the base of the mountain.

For when she was alone, Leto did often visit the grave of the mortals to shed tears for the evil she had done. Many times had she thought to abandon her sisters in their murderous rampages, but always she remembered the promise that she had made to her mother.

One day a great ship lost its way and sailed into the treacherous hunting ground of the Sirens. Many oarsmen were aboard the ship, and the seductresses revealed their beauty to the mortals, guiding them with their glorious voices. As the men began begging the Goddesses to board the ship, Leto suddenly noticed a mortal unlike any other she had ever seen. He stood as tall as a Cyclops with fair hair that looked to be spun of gold. His eyes were as blue as the topaz of Zeus's crown.

"Leto," beckoned Parthenope, "what causes you to cease your song? Have you begun to doubt your desire to destroy the mortals?"

At the sight of the beautiful sailor, Leto's heart began to pound. He had not yet fallen upon his knee to beg knowledge of the glorious Goddesses, suggesting a superior strength of heart and mind.

"Dear sisters," she spoke sweetly, "many years have we destroyed men aboard their own ships, carrying their bones to our meadow and rejoicing over our conquests. Shall we not beckon these men to dwell on our island for a time? For surely there are things about mortals that we may learn from these oarsmen."

Leto's words found favor with her sisters, who lured the sailors to the island. There, confused as a herd of cattle, they cast their weary feet onto the green grass of the meadow.

Many months dwelt the mortals among the Sirens, doing any manner of thing commanded by the seductresses. They played instruments for the Goddesses as Marsyas had once done. They slaughtered the animals, which then they prepared with flowers and herbs for the Goddesses. With axes of golden handles, they chopped down trees and built the prison in which they were forced to remain.

All these long days, Leto observed the beautiful mortal who had captured her heart. She learned that his name was Nereus, and that he was the commander of his ship. Many wars had Nereus seen, and great wisdom was his. Leto was amazed at the beauty of the mortal who spoke ever sweetly to his men, offering them hope for a safe return to their homeland. He begged them to resist the powers of the Goddesses, but his men were weak.

Only Nereus remained sound of mind when the sweet songs of the Sirens filled the air.

Leto and Nereus escaped together whenever the sisters turned a blind eye, forming a deep and pure love for one another. The lovers explored all corners of the lush island, Nereus riding on the back of his beloved winged Goddess.

Alas, the lovers' bliss was not to last long, as one fateful day Parthenope questioned her sister:

"Leto, what manner of game have you played these many months with the one they call Nereus?"

Ligeia let escape an evil laugh, for she had spotted the lovers many times lying together in the grassy fields.

"What matter is this to you, dear Parthenope?" responded Leto.

Parthenope bared her snow white teeth and said "I have grown weary, Leto, of this flock of mortal men that lives among us. Come, let us now destroy them, for too long have we waited for the taste of mortal flesh."

Ligeia laughed once again, anticipating the great sorrow her sister would feel at the loss of her mortal lover.

Great tears of silver now fell from the emerald eyes of the lovely Leto.

"I beseech you, Parthenope, do not be hasty in dealing with these men, for now am I even in love with the one they call Nereus. I beg you, spare his life, Parthenope, so that we may live our days together."

Parthenope laughed at the desperate pleas of her sister.

"A foolish girl you are, Leto, to think that love can be shared between *a mortal and a Goddess. Let us make haste now, Ligeia, and destroy these men. No longer am I willing to encourage such a foolhardy love."*

Thus emerged the white wings of the Sirens as they flew to the wooden cage where the men did sleep.

"No!" screamed Leto. "I beg you! Cease this evil, my sisters!"

Her wings emerged at once as she flew with great speed to keep pace with her sisters. But the strength of two immortals is far greater than that of one. And though Leto implored the almighty Zeus that he might intervene on her behalf and spare the life of her beloved Nereus, her plea fell on deafened ears.

Leto flew above the olivewood prison, circling slowly, singing a song of comfort to the men who were now to become forgotten souls. She sang in a voice as pure as snow while her sisters began to tear apart their human flesh, filling the evil hunger that had mounted inside them these many months. Leto begged the men not to resist death, as their efforts would only worsen their suffering.

Nereus stood tall in the center of the olivewood cage. Longingly he gazed heavenward at his lover. The tears that spilled from Leto's eyes fell upon his golden curls, creating a sun-kissed blend of silver and gold. As he heard the song escape the lips he had kissed so tenderly, he knew for certain that death was upon him.

He brought his hands upward, longing to touch her once again, when all at once Parthenope and Ligeia were upon him. They ripped him limb from mortal limb and feasted on his flesh, all the while Leto singing above them. When at last the massacre had ended, the evil sisters flew up to Leto and threw her lover's bones into her quivering arms.

And so Leto's pain was so great at the loss of Nereus that she could no longer dwell with her evil sisters, who had murdered him before her very eyes. Even the promise she had made to her mother could no longer force her to keep company with the murderous Goddesses. In a wooded cave the Siren hid, ever weeping for the loss of her lover. One day Athena, the great Goddess of compassion and wisdom, appeared to Leto, taking the form of a wild boar, lest the evil sisters spot her and try to bring her harm.

The wild boar approached Leto, who hoped the animal would make quick her death so that she could be with her beloved. But she knew she hoped in vain, as the only sure death for a Siren was to drown in the open sea.

"Leto," said the boar unto the sullen Goddess, "do not sit here any longer shedding your lovely tears of silver. Let us leave this island at once, for soon Parthenope and Ligeia will make leave for the depths of Hades.

"But you, my sweet Leto, grow inside you now a daughter, born of the love that you shared with Nereus. So I bid you, come live with me so that you and your daughter will know happiness."

Athena's words greatly comforted Leto, whose giant wings emerged at once. The wild boar climbed upon her back as they made ready to fly.

Through heavy tears, Leto said these words:

"Athena, long have I waited for kind and inviting words such as you have spoken. Before we depart, I beg you, help me to solve but one mystery. When will the next one come? The one with the olive skin and the lapis eyes?"

"I cannot say, sweet Leto, but I do know that when she arrives, all who know her will question whether they had ever really known the beauty of music before her…"

Leucosia glanced at the skylight, determining the sun's position overhead. This was still the most reliable way for her to tell time, a fact she lamented as it meant she just couldn't justify spending the money on one of the new Cartier timepieces that had recently caught her eye.

It was 6:30 a.m. Where was he already? She had to get to school in an hour, and she knew the meeting with her father could run long.

Finally she heard him enter the house, and she rose up to greet him.

"Father," she planted a kiss on both of his heavily bearded cheeks. "You look wonderful."

"As do you, my dear Leto. The years have been your kind friends."

"Father, I think I'm a bit old for that nickname by now,

don't you?"

"Ahh, no, my dear. You will always be my Leto, my 'hidden one.' For in you, Leucosia, there is a humble flame that warms the hearts and souls of all who come to know you."

He leaned in once again and embraced his daughter heartily, feeling her wince slightly at the touch of his hands on her back, so sore from the many years of bearing the weight of her lofty wings.

"Have you still the breakthrough pains that have often afflicted all winged Gods?" Achelous questioned his daughter.

Leucosia was frustrated by the antiquated verbiage of her father.

"Father, in this day and age, if anyone heard you speaking like that they would probably lock you up in a loony bin."

Achelous maintained an uncomprehending stare.

"Oh, never mind," she said, eager to tell him of Portia's recent developments.

She turned around and arranged the silver tea set on a tray, which she carried over to the coffee table. Pouring a cup of his favorite lavender tea, she topped off the steaming drink with some fresh chopped mint, her father's signature twist. She handed him the delicate teacup, which looked positively Lilliputian in his enormous hand.

"How is the tea, Father?"

"Lovely, Let—I mean, Leucosia. The mint is especially fragrant—"

"The lavender reminds me of the ointment I had to apply to Portia's back the other day," she interrupted her father, bursting at the seams to speak of her young charge. "She came to my office—growing pains, you know—and it was so lovely to have the one-on-one time with her."

"Ah, so she's evolving?" Achelous took another sip of the tea.

"Oh, Father—she's practically a woman!"

Leucosia knew she sounded like a gushing mother, but she couldn't help herself.

"She's beautiful and intelligent and at the same time humble and shy. She has nothing of the 'silly schoolgirl' in her, well, except for the fact that I think she's developed a recent crush. But anyway, she is just an absolute gem."

Achelous smiled at the great joy of his remaining daughter, but still he seemed concerned.

"And your, um, sisters? Has she any of the poison that did flow through their very veins?"

This time Leucosia ignored her father's ancient language. Her heart went out to him as his face crumpled at the mention of Parthenope and Ligeia. Determined to reassure him, she conjured up an image of Portia in her mind's eye. She could see clearly the beauty of the girl. Her sculpted face, now freed of any remnants of childhood pudge. Her brilliant blue eyes—Nereus's eyes. Her piles of brown silken hair.

And the mouth.

That full mouth—about to be released from its prison of silence.

"No, Father, there is not a trace of evil to be found in the young Siren…"

Part Three

Siren

Chapter 11

"This isn't the paper I e-mailed you!" Portia had waited until after class to clear up the confusion with Mr. Morrison. A "B-" certainly wasn't going to cut it for her. And his comments:

"A most lackluster effort, Portia. I expect more of you..."

His bold writing and the red ink had infuriated her. She had officially gone crazy trying to compile a reasonable paper about the three sisters. Never mind that Homer never specified who exactly the Sirens in *The Odyssey* were. After the virtual barrage of information that had assaulted her, Portia was convinced that Homer could only have been writing about the sisters Parthenope, Ligeia, and Leto.

But what exactly were her sources? The few times she had tried revisiting the storytelling sites or the iTunes gift from Marsyas, she found herself lost in the virtual beyond. She had even tried inviting Marsyas back in for a video chat, but his name had disappeared from her buddy list. Finally she had decided to invent a few of her own "sources" for footnoting. The least she deserved was an A for effort.

But when she started rereading what she had written, she realized that this was not the paper she had launched into cyberspace to land safely in Mr. Morrison's inbox. And yes, whoever paper this was, it was lackluster.

Portia had asked Ellen Chadwicke to stay behind to help her converse with the teacher.

"These are not my words. I did not write this paper." She signed out the words and was impressed when Ms. Chadwicke vocalized them with the same measure of rage that she was feeling. "My paper was about the sisters, you know? Parthenope, Ligeia, Leto..." This stumped the sign language interpreter a bit as she tried to do justice to the strange names Portia was spelling out.

"What sisters?" Mr. Morrison asked. "You see, that's the problem with you kids today—you probably used some crazy web source or a bog—"

"Blog," Ms. Chadwicke corrected him.

"Whatever, and read something that you decided had to be true, simply because it was posted on the Internet. It's lucky that that was not the paper you handed in or else you probably would have gotten an F. Now, I know you're a solid student, Portia. A 'B-' is hard for you to accept. But maybe for your next essay you'll try a little harder."

"Yeah, well, maybe for my next essay you won't be such an asshole." She signed the words, fueled by the rage that had been coursing through her veins with greater frequency these past days.

Ms. Chadwicke did a double take, but recovered herself quickly. "OK, thanks. I'll try harder next time," she offered the teacher, glaring at Portia.

"Whatever," Portia signed out and stormed away.

She had an inexhaustible headache. What was she supposed to do? Start telling her teacher and the sign language interpreter that someone, something had been virtually messing with her on such a grand scale that the best case scenario would be that it was just some freak cyberbully who was getting his or her jollies by making her squirm. The worst-case scenario, and the more likely, she feared, was that she was completely losing her mind.

And so the charade continued. It was one thing to have to hide her voice from everyone, but keeping her nervous breakdown under wraps was causing her to literally be physically ill. The only relief for her these past couple of days were the moments spent with Max.

When he returned from seeing his father, Max had headed straight for the Griffin house. Portia was relieved that her father was away on business—when it came to boys, Joshua was old-fashioned, to say the least, and had a strict 'no boys in the bedroom' policy. But Helena was instantly charmed by Max's swag and feigned a sudden desperate craving for a sugar-free vanilla latte at Starbucks, despite the late hour.

Portia ushered Max into her father's library. She had always loved the hunter green walls and overstuffed leather chair and a half. The room was a cozy sanctuary that she hoped read as "let's snuggle" and not as "let's get it on."

Max collapsed into the chair and perched his legs up on the ottoman, stretching his neck from side to side, releasing an audible crack in both directions. He was so tightly wound that Portia was unsure how to approach him. But then he reached for her hand and drew her into his lap, where she instinctively curled up, resting her head on his chest, enjoying the thrumming of his heartbeat.

"It was bad," he offered.

She looked up at him expectantly, afraid to push.

"It was really bad," he repeated, "My dad, he just—" He had been stroking her cheek while he tried to get the words out. She placed her fingers over his, stilling them on her skin, tilting her chin up to meet his gaze.

"He, um…you know, I forgot what I was going to say…"

"I'm sorry," she mouthed.

But he interrupted her with a gentle brush of his lips, first on her forehead, then her eyelids. And finally down to her lips, where he lingered, unhurried, like he had just tasted the most wonderful dessert on earth and wanted to savor it forever.

"Better than I even imagined," he mumbled when at last he pulled away.

Portia responded with a crush of her lips. She was as shocked as he was by the sudden gesture, but once she had initiated, there was no backing down. He pulled her face into his hands and poured every bit of stress and frustration into that kiss. His hands traveled down her back, drawing her further into him until they were welded together by their own heat.

She wished he would take it further. Her body ached to be touched, to be kissed by those lips that had sung so sweetly to her, about her. The more lost she became in his touch, the more distant were the events of the last few weeks, the feeling that she had been going crazy. She brought him even closer, placing his hands around her waist, willing them to travel north underneath her shirt.

At the touch of her bare skin, he recoiled and reluctantly pried his lips from hers.

"What?" she mouthed, embarrassed. She could feel her face turning red and realized that this was that after-kiss awkwardness she had always dreaded.

"I, um, I won't be able to stop, Portia. I want you—" he choked out while caressing her hair, inhaling deeply as his mouth skimmed the base of her throat "—so much that I won't be able to stop."

They held each other's eyes, each unsure of where to go with this revelation until Max finally eased her away gently.

"I should go."

She nodded, confused but relieved. She got up to walk him to the door, but he politely refused.

"I can show myself out. That whole, um, wanting you thing? No need to prolong it, right? Need me some cool-down time, you know what I'm sayin'?"

The urban rhetoric procured a smile from her, and he hurriedly pecked her on the cheek and headed out.

After he left, Portia realized that she needed herself some cool-down time, too. Her body was suddenly speaking a foreign language, exotic and sultry. Her brain needed some time to translate.

When she came down a bit, she realized that she had never found out what was going on with Max's father. She tried making up for it by asking him about it over the next couple of days. But they had already gotten a taste of each other and were in that place where conversation just seemed an awful waste of time. The air around them was so charged that she wondered if her friends could pick up on it.

Certainly the white bird creature who had become an expected visitor to her sleep had caught wind of it. Her dreams had become a melee of horror and erotica, awakening her in a cold sweat that was not altogether unpleasant.

So why was she still so easily pissed off all the time? Was it the sleep deprivation? The new awkwardness with Felix?

I mean, calling a teacher an asshole?

Portia made a mental note to thank Ellen Chadwicke for saving her as she entered Mr. Rathi's classroom. Max's left dimple did the flexing thing when she walked in, and she sat herself down next to him.

Throughout class they coiled and recoiled their pinkies around each other's, enjoying the feel of each other's touch, until Rathi caught on and asked Portia to move her seat so that she could, "um, focus."

Once she was reseated away from Max, her exhaustion caught up with her. As Rathi droned on about Eleanor Rigby, she laid her head down on her desk, praying that if she drifted off to sleep and dreamt of Max, she wouldn't cry aloud and betray the secret that had been unraveling her, thread by silken thread…

Chapter 12

Leucosia felt like she was walking a tightrope.

How could she have been so foolish?

When she met with her father just a few short weeks ago, she was so confident that everything was moving along remarkably well. She had reported to him the many details of her charge's seamless transition into womanhood and, more importantly, Sirenhood.

Since that first day of school, Portia had not been back to her office with any more coughing fits, leading Leucosia to believe that the young Goddess's syrinx had finally finished developing.

Leucosia felt blessed knowing that she and her kind possessed both the larynx and the syrinx, the combination of which produced a voice unparalleled by Gods or mortals. The slow development of Portia's syrinx seemed to have finally capped off. The seasoned Goddess wished that the final stages of Portia's vocal development had not been so frightening, but that sense of overcrowding in the throat was inevitable with this particular anatomical development. And now that everything appeared to be settled into its place, Leucosia looked forward to hearing Portia's glorious voice very soon.

She had assumed that all was continuing to progress according to plan, especially when she caught Portia considering the audition for the school musical. And then Mr. Rathi had sent Portia to her office on Monday with a note that he was concerned for the girl. Apparently she had fallen asleep during class, and the teacher wanted to make sure she was all right, considering that she was usually one of his most engaged students.

"I haven't been getting much sleep," Portia casually signed out to the concerned nurse. Leucosia's hair stood on end as

Portia's hands explained the reason for her lack of sleep.

"I've been having crazy nightmares. It's like this giant white bird creature is trying to get me to lower myself into some kind of evil abyss. I mean, most girls my age are dreaming about RPats—" she took in Leucosia's confused expression. "That's short for Robert Pattinson."

Leucosia tried to offer a look of understanding, but at the mention of the white bird, the blood must have drained out of her face.

"Are you OK, Ms. L?"

"Yes, yes. Sorry, dear. Can you tell me more about these dreams you've been having?"

"I'm so tired," signed Portia. "Do you think I could rest first, before we get all Freudian?"

Leucosia forced a smile and said, "Of course, dear. Why don't you lie down and close your eyes for a bit. I have to organize the results of my lice tests anyway—my least favorite part of the job…"

The nurse shuffled some papers around on her desk, humming distractedly and pretending to look busy while Portia let her muscles relax on the paper that covered the vinyl gurney.

Portia's lids grew heavy as the sound of Ms. Leucosia's sweet voice engulfed her, ushering her into the world of dreams.

Once Portia fell asleep, Leucosia shot out a quick text message to the great God Morpheus, ruler of dreams. She'd been smart to gift Morpheus an iPhone for his recent birthday and considered Face Timing him but wasn't sure if the God had yet mastered this new mode of communication. With all of his omnipotence, Morpheus still fell into the "technologically challenged" category.

"Morpheus," she wrote, "It is emergent that I gain immediate access into the dream of my young charge, Portia Griffin."

In a flash his response came back. "Close your eyes, dear Leucosia," and then a winking emoticon. Wow, he really had come a long way, Leucosia thought. Next stop, Siri—although Leucosia still maintained that Siri was really just a code name for her oldest and wisest friend, Athena.

The Goddess continued to hum, lulling herself into a trancelike state, allowing her spirit to be carried away by Morpheus, who had often visited her own dreams once upon a time.

An invader of Portia's privacy, she trespassed gently onto the set of Portia's dream. She was not surprised that the first person she saw was Max Hunter, a guitar slung lazily around his shoulder. The boy really was alarmingly good looking.

He seemed to be lost.

"Portia? Where did you go?" He was standing in an open meadow.

Portia suddenly appeared. Or at least her seductively altered twin appeared.

"What happened to you, Portia?" Max questioned her.

The young girl's eyes were heavily outlined in black, emblazoning the blue of her irises. And the black shirt she wore ended abruptly, revealing a good two inches of flat, tanned torso above her abbreviated denim shorts.

"Hi, Max." Her voice was splendid.

He looked at her in shock.

"What—a girl can't dress up once in a while?"

Max stumbled over his words. "Portia, I thought you couldn't speak."

"Oh, that," she replied as she moved in closer to him. "I forgot to mention to you that I recently picked up a little something I like to call 'a voice.'"

She was standing right in front of him, moving in closer, pressing herself up against him. Max tried pushing her away, and Leucosia admired his resolve.

"Max, there's no sense in trying to resist me." She sidled back over to him, trapping him in the force field of her seduction. "You can't even imagine the powers my voice has."

"What are you talking about, Portia? What powers?"

"My voice, Max. It came on one day like a volcano that

had finally erupted. At first it was like it belonged to somebody else—like a force of nature had taken over my body. But then my brain caught on, you know? It was mine—this voice, this power was actually mine. And, well," Portia giggled, "the next thing I knew, I was leading Charlotte's father to his death. That bastard deserves to die. But I spared him. At the last minute, I spared him. But he knows. He will forever know that my voice can destroy him. It can destroy anyone."

Leucosia was just as shocked at this revelation as Max was.

Portia reached for the guitar, easing it from Max's shoulder.

"Portia, this doesn't make any sense." The boy's confusion was pitiable.

Portia placed a finger over her painted red lips.

"Shh. You won't want to miss this," she assured him.

She started experimenting with the strings of the Gibson, acclimating herself to the feel of the acoustic instrument.

"Have you ever been on a ride, Max? I'm not talking the London Eye. I'm talking like Kingda Ka. The kind of ride that makes you wonder why the hell you ever got on in the first place? The one that when they're strapping you in, you want to say no, let me off, but then it's just too late—the car's already moving…"

She strummed the guitar.

"You can either cry and scream or just sit back, close your eyes, and enjoy it. We're about to go on a ride, Max, you and me. So buckle up and decide now—are you gonna enjoy it?"

Max was too disconcerted to speak. He stared open-mouthed at this hyperbole of his girlfriend. She strummed the guitar more deliberately now and started to sing in a low throaty voice.

> *"Most have blood coursing through their veins,*
> *But I've got fire and ice.*
> *Hear me now and hear me plain,*
> *You're gonna need this advice.*
>
> *I'm the one they warned you about,*
> *The one who spreads like cancer.*

Go ahead, baby, scream and shout.
You'll never find the answer…"

Leucosia was stupefied by Portia's voice. It was beyond what she ever imagined it could be—melodic, harmonious, dangerous. It was the Mormon Tabernacle Choir and Janis Joplin rolled into one. And the lyrics? Where were they coming from?

"Well, I'm three parts devil, one part girl,
And there's a heat that's always mixed in.
Call me snake and I will crawl,
But best to call me Vixen…"

Leucosia pitied the young mortal as he became caught in the web of Portia's song. He moved in closer to her, drawn in by the glorious sound.

"And you can try to run away,
And you can try to fight it.
I'm that dragon you must slay,
Come on, I dare you, try it…"

He leaned into Portia's face, the venom of her words poisoning his blood. His face held the longing of a man stranded in a desert and suddenly finding himself before an oasis of cool waters.

"What you can't know, will never see,
Is that there is no choice.
First blood's been drawn, there's only me,
And the blade that is my voice…"

His breathing grew heavier, and his hands migrated around to Portia's front, caressing her every curve.

"PARTHENOPE! LIGEIA! MAKE YOURSELVES KNOWN UNTO ME NOW!" Leucosia screamed.

"I'm three parts devil, one part girl,
And there's a heat that's always mixed in.
Call me snake and I will crawl,
But best to call me Vixen…"

Max was on his knees, running his hands up and down the length of Portia's legs. He placed his head on her concave belly as she abandoned the guitar and wove her fingertips through the gloss of his hair.

Leucosia could hear familiar laughter in the background.

"In the name of the Almighty Zeus, I beseech you, my sisters, to show your face unto me!" Though she wanted desperately to wake Portia from the dream, she felt compelled to confront the spirits of her sisters, who were surely guiding the innocent ingénue down this dangerous path.

"Ahh, sweetest Leucosia," a familiar voice suddenly said, "it has been many years since upon your lovely face we have laid our weary eyes."

Parthenope then appeared to Leucosia, resplendent as ever, her face unchanged from the days of her youth. She was flying above Portia and Max, who were lost in the throes of their sexual frenzy.

> *"You think you've lived? Have drawn true breath?*
> *Have tasted all the flavors?*
> *Well, I'm dessert. I'm crystal meth.*
> *The one to grant you favors…"*

With each word the girl sang, Parthenope laughed even louder.

"Ligeia," Parthenope called out to her younger sister, "come show your face to us, for Leucosia beckons us now into the dream of her blessed descendant, Portia."

Suddenly Ligeia appeared as well. Leucosia was not surprised to see that her other sister had also not aged, her beauty as ethereal as ever.

> *"And you can try to get clean,*
> *To rehabilitate,*
> *But off of me you'll never wean.*
> *You're a junkie, it's too late…"*

Max's moves grew frenzied and fevered. His grip on Portia's hips was firmer as he pulled her closer to him.

Leucosia produced her wings and swooped down, flying abruptly past Portia. She produced a swoosh of air that sent Portia reeling slightly. When she recovered herself, Leucosia could detect a sudden shift in Portia's confidence as Max continued to lose control.

"Parthenope, Ligeia, I beseech you. Do not lead Portia down the destructive road upon which you have both traveled! Why must you persist in your evil ways?"

Ligeia addressed her sister's question.

"Leucosia, do you dare to deny that you stole the love of our very mother for your own? You must have known that the day would come when you would pay for your crime."

"I stole nothing, Ligeia. But even if as such you did believe, is it not enough that you killed Nereus before my very eyes?"

Ligeia and Parthenope laughed and joined hands, floating above the lurid scene intensifying between Portia and Max.

"Dear sisters," continued Leucosia, "Portia Griffin is an innocent among the immortals, knowing not even the powers that are hers. I beg you, spare her from your evil clutches and allow her to use her powers for the pure and good purposes for which they were intended."

> *"Cuz I'm three parts devil, one part girl,*
> *And there's a heat that's always mixed in…"*

Portia's voice grew lovelier as tears of silver began to stream down the valleys of her face. She was trying to pry Max's hands off of her, to stop him from pawing and disrespecting her, but she was powerless to stop singing, and he continued to grope her lustily.

Parthenope and Ligeia were circling above the youngsters, enjoying the tawdry spectacle. As they spun around and around, Leucosia maintained control, determined to remain civilized.

> *"Call me snake and I will crawl,*
> *But best to call me Vixen…"*

Portia became hysterical as Max tried to fumble with the belt that was holding up her skimpy shorts. She kept singing through her tears, the sultry words gushing forth from her mouth like waters from a broken dam. Max continued his advances, goaded on by her voice.

"Yes, you will call me Vixen…"

"SISTERS, I BEG YOU! SHE IS BUT A CHILD!"

Parthenope spoke then, relishing her own words.

"Dearest Leucosia, why should you fear so? We are but mere spirits in a dream. Surely we cannot do any real harm—though it is curious that even your beloved Morpheus cannot keep us out of Portia's reveries, don't you think?" The sisters snickered menacingly and dropped each other's hands. "But no matter—did not even the great Penelope, wife to Odysseus say, 'dreams are very curious and unaccountable things, and they do not by any means invariably come true'?"

Leucosia's mistrust of the sisters grew even greater at their mention of Odysseus, the very mortal who sealed their fate. She opened her mouth to question them, but their flight grew even faster and in a flash they vanished.

As soon as they were gone, Portia stopped singing.

Max immediately fell back, a look of deep confusion running across face. He noticed Portia crying and moved toward her, gently extending his hand to brush her tears away.

"Don't even think about touching her again."

The voice belonged to Felix. He grabbed Max's hand in his giant fist, his eyes filled with rage as he dragged Max by the arm over to a foggy corner of the meadow. Suddenly the fog lifted, and a mountain of bones appeared. The boys were wrestling at the edge of the hill, Felix's strength winning out, threatening to add Max's corpse to the grotesque heap.

"Please, Felix," Portia tried reasoning with her friend. "It wasn't his fault. It was me, Felix. It was all me…"

Leucosia traveled out of the dream and back to the nurse's office, jolted by the vision of the bones. She petitioned Morpheus, once again, to grant Portia some selective amnesia. It would be better for the young girl not to remember the details of this dream. They had enough to deal with.

"Portia, wake up, dear. Come on, Portia. No more sleeping…"

"We have our work cut out for us," Leucosia murmured.

"What do you mean 'we have our work cut out for us'? Why does everything you say always sound so mysterious?" Portia signed. She couldn't help but notice that Ms. Leucosia looked suddenly rattled.

"Um, I'm sorry, my dear. My thoughts were elsewhere for a moment. Tell me, did the monster reappear in your sleep just now?" Leucosia seemed distracted and nervous as she began to write out a permission slip for Portia to be readmitted to class. In her haste, she accidentally dropped her pen, and when she bent over to pick it up, a bloodstain seeped through her crisp white shirt.

Portia thought that maybe she was hallucinating again, but as Ms. Leucosia bent down further to the floor, the bloodstain expanded, evolving into a bright red streak that stretched from her shoulders down to her waist. The wound was painful to look at, and Portia could only imagine how much more painful it was to actually sustain.

The nurse was oddly indifferent to it.

Portia motioned to get Ms. Leucosia's attention and signed, "Are you OK? Your back is bleeding!"

Leucosia hesitated for a millisecond and then offhandedly dismissed Portia's concern.

"Oh, did that scab open up again? Darn. My cat gave me a whopper of a scratch the other day when I wouldn't get out of bed to feed him. Nasty feline."

She avoided Portia's eyes and carelessly stuffed a wad of paper towel into the collar of her shirt. "Now—where were we? Oh yes, the dream. Did the monster come back to you in your dreams just now?"

"I don't know—I don't think so." She was still a bit queasy from seeing the blood that had seeped out of the nurse's back and was overcome by an odd sense of déjà vu. "I can't seem to remember having a dream just now. But I still feel like when I sleep, I can't really get a good rest. It's hard to explain."

Leucosia came back at Portia with something completely unexpected:

"Portia, at your age it's very common to go through changes—changes that you didn't ever anticipate. I want you to know that you can come to me about anything that you are going through, no matter how um—" she cleared her throat, "how supernatural your symptoms might be."

Portia looked up in shock. How did she know? The beautiful school nurse seemed to have a sixth sense devoted entirely to diagnosing the mysterious maladies of Portia Griffin.

She decided to dip her toe in the water. It would be so nice to gain a little bit of insight into her sudden change by someone who had a medical background. She told Ms. Leucosia about the stretching feeling she had been having at the base of her throat, which, thank goodness, had subsided over the last few days.

"Now it's more like a weird feeling. My throat doesn't really hurt, but it keeps having, like, an occasional vibration. It hasn't been as bad the past couple of days, but I don't know, I feel like I went through some kind of change."

She signed out the confession hesitantly, scaling the wall of truth, wanting so much to take a leap and reveal everything to Ms. Leucosia, to anyone who could help her make sense of it all. Something was holding her back, though. The wall felt stable, but what was on the other side was terrifying.

Leucosia extended her slender hand to the base of Portia's throat. Portia could feel the nurse's fingers rest on a certain spot—a dense spot.

"You know, I've heard stories about girls like you, Portia. Girls who couldn't speak for a long time and then suddenly started going through changes. It's possible that these changes might even result in the acquisition of a voice."

Portia looked away. She had been caught red-handed.

"Well, anyway, I'm not a doctor or anything," Leucosia continued dismissively. "I'm sure you've just been experiencing general 'growing pains.' It's part of life. I do think, though, that you should probably get as much rest as you can in the next few days."

Portia thought about the week ahead of her.

"That shouldn't be a problem. I only have plans for Wednesday night. Otherwise I'll definitely take it easy."

Leucosia asked with a casual indifference "Anything exciting on Wednesday?"

"Just Open Mic Night at the café," Portia signed. "Shouldn't be too late of a night, don't worry."

But the nurse did look worried.

"Don't worry, Ms. L, it's not like I'm going to be drinking or anything."

This brought a smile from the nurse that was not altogether convincing.

"No, of course not. OK, well then, Portia, I'd like you to come back and check in with me later on this week. Gotta keep my eye on you…"

Once again Portia sensed that Ms. Leucosia's words were layered with innuendo. She nodded her head, agreeing to visit again soon. When she got up to leave, she suddenly remembered the tune that Leucosia was humming before she fell asleep.

"By the way, what was that that you were humming before? It was so familiar."

Ushering Portia toward the door, Ms. Leucosia mumbled something about an old lullaby that her own mother used to sing to her.

But when Portia walked out into the busy hallway, something was still agitating her.

I know that melody from somewhere.

The bell had just rung, and everyone was clamoring to get to their lockers. In a cloud of thought, she floated over to her own locker, where Felix was waiting.

"Were you in Ms. Leucosia's office again?" he questioned her. "What's going on with you?"

"I fell asleep in Rathi's class," she signed back. "So unlike me, right?"

"Seriously. You would think you had Mrs. Crebbs."

She exchanged a few more idle words with Felix but was

still distracted by the frustration of not being able to place the tune. As she and Felix walked into their next class together, it suddenly dawned on her where she had heard it before.

It was the melody she had sung when she had almost killed Harold Trotter.

Chapter 13

At lunchtime Portia asked Jacqueline and Charlotte if they wanted to do a little shopping after school that day. She wanted to explore her fashion options for Wednesday night. Charlotte begged off, claiming too much homework. Portia suspected, though, that really she wanted to go home and be with her mom—the tough love stage had kicked in, and Charlotte had been remarkably diligent about it.

Jacqueline, on the other hand, was always up for some retail therapy. Portia loved going shopping with Jacqueline, who had that French knack for making everything she wore, including the RPA uniform, look like couture.

When school was over, the girls walked the short distance into town and decided to kick off their expedition in Jacqueline's favorite boutique, Haute. Perusing the many racks of edge-of-the-envelope ensembles reenforced Portia's gratefulness that RPA had uniforms. She hated to have to make fashion decisions.

"How about this, ma cherie?" asked Jacqueline. She was holding up a black stretchy tube that Portia guessed was meant to be a dress but really looked more like a leg warmer.

Portia took out her phone and started typing:

"R u crazy? If my parents saw me in that they'd lock me up! A little more subtle pls."

The girls continued to scan the shop, Portia fending off Jacqueline's racier suggestions until they came across a blue silk charmeuse halter top. The blousy shirt had a slight ruffle at its high collar, above a distinct absence of fabric in the back. More comfortable showing off her back than her front, Portia held the shirt up for her friend's approval.

"That could work—it's very YSL." She said the letters in

French, and it took Portia a minute to realize she was referencing Yves Saint Laurent. "With a pair of jeans and some strappy heels, it will be parfait!"

Portia grabbed a pair of tissue-thin jeans and headed for the fitting room, delighted to find that the outfit was a perfect call. The blue of the shirt brought out the blue of her eyes, and the drapey fabric fell across her torso perfectly. The three-way mirror afforded her a great view of her shoulders and back, all of which took quite well to such flagrant exposure.

As Portia admired her reflection, she felt an unwelcome return of an odd warmth flowing through her body. She placed her hand in front of the vent on the wall and was relieved to feel some cool air flowing in. But still, she felt a heat—a heat that was alarmingly similar to the one that had attacked her on those first days of school. Her mouth was suddenly dry and pasty, and her palms were slick with sweat. The lights in the fitting room were obscenely bright, blinding her momentarily.

She blinked her eyes purposefully, trying to clear them. When she regained her vision, she was terrified at what stood before her.

Portia touched the glass with her hand and when the mirrored image reached out its hand in time with hers, she knew that it was indeed her own reflection staring back at her.

Only this was not Portia Griffin.

This was Delilah coming at Samson with shears in her hand.

The reflected Portia was taller and shapelier. Her hair seemed twice its usual thickness and fell long onto a chest that could only be described as ample. Her eyelashes formed mascara-laden question marks, which brought out the jewels of her eyes.

Portia stood before the mirror, expressionless from the shock of seeing this alter ego of herself. She wanted to look away, but the image held her transfixed. Exhausted from her sleepless nights and convinced now that she had officially gone crazy, she began to cry. But the tears were not reflected in the face looking back at her.

Instead her alter ego grinned from ear to ear.

Feeling faint, she tried steadying herself by grabbing hold of the chair in the corner of the dressing room. Despite her movement, her reflection remained still except for the widening of its evil smile. Regaining control of herself became out of the question. Portia could feel her heart pounding as the tiny mirrored room spun around her. She wanted to run from the dressing room but couldn't take her eyes away from her reflection. She thought about screaming out for help but in a fleeting moment of lucidity knew that this was certainly not the way she wanted to debut her new voice.

She was helpless. There was no escaping the smiling specter.

Portia had never fainted before, but that record was about to be broken. Right before she went down, her reflection spoke in a voice that was an uncanny clone of her own:

"The stage is set, Portia. Are you ready?"

She hit the floor of the fitting room with a loud thud.

Jacqueline Rainier was sounding off all kinds of French expletives when Portia began coming to. She was tapping her unconscious friend's cheeks, not without force, and blowing on her face.

Portia's eyes flung open. She was still lying on the floor of the dressing room. Somewhere on the periphery, she heard the salesgirl telling an incoming customer that the shop was closed for an emergency and would reopen again soon.

She reached for her phone.

"Did u call 911?"

"No, not yet," said Jacqueline, "you were only out for *un moment*. What happened?"

Portia was not about to describe the bizarre apparition to her friend. She quickly scrambled through a list of plausible excuses in her head and decided that lack of food would probably appeal most to Jacqueline's model-thin sensibilities.

"My stomach was bothering me this morn—I haven't eaten all day. I think it just caught up with me."

Jacqueline asked the salesgirl if she had any juice or something, and miraculously the waif-like brunette produced a banana from her bag.

Portia wolfed the fruit down quickly, taking great care not to smear the silk of the halter top, which she was still wearing. She noticed for the first time that Jacqueline was wearing a black strapless bandage dress. Though it barely reached mid-thigh, somehow her friend's interpretation of the dress was chic— merely teetering on the edge of trashy.

"You should def take that," Portia typed out. Luckily Jacqueline was easily distracted by any talk of fashion.

"It's a great copy of a Leger, don't you think?"

Portia had no idea what her friend was talking about but nodded her agreement anyway. Jacqueline started telling her about a pair of shoes she had her eye on that would go perfectly with the dress.

"Are you feeling better? Do you think we can go to the shoe store now that you ate something? We can stop first for a café, no?"

Portia rose to her feet and made a great show of brushing herself off. Her breath had steadied, but still she didn't dare look in the mirror again.

She nodded her consent to Jacqueline with a weak smile.

The girls paid for their purchases at Haute and thanked the shell-shocked salesgirl for all of her help. They walked in the direction of Footnotes, Jacqueline's head filled with thoughts of mules and pumps while Portia's thoughts were consumed by all things that go bump in the night.

On Wednesday morning Portia woke up feeling queasy. She was completely stressed about the day to come. Well, not so much the day as the night. So much was riding on this one silly night at Café on the Ridge. With all the tension between Felix and Max, she felt like a spider caught in a web of male testosterone.

After the events at Haute, though, the cockfight between

the boys was the least of her problems. 'Portia the Vixen,' who had spoken to her from some hellish hallucinatory universe, was hovering over her shoulder.

"The stage is set—are you ready?"

Are you ready?!

Of course she was ready. OK, OK, so there might be a little teen drama in the backdrop, but that was no cause for her to be suffering hallucinations.

She considered telling Helena that she wasn't feeling well but knew that if she stayed home from school, there would be no way she would be allowed to go out that night. Deciding to suck it up, she forced herself out of bed.

That morning, though, she did not look in the mirror, and Charlotte seemed puzzled when Portia quietly whispered to her on the bus to school.

"Do I have any, like, pimples or anything I need to know about on my face?"

Charlotte started rummaging through her bag. "No. But I definitely have a mirror in here some—"

Portia grabbed her friend's hand, and Charlotte looked up at her with terror in her eyes.

"Don't touch me like that, Portia." Her voice was loud but shaky.

Portia dropped Charlotte's hand. Other kids on the bus looked over at them, and she quickly took out her phone.

"I'm sorry. I didn't mean to do that. I just don't wanna look in the mirror right now."

Charlotte had turned pale and moved as far away from Portia as the window seat would permit.

"I'm sorry." She typed the words again.

"It's OK." Charlotte smeared away tears with the back of her hand. "It's just…I can't let anyone ever touch me like that again…you know—in any kind of harsh way. God, I don't know if I'll ever even be able to let someone touch me in a non-harsh way."

"Even Caleb Samuels?" Portia tried lightening the mood by mentioning the senior who was the object of every RPA girl's high school crush.

Charlotte smiled. "Well, I don't know…maybe Caleb. It depends if he's wearing his rugby jersey."

Relieved that the moment had passed, Portia decided to try convincing Charlotte once more to come to Open Mic Night. Surprisingly this time her friend agreed.

"Yeah, my mom told me that if I don't start going out with friends once in a while, she's going to 'take matters into her own hands'—whatever that means. I guess tough love can go both ways, right? So I figured I'd go. Wanna come get ready at my house?"

"Sounds like a plan." Portia typed out, and suddenly a text popped up from Max.

"Hey—on train back from NY. My aunt drove me out at midnight last nt—we got an urgent call from his nurse. Not sure how much longer I can do this…"

After passing out yesterday, Portia had failed to notice the absence of a customary late-night chat with Max. Now she felt guilty for not being more plugged in.

"Sorry, didn't realize—was feeling a little sick yesterday, but all OK now. As for your dad, I'm sure your visit meant a lot to him."

She was saddened by Max's response:

"I don't think so. I'm not even sure he knew it was me."

"I don't know what to say, Max. I'm so sorry."

"There's nothing to say," he wrote back, "I just wanna get back…and see you."

She couldn't help but smile.

"R U still planning on going to the café tonight?" she wrote back.

"Def. Need to blow off some steam. First I'm gonna go home and sleep—I hope the boys are not all hyped up when I get there."

Max was referring to his little cousins. His aunt and uncle had two rambunctious sons, five and six years old. Max usually referred to them as "the Irish twins" until one day the O'Reilly boys thought he was talking about them. In a moment of frustration, Max had declared, "those Irish twins can really be a couple of pains in the ass!" Luke and Lance had their fists balled up immediately until Portia quickly signed to them that Max was talking about his cousins. Ever since then, Max ditched the "Irish twins" nickname and started referring to them innocuously as "the boys."

"I'm sure you could use some R&R," Portia wrote back. Then she added, against her shy judgment, "I can't wait to hear u perform tonight."

"And I can't wait to sing to you, Portia. C U later."

"C u." And then an "XO" for good measure.

She must have still been smiling to herself after the exchange because Charlotte suddenly broke out into a rare grin and said with great flair, "Ahh—ain't love grand…"

Portia nodded in agreement and took a chance by whispering when she was certain nobody was looking. "Yes, Charlotte, it really is…"

Portia spent the whole day trying to keep all her balls in the air. Yesterday's hallucination, the incident with Charlotte that morning, and the knowledge that she would be seeing Max that night were enough to keep her on her toes. But the toughest part of the act was the walking on eggshells she had to do around Felix. She almost wished he wasn't going at all tonight.

That's pretty selfish, Portia. Where the hell are your loyalties?

But why did it have to be a question of loyalties? Putting her tray down on their usual lunch table right next to Felix, she elbowed him playfully.

"What's up?" he said. He seemed like his usual self.

"Nothing much," Portia mouthed. "Stressing from that chem review."

"Lucky you've been studying so hard with Charlotte."

Was there a cynical edge to his tone?

She attempted a change of subject:

"So what time are you going to pick me up tonight? I

already told my mom that I'd be skipping dinner. I'm assuming Wendy will hook us up with all kinds of food—"

"Yeah, about that," Felix said, "Why don't we just meet there? This way it will seem less like a date. I might actually pick up Gabrielle on the way."

His words stung, but frankly Portia was too tired to deal with one more unpleasant assault.

"Fine," she signed. With that she grabbed her tray and stormed away from the table.

She wished he would come after her, tell her that nothing had to change just because Max had entered the picture. Or Gabrielle. She wished that he could hear her. Really hear her, not just her voice, but the stuff she was unable to say by signing or speaking.

But when she turned back he was facing the other way, joking around with Luke and Lance. He shot her a quick glance, his eyes mirroring the confusion they were both feeling.

And then that mask he wore returned and Felix turned away again, focusing all of his attention on the antics of the true Irish twins.

Chapter 14

When Max Hunter walked into Café on the Ridge, he thought of horses. Well, one horse, in particular. His mother's American Saddlebred, Juliette. When he was a kid, they used to go out and ride "Juju" until mare and boy couldn't catch their wind. And then one day he heard his parents talking about the horse's anhidrosis.

"Horses can't sweat like people, sweetie," his mother had explained when he asked her about the new word that sounded like some fatal disease.

He never rode Juliette again. How could he put that poor creature through her paces with no release? No exit for her own buildup of heat?

That was pretty much how he felt tonight. These past few days with his father had sparked a raging heat within him, and his only release was music. If he couldn't perform, couldn't get lost in a world of chords and runs, there was no doubt he would overheat.

When he had arrived at the hospital his father had been completely delusional.

"I saw her, Max. She was here. I told you we would find her. She was here, and she asked for you."

Max had tried easing his father back into reality. "Pop, listen. She's gone. She wasn't here. She's never going to be here…"

But that just furthered the hysteria. His father had grabbed him by the collar. "Don't you ever say that, you ignorant little shit. I'm telling you, I know what I saw. She was here!"

The nurses had had to restrain him, and by the time Max left, his father was so doped up that he doubted he would have been able to differentiate between his son and the

Havenhurst custodian.

Max made his way over to the stage area and watched as Lily Wilson, the owner of the café, moved the last of the sofas off to the side, clearing more space for a dance floor. He considered offering to help but was impressed at how deftly Lily unlocked the casters and rolled the heavy piece of furniture away.

"It's all rigged that way," she said to him. Her voice had a smoker's rasp. "I could have this place cleared out in less than 5 minutes if I needed to. So what are you planning on singing tonight, Mr. Hunter?"

Looking over at the Kawasaki upright, Max decided that tonight didn't feel like a six string kind of night. Right now he was all about the ebony and ivory.

"Thinking about giving that upright a proper workout."

"I like the way that sounds, honey."

He granted her a quick flex of his dimples and then politely begged off the flirtation, walking over to the piano. Gently touching the cool keys, he could feel the pressure swell inside him, the sweat rising to the surface.

He glanced at his watch, a Breitling that his dad had given him when they had moved to New York. "To keep track of the time until we find her. Then you can throw it away, Max. Once we find her, time won't matter…"

He played out a few chords, closing his eyes, introducing himself to the instrument that would be his artillery for the evening. His mind flooded with mental snapshots of his mother. She had been so encouraging of his musical pursuits.

"Your great-grandfather used to tell me a wonderful story, Max. Do you want to hear it?"

He had lived for her stories, so often crawling into the safety of her lap.

"Once upon a time there lived a God named Marsyas. Marsyas had music running through his veins just like you, Max…"

He couldn't remember the rest of the story and, as always, his memories always came to an abrupt halt with a conjured image of his mother's lifeless body lying in a pool of her own blood.

When he opened his eyes again, Max scanned the room. Patrons were starting to trickle in, ordering all manner of yuppified coffees and cappuccinos.

God, he missed his mother. At Performing Arts he had skipped from girl to girl, always looking for that one that would make him feel whole again. When his dad flipped out, he had sworn off any relationship that could ever potentially wound him again.

And then came Portia.

What was it about this damned girl that had him so unhinged? He couldn't stop thinking about her, replaying every gesture between them, conjuring her aroma, the feel of her skin.

He'd been a little hurt that she didn't show more concern while he was off with his dad. But then again, a phone conversation was not within her scope, and she had probably had too many questions to text.

Well, there was plenty of time for him to explain things to her.

He played out a few more chords on the piano, the pedals a welcome obstacle underfoot. Yes, it was definitely an ebony and ivory kind of a night.

Now, where in the bloody hell was Portia Griffin…

Banging out the last of his chemistry homework, Felix considered blowing off the whole night. He could always use more studying, right?

He knew he was acting like a baby but just didn't feel like seeing a bunch of women swooning over the gorgeous musical prodigy Max Hunter.

He slammed his book shut and threw it into his bag.

Why was he so goddamned angry?

Admittedly he had been treating Portia unfairly. So they had had a moment a few months ago—big deal. He should have manned up at the time and told her that he was feeling something.

He wasn't sure what exactly *it* was, but he was definitely feeling something. Instead he had said nothing, pretended everything was status quo.

And now it was too late. Of course some guy was gonna come along and snatch her up. Felix was deaf, but he sure as hell wasn't blind. In the looks department, his best friend had basically become something of an overnight sensation. He wondered, though, if she knew that he loved her before all that. That he had always thought her to be the most beautiful girl in existence.

No, she doesn't know—because you are too much of a wuss to tell her.

So he'd have to settle for friendship. But Felix was just not a settler. He couldn't settle for not being able to speak as clearly as a hearing person. He couldn't settle for not being able to hold his own on a dance floor. How the hell was he supposed to settle for 'just friends' with the only girl who had the ability to make him feel whole?

His thoughts turned to Gabrielle. *"I might actually pick Gabrielle up on the way?"*

Why did he have to say that to Portia? He hadn't even mentioned Open Mic Night to Gabrielle and found himself hoping that she wouldn't actually be there. Gabrielle was pretty and sweet but so…one-dimensional.

He just couldn't think straight around Portia anymore. There was something different about her. He suddenly felt like he didn't know her like he used to. And he couldn't rid himself of that persistent nagging feeling that Portia and Charlotte were keeping something from him. He was probably just being paranoid. It was strange, though, the way all of a sudden the once-silent Charlotte was now so enamored of Portia. Something must have prompted the sudden friendship.

When Felix had questioned Portia about it, she had offered him a vague, "Oh—I guess she was just ready to come out of her shell."

Stop it! You sound like a freaking schoolgirl!

He pushed himself away from his desk, accepting the inevitability that tonight would be happening. He would just have to suck it up, the same way he had been doing these past weeks.

Opening his closet to throw on a clean change of clothes, Felix was not surprised to find a note from his sister Wendy that said: "Wear This!" His self-appointed stylist had stuck a Post-it onto a navy and white gingham Abercrombie shirt, super slim. An identical note rested on a pair of faded jeans.

"And these!" said another note at the bottom of the closet, stuck to a pair of loafers that Wendy had made him buy before he had gone to Canada.

Gotta admire her persistence.

He threw on the outfit and took a long look in the mirror.

"OK, OK, not too bad," he said the words aloud.

He went into his bathroom to take a quick shave and when he opened up his medicine cabinet, there were two more notes in his sister's manic handwriting.

OK, this is getting ridiculous.

"Don't do it—the five o'clock shadow thing is very George Clooney." The note was stuck to his can of shaving cream.

And then there was an unfamiliar small jar of styling wax, which she must have snuck in on the down-low. "And use some of this!"

He conceded on the no shaving but refused to do the hair styling thing.

He went back to his room to retrieve his wallet from his night table, where he found one final note from his sister "If she doesn't want you, she's a fool."

Jesus, Wendy.

Felix hurried back into his bathroom and indulged his sister by threading a miniscule amount of wax into his mess of hair. Knowing he had done her proud, he headed out the door to face the night head-on.

Leucosia still had trouble acclimating to modern styles. She had been so happy in years past to just while away her days in white robes of linens and silks. Now it was all about belly shirts and True Religion, a name she found most laughable. Rifling through her closet, she settled on an embroidered green peasant shirt and a pair of black trousers.

Do people still use the word trousers?

She had to admit she felt a bit of a thrill when she put on the high Louboutin black heels, an indulgence she had allowed herself a few months ago.

Spotting an ancient pair of gladiator sandals in the corner of her closet, she remembered back to when gladiators had come back into fashion last year. Leucosia had been delighted to dig out the handmade relic. A few of the girls at school had even commented on them and wanted to know where she had bought them.

"I actually got them a long time ago from the cobbler," the school nurse had responded.

"Oh, is that that new boutique on Upper Madison?" Jacqueline Rainier had asked her.

Glancing in the mirror, Leucosia was satisfied that her appearance was au courant. The green of the blouse highlighted her eyes, and the neckline was cut high enough so as not to reveal the scar from her weighty wings.

She grabbed a small clutch bag from her closet, a Judith Leiber in the shape of a Persian cat. It had been an impulse purchase, but the jeweled bag had reminded her so much of her beloved Hermes that she had simply been unable to pass it up.

Just admit it, Leucosia. You love modern-day shopping!

She smiled at the lighthearted realization, which was such a welcome departure from the constant fear that had been hovering over her since Portia's dream.

Portia's last office visit had been a terrifying wake-up call for the weary Leucosia. The sight of her sisters' faces and the sounds of their laughter had overwhelmed her in more ways than one. Not to mention the knowledge that Portia had almost killed Harold Trotter.

With that dream, the full magnitude of her responsibilities was suddenly upon her. And she wasn't sure how to proceed. She didn't want to overwhelm Portia with too much information at once, but she also couldn't take a chance that the young Goddess might abuse the powers of her voice unknowingly.

The night after Portia's last visit, she had texted Morpheus angrily, admonishing him for not forewarning her about the turmoil of Portia's sleep.

He had texted back:

"Leucosia—when I was gifted by the Almighty Zeus with the power to visit the dreams of Gods and models—"

Models? The Siren did a double take at her phone.

"I meant 'mortals,' my dear. Autocorrect be damned. Anyway, I was warned that any abuse of my power could result in my gift being taken away."

Leucosia understood the divine Hippocratic oath that bound the Gods to maintain the privacy of mortals.

"My apologies, Morpheus. I am not angry with you. I just fear for the well-being of the young Siren. Tell me, what exactly are the dangers of these dreaded dreams?"

"The venom of the dream depends on the snake who takes the bite, Leucosia. I fear that your sisters are the most poisonous of snakes…"

With that Morpheus had begged off—he had to go visit a mortal who was struggling to wake up from a month-long coma.

As Leucosia put on her makeup, she replayed his words. Her sisters were indeed snakes of the worst kind, but how exactly were Parthenope and Ligeia planning on exacting their revenge?

They've got something up their sleeve.

Her cat sat at her feet, looking up at her with his copper eyes.

"Yes, I know, Hermes. I am over three thousand years old and am trying to walk in a pair of six-inch platforms…"

She leaned down to give the cat a quick rub.

"I'm getting too old for this…" she whispered to her whiskered confidante.

Since Helena and Joshua were having their standing dinner date with the Feins, Janie Trotter gave the girls a lift to the café. Embarrassed at being chauffeured by her mom, Charlotte insisted on being dropped off a block away. Mrs. Trotter didn't seem to take offense, though, as she handed Charlotte some extra money, despite her daughter's insistence that she had enough. Charlotte planted a kiss on her mom's cheek and allowed herself to be pulled in for a prolonged hug.

"Don't worry, Mom," she said. "I'll be fine, and if you need me, just call me on my cell."

"I won't need you," assured Janie Trotter. "I only need for you to have fun."

With that the girls hopped out and started walking in the direction of the café.

Though she tried maintaining a carefree pace, Portia felt like an idling engine on the racetrack, knowing that Max might be just a few yards away.

What, so now you're a car enthusiast?

When they walked in a little bit before 8:00, the room was already full. Portia caught a glimpse of Wendy Fein out of the corner of her eye. She waved to Felix's sister, who returned the greeting with a cold nod.

Et tu, Wendy?

But she ignored the gesture for now, scanning the crowd for the one person she wanted—no, make that *needed*—to see most. A smile came to her face when she glimpsed Max sitting in a corner, leafing through some sheet music.

She gestured to Charlotte, a slight tip of her head in Max's direction.

"What are you waiting for? Go, go already."

As she neared him, Max looked up at her.

"Holy hell," he offered. "You look incredible, Portia."

She felt the heat rush to her face and tried making light of the compliment as she sat down and took out her phone. She was about to start typing when Max took the phone and said, "Why don't you try mouthing the words to me? If Felix can read your lips, I don't see why I can't." Clearly he had planned for this line of attack.

She felt a brief stab of pain at the mention of Felix and

wondered if he had gotten to the café yet. If she knew Felix, and she did know Felix, he was probably planning on doing the whole fashionably late thing, just to prove his nonchalance.

"OK," Portia mouthed, "I was just going to say that you look exhausted. Did the boys let you sleep when you got home?" She stretched the elastic of her lips over each word so that he would understand her.

"Actually, I can't blame it on the boys." Their hands had instinctively found each other's, their fingers interlacing and rotating as if trying to solve a Rubik's Cube. "I mean, yeah, they were running around like bats out of hell, but the truth is I can't come down from the visit with my dad. It was all too crazy. The things he said to me, Portia, it was insane."

She broke the contact, wanting to offer him her full attention. But with a brief shake of his head, Max combed his hair back with his fingers and tried to collect himself.

"Anyway," he said, "Let's try to enjoy the night. What's been going on with you?"

"Not a lot, Max. I'm worried about you."

"Ah, no need to worry about me, Portia. I've got a thick skin. Besides, I knew you would be here when I got back and I gotta admit, that really helped."

She looked away, picking at an imaginary piece of dust on her jeans.

"You have to stop doing that."

"What?" Portia asked him.

"Looking away from me every time I say something nice about you."

"Oh, was I doing that?" she mouthed with exaggerated innocence.

"Yes, you were," he wrinkled his nose at her. "Now, let's see if you can look straight at me while I do this."

He reached his hand out and slowly passed the soft pad of his thumb over her lips. Portia held his gaze despite the tremor he had sent through her body. Max leaned in and kissed her gently. She closed her eyes and savored the feeling of his mouth on hers. He started to pull away, but she brought his face back in, forgetting that they were in a room with about two hundred people. They might have been the only two people alive at the moment for all she cared.

Suddenly Lily Wilson was speaking into the microphone, trying to gain the attention of the audience. Reluctantly Portia and Max drew apart as Lily welcomed everybody and gave them the lowdown on the young talent that would be performing that night. Scanning the room, Portia saw Felix standing with Charlotte and Jacqueline, who looked awesome in her new ensemble. Luke and Lance were there, too. And Gabrielle. She wondered if any of them had seen her and Max kiss.

The audience quieted down as Wendy Fein sat down on a high stool, guitar in hand, and performed a beautiful rendition of Cat Stevens's "If You Want to Sing Out, Sing Out."

When she was finished, the audience applauded enthusiastically. Portia saw Felix twisting his hands in the air, the universal deaf sign for applause. She ached then for her friend who couldn't actually hear his favorite sister's performance.

"Max, I'm going to let you prepare," she mouthed, "Good luck."

She bent over and kissed him on the cheek, more self-conscious suddenly about being spotted by the watchful eyes of her friends.

As she made her way through the crowd, a woman in an insanely high pair of platforms tripped and bumped into her.

"Excuse me," said the slight red head. When she looked up, Portia was taken aback to see Ms. Leucosia, so out of the context to which she was accustomed.

"Oh, hi there, Portia," said the school nurse as if it was the most natural thing for her to be hanging out at the student watering hole. "I'm just meeting a friend," she offered quickly.

Portia nodded and smiled. She pointed to the nurse's shoes and gave her a big thumb's up.

"Thank you, dear."

The use of the word "dear" was so incongruous to the striking looks of a woman like Leucosia.

"Well, have fun," Portia signed—she was eager to get over

to her friends.

"You too, dear."

She continued to make her way over to Felix. As she neared him, the walls of her stomach felt much like that purple hedge in Charlotte's garden—flooded with butterflies.

Calm down. It's just Felix.

She tapped his shoulder from behind, and Felix turned around.

"Jesus, Portia, you look amazing." For the first time in a while, she could tell he was being completely honest.

Gabrielle excused herself, heading over to some of her freshmen friends.

"Shouldn't you go after her?" Portia signed.

"Who?"

"Oh, never mind." She was pleased that he approved of her getup and didn't want to mess up the first pleasant exchange they'd had in a while.

"You look amazing, too, Felix," she signed, "Looks like Wendy hooked you up."

"Yeah, she pretty much ambushed me with Post-it notes all over my closet and bathroom—"

Just then Luke punched Felix on the arm.

"Hey, man," he said, "you gotta stop talking—next performer's up."

Felix was notably embarrassed at having to be quieted.

"…and so this Adonis walked in the other day and asked me if he could try out," Lily was saying. "I'm sure you'll all find him to be every bit as impressive as I did. Everybody, give it up for Max Hunter."

A sudden hush fell over the room as Max sat down in front of the upright. He leaned into the mic and said:

"I want to dedicate this song to my dad, who couldn't be here tonight. I just hope he knows I'm thinking about him."

He started to play out a soulful introduction…

'The traffic light's saying 'Don't Walk,' but you're walking. Memories, voices, smells always stalking.

Horns are blaring, angry and loud,
Threatening to poke holes in her shroud.
Subways and cabs won't get you there,
No bus driver calling 'next stop, no despair.'
Roads intersect and highways converge,
A vehicle of sorrow, refusing to merge..."

Max's graceful fingers floated over the keys. Portia had never seen him play the piano before and was amazed at his command of the instrument. His voice was layered with emotion as each poignant lyric resonated with his buttery voice.

"But I'm reading the signs,
And I'm swimming upstream,
And I'm getting old for my years.
Can't you lead our team?"

There was a slight break in Max's voice as he sang out the last line of the chorus, isolating himself in the capsule of his own thoughts.

"And no one is meant to go it alone.
We all have our person, the one we call home.
Your home destroyed, vacant streets you wander,
Where is that place that will take you beyond her?
Inventing a world inside of your head,
Where longing alone might bring back the dead.
Well, I've looked for that place, but it doesn't exist
So I swallow hard and I uncurl my fist..."

The hush that had fallen upon the room was eerie, his pain floating through the air, filling the silence. Portia turned toward Felix just long enough to note the defeat and frustration that was plastered on his face.

"Instead I'm reading the signs,
And I'm swimming upstream,
And I'm getting old for my years.
When can you lead our team?"

Max's voice gained strength as he continued to sing his

story. His fingers eked out angry chords from the upright, and his knee tapped to the beat in his head.

> *"Hanging off the edge of the 'cliff of dashed hope,'*
> *Knowing your fear, I throw you a rope.*
> *But taking that rope means she's left us for good,*
> *Time to resettle, find a new neighborhood.*
> *Can't I be your home? Help you climb out of your head?*
> *With so much to live for, why waste time playing dead?*
> *And we'll cry together if you'd just return.*
> *There's so much from you that I still have to learn…"*

As the conclusion of the song drew near, Portia wished she could sit beside him and help him get through the rest. If not with her voice, then at least with her touch.

> *"And I'm reading all the signs, Dad,*
> *And I'm swimming upstream,*
> *Making music that hurts me,*
> *Building up my regime.*
> *And I'm shedding my blindfold,*
> *Cause I choose to see.*
> *And I'm unlocking doors,*
> *And I'm entering me,*
> *But I'm getting old for my years.*
> *So I hold on to the dream*
> *That one day you'll return,*
> *You'll be back on our team…"*

The room was silent as Max finished playing the last note and slowly opened his eyes. He abruptly stood up, scraping the bench against the wooden floor, the only sound that could be heard before the audience erupted into explosive applause.

He closed the lid on the piano and walked away without lifting his head. It was the first time Portia had seen him so humbled.

It made her love him all the more.

"That was awesome, man," Luke gave Max a man hug followed by two loud thumps on the back.

"Yeah, Max, that was seriously brilliant." Charlotte's cheeks were wet, her mascara slightly smudged.

Max accepted the compliments graciously. Portia's comments, though, were the only ones that seemed to matter to him. He looked at her expectantly. She squeezed his hand in response, her eyes telling him everything he needed to know.

"Isn't anyone going to ask me what I thought?"

The friends exchanged an awkward look, and Lance tried distracting Felix with a playful slap on the back and a request to go get some coffee.

"Get off of me, Lance. I'm serious. Isn't anyone gonna ask me what I thought of the song?"

Max broke into the sudden heaviness with an, "I hope it wasn't too boring for you, man."

Portia held her breath.

"What the hell is that supposed to mean?" Felix hovered within an inch of Max's face.

"Nothing, man, I just figured if you were going the sarcastic route, then we might as well all join in on the fun."

"Well, next time, don't figure anything."

Portia noted the throbbing vein in the right side of Felix's neck, a telltale sign of his impending rage.

"Felix, why don't we go see if Wendy can hook us up with some good eats?" she signed.

"Don't patronize me, Portia," he glared at her hard, his eyes a pair of grenades whose pins had just been pulled.

"Yo, dude, lighten up, will you?" Max stepped in front of Portia, stretching himself to his full height, which still came up inconsequential next to Felix.

"Yo, dude, go screw yourself, will you?" Felix was gunning for it.

Portia scrambled to think of something to ease the tension but before she could say or do anything, Max drove the final nail into the coffin with, "This whole jilted lover thing doesn't really suit you, Felix."

Felix pounced with lightning speed, toppling them both to the ground, landing a few good blows into Max's ribs before Max could even regain himself. A crowd formed around them as Luke and Lance tried to pry them apart. Their pent-up anger, though, was more than the twins could handle, so they backed off in defeat.

Portia was sick at the sight of them pummeling each other. She herself tried getting in between them, but they were too tightly intertwined. She scanned the room and saw that Lily Wilson's boyfriend, a cop who had recently pulled Helena over for speeding, was rounding up his buddies and heading over to the brawl.

She had to do something. The last thing anyone needed was for Max and Felix to be locked up together in a holding cell, staining their permanent records with acts of disorderly conduct.

She looked up at Charlotte, shrugging her shoulders, begging her advice.

"I think you know what you have to do, Portia. I think it's time."

The boys continued throwing punches, drawing blood and blackening eyes, as the cops pushed their way closer.

Nobody noticed when Portia nodded at Charlotte and snaked her way to the other side of the room where the microphone rested in its cradle.

She felt like she was walking the plank into an ocean full of piranhas.

Things will never be the same for me. I will never be the same.

The ramifications were both terrifying and thrilling. Looking back at the raging Max and Felix, their fight gaining momentum, she had no choice but to take the plunge.

With a quivering hand, she eased the microphone off the stand. Everyone's attention was diverted away from her, focused on the fight. As she opened her mouth, Portia did notice, though, that Ms. Leucosia seemed to be following her every move. The two women locked eyes and to Portia's amazement, the school nurse gave her an encouraging nod, not a hint of surprise in her expression.

Drawing in a deep breath, she had no idea what was going to come out of her mouth. She just knew that it would be something other than silence.

"Is it underneath your skin?
The pain you're living in?
Or do you bear the scars?
Are you seeing stars?"

Max instantly stopped fighting Felix as the first lyrics floated out of Portia's mouth. The entire room grew still at the sound of her virginal voice.

"Mine is all around me.
It confuses and confounds me,
It shakes me and it quakes me.
Over burning coals it rakes me."

Felix stopped throwing punches, sensing that something had shifted in the atmosphere of the room, the atmosphere of the earth. He scanned the café and saw Portia cradling the microphone in her hand and moving her lips.

"Is there a stain upon your shirt?
A place where your blood spurt?
Please, oh, please, just tell me,
Oh—show me where it hurts…"

He looked around at the faces of the audience, frozen, as if they were witnessing a modern-day miracle. Pushing his way through the crowd, he tripped over himself toward one of the giant speakers, placing an unwilling hand on top of it. The vibrations that met his fingers coursed through him like an electrical current. A punitive current. The kind that would penetrate someone in an electric chair.

"Growing pains can shatter,
Cause your teeth to chatter,
And the heart bleeds like no other,
Begging kisses of a mother."

The audience was hypnotized by the raw beauty of her voice. Portia was sounding off bass notes along with their coordinating harmony with an ease that spoke of years of vocal training. Her range was mind-blowing as she wove a musical tapestry. The crowd drew nearer to the singing Goddess. Everyone, except Felix, who stood rooted to his spot at the speaker.

> *"Wounds of silence pierce,*
> *Holding a dissonance that's fierce,*
> *And loneliness can kill,*
> *But look, you're standing still."*

The unfamiliar melody was carrying Portia through the song as she scanned the room to find Felix. She spotted him, standing off to the side, his hand on the speaker, tears streaming down his face. Seeing his hurt added another dimension to her voice.

> *"And though the words we skirt,*
> *The pain you can't divert.*
> *So, show me, baby, show me,*
> *Oh—show me where it hurts…"*

She stared at Felix, waiting for his reaction. His face was so twisted with pain and confusion that he no longer even resembled her Felix.

Suddenly, from the back of the silent room, she heard a familiar voice.

"Portia?"

She looked up and saw a dumbstruck Helena standing in the entrance of the café. She was with Natalie Fein, whose cheeks were stained with tears.

Chapter 15

Portia felt like an action hero who had tried to traverse two buildings and had plummeted right into the gap.

She needed out.

Fast.

She remembered Wendy once sneaking her and Felix into the café through a rarely used back exit, which thankfully was unlocked. The cool breeze stung her skin as she tried to inhale deeply into her lungs.

What the hell was she thinking?! This was it. There was no going back now. Felix would probably never talk to her again. And her friends? And Max? They probably all thought she was some kind of hypochondriacal freak. How would she ever bridge the two worlds of her life? The voiceless and the voiced?

Hyperventilating, she recalled the pained look on Felix's face when he had laid his hand on that speaker. She wished she could turn back the clock. How could she have made such a hasty decision? As her breathing growing more labored, a wretched bile threatened to rise up out of her throat.

And Helena? Why had her mother been there? She suddenly remembered the tears on Natalie Fein's face. Had something happened?

Portia started to scream into the darkness, great stabs of anger piercing the emptiness around her. She crouched down to the floor as her screams gave way to clamorous sobs.

A sudden hand on her shoulder interrupted her solitude.

She looked up to see the endless green eyes of Ms. Leucosia gazing down upon her, much like a mother admiring her newborn baby.

"Portia," the Siren said, her voice as smooth as silk, "we need to have a talk…"

"What's going on, Ms. Leucosia? How did you know I was back here?" Portia's voice was heavy with tears.

"Portia," Leucosia began awkwardly, "I heard through the grapevine that you placed into Mr. Morrison's elective about *The Odyssey*."

Portia looked at the school nurse as if she had completely lost her mind.

"What are you talking about, Ms. Leucosia? I'm a little preoccupied right now, you know," she responded, exasperated. "Weren't you just inside? Didn't you see what happened?"

Leucosia slunk down to the ground next to Portia, hugging her knees into her chest.

"Yes, Portia. I was inside, and believe it or not I've rehearsed these lines in my head so many times. Now that this moment has finally arrived, I'm feeling quite nervous, actually—uncertain about where to begin."

"What the hell are you talking about, Ms. Leucosia?" Portia was losing her patience.

"Did Mr. Morrison get up to the part about the Sirens yet?"

At the mention of the Sirens, Portia receded further away from the nurse, a blaring alarm sounding in her head. Something was off. Very, very off.

"He referenced it—why?" It came out as a whisper.

"And I think you already know that the names of the Sirens who unsuccessfully tried to lure Odysseus in were Parthenope and Ligeia, right?"

"I know those names…but…but it never said in the book or anywhere else that they were the ones who tried to lure in Odysseus. Wait—it was you? It was you messing with me whole time?" A look of shock ran across Portia's face. "Why would you do that? Why was it so goddamned important that I know a twisted fairy tale about some crazy made-up Sirens?"

"Because, my dear, those crazy made-up Sirens were my sisters. Parthenope and Ligeia were my sisters."

Portia stared at Leucosia like she had just sprouted a second head. If she wasn't so distraught over the events of the last hour, she might have even laughed.

"Ms. Leucosia, have you taken leave of your senses?" This was an expression Helena favored. It seemed fitting at the moment.

Of course this was the reaction that Leucosia expected from the young girl. She herself could hear how laughable she sounded. Rethinking her strategy, she tried backtracking a little.

"Portia, do you remember when you were last in my office, I placed my hand over your throat? The reason I did that was to see how far along the development of your syrinx had come."

"My what? Only birds have syrinxes, Ms. Leucosia."

The older Goddess was visibly impressed at her charge's knowledge of bird anatomy and decided to stick with birds as a segue into the inevitable bomb she was about to drop.

"Ahh—so you're a bird person. Then you already know that the syrinx is an anatomical wonder—a magical voice box that splits into two bronchi, enabling two different notes to be sung at the same time—"

"Ms. Leucosia," Portia interrupted the nurse impatiently, "I'm kind of not in the mood for a biology lesson right now." Her mind was racing, her thoughts fragmented like fireworks through her head. She really needed this lunatic to leave her alone.

The nurse continued as if Portia hadn't even spoken. "Well, the syrinx is what enables birds to call out as they do. But Sirens have both a larynx and a syrinx, making something like this possible…"

Leucosia looked up at the night sky and let escape from her mouth a simultaneous symphony of notes.

Portia stared wide-eyed at her, mouth agape.

"That was beautiful," she admitted when she recovered herself. Was there no end to the bizarre ways in which this day was unfolding?

"Thank you," responded Leucosia, "Although I suspect that you've been able to execute the same vocal feats lately."

Portia nodded reluctantly.

Leucosia took Portia's hand and placed it at the base of her own throat. She emitted another glorious sound, a silkworm releasing a melodic thread, and Portia could feel an intense vibration travel through her hand. She wanted to move her fingers away, but the nurse's delicate throat was like a magnet. Finally Leucosia stopped singing, and Portia dropped her hand immediately.

"OK, so maybe somehow we have the privilege of having syrinxes. So what?" She knew she was being rude—she never spoke to adults this way. Well, at least not until her recent run in with Mr. Morrison. But her emotional well had run dry, and she just didn't have the energy to check herself.

Leucosia decided to go in for the kill.

"Portia, I know you tried to kill Charlotte Trotter's father."

Portia looked up at her in shock. The nurse suddenly had her full attention.

"Portia, listen to me. For as crazy as this might sound to you, you are indeed a Siren, just like the ones described by Homer. Not that he even knew everything about Sirens, but boy, he did like to hear himself talk. My dear friend Athena—you know, the pale-eyed Goddess from *The Odyssey*; actually they're more of a grayish tone—anyway, she can shift her shape, remember? So we caused Mr. Morrison to have a slight case of food poisoning for the first couple of days, so that Athena could deliver his lectures for him. As him. She needed to start planting the seeds in your head that the world of the Gods is a real one."

"That's impossible," Portia replied.

"Portia, all these Gods—Athena, Morpheus the God of Dreams, and others whom you will come to know—made a collective decision at your birth to slow the development of your syrinx so that you would not achieve your full powers until you were mature enough to handle them. They—we—couldn't risk you turning out like my sisters. But now, here you are, a young woman with a voice whose powers are…are…immeasurable. And I am going to help you learn how to master your tool."

Portia did begin to laugh then—a nervous laughter that one

might let out at a funeral. Scanning the alley surrounding them, she began planning her best escape route from this lunatic, who she prayed to God was harmless.

"You can run, Portia, but you'll be doing yourself a huge disservice. There are forces out there that would have you use your voice purely for purposes of destruction. Parthenope and Ligeia are trying to encourage you down the same path of evil upon which they traveled. You must trust me so that together we can ensure that the goodness in your heart remains there. Forever."

"Ms. Leucosia," Portia tried to be as diplomatic as possible, "you are talking to the only teenage girl on the planet who never truly obsessed over Team Edward or Team Jacob—OK, maybe I did a little. But do you know why I never lost sleep over it? Or bought a T-shirt? Because ultimately vampires and werewolves don't exist! And neither do Sirens. I'm not sure what exactly is going on with me, but I guess now that the cat is out of the bag, my parents will force me to do the whole doctor circuit again, and then we'll find out."

"I wouldn't recommend that." Her tone was menacing. "Unless you want to spend the rest of your life visiting a steady stream of doctors who are determined to figure out what makes you so 'special.' I think you've had enough of that in your childhood already, right?"

"All right, that's it. I have to go." Portia stood up and readied herself to make a break for it when Leucosia once again began singing. Willing her feet to start walking, running even, she found that she was paralyzed. She focused all of her energy on taking the first step that would lead her back to the real world, but as Leucosia's voice grew louder, Portia's legs became more inert.

The redhead's voice was glorious as foreign lyrics spilled effortlessly from her mouth. To her horror, Portia found that she was not only unable to take a step forward, but was also unwittingly slumping down along the alley wall again as Ms. Leucosia continued to sing. When her fingers felt the cold stone of the pavement beneath her, her mind suddenly flashed an image of Harold Trotter's bloodied knuckles scraping the stone edge of the well.

She scrambled through her memories of the past few weeks, wondering if maybe Ms. Leucosia might be on to something. Nothing mythological, of course, but perhaps some kind of spiritual or karmic explanation for her sudden metamorphosis.

"Please start at the beginning." She couldn't believe she was encouraging this madness.

"You already know the beginning, Portia. Let me start where we left off…"

Leto bore a daughter from the great love she shared with Nereus. The child was called Melina, for she was as sweet as honey and was the greatest source of joy that Leto had ever known. But though Leto prayed to the almighty Zeus to grant her daughter immortality, it was not meant to be.

Melina was beautiful among mortals and found love with a man, Nikolas, who knew only goodness in his heart. Four daughters did they bear, one more mortal than the next.

Leto's heart was ever filled with sorrow as she appealed to Zeus in her every waking moment to spare her the pain of burying her own child.

But there are chapters in the books of the Gods that can never be rewritten.

And so came the dreaded day when Leto held her dying daughter in her ageless arms. Snowy gray was the once-red hair of the aged Melina, her skin deeply lined and freckled with brown spots.

"Dearest Mother, for my mortal soul I beg you, do not weep. For I have known great happiness with Nikolas and the many daughters with whom the Gods have blessed me. And above all, I have known the love of a mother who has never once uttered a harsh word unto me."

Leto felt a pain such as she had never known.

"Mother," continued the dying mortal, "as the hour of my death is upon me, I beg you only one request."

Her heart brimming with love and sadness, Leto said to her daughter, "Dearest Melina, be not humble in your request, for there is nothing I could deny a daughter such as you."

Melina then spoke these words:

"Though we have not often spoken of it, Mother, well known among Gods and mortals are the evildoings of your sisters, Parthenope and Ligeia. I beg you, remain upon this earth until the next Siren emerges. You must guide her down the path of goodness, so that she does not follow in the evil footsteps of your sisters."

A great panic descended then upon Leto, who was ever exhausted by the trials of her immortal life and by the very oath she had already sworn to her own mother, Terpsichore. But her love for Melina was great, and she could deny her daughter nothing.

"My sweet Melina, I swear to you that I shall guard our kin like the lioness guards her cubs."

Melina then spoke the words that carried the great Goddess Leto through her many years on earth.

"When the next one does emerge, speak to her of your daughter Melina, who even now at the hour of death feels she has been a great disappointment. For always I wished to possess the Godliness that has blessed you."

Leto's heart shattered into a million pieces.

"Melina, a better daughter than you a mother has never known. You are kind and true, so much like your dear father, Nereus."

Leto stroked the aged cheeks of her daughter with a hand young and supple.

"Mother, I feel the grip of death growing ever stronger upon my wretched aged body. I beseech you, each of your days shall you imagine the many words that you will one day speak unto the next, telling her of all the goodly mortals that came before her…"

With these words, the timeworn eyes of the once-lovely Melina were sealed shut with the kiss of death.

"You're Leto." Portia blurted out incredulously. "Is that why I could never see her clearly?"

"You did see her, Portia. You saw the whole thing, the whole story. It's just that, well, Sirens can develop this ability to erase a memory—you'll get around to it. And I'm a pretty experienced Siren, so I can actually do some selective memory erasing—it took me two centuries to master that one. Anyway, remember that song that would play at the end of each video segment—you know, while the credits were rolling? That was sung by me—a song meant to make you forget parts of what you saw until it became time to remember." Leucosia took Portia's hand and gave it a not altogether gentle squeeze. "And now it is time to remember," she commanded.

And then, like a defroster had suddenly been activated in her brain, Portia was able to remember the face of the third sister. It was indeed Leucosia's face. Down to the last freckle.

"I am Leto, Portia. Leto is my, um, nickname. It means 'hidden one'—a nod toward my reluctance to be in the spotlight, I suppose."

Portia's shock began to transform into full-fledged fear.

"So what?" she attempted, "You could put anybody's picture on one of those sites, right? And maybe I just didn't remember because…because…" But her words trailed off into the abyss of the inexplicable.

"Don't you see, Portia, all those links, all that storytelling, the appearance of Marsyas—well, that was actually Athena who shifted her shape into Marsyas's form for purposes of the story. After all, he was the first to notice the evil in my sisters. It ruined him for his whole life—it was such a shame, too, because he was so gifted. But the rest was all me."

"I can't believe that *you're* the cyberbully—"

"Oh, I don't know if I would use the word 'bully.' You know RPA has a strict anti-bullying policy."

Portia was incredulous. "Have you been, like, reading all my e-mails? Spying on my conversations?"

"No, I would never do that—well, wait, I did have to intercept the paper you e-mailed to Mr. Morrison. Sorry about the B-, by the way—I told you, I'm just not a Homer fan."

"This is not happening. You're crazy, Ms. Leucosia. You really think that I'm some kind of immortal God? And by immortal, I mean, like *immortal*? You're telling me that I'm never going to die?!"

"Portia, it is both the blessing and the curse of the Gods to live a life of immortality. Many a God has perished, but never in the ways that humans die. There is no illness, no aging, no starvation. There is only death at the hands of another immortal, or in our case, drowning in the open sea."

"So what's going to happen to me? This is it? I'm going to remain a sixteen-year-old for the rest of my life?" Her voice was shrill, a sieve leaking out fear and desperation.

"Well, not exactly." The nurse's lack of hysteria only reinforced the verity of her words. "You have more or less reached your physical peak. However, as the powers of your voice continue to unfurl, your physical beauty will increase. So, too, as you gain wisdom—the wisdom that inevitably comes to all Gods and Goddesses—your physical person will develop something of an agelessness. I mean, think about it, has it ever occurred to you that you've known me for years, and I have not shown any signs of aging?"

Portia kept shaking her head, trying to block out the well-rehearsed tale that was being flung at her by this apparent psychopath.

Leucosia took Portia's hand, a natural motherly gesture.

"Portia, when I was in your dream the other day—"

"—my what?"

"Yes, well then, I'm so sorry about that. I promise not to make a habit out of it, but I was so worried for you the other day when you came into my office and described your dreams to me. With a little help from Morpheus—remember I mentioned him? The God of Dreams? Well, with his help, I traversed into your dream to see if my sisters were indeed trying to—what is it you kids say—oh yes, mess with your mind. Anyway, I realized that their jealousy and resentment has not waned at all over these many years. They believe that I usurped the love of our mother for my own, and apparently the murder of my mortal lover, Nereus, was not enough to sate their desire for revenge—"

Portia had begun to cry, offering intermittent pleas between sobs for Ms. Leucosia to stop playing games with her.

"Why would you taunt me like this?" she petitioned the beautiful nurse. "What have I ever done to you?"

Leucosia took Portia's heart-shaped face into her hands,

brushing away her tears, which unsurprisingly had begun to show traces of silver.

"That's precisely the point, Portia. Why would I make any of this up? I have known you since you were a small child. I have watched you grow into a beautiful young woman. Why on earth would I want to hurt you, Portia?"

Portia continued to cry. "But why me of all people? What makes me so special?" The questions tasted sour on her tongue, knowing that they somehow leant credibility to the story.

"Ahhh. That is an excellent question. One which I have sought an answer for over many years until one day Athena explained to me that the next Siren will only be born out of a love as pure as the one I shared with Nereus. A love that defies the odds. A love that is usually reserved for fairy tales."

Portia wished her limbs were not paralyzed by Ms. Leucosia's enchanting voice. She needed to get away now. Before her parents were dragged into this madness.

"Portia, I'm sure I don't need to tell you that your parents are ridiculously, wholeheartedly, and wonderfully in love with one another. So much so that when Aphrodite caught wind of them—she's the Goddess of Love—she ventured a guess that you would be arriving imminently."

These words, so undeniably true, only furthered Portia's confusion. She would have done anything for any of her friends—Charlotte, Jacqueline, Max, Felix, oh God, Felix—to come out back and save her from the maddening story, which to her great horror so snugly fit as the missing pieces to the puzzle that her life had become. She was running on fumes. Exhausted, confused, noxious fumes. She needed time, a good night's sleep, and some clarity of mind so that she could decide if what Ms. Leucosia was telling her could even be remotely possible.

Through all of her skepticism, one question did continue to coil its way around her mind. She weighed the pros and cons of asking it, knowing that she probably didn't want to hear the answer.

Finally she garnered her courage.

"Ms. Leucosia—"

Leucosia interrupted her:

"I think you can start calling me just Leucosia, dear. The 'Ms.' seems kind of formal considering our circumstances."

"OK, Leucosia. Let's say I am this Siren you've been waiting for. What exactly do your sisters want from me?"

Leucosia had been asking herself the same question over and over.

"I'm not sure yet, dear. But I'm sure it's nothing good." Leucosia looked down at the pavement as she spoke these words.

Portia scrutinized the flawless face of the alleged three-thousand-year-old Goddess.

"What is it? What are you not telling me?"

Leucosia looked back up at her charge and hesitated before detonating the final bomb.

"I think they want you to kill Max Hunter..."

Chapter 16

Portia had ignored her texts during the ludicrous exchange with Leucosia, but her phone kept signaling her, and finally she decided to plug back into the real world. The world that actually did exist.

She had about a million missed calls and texts from Helena. "Portia, where are you? I'm worried about you! Dean Fein was in a terrible accident. We're all here at the Feins helping them prepare to fly out to Canada. Where are you? Felix needs you, and we need to talk. That was crazy at the Café—what I saw, what I heard! Where r u??"

"Oh, shit!" she said aloud.

"What is it?"

"Leucosia, I need you to drive me over to Felix's house."

Without a moment's hesitation the two women followed the alley back out to the street and got into Leucosia's car, Portia explaining the little she knew about what had happened to Dean Fein.

"Dean and Felix are like brothers. Oh God. Oh God. I knew he shouldn't have gotten that dirt bike. I told Felix…"

Driving in silence for a couple of minutes, Portia had a sudden epiphany.

"I should be able to save him, right? If I'm really what you say I am, Leucosia, then my voice should be able to save Dean, right?"

Leucosia's eyes remained fixed on the road.

"Portia, it is not within our powers to save the lives of mortals. If it was, I would have saved so many…"

"Come on, Leucosia, can't you call in a favor with one of your God friends? Maybe the dream guy, Morpheus, knows someone? Or Athena? Maybe she has a few connections?" She could feel herself poking holes in Leucosia's obscene story, and it felt good. For a minute she had actually been caught up in the twisted fairy tale.

"Portia, you cannot change what is written by the Gods. The best you and I can do right now is hope that Felix's cousin is strong enough to pull through."

They pulled up in front of the Fein house, and Portia leapt out of the car. She leaned into the open window.

"Thanks for nothing, Leucosia. You know, that place where Max's father is staying might have an opening for you—'Havenhurst,' I think it's called. Why don't you use your magical voice to book yourself a room there?"

She couldn't believe the cruelty that was spewing out of her own mouth. But she couldn't stop it either. And the unflinching look on Leucosia's face only spurred her on. "I'll buy you a Kindle before you go, and you can download all the Greek Mythology you want. Maybe you'll even find Nereus and Melina again." At the mention of the names of her lost loved ones, Leucosia's eyes released a creamy silver liquid.

Portia turned on her heel and swatted her own tears away with the back of her hands. She needed to be strong now for Felix.

Just as she turned the knob, she caught her reflection in the brass doorknocker. She didn't like what she saw—silver tears that looked awfully similar to Ms. Leucosia's were streaming down the planes of her face.

The Fein house was so chaotic that no one even noticed Portia sneak in and head up the stairs. When she walked into Felix's room, he was throwing some clothing into a duffel bag, his back to the door. She tapped him gently on the shoulder.

Turning around, his face crumpled at the sight of her, and he surrendered himself to a torrent of pent-up tears. Portia pulled her friend in tightly and held him for as long as he would allow.

After a few minutes he pulled away, and Portia signed to him, "How bad is it?"

He signed back, "Best-case scenario would be that one day he'll be able to walk again. That is, if he ever regains consciousness. They're not sure yet how much brain damage there was. It's hard to tell yet because of the swelling…" He went into his bathroom and grabbed a bunch of toiletries, tossing them carelessly into his bag.

Portia handed him his laptop, which he slipped into a carry-on. "Good that you're taking that. This way we can chat when you get there. How long do you think you'll be gone?"

Her use of the word "chat" detonated the bomb that had been ticking inside of him. "Why do you care, Portia? Seriously! Why do you give a shit?! Max will be here and you guys can 'chat' with each other all day long!" His voice was thunderous, his words sizzling with resentment. "You can sing to each other. You can share secrets. A regular fucking CW romance!"

His anger stung, but Portia just accepted the hurt he was inflicting. At least he was evening the playing field.

She started signing with lightning speed. "Felix, I—"

He grabbed her hands, squeezing them hard in the vise of his grip.

"DON'T EVEN!"

"Felix, you're hurting me…stop!" She spoke the words aloud, knowing he wouldn't hear them.

He pinned her hands behind her back. "You want *me* to stop hurting *you*? You, Portia Griffin, Queen of Pain? Queen of Secrets! How long have you been playing mind games? Have you just been pretending your whole life? Some kind of sick charade to gain pity? Pretending to be mute as an excuse not to have to make any normal friends?" He moved in on her, pushing her toward the door until she was sandwiched in. Her fingers ached in his, but still she held his gaze, welcoming his rebuke.

"You think I haven't noticed that something changed? How long has Charlotte known?! And Max? Did you tell him, too? Have all our years of friendship meant nothing to you? You think because I'm deaf that I'm also blind? That I don't see you?

Smell you? Dream about you?" He was towering over her, his height exaggerated by the tension of his posture.

And then suddenly he went slack. The well of his words ran dry, and he eased his grip on her hands. Still he didn't make any move toward letting her go. They stood there for an endless moment, their breath coming hard, the rise and fall of their chests defining the passage of time.

He leaned his face in close to hers. She closed her eyes, anticipating the feel of his angry lips on hers. Wasn't this what it was all leading up to anyway? All that anger, all that hurt? Couldn't it all be erased by a kiss?

But his lips never came.

She opened her eyes and when she read his face, she realized that a kiss would have been an insult. What was held in those black eyes could never have been expressed by one kiss, by one moment. She brought her hand up to touch his face.

But the masked man was back, his face a beautiful slab of cold stone. And as much as Portia wished her fingers could chisel away at that stone, they remained mere fingers. Fingers that ached from his rough handling of them.

He pried her hand from his face. "Go home, Portia."

She pushed him away and ran out of the room.

When she got down the stairs, Portia lost any hope that the exchange between her and Felix had flown under the radar. All the scheduling and airline calling came to an abrupt halt as soon as she came into view. Wendy, Kate, and Julia were glaring at her like a pack of mother lions whose cub had just been threatened.

Portia wished she was invisible. She wished she was dead.

Helena broke the silence. "Natalie, we're going to take Portia home now." She gave Joshua's hand a squeeze. "Please keep us posted about Dean. Anything we can do to help— you know we're here for you…" Her words trailed off into the awkwardness.

Portia walked over to Felix's mother. She had known

Natalie Fein for as long as she could remember. She wondered if Felix's parents hated her now. She wondered if Natalie would reciprocate an embrace. Cautiously she folded her arms around her and felt a great sense of relief when the hug was returned.

"I'm so sorry, Natalie. For everything."

She could not believe that these were the first words her voice would carry to her loved ones.

Chapter 17

One day Ares, the great God of War, drew his blade and carved a crescent moon into the left cheek of Proteus, a great shape-shifting God. Proteus then soared out of the grip of Ares, turning into an eagle, his favorite form of all.

As he flew further away, Proteus found himself above a lush island when suddenly he heard the most beautiful sound ever known to him or any God. Swooping down to the meadow, he transformed back into his own person, boasting a strong build and a fine face, excepting the mark on his cheek.

At the edge of the meadow he beheld a Goddess of immeasurable beauty, passing her graceful hand through the clear waters of a shimmering pond.

"Please forgive my intrusion on your glorious song," said Proteus. "I hoped you would allow me to cool my weary feet in the waters of this pond."

"A fair God are you," replied Ligeia, her teeth glowing white as the moon. "Thus I will not deny your request. But I must warn you that the waters of this pond have come from the many tears I have shed."

Proteus was further enchanted and transformed himself into a swan, diving gracefully into the salty waters. Ligeia was pleased by the feat of the shape-shifter, watching him float as a swan and then resume his manly form.

Proteus swam to the edge of the pond and offered his gratitude to the Goddess.

"I must thank you for the gift of these waters, which do ease my well-worn muscles. I pray, tell me your name and why so many tears you have thus shed."

"I am called Ligeia," spoke the Siren. Her voice was as soothing as the waters in which Proteus floated. "I am one of three daughters of Achelous and Terpsichore. Just here I sat some years ago when I learned that my sister, Leucosia, was best loved by my mother."

Ligeia's eyes became greener with envy.

"A final good-bye I never said to my beloved mother for she did not desire to see myself or Parthenope. Only Leucosia."

With a delicate hand she swiped away her fresh tears.

"Only Leucosia…"

Proteus's heart grew heavy at the tale of the Goddess's great rejection. Out from the salty waters the shape-shifter climbed, settling himself alongside the magnificent Siren.

Ligeia then told him of the murder of Nereus and the sudden disappearance of Leucosia.

Proteus was already smitten and could not see the evil that dwelt within the Goddess—only the great pain she had suffered. The seeds of their ardor had been planted and secret lovers they became, never wanting to share their moments with another.

But, alas, the evil that bloomed in Ligeia's heart would not be staid by Proteus's great love for her.

The Siren's heart floated further and further away from Proteus, consumed by hurt and revenge. He performed great feats of shape-shifting for his lover, trying in earnest to draw her attentions back to himself. But his efforts were fruitless, and Ligeia continued down her path of self-destruction, her murderous frenzies becoming ever more frequent.

One day, after Poseidon blew a great storm out to sea, Ligeia sought out Proteus in the spot where they had first met. The waters of her pond of tears had turned murky and sulfurous, a dense steam rising from their wake. Proteus swooped down to meet his beloved but could barely recognize the Siren who stood before him.

"Ligeia, in my eyes you will always be beautiful. But even now do you appear unto me quite mad. For your hair, which once could shame the brightest flame, is now streaked with gray. And your eyes, once clear as a flawless emerald, are now reddened and filled with fog. Tell me, why do you now bare teeth of yellow and the odor of festered roses? What troubles you so deeply that has rendered you a mere ghost of the great beauty you once were?"

Ligeia's fury came at Proteus like a sword unto his heart.

"Have you not heard, Proteus? Have you not heard that the great mortal Odysseus was not drawn in by our song?" In frenzied circles the Siren paced about as she ranted onward. *"We are ruined, Proteus! A mere mortal has passed before us and resisted our seduction. We have*

suffered a shame that can never be healed! No mortal has ever resisted the Siren's song!"

Ligeia pulled at her hair, dropping tiny tufts at her lover's feet. "Parthenope and I must now take our own lives, Proteus. We cannot bear the shame. Never again will we know true happiness. For the rest of time, Gods and mortals alike will speak of Odysseus' power to resist us. We will forever be a failure..."

She placed her quivering hand on the face of her lover, fingering his golden locks. Her fingers were peeling and bloodied, chewed to the very quick.

"I have come to bid you farewell, Proteus. I have loved you truly, but that cannot be enough to make me live with the shame of my failure."

Proteus felt great panic, knowing that Ligeia had chosen to take her own life. He beseeched her with wise and loving words, saying:

"Ligeia, of what madness do you speak? Loveliest among the Goddesses are you ever still, your voice sweeter than ambrosia. I beg you, do not take your own life for the rejection of one mere mortal!"

Ligeia's giant wings emerged from her back, creating a great wind, which blew the words of Proteus fast out to sea.

"There is nothing you could say, Proteus, nor any shape into which you can shift, that can rid me of the great unrest that now lives in my heart. I bid you, say farewell unto me without anger or fear, for we have shared a great love. Perhaps one day our paths shall cross again among Gods or mortals."

The Goddess then flew away, carried by her giant wings.

Proteus immediately shifted his shape into the eagle that had first brought him unto Ligeia. He flew in silent desperation and then hovered in the sky, helpless to halt her. He felt as if he had fallen upon the sword as he beheld his lover and her sister join hands and soar with maddening speed into the dark wine waters of the great sea.

Before they broke the surface of the water, the sisters sang unto one another with voices that remained glorious. The melody that they sang as they descended into the waters haunted Proteus for many years to come.

He had to admit that when Leucosia sang it to Portia, behind the Café on the Ridge, it sounded just as beautiful as though it were escaping the lips of his lost love...

Chapter 18

The short car ride home with her parents exhausted Portia beyond reason, especially since none of the Griffins even moved to get out of the car once they pulled into their driveway. There were so many questions, so many tears. Tears of joy for the gift of their daughter's voice, and tears of sadness for the pain she and Felix were feeling, for the injuries of Dean Fein. None of it was like the fantasies in which she had indulged as a child.

When they finally entered their house, Portia had delighted her parents with an "I love you both so much" before heading up to her room. Ok, so maybe there was a little fantasy there. Hopefully her parents would be distracted enough by the declaration to forget about all the doctors' visits they had been planning in the car. At least for now.

Burrowing her head into her pillow, Portia couldn't help but think about the Kübler–Ross model that had been presented to them in last year's Psych elective. The model offers five stages of grief through which a person travels upon hearing devastating news. Portia felt like a Ping-Pong ball, bouncing from one stage to the next, moaning into her pillow and taking a modicum of comfort in the sound she was producing.

I've been dreaming, she thought. *There's no way any of this could be real.*

Stage one: Denial.

There's no such thing as a Siren or a human syrinx or any of the stuff that Ms. Leucosia was ranting about tonight. I mean, I feel fine. Sure, the whole voice thing is a little weird, but it doesn't mean that I'm a freak.

This brief stage of denial was so comforting to Portia.

I'm not going to outlive everyone I know. I am a normal teenage girl who is going to go through adolescence just like everybody else. I will go to college, fall in love, get married, grow old with somebody, and die of old age with deeply wrinkled skin and a mind riddled with senility.

Portia pushed her face further into her pillow, willing her thoughts to be real, to negate anything Leucosia had told her that night.

Coming up for air, she caught a quick glimpse of the picture she kept on her night table of her and her parents. That's when the anger set in.

Stage two: Anger.

What the hell is going on here?! Why is this happening to me? Because my parents are nauseatingly in love with each other? What kind of reason is that?

Of all the people in all the world, why am I being singled out? I'm a good girl. I've loved and respected my family and friends. And now I'm being told I'm going to outlive them all?

Sure, it's natural for my parents to go before me, but how the hell am I going to explain my lack of aging to them? How am I going to stand by and watch all of my friends, maybe even my own children, die before me?

Adding to her fury was the realization that if anything Leucosia said was true, her whole identity would now have to become a secret. Living a lie was going to be a nightmare—she had already had an unpleasant taste of it when she had regained her voice. How was she supposed to guard every word that came out of her mouth now? Every action? Every sound? The anger rose up in her as she thought about the burden that had been placed upon her.

But just as quickly, the fury segued into panic, which led to the next stage.

Stage three: Bargaining.

Oh, please God, or whoever it is that is controlling this, please don't let this be true. I will be good. I will never use drugs or drive drunk. I'll even take premarital sex off the table if you just give me a sign that I am actually normal.

Please just let me age at a normal pace. Let me enjoy normal friendships and romances. I'll do anything. Anything at all. Just please, please let me be normal.

And then:

Even just a few more years. Let me have a few more years of an ordinary life so that I don't have to bury the old Portia just yet. Is that too much to ask? Just a little more time?

But Portia wasn't even certain with whom she was bargaining. She had always struggled with what it was she actually believed in, and now any theological infrastructure that she had developed over her short life had been blown to bits.

Stage four: Depression.

She sobbed into her pillow. Overcome with the grief of knowing that the Portia Griffin who existed before tonight might actually be dead forever, Portia's tears came fast.

Why should I even bother trying to make a life as this thing that I don't want to be? Didn't Leucosia mention there was one way out? Maybe I should just drown myself now, before having to endure any of the pain that's waiting out there for me.

This stage was the most inviting. Portia indulged in the deep depression throughout an entire sleepless night. She alternated between crying and moaning and just lying listlessly in her bed, staring into space. She indulged in imagining how she would do it. The bathtub, perhaps? A vertical cut to an obvious artery? Or should it be horizontal? Maybe a hefty dose of pills before getting in…But wait, are Goddesses immune to prescription drugs?

Any iChat invitations that interrupted her reflections went unanswered. Finally, at about three in the morning, she glanced at her computer to see who had tried reaching her. She wasn't surprised to see that Charlotte, Jacqueline, and Max had been trying her all night. It was a slight comfort to know they cared, but she was still shattered.

Feeling so disconnected from them all, she posted a new status.

"Bad night, everyone—Felix's cousin might not make it. As for me, let's not talk about the voice thing at least until tomorrow. I'm wiped."

She hit the enter key and continued to lament the life of misery that awaited her.

By the morning, she was on her way to the final stage.

Stage five: Acceptance.

With the rays of the morning sun she felt a new hope rise up within her.

It's going to be OK. Whatever is going on with me, it's all going to be OK...

Getting up to brush her teeth, Portia looked into the bathroom mirror and caught a quick unexpected glance of demonic Portia smiling back at her, a carbon copy of her reflection at Haute.

It was then that she knew that Kübler–Ross had been a waste of her time—particularly Denial.

Placing her hands over her evil reflection, who did not even attempt to mimic the gesture, the young Goddess knew that there was no denying it.

Everything Leucosia had said was true.

Somehow Portia managed a quick shower and a fresh change of clothes. Glancing at her clock, she noted that it was only 6:30 a.m. and wondered if it was too early to iChat Max.

He responded immediately.

"Hey," he said. His left eye was completely swollen from the altercation with Felix, and his bottom lip was about twice the size that Portia remembered it to be. Still, he looked beautiful to her, and to make matters worse, he wasn't wearing a shirt. She wished he would put one on as she was finding this glimpse of his body to be extremely distracting.

"Hey," she typed back.

"Portia, no more typing. I was there last night. I heard you. Talk to me."

"Hey," she said aloud.

"That's my girl." She liked the sound of that. "Wanna explain now or do you just wanna talk?"

"I just wanna talk."

Especially since any explanation I have would send you running for the hills.

"OK. What do you wanna talk about? I can handle anything from why Salieri was undoubtedly Mozart's murderer to why Ayn Rand is not as much of an objectivist as she claims to be. What's your poison?"

Portia smiled at this bizarre menu of topics. What came out, though, was:

"Felix's cousin might die."

"I know. I read your status before. I'm so sorry. How is the family holding up?"

"I guess OK. You know, Felix and Dean have the same birthday. He goes to Canada every summer; they're like brothers. He flew out with his family last night. His grandfather isn't holding up too well. He bought Dean the bike, you know…"

"Jesus. That's a lot to deal with." He attempted an encouraging smile. "So are you gonna try to go and visit, too?"

Portia thought about the confrontation with Felix.

"I don't think so. Don't think I'd be a very welcome guest right now. Anyway, I've obviously got some of my own stuff to work out right now, too, so I think I better stay put."

"Yes, that sounds about right. And about that," Max ventured, "I know you don't want to get into any major conversations now, but I just want to say one thing about your new, and might I add, totally mind-blowing voice."

He sat up further in his bed, a fresh spark igniting his eyes.

"When I first saw you, Portia, I literally could not breathe. I swear to God. I mean, the way I attacked you in Rathi's class? I may as well have pulled your pigtails on the playground. And then—well, then, I mean, that night at your house, I've relived that night in my head so many times that I'm, like, afraid I'm gonna wear out the memory or something. And all that time you were silent. I mean voiceless, never silent. I felt you speaking to me in so many other ways, right? So imagine that—this girl who I already thought was perfect just became even more unbelievable. I mean, getting used to speaking Portia and singing Portia is going to be absolutely no problem for me. So if for some crazy reason you thought I'd back off, I'm asking you to cross that off your list of worries. I'm not going anywhere."

While Max poured out this proclamation, Portia forgot about everything else. His unconditional feelings for her were a welcome silver lining to the storm cloud that had hovered over her these past weeks.

"Max, thank you. For saying all that, I mean. I, um, wasn't really sure how this conversation would go, and you made it a helluva a lot easier than I imagined. But I think I need some sleep now. Helena said I could skip school and take a mental health day. Try to take good notes for me in Morrison's class, OK? That B- is really bugging the hell out of me."

Not to mention that it wasn't even my paper he graded…

"Mmmm, I don't know if I can promise that. I'm not the best note taker, but I'll definitely copy somebody's notes for you. Hey—I've gotta babysit the boys tonight. My aunt and uncle are having a 'date night.' It's crazy what goes into planning dinner and a movie once you have kids. Anyway, I could use some company. What do you think?"

Portia relished the thought of doing something normal like babysitting. Especially if it meant being with Max.

"Maybe…" she said, knowing that she would definitely be there.

Always keep them guessing, right?

She signed off and for the first time in a long time, enjoyed a few hours of dreamless sleep.

Morpheus had obviously decided to cut her a break.

After her long sleep, Portia and Helena spent the day together, lunching, shopping, and most importantly talking. Joshua met them for lunch and just made Portia repeat things over and over again, pointing to different objects around the room and having her name them out loud.

They lamented Dean Fein's precarious condition, and Portia even offered up a few details about the strain between her and Felix. She hadn't planned on getting into it with them but had just gotten caught up in the moment.

By the end of the day, she was spent. As much as she was looking forward to seeing Max, she could have done without the babysitting part of the evening. When her mom dropped her off, she prayed that the boys would go easy on them.

As soon as the door opened, though, all hopes of smooth sailing were dashed.

Ryan, the five-year-old, answered the door after Portia rang the bell about a hundred times.

"Ryan," Max called out from somewhere beyond, "you know you're not supposed to answer the door before I—oh, hey." Max looked completely disheveled, weaving his way toward the open door with Jonah, the six-year-old, dangling from his shoulders.

"Jonah, get off of me. I already told you we are not watching *Gladiator*. If your parents found out I showed you that movie, they'd kick me out. And I wouldn't blame them, either." Max shook the boy to the ground as he leaned over and gave Portia a peck on the cheek.

"Eeewww—don't kiss a girl, Max," Jonah warned.

"Yeah—don't kiss a girl," Ryan echoed.

"Ok, guys, I'll tell you the same thing in about twelve years, and we'll see how you feel about that then." He turned to Portia. "Help me!"

She walked into the foyer of the house, which was littered with Dunkaroos wrappers and half-empty juice boxes. The boys had chocolate frosting on their faces, and their shirts were stained purple with grape juice. It was an absolute disaster.

"What's going on here, Max?"

"They're out of control." He was legitimately clueless.

"Well, maybe if you weren't giving them Dunkaroos and grape juice at 6:30 at night, they wouldn't be bouncing off the walls. Why don't you just inject them with sugar and caffeine?"

"That sounds cool, Max," Ryan said, "Can we try that?"

"OK, boys," Portia commanded, her voice resonating as if she were speaking through a bullhorn, "let's clean this place up and take a bath. Then we are going to have a *real* dinner. I'm talking, like, beyond Dunkaroos, you know. Afterwards, when you're done with bath and dinner, I promise to tell you a story that will blow your minds."

The authoritative tone of her voice warned the boys that there was no room for their usual negotiation here. Max stared at them in astonishment as they began picking up their mess.

"Can we use the dino magic bubbles in the bath, Max?" Ryan asked.

"Sure thing, dude. Go up with Jonah and start picking out your pajamas. I'll be up in a minute to pour in, like, a whole bottle of dino bubbles."

The boys started running for the stairs.

"You're such a baby that you still ask for dino bubbles," Jonah taunted his brother.

"Shut up, Jonah!" Ryan landed a dead arm on his brother's bicep.

"Hey!" Portia interjected. "Keep it moving and hands to yourselves." The boys laid off each other and marched up the steps.

"I don't understand why they're listening to you—it's like you're the God of Babysitting…"

"Something like that," she offered, marveling at the irony of it all.

He followed Portia into the kitchen, where she began scrounging around the cabinets, taking out a box of pasta. From the fridge she extracted a stick of butter and some milk.

Why not? Those boys could use some meat on their skinny bones.

She turned to Max. It was so liberating to not have to rely on her cell phone to communicate with him. "How 'bout I make some kind of creamy pasta while you get the boys cleaned up? You know, something with a roux-based sauce."

"I love the way you say 'roux,' Portia. I actually think I detected a bit of a French thing happening with your 'r.' You must be hanging out with Jacqueline too much. Say it again," he demanded playfully.

"Je vais preparer un repas merveilleux—allez!" She executed a perfect French accent, which surprised her as much as it did Max. It was as if she had been speaking French all her life. Portia made a mental note to ask Leucosia if multilingualism was part of the gig.

"Wow," Max said. "Where did that come from?"

"I have no idea," she admitted. "Can you point me in the direction of some flour?"

Max quickly helped her pull together some ingredients and then ran upstairs to tend to the boys. A few minutes later, Portia could hear bits of their bath time conversation from downstairs. It was endearing the way Max was using bribery to get them into the bath.

"Look, little dudes, if you get into the tub now, I promise I'll talk to your parents about getting you Xbox Live."

"No, you won't," Portia couldn't tell if it was Ryan or Jonah. "You just wanna get back to that girl downstairs. The one with the voice."

"What do you mean, 'the one with the voice'?"

Portia strained her ears.

"Didn't you hear her, Max? You gotta do whatever she says. Even if you wanna say no, you still have to say yes."

"Yeah, it was like, creepy."

Max must have dismissed the observations of his cousins, as Portia heard the bath water start running again. She was not as dismissive, though. Could it be that by merely talking she could procure her vocal magic?

About a half hour later, Max reemerged with two squeaky-clean boys in matching Buzz Lightyear pajamas.

"Wow, don't you boys look handsome. Come sit at the table and have some pasta." The boys looked at each other and shrugged their shoulders in defeat. They took their places at the table, which Portia had set hurriedly while they had been having their bath.

"Jesus, you really are like Mary Poppins." Max said.

"Hey, you're not supposed to say Jesus like that Max," Jonah warned his older cousin.

"You're right," Max conceded. "Sorry about that. I think I went crazy for a minute by how good it smells in here." With hungry eyes he ogled the pasta that Portia was spooning into a bowl. It was drenched in a smooth white sauce, emitting a mild garlicky aroma. In the fridge she had found some kielbasa, which she had sliced and seared. The boys' mouths were watering.

"OK, here's the deal," she made an effort this time not to sound too bossy. "I found some carrots in the fridge, and I roasted them with some maple syrup, which means that they are like totally kid-friendly. You each have to at least try one before you start filling your bellies with creamy noodles. Deal?"

Once again the boys looked defeated.

"Deal," they responded in unison.

Portia took the carrots out of the oven and placed a few on each of the boys' plates.

"Hey, don't I get any?" Max sounded childish himself.

"Look, I'm babysitting here, Max," Portia said playfully. "You gotta help yourself." She was doling out big portions of pasta to the two boys, who were both on their third carrot.

"This is really good...um, wait, what's your name again?" Ryan asked.

"It's Portia," Max answered. He spoke her name like it was the two most magical syllables he had ever uttered.

The boys stuffed themselves silly while Portia and Max made googly eyes at each other. Max was actually just about to go for a second helping when Portia suddenly detected a yawn escaping Ryan's mouth. Jonah caught the bug and yawned, too, not nearly as subtly as his brother.

"Max," she suggested, "How would you feel about me taking the boys up and putting them to bed while you finish and clean up in here?"

Max couldn't believe his luck. It was only 8:00. The little monsters usually made him wait until at least 9:30 before even considering the commencement of bedtime routine.

"That sounds like an awesome idea. What do you boys think?" Max looked at the sleepy overstuffed faces of his cousins. They looked so much alike that sometimes it was hard for him to remember that they weren't twins.

"But Portia promised us a story," Jonah argued.

"And I will deliver on that promise. I promise. But only after you guys brush your teeth and get into bed. And don't try to trick me. I know someone who knows how to test toothbrushes to see when they were last used."

The boys looked at each other suspiciously and bolted for the stairs.

Portia turned to say something to Max when all of a sudden she felt his mouth on hers. His lips tasted spicy and his hands cupped her cheeks as he moved in closer to her. She forfeited herself to the kiss, enjoying the way he was stroking the sides of her neck, tracing her collarbone with his fingers.

Kissing and nibbling Portia's bottom lip, he savored every millimeter of her full mouth. Much to her horror, a soft moan escaped her throat.

He stopped and smiled, "God, I'm happy you found your voice."

Portia reached out to touch his dimples. "Are those things real?—"

"Portia, we're ready!!" The boys were screaming from upstairs.

"Duty calls." She must have said it loudly because as she bolted for the stairs, she could hear one of the boys:

"She said doody…"

As Portia walked up the stairs, something Leucosia had said to her behind the café suddenly came back to her.

"*But now, here you are, a young woman with a voice whose powers are…are…immeasurable.*"

Come on, voice, don't fail me now, she thought as she started forming a plan. *I need these kids to go to sleep…*

When Portia found the boys, they were snuggled under the covers of what was obviously their parents' bed.

"Whoa, fellas, I'm sure in this giant house you guys must

have your own awesome bedroom."

"We do," Ryan said, "But Mommy and Daddy always let us fall asleep in their bed when they go out."

She was afraid they were taking her for a ride but found the boys so endearing that she didn't have the heart to relocate them.

"Did you guys brush your teeth?"

They blew their minty breath in her direction.

"Great, now I can call my friend back and tell him I won't be needing his services after all."

They smiled as she settled herself at the foot of the bed.

"So what kinds of stories do you guys like? Cops and robbers? Cowboys and Indians?"

"We like scary stories."

"Yeah, like with blood and guts."

For a moment she considered regaling them with the story of Parthenope and Ligeia's murderous rampages but then scanned her brain for something a little more appropriate. Suddenly remembering a favorite Ogden Nash poem that her parents used to read to her, she decided that "The Adventures of Isabel" would be a safe bet.

"I've got one, guys. It's about a little girl named Isabel."

"No way, we don't want to hear about a dumb girl," they protested.

"Trust me," said Portia. "This is a really good one. It was written by this guy who had a daughter named Isabel, and I used to imagine that all of these things really happened to her. Just give it a chance."

Portia hoped that her instincts were right. She dimmed the lights and cleared her throat, instructing the boys to listen closely.

Here goes nuthin', she thought.

> *"Ok, so Isabel met an enormous bear,*
> *Isabel, Isabel, didn't care,*
> *The bear was hungry, the bear was ravenous,*
> *The bear's big mouth was cruel and cavernous.*
> *The bear said, Isabel, glad to meet you,*
> *How do, Isabel, now I'll eat you!"*

"This is dumb," Ryan interrupted.

"Oh, yeah? Just wait," Portia responded. She poured all of her energy into the story and suddenly a giant holograph of a bear was sitting on the white chaise lounge in the corner of the room. Even Portia was delighted with the cinematic effect she had procured.

A small girl with curled black pigtails and gigantic brown eyes appeared as well.

"Whoa," Ryan said as he moved closer to Jonah.

"Awesome," Jonah said. He put his arm around his brother protectively.

Suddenly the girl got up. Portia continued.

> *"Isabel, Isabel, didn't worry.*
> *Isabel didn't scream or scurry.*
> *She washed her hands, and she straightened her hair up,*
> *Then Isabel quietly ate the bear up."*

The boys could hear water running as Isabel washed up at an imaginary sink before her. Suddenly the bear was encapsulated in a giant bubble, which floated into Isabel's mouth, eliciting a huge burp as the bear disappeared into her belly. The boys started laughing hysterically.

"Should I go on?" Portia asked, "or do we still think Isabel is stupid?"

"Go on, go on," they begged in unison.

> *"Once in a night as black as pitch,"*

The room suddenly turned pitch-black except for one beam of light illuminating the new character that had entered stage left.

> *"Isabel met a wicked old witch.*
> *The witch's face was cross and wrinkled,*
> *The witch's gums with teeth were sprinkled.*
> *Ho, ho, Isabel! the old witch crowed,*
> *I'll turn you into an ugly toad!"*

The evil witch looked just as Portia had imagined her all the many times that Helena and Joshua had told her this story.

Holographic Isabel marched straight over to the witch, not a trace of fear on her angelic face.

> *"Isabel, Isabel, didn't worry,*
> *Isabel didn't scream or scurry,*
> *She showed no rage and she showed no rancor,*
> *But she turned the witch into milk and drank her."*

The little girl plunked a glass down on the end table next to the chaise. Then she produced a linen napkin from the pocket of her dress and dabbed at the corners of her mouth.

"I liked it better when she burped," said Ryan.

Jonah elbowed him and told him to shut up.

Suddenly the boys felt the room shake as a mammoth giant entered the tale.

Portia continued:

> *"Isabel met a hideous giant,*
> *Isabel continued self-reliant.*
> *The giant was hairy, the giant was horrid,*
> *He had one eye in the middle of his forehead."*

Portia stopped momentarily, realizing for the first time that this character must be based on the Cyclops of *The Odyssey*—what was the name of the one who Odysseus blinded? Polyphemus, was it? She wondered if he was actually the very same Cyclops who had killed Leucosia's mother. As her thoughts trailed off, the animated images in the corner started fading.

"Hey, turn it back on," Jonah demanded.

"Oh, yeah. Sorry. Where was I? Oh, OK."

As she came back to the poem, the giant began to circle Isabel.

> *"Good morning, Isabel, the giant said,*
> *I'll grind your bones to make my bread."*

Ryan let out an almost undetectable shudder at the mention of the bone grinding.

"Well, you wanted blood and gore," she told the brothers.

"We do, we do. Go on. What happens with the—well you

know, him?" Jonah motioned with his thumb over to the giant, who was hovering over the tiny figure of Isabel.

> *"Isabel, Isabel, didn't worry,*
> *Isabel didn't scream or scurry.*
> *She nibbled the zwieback that she always fed off,*
> *And when it was gone, she cut the giant's head off."*

Luckily imaginary holographic creatures don't exactly bleed. When Isabel triumphantly held up the head of the giant, his severed neck was as sealed up as a knotted balloon. The rest of his body had collapsed with a thud, which Portia hoped Max didn't hear downstairs. She had a feeling, though, that what happened between her and the boys stayed between her and the boys.

Portia decided to skip the last verse—it was about Isabel going to a scary doctor, and she had never particularly liked that part, considering her own history. And so Isabel swiped her hands together, a sure indication that her work here was done. She waved good-bye to the boys and spread out on the chaise lounge, cuddling into herself and closing her eyes. Her image vanished, and suddenly the boys were back in the real world.

"Do another one, Portia," Jonah begged.

"Yeah, one more!" Ryan echoed the plea.

"Not tonight, boys. It's late. You gotta get some sleep so you can grow and be strong like Isabel."

At the boys' request, Portia left the bathroom light on with the door open and began to walk out of the room.

"Portia," Jonah called after her, "that was the best magic we ever saw. What's your secret?"

She looked into the boys' expectant faces.

"I'm afraid I'll never be able to reveal my secret, guys."

The truth of this statement plagued her as she headed back down the stairs.

Chapter 19

When she got downstairs, Portia found Max settled on the sofa, strumming his guitar and singing the first verse of Glen Hansard's "Falling Slowly." She eavesdropped quietly for a moment, admiring the way he handled the instrument.

Clearing her throat, she sat down next to him on the couch. He stopped singing, but his hands continued to strum the six-string absentmindedly.

"You know, when I saw the movie *Once* for the first time," Portia began, "I was completely obsessed. I must have watched it like a thousand times. And that scene in the end when he sends her the piano? Massive. I felt like nobody else had seen the movie, though, and then Kris Allen performed that song on *Idol*. I have to admit that that night I actually texted in my vote." She couldn't believe she was admitting to actually casting a vote for *American Idol*.

Next thing I know, I'll be telling him that I'm a Siren...

Surprisingly Max came back at her with, "Yeah, Allen's performance was good, but that DeWyze–Bowersox duet was mind-blowing, wouldn't you agree?"

"No way! You're an *Idol* fan?"

Max tried placing the blame on the boys. "They'll watch any kind of reality TV. Their recent favorites are *Pawn Stars* and *Deadliest Catch*."

"That's so cute. They really are such great kids, Max." She fell silent for a moment. "I always wanted siblings." It sounded more pitiable than she had intended.

Max shifted over on the sofa, and she maneuvered herself closer, nestling into him. "I always wanted siblings, too," he offered.

"Well, at least you have the boys. And I always get to hear about the drama with Felix's sis—" she stopped herself immediately.

Max stopped strumming. "Portia, he's part of your life. I don't expect you to just drop him because of me…"

She traced the outline of his blackened eye with her fingertip.

"I can't believe he did this to you."

He took her finger and kissed it gently, making it almost impossible for her to stay on topic.

"…It really doesn't hurt as much as you'd expect. Besides, Felix and I needed to get that fight out of our systems. You know, marking our territory and all that."

"Men are so primal." She elbowed him playfully, and he feigned great pain at the gesture. "Oh my God, sorry—"

Max smiled. "You gotta lighten up, Portia. I mean, the guy's big, but I had a few moves socked away, you know."

"Oh, so now you're Lenox Lewis?"

He put down the guitar. "You're such a girl. Lenox Lewis hasn't been in the ring in like a thousand years."

"Yeah, well, he's British though, right?"

"Yes, he is. But he's also six four and black, so I'm not banking on the British thing as a common thread. Anyway, I've got my own unique fighting style." He flexed his arms exaggeratedly. "Wanna see some of my moves?"

He threw a few mock punches her way but then brought the topic back to Felix.

"Anyway, have you spoken to him at all? How's he doing?"

Portia had iChatted with Felix just before she left the house. Their conversation was incredibly strained, but at least she was able to get an update on Dean's condition. It was not looking good. The list of his injuries was endless, as was the sixteen hours of surgery to try to correct them. Now all they could do was wait.

"My grandfather's a mess," Felix had said. "Everyone is. It's crazy to see my uncle crying, you know?"

In a feeble attempt to smooth things out, Portia had offered to be on the next flight out.

"No. Don't do that. I need some time to figure stuff out, Portia," he had told her. "Besides, you should be working on honing your new voice."

At least this time when he referred to her voice, it was without palpable rage. But she had wanted to talk it out with him—the last time they had avoided talking something through, it had festered away, ending disastrously.

"About that," she signed into the webcam, "what you said before you left. Felix, the voice came about a month ago, and your suspicions about Charlotte were right. She was the only person who knew. I can't explain to you why—I mean, why Charlotte. Please don't ask me to. But I was planning on telling you—I was just trying to figure out how to, you know?"

"Well, you certainly picked an interesting approach." His tone made it clear that they were still eons away from any kind of truce. "Anyway, Portia, I can't be about you right now. I've gotta deal with my family."

I thought I was family, she had wanted to say. But the conversation had just trailed off, a giant abyss of unsaid words and silent apologies hovering between them.

She looked at Max, who was patiently awaiting her response.

"As best as can be expected, I guess." A comfortable silence hung in the air as Portia settled her head more comfortably on Max's shoulder.

"Max," she broke the silence, "aren't you at all curious about my voice?"

"Of course I am." Max said. "But I didn't want to push you to talk about it until you were ready."

"I appreciate that. And I guess I really don't have much of an explanation for you anyway." She avoided his eyes. "A few weeks ago, I just started feeling a change come on—like a stretching sensation at the base of my throat. Then the other day I just tried it. I was as shocked as anybody else to hear my voice—more, even. Helena—I mean, my mom. I guess now that she can hear me, I better not call her by her first name anymore. I used to refer to her that way in my head—it made me feel more grown-up since I was so, like, infantilized by my handicap. Anyway, my mom wants to take me to all kinds of doctors now, but I've been refusing. I figure, why look a gift horse in the mouth?"

That and the fact that the last thing I need is for a doctor to see that I have some kind of extra organ in my throat, causing my anatomy to be alarmingly similar to that of a bird…

"Anyway, if I have to be completely honest with you," she let out a slight cough when she said the word honest, "the thing I'm most concerned about is how this is going to affect my friendship with Felix."

It was a relief to find not the slightest hint of anger in his face. She needed to talk to someone about this. To him.

"Go on," he said.

"I don't know—I feel like he's so far away from me. I don't just mean the Canada thing. I mean everything. I've had Felix for as long as I can remember, you know? And since you came around, I feel like our whole history has been erased. And now I'm afraid this voice thing is going to be the final nail in the coffin."

Max allowed a pensive pause before speaking. "Portia, don't take this the wrong way, but why do things have to be so different for you guys if Felix can't even hear you one way or the other?"

"It's the abandonment, Max. I've abandoned him. Felix and I have always kind of been like twins in a way; you know, inventing our own language. 'Smanglish,' we would call it— signing and mouthing English. We even had—have—our own signs for some things. But now I can talk just like everyone else… and he's still using Smanglish. So I understand if he feels like I've abandoned him…"

"You haven't abandoned anyone, Portia. I know it's easier said than done, but if he's a true friend, he'll get over it. He should be happy for you, shouldn't he?"

"I don't know. It's complicated." The mood was growing heavy—definitely not the direction Portia had intended the evening to take. "Let's change the subject. How was Morrison's class today? Did I miss anything special?"

"Nope, not too much. He actually spent most of time talking about the powers that women have over men."

Portia's ears perked up. She wondered if Athena had pulled another body-snatching invasion of her *Odyssey* teacher. "What do you mean?"

"Well, there are so many women in *The Odyssey*, right? Calypso, Circe, the Sirens. They all have crazy powers over Odysseus and his mates. Seems Homer was something of a misogynist. For him there was no end to the evil ways of women. He wasn't a chauvinist, though. I mean, he understood that women can have crazy powers over men."

Yes, that had to be Athena. Had she been trying to warn Max to be careful around her?

"Well, what do you think about that?" Portia ventured.

"What? Do women have power over men? Well, without a doubt you have some crazy powers over me, Portia."

"What do you mean?" she ventured. Maybe if she could understand how she was affecting him, she could try to keep it in check.

"Well, for example," Max leaned over and inhaled the scent of her hair. "When I smell your hair, I feel like there's nothing I could refuse you."

Well, I don't need to keep that in check, she thought as she tousled her hair playfully.

"And when I see those eyes," Max planted a gentle kiss on each of her eyelids, "I would literally give you the shirt off my back."

"That sounds like a fair bargain…" She fingered his shirt collar, forgetting all about the power-checking strategy.

"And those lips," he ran his thumb over her lips. "I would enter the eye of the storm for those lips."

"Luckily you won't have to do that," she said aloud, hoping that indeed he wouldn't have to.

"But I would…" Max leaned over and kissed her.

She could not believe how good his kiss felt. It sparked a relay race of thoughts in her head.

…I'm so happy I wore a tank top…Should I be embarrassed

by the goose bumps, though?…God, I hope I'm measuring up to those NYC girls…

Finally she just decided to try to clear her mind and focus entirely on the kissing. No worries, no expectations. To her great relief, she found that she was actually able to relax after a bit. She surrendered herself entirely to the moment.

"Claw him!"

The thought popped into her head out of nowhere and was accompanied by a similar rage to the one she had felt with her father the other morning.

"Come on, you have nails, leave your mark on his back, on his neck, anywhere."

Her hands clenched—she abruptly pulled herself away.

"What's wrong?" Max asked her.

"Nothing, nothing," she plunged the rage deep down enough so that it wouldn't surface, leaning back over and kissing him again.

"You think the kiss tastes good? Wait until you taste the pain."

She bolted up from the couch.

"Ummm, sorry, Max, I have to use the bathroom." She ran out of the room before he could say anything.

"…Last door on the left," he called after her.

Portia had already found the powder room and slammed the door behind her. She slumped to the floor, trying to catch her breath.

"I am losing my goddamned mind," she said out loud.

Allowing herself a few minutes to regroup, she heard Max's voice outside the door.

"You OK in there?"

"Yeah, I just need a minute." She stood up and splashed her face off with some cool water. She looked into the mirror over the sink and instructed herself:

"Get a hold of yourself, Portia. Just clear your thoughts and get a hold of yourself."

But as she said the words aloud, her reflection did not follow suit. The fear started rising up in her throat.

"Get out of here!" she commanded the mirrored image of herself, but the reflection remained stationary.

Portia's breath was coming fast, and she feared she would end up passing out again.

"Get the hell out of here!" she said again.

The reflection smiled back at her, a giant evil grin that surrounded the words it spoke:

"He's totally helpless out there…"

She gripped the sides of the sink and shook her head, willing the reflection away.

Evil Portia started to laugh.

"You're kidding yourself if you think you've known pleasure. The truest pleasure is in the destruction."

Her reflection held up its hands. They were dripping blood.

She was going down. Unless she turned away right now, she was definitely going down. Her feet unsteady beneath her, she shakily reached for the door.

"Portia?" Max was knocking.

She flung the door open, a look of sheer terror in her eyes.

"Portia, what happened? What's the matter?" He reached out a hand to touch her.

"Don't!" she screamed and grabbed his hand with hers, digging her nails into his skin, drawing blood. He looked down at his hand, open-mouthed, and then up at her in shock.

"Oh God, I'm sorry. I have to go. I have to get out of here."

She pushed past him, bolting for the door.

"Portia, wait a minute—"

But it was too late. She was already down the front path, running at lightning speed, the outdoor lights illuminating her fading form.

Max stood staring as he watched her fade away.

"Max, are Mommy and Daddy home yet?" Jonah was standing at the top of the stairs. "Whoa, what happened to your hand?"

Max looked back down at his left hand. Five arcs marred his skin, tiny crimson rainbows streaming thick droplets of blood.

Portia was running hard, her lungs burning, her eyes stinging from the salt of her sweat. She had no idea where she was headed, only that she had to keep running.

She could feel the blood from Max's hand caking up under her fingernails.

He's never going to want to see me again.

Unable to catch her breath, she was forced to slow her pace.

The look on his face—how was she ever going to explain what she had done? She couldn't even explain it to herself.

On the periphery, a pair of headlights was flashing her and a familiar voice called out her name.

Portia stopped in her tracks and looked past the headlights into the driver's seat. She was not surprised to see Leucosia.

When she got into the car, Leucosia procured a Kleenex, which Portia accepted as floods of tears escaped her eyes. The darkness in the car veiled the metallic stains on the tissues.

"Tell me everything," the elder Goddess seemed never to lose her composure.

"How did you know where to find me?" Portia asked.

"I've got a few tricks up my sleeve, Portia, ancient as I may be."

Portia didn't have the energy to press the issue. She just couldn't handle one more paranormal revelation.

She began to recount every detail of the night with Max. Leucosia was not familiar with Ogden Nash's *Adventures of Isabel*, but was happy to hear that Portia had experimented with her vocal powers and had yielded such fantastic results.

"The boys must have loved that," she assured her young charge. "That's pretty advanced for a newbie…very promising…"

Portia had forgotten about the boys. What if they had heard her hysterical fit? What if they had actually seen her claw Max's hand?

The rest of the evening's details gushed out of her in a torrential downpour.

When Leucosia heard about the reappearance of the distorted reflection in the bathroom mirror, her composure visibly faltered.

"Portia, I hate to be a bad influence, but do you think Charlotte Trotter would cover you for a sleepover tonight? There are people, well, actually immortals, who might be able to help us. We need some time to get this sorted out."

Portia did not relish the thought of spending the rest of the night surrounded by a group of ancient Gods, but the look on Leucosia's face told her that she didn't have much of a choice.

She dialed Charlotte's cell.

"Hey, Portia, how's it going with Max—"

"Charlotte, I need to ask you a huge favor, and I'm hoping we can avoid the millions of questions that you're for sure gonna have."

"OK," Charlotte said cautiously.

"I need to tell my parents that I'm sleeping over at your house tonight. I'll tell them you called me all worked up about the chem test, and that I told you I would come help you at your house because you didn't want your mom to be alone."

Charlotte hesitated for a quick moment. "Um, OK—as long as you're safe, Portia, it's done. But you'd tell me if you were in trouble, right?"

Portia thought for a second and realized that if she were to tell anyone that she was in trouble, it would actually be Charlotte. But with everything on Charlotte's plate, she thought it best to spare her the more implausible details of her life.

"I'm OK, Charlotte—I mean, I'm safe. I promise. I just have to work a few things out." She hated sounding so cryptic.

"OK, Portia. I'll do it. But, please, be careful, whatever it is you're doing."

Portia hung up with Charlotte and started nervously dialing Helena.

Leucosia offered her a nod of encouragement as Portia braced herself for the lie she was about to tell.

"Hi, sweetie. How's it going over at Max's?"

"Hi, Mom," she drew in a sharp breath at the mention of

Max's name. "Actually, I'm on my way to Charlotte's now with Mrs. Trotter. Charlotte was stressing about the chemistry test tomorrow and wanted to know if I could come study with her. I have a feeling it's going to be a late night, so I'm thinking maybe I should just sleep over."

"OK, honey. Do you want me to drop off a clean uniform for tomorrow?"

"No, that's OK, Mom. I'll just borrow one from Charlotte." The lies produced a sour taste in her mouth.

"All right then, but try to get some sleep. It's never good to take a test after pulling an all-nighter."

"I know, Mom. Don't worry. I love you."

"Love you too, sweetie. Oh, and let me speak to Janie for a sec."

Oh God—now she was screwed. She shouldn't have lied.

Putting her hand over the mouthpiece, she whispered to Leucosia. "I'm dead. She wants to talk to Mrs. Trotter."

Leucosia smiled, grabbing the phone gingerly.

"Hi, Helena. How are you?" Her voice was an exact clone of Janie Trotter's—even down to the slight quiver it always held. "Oh, no problem—I was out anyway." Pause. "I won't, don't worry. Yes, yes, thank you. I think we're good for now, though." Pause. "Ok, Helena, I'll talk to you soon. Bye."

Portia was dumbfounded.

"Wow, I guess Homer really didn't have you guys figured out, did he?"

"My dear, you ain't seen nuthin' yet…"

A few minutes later they pulled up to a lovely white stucco house with black shutters and trailing green ivy scaling the walls. It was exactly the kind of house Portia would have expected Leucosia to live in.

When they walked in, Leucosia was immediately greeted by a fat charcoal gray snowball.

"So you actually do have a cat. I was wondering if that was

just an excuse you gave me in your office that day."

"Yes, I do have a cat, but that *was* just an excuse, Portia. This is Hermes, named for the God, not the store. He would never scratch me. He's about love, not war. I actually felt so bad when I blamed my bleeding on him."

The cat was sidling up to Leucosia's leg, purring loudly.

"He's cute," Portia offered. "Does he let strangers pet him?"

"Are you kidding? Hermes will do anything for a good rub."

Portia leaned over and started scratching the flat-faced Persian cat under his chin. Hermes stretched out his neck encouragingly. Against her better judgment Portia asked, "So what was the bleeding actually from?"

Leucosia was nervous about overwhelming her young charge with too much information at once, but it was inevitable that Portia would see her wings, and she figured now was as good a time as any.

She closed her eyes and within a millisecond, two giant wings emerged from her back, piercing matching holes in the back of her blouse.

"Holy shit!" said Portia.

Leucosia was not accustomed to hearing people swear, and Portia was not usually the swearing type, but in this instance they both felt the expletive was warranted.

"Portia, I realize this must look totally out of the ordinary to you—"

"Out of the ordinary? It's completely messed up."

"Yes, well, feeling that way is understandable. For me, the emergence of my wings is as mundane as brushing my teeth. The bleeding you saw in my office is called breakthrough bleeding. It's common among all winged Gods who have been sustaining their wings for so many years. I had taken a long trip the night before I saw you in my office—Zeus needed me to check on a disturbance coming from my old neighbor, Scylla—"

"The one with the six heads?"

"The very one…wow, you really have been paying attention in Mr. Morrison's class. Such a shame about Scylla, you know. She used to be a beautiful Goddess, only one head, and then

Circe interfered and well, it's not pretty. Did you know that after Odysseus sailed by my sisters, Scylla actually killed six of his oarsmen? Just plucked one per head, right out of their ship and killed them. Anyway, the reason I had to go is that Charybdis, Scylla's neighbor, kept complaining about too much noise coming from Scylla's rock—lots of screaming, she said—and I guess because it was my old stomping ground, Zeus wanted me to check it out, which was no easy task. Scylla was less than welcoming to me, I'm not sure why. I mean, what did I ever do to her? But forasmuch as she would let me see, everything seemed fine to me—a bit overgrown and unkempt, maybe, but nothing suspicious that I could see…"

Portia nodded her head as if she understood, but her head was spinning at the crazy story.

Leucosia caught herself. "Yes, but I'm off on a tangent, I suppose. Sorry about that—I'm really trying not to overwhelm you. Anyway, the pains you were having in between your shoulders were preparatory pains. As your syrinx neared its full development, the muscles in your back began to ready themselves for the burden they sensed coming. Wing emergence, though, does not have to be at the top of our worry list."

With these words Leucosia's wings disappeared as quickly as they had come out. She reached her hands to her back and felt the holes that were left in her blouse.

Portia kept nodding methodically, a resigned look in her eyes. "So I'm, um, going to grow wings one day?"

"Well, not so much grow as sprout. And I can't say that it's a painless acquisition. But totally worth it."

The nodding continued as Portia retreated back to that place of 'this cannot be happening.' The fact that she might one day sprout a pair of wings from her back was…well, laughable.

But when Leucosia turned around to put water in Hermes's bowl, the holes in her blouse brought Portia back to the reality at hand.

"What is at the top of our worry list?" she demanded.

"Well, for starters, I think we need to prevail upon some of the other Gods to help us figure out what exactly my sisters are up to."

"OK," Portia conceded. "Why don't you go change into something, um, that doesn't have, like, two gaping holes in it, and then you can explain to me how exactly we're gonna do that. Where's your closet—I could use a pair of sweats, myself…"

Portia started heading toward the nearest bedroom, trailed by a disinterested Leucosia. There was a huge walk-in closet off the entry to the room. Its door was ajar, so Portia peered in and felt like she had just stepped into the mother of all costume studios. Even she could not pass up the opportunity to scan its contents.

"Oh my God, Leucosia! This is insane! Can I look?" she asked, already fingering the vast wardrobe.

Leucosia shrugged her consent.

Portia tried taking it all in. The simple white sheath dresses, complementing ivy wreaths clipped onto their hangers. The ornate scalloped lace collars of the elaborate Elizabethan dresses. The silks and brocades of the empire Victorian garb, whose coordinating hats were striking not only because of their largesse but also because of their lifelike flowers and variegated silken ribbons. There were Chanel suits and Pucci prints. Bell-bottoms and leggings. Ruched velvet tunics and worn cotton T-shirts.

And the shoes! The sandals, the silken slippers, the lace-up booties, the kitten heels, the platforms, the thigh-high boots.

It was all there. Every trend that had ever existed in fashion was right there on display in Ms. Leucosia's cavernous closet.

"This used to be a bedroom," Leucosia admitted, a hint of mischief in her face, "and then I realized I was going to need a bigger closet space, so I had it converted." The Goddess suddenly sounded like a teenager as she broke out into a huge smile and said, "Isn't it wonderful?! My favorites are the Victorian hats! Wait, no, I take that back—the flapper dresses, or actually the Elizabethan collars. Will insisted I wear this one to the opening of Hamlet."

She picked up a gold brocade corseted dress with a protruding stiff lace collar and an enormous crinolined skirt.

The hanger bowed dangerously under the weight of the dress.

"Will, as in Shakespeare?"

Leucosia nodded as if attending an opening of Hamlet with William Shakespeare was as mundane as catching a Saturday night movie. Placing the hanger back on the rod, she retrieved a striking black columnar cocktail dress—sleeveless, dropped waist, the high neckline edged by tiny black and white flowers.

"And Coco designed this for me herself," Leucosia beamed.

"Coco Chanel?"

"The one and only. Very elegant—heavy smoker, though, I was always trying to convince her to quit."

Taking in the contents of Leucosia's closet, Portia felt overwhelmed at the thought that she, too, would accumulate an extensive wardrobe like this one, albeit with far fewer bustiers. How many people would she meet over the course of her interminable life? Abruptly she closed the closet door, trying to shut out any thoughts that revolved around her immortality.

"Oh, wait—you didn't grab a change of clothes." She opened the door again. "Your, um, wings really destroyed that shirt you have on."

"Portia," Leucosia said dismissively, "I've already ruined one blouse tonight. I don't see why I should ruin another."

"What do you mean? Don't you want to throw on some comfy sweats or maybe a corseted ball gown?" Something told her that her attempt at a joke was not going to lighten things up.

"Portia, in order to beseech the Gods, we actually have to go see the Gods."

Portia started shaking her head.

"No way, Leucosia. I'm not traveling anywhere on wings that are not attached to an airplane."

"Portia, I have only your best interests at heart. We must implore the Gods to help us before it is too late. I promise to return you safely home. But for now you must trust me."

"No way. I can't do it, Leucosia. There's just no way." Her voice was loud and shrill. She was terrified. There was no way around it. There was too much to learn, too many issues to contend with.

"I promise you, Portia, I'm an old pro at this."

"It's not just the flying, Leucosia. It's everything! I'm terrified about what happened with Max tonight. I'm terrified of losing Felix. I'm terrified of outliving everyone I love. I just can't process all of this. It's too much."

"Portia, I promise you that after tonight you will feel more settled. Knowing there are others out there like yourself will be a great comfort. You just have to trust me. Do you think you can do that?" Leucosia's wings suddenly emerged once again, as breathtaking as they had been just moments ago.

"Please," she extended her hand toward Portia, "I've traveled with all manner of being on my back—mortal men, wild boars...don't ask."

Portia inched her way over to Leucosia and extended a cautious hand to the tip of one of the giant wings. The feathers felt silky to her touch, and she had to admit that the flutter of the wing against her hand was exhilarating.

"What do they feel like?" she asked cautiously.

"You'll know in time, Portia."

"Yeah, I figured you'd say that." She stroked the full length of one wing, then the other. "So how does it work? Do you have to take a running start? Or is it more like a helicopter that just shoots straight up? God, I can't even believe I'm considering this."

"No running starts, Portia. And not quite a helicopter, either. Look, I have waited thousands of years for your arrival. Do you really think that I would do anything now to put you in harm's way?"

Portia measured the sincerity in Lecousia's eyes. She did have a point.

Ok, let's do it." The words surprised even herself as she walked around to Leucosia's back and gripped her shoulders before she could change her mind.

"I don't usually fly through walls, Portia. It would be better if we started from outside."

Portia ignored the remark, which just emphasized how much she still had to learn. The two Goddesses walked out through a wide set of double doors, which opened onto a generous stone veranda. The night sky was clear, a black velvet case strewn with diamonds.

"Ready?" Leucosia asked her terrified charge.

"As ready as I'll ever be," she perched herself onto Leucosia's back, wrapping her arms around the slender neck of the woman who, until recently, was just an incidental fixture in the backdrop of her life.

Closing her eyes, she suddenly felt herself soaring up into the air, her stomach lurching as they flew higher and higher. She dared not ask her mentor where exactly they were headed.

The truth was she didn't really want to know.

Chapter 20

Portia counted fifty-two peaks jutting out of the mountain range toward which they were headed.

No, not headed—flying!

Some peaks were covered with frost, some densely blanketed with lush forests of trees. Some of the peaks were sprinkled with cattle grazing off their green carpets of grass. But as they neared the peak where it appeared Leucosia was planning to make her landing, Portia couldn't make it out at all for the thick fog that thwarted any bird's-eye view.

And I certainly can't get any more bird's-eye than this…

She learned later that the mountain peak was known as Mytikas. Apparently Poseidon, a.k.a. the Great Earth Shaker, blew an eternal fog onto Mytikas so that mortals would think that this Grecian mountaintop was uninhabitable. But when they landed softly on the velvety grass of Mytikas, Portia realized that in terms of habitability, no other place on earth could compare.

Her senses were immediately flooded by the wonders of the unfamiliar surroundings. The aroma, a combination of wildflowers and herbs, was intoxicating. No wonder this was a favorite dwelling of the Gods.

Oh no, did I just form a thought with the word 'dwelling' in it?

Her ears filled up with the soothing gush of distant waterfalls and cicadas singing out to one another. And the views! Though the mountaintop was sheathed in fog, the views were crystal clear, stretching to the four corners of the earth.

As she marveled at the vista, she was also struck by a distinct sense of timelessness. She felt caught somewhere between dawn and dusk, sun and moon, suddenly completely unsure of how long her journey on Leucosia's back had taken. Though this ambiguity was disorienting, Portia found it refreshing to have a brief respite from the tethers of time.

While she was gaining her bearings, a statuesque woman approached to welcome them, clad in a column of ice blue silk, which reflected the colorlessness of her eyes. Leucosia introduced the Goddess as Athena, embracing her heartily and chatting her up like a silly schoolgirl.

Leucosia was right—her eyes are actually gray, Portia thought as she stood in her faded jeans and Abercrombie sweatshirt, a complete fish out of water.

I should have grabbed something from Leucosia's closet, she admonished herself, remembering the vast array of dated garb that had been ripe for the picking.

About five minutes into her conversation with Athena, Leucosia suddenly remembered the real purpose for their visit and began to make formal introductions.

"Zeus, allow me to introduce my young charge, Portia Griffin. Portia, this is Zeus, the father of Athena and king of all the Gods."

The sharp eyes of the impressive God scrutinized her, but there was a kindness in his gaze that stopped her knees from completely buckling beneath her.

"So you are 'the next one'?" he questioned.

Portia could have sworn she felt the earth quake when Zeus spoke to her, his voice thunderous though not quite threatening.

"Yeah, I guess. I mean, I think…yes, I am," she said meekly. An awkward silence ensued for a moment until Leucosia broke it by introducing the God who had been filling Zeus's goblet.

"Portia, this is Dionysus, the God of Wine and Pleasure."

"And Madness," added the effeminate God.

"Yes, well I try not to think about that part, Dion," Leucosia responded.

Dion?

Dionysus appeared slight next to Zeus's imposing form. Though what he did not possess in girth, he made up for in color. He wore a velvet robe in the richest shade of purple Portia had ever seen. She wondered for a moment how the color would be named in a Crayola box—*Violent Violet? Alarming Amethyst?*

Dionysus offered Portia a warm, slightly inebriated smile. His eyes were as chromatic as his robe, a rich deep blue, and his lips were stained burgundy, which Portia could only assume was because he was constantly sampling his own wares.

She liked him instantly.

Uncertain if she should bow down or extend her hand, she did something that could have been classified as a sort of a curtsy.

Did I actually just curtsy?!

She looked to Leucosia for some much-needed counsel.

"Leucosia," she whispered, "please help me out here. I have no idea what to do."

Leucosia smiled at her reassuringly. "Just do as I do, Portia. We begin with a material gift."

The elder Siren then presented both Zeus and Dionysus with a golden pendant. For Zeus there was the shape of a crown, boasting tiny rubies and sapphires. For Dionysus, a tiny goblet overflowing with diamond champagne bubbles.

"When did you get those?" Portia whispered. "You're making me look really bad! And what about for Athena?"

"Oh, Athena would never accept a gift from me. We are way past gift exchanging."

Portia looked over at the Goddess with the clear gray eyes. Indeed she did not look at all expectant of anything more than Leucosia's friendship.

"My fellow cherished immortals," Leucosia began, "please accept these gifts which have been bestowed upon you not only by myself, but also by my young charge, Portia Griffin."

Portia curtsied again at the mention of her name.

I have got to get a grip!

Zeus spoke out and this time, Portia definitely felt a rustle underfoot.

"Leucosia, we offer you many thanks for these lovely tokens of gold. You have our full attentions, for even now have we heard from Athena that your heart is heavy with worry—"

Just then two other figures emerged from the thick fog.

"What gathering is this?" asked one of the newcomers. "If of dreams you do speak, let me provide counsel, for no one knows the world of dreams as I do. Though Leonardo DiCaprio might think he does."

He directed his joke at Portia, who actually smiled at the God's reference to the movie *Inception*.

"Many young girls of Leo do dream," he explained.

Portia surmised that this must be the famous Morpheus who had been Leucosia's accomplice in invading the privacy of her dreams. The God looked much like Portia had expected, boasting a long white beard and silvery white curls. But he moved with a sprightliness that did not jibe with the color of his hair. Still, Portia was mildly intimidated by the God of Dreams, knowing that he had been privy to her most secret thoughts.

Not wanting to be upstaged by Morpheus's modern humor, Ares, the God of War, introduced himself by raising his shield and sword with great fanfare.

"But should you seek guidance in matters of battle or warfare, I am surely the God to whom you must turn, for many great battles have I known even among mortals and immortals."

Portia tried offering Ares a smile but had to admit she was more than a little put off by the way he was brandishing his weaponry. A blinding glint of light bounced off the steel of the sword, and Portia remembered Leucosia telling her that Ares's sword had been blessed with a spell from Zeus, enabling it to actually take the life of another immortal, which apparently was no easy feat. She wondered, though, what the blade could do to immortals who were already deceased. Immortals named Parthenope and Ligeia, to be specific.

Leucosia addressed the new Gods:

"Our deepest gratitude, Morpheus and Ares, for meeting with us here today."

At that, Leucosia presented Ares with a golden locket in the shape of a shield. When opened, the locket revealed a tiny sword with a ruby-encrusted handle. The God of War was delighted with the gift. For Morpheus she had an intricate pendant of a tiny child enjoying a blissful slumber on a billowy cloud of sapphires and aquamarines. The God of Dreams was equally thrilled.

Leucosia continued:

"Wise are you all in knowing that we will be calling upon you to aid us in our battle against my evil sisters, Parthenope and Ligeia. Before we make known to you our deepest woes, however, may we not sing for you a song to show our gratitude for your wise counsel?"

"Ummm, excuse me, Leucosia, could you come over here a minute?" Portia stepped out of earshot of the intimidating gathering of deities. "With all due respect, and I do mean respect—because what I am seeing here is awe-inspiring, to say the least—but, um, are you crazy? I'm not going to sing in front of all of these Gods! Why would you even offer such a thing?!"

Leucosia's expression remained steadfast. "Portia, it is customary among Gods to bestow gifts, not only of a material nature but also of a spiritual nature. Let us not deny the Gods the beauty of our voices, which have been ever blessed with immeasurable glory."

Portia noted Leucosia's regression back to her ancient vernacular. She had some trouble following her mentor's words but got the basic gist—singing for the Gods would be happening.

Dionysus approached them, offering up a glistening golden lyre, which Leucosia plucked at gently.

"A lyre?" Portia whispered. "Really?"

Leucosia flashed her a mischievous smile and then turned the lyre sideways. She started to strum it like a guitar and brought forth a timeless sound peppered with modernity.

"Dear friends, today let us not concern ourselves with the trials of Helen of Troy or the chronicles of Orpheus. Today I would like to sing a song of a more, um, current nature. You see, I would like to reassure the young Portia Griffin that the world is filled with flaws. Hardships are a tale as old as time. And yet time marches on and we overcome. There is no such thing as a perfect world—or a perfect anything—"

Zeus let out a gruff "ahem."

"Well, perhaps excepting you, Zeus. Anyway, I hope that

this song does remind Portia, and all of us here, that we mustn't take life too seriously. Somehow we will muddle through."

Portia couldn't imagine where this was headed. Leucosia tuned the lyre a bit more and then exacted a compelling rhythm.

The ancient Goddess then began a delicate melody.

> *"The greenest of emeralds*
> *Are most often flawed,*
> *And you might cry 'fake,'*
> *And you might cry 'fraud.'*
>
> *But look into that stone,*
> *It's plain to see,*
> *That flaws are a part*
> *Of our reality."*

She paused for a moment, catching the eye of all who were gathered, and then began what could only be described as, well, a glorious melodic form of rapping:

> *"Sing it—*
> *Why must a salmon*
> *Swim up the stream,*
> *Only to realize*
> *A procreational dream?*
>
> *And what about Krispy Kreme—*
> *Why can't it just be*
> *That iced, glazed, and sprinkled*
> *Has one calorie?"*

She picked up lyrical speed, shocking her fellow Gods, who looked more than a little discomfited. She was a freestyling Sarah Brightman. Seeing her mentor this way made Portia feel like everything was just a little bit less dire.

> *"The price of good shoes—*
> *Oh, such a pity!*
> *I blame it on Carrie*
> *From Sex and the City.*

> *Let's face it head on:*
> *The system is flawed.*
> *But at least there's a system,*
> *And for that we applaud."*

Leucosia gestured to Portia as though passing her a microphone. Portia could think of a few grievances she had with the world these days and found, to her great disbelief, she couldn't wait to chime in:

> *"The GW Bridge toll*
> *Is up to twelve dollars!*
> *Try posing that one*
> *To wise men and scholars!*
>
> *"And why SATs?*
> *I mean, let's be real!*
> *A standardized test score—*
> *What does it reveal?"*

They joined in on the chorus together, Leucosia manipulating the golden lyre, Portia drumming out a beat on the leg of her jeans.

Leucosia took the reins again:

> *"Rainbows can erase*
> *Most feelings of pain,*
> *But to behold a rainbow*
> *You gotta traipse through the rain!*
>
> *'Like' is now standard*
> *In every teen's diction—"*

Knowing she was guilty of this particular transgression, Portia chimed in to try to salvage her intelligence:

> *"Newspapers purport*
> *Less fact and more fiction."*

"Nice one, Portia!" Athena called out.

"I thought so, thanks."

Portia and Leucosia started giggling, heady with their clever lyrics and magical voices.

The two Sirens looked at each other, reading one another's thoughts. In unison they harmonized the last verses, the sound of their combined voices explosive and powerful. There was an indescribable high in knowing that without ever rehearsing or even discussing the song, the Sirens could intuit what the other would say:

> *"Some turn to evil*
> *To get their kicks,*
> *So we gotta keep figuring*
> *New defensive tricks."*

Leucosia offered the last verse:

> *"And that's why we're here,*
> *Because I must uphold*
> *This contract that binds me,*
> *What my mother foretold."*

And in unison they completed:

> *"To show you firsthand*
> *That the system is flawed,*
> *But we have all of you,*
> *And for that we applaud…"*

And just for good measure, from Portia:

> *"Word."*

Dionysus was the first to speak.

"Well, so long has it been since I have heard the blessed voices of the Sirens. Now do I remember that no other sound in heaven or on earth can compete with your glorious song, though it was—um—modern, to say the least. My deepest gratitude for this priceless gift, fairest Leucosia and beautiful young Portia."

Athena brought two goblets of wine over to the Goddesses.

"Oh, no thank you, I'm underage," Portia offered.

Charmed by her refusal, the pale-eyed Goddess went instead to fetch the young Siren some ambrosia.

The almighty Zeus spoke then:

"How can we thank you for these blessed gifts? For now that our hearts are lifted and filled with the glory of music, surely there is nothing we can refuse you."

While Zeus was speaking, Portia accepted the glass of ambrosia from Athena and was immediately seduced by the most delectable combination of flavors she had ever tasted. She felt a bit more at ease after the impromptu performance and drank greedily as Leucosia addressed Zeus.

"We are so pleased, Zeus, that you enjoyed our song. We hope it did please all of you. It is with a heavy heart that I must bring our conversation to the matter at hand. I fear that an evil I thought forever gone—my sisters, the very Parthenope and Ligeia—has reared its ugly head once again."

Ares interjected:

"But long have your sisters been banished to the depths of Hades. How is it that now they have reappeared?"

At this, Athena chimed in:

"I've heard it said that Ligeia and Parthenope have not been always harshly judged in the underworld. They have not even yet been banished to Tartarus—that, Portia, is the deepest underlayer of Hades. The most evil spirits are banished there, never to be seen or heard from again."

"Yeah, so then shouldn't Leucosia's sisters automatically have gone there?" Portia was having trouble following.

"Actually, Parthenope and Ligeia have dwelt these many years in a state of limbo, for some Gods do take pity on the Sirens who were cheated their very mother's love. That is why their spirits are ever mobile."

"But that's ridiculous," Leucosia spit out. "They weren't cheated out of anything. My sisters dug their own grave."

Ares turned to Dionysus, "I like that…'dug their own grave'…ever must I use these words soon."

Then Zeus weighed in on the matter:

"I fear that the laws that guide the underworld are ever mysterious, even unto the most powerful of Gods."

Portia tried to shed some light on the situation. "Well, does it help clear things up at all if I tell you that they've also been showing up in the mirror—at least I hope it's them or else I've become a complete slu—"

Leucosia cleared her throat loudly.

"Oh, sorry, I mean their appearance in the, um, looking glass, was most unwholesome. And very real."

I will never get used to speaking like this.

Portia was starting to tire. She wasn't sure what time it was—really, she had no idea at all—but suddenly all the events of the last forty-eight hours were upon her.

"Umm—excuse me, great kings—"

"—Gods," Leucosia corrected her, "not kings—only Zeus is a king."

"Oh, sorry. Great Gods, can we cut to the chase? I know this might sound ridiculous to all of you, but I have a chemistry quiz tomorrow."

They stared at her blankly.

"Um, so, I was wondering if I could try to sum up our situation," she continued cautiously. "I, um, really do have to get back and study."

"Do go on," Zeus beckoned, inciting a fresh case of nerves in Portia's stomach.

"Well, it seems like we are saying that because Leucosia's crazy evil sisters were deprived of their mother's love, whoever is running things in the underworld has taken pity on them? And that we're not even exactly sure what that means or how far their powers can go?"

Zeus nodded. "Leucosia, you have not exaggerated your muse's great intelligence. For even now do I see that she is quick to grasp the perils that face her."

Portia blushed at the compliment.

Can't get any higher praise than that...

Fueled by Zeus's kind words, she continued: "But all of

you can stop them, right? I mean, all of these mood swings I'm having and the ghosts in the mirror." The urgency in her request could not be veiled by the fog of Mytikas. Her fear was palpable, even unto the Gods, who exchanged knowing looks with one another, a shared sense of pity in all of their faces.

"What? What am I missing? Oh, God—I mean Oh, Gosh—what am I missing here?"

Athena moved toward her, extending a reassuring hand to Portia's cheek. "Portia," her tone was even, her voice steady. "So much have you had to absorb these many days—more than anyone should have to process in so short a time. Let us not yet delve into the actual strategies that will finally obliterate the spirits of Parthenope and Ligeia. For there is much to consider—"

The way the assembled Gods were skirting the details of how exactly they were going to annihilate Parthenope and Ligeia caused a fresh wave of panic to course through Portia's veins like a tidal wave.

"With all due respect," she interrupted, her voice steadily rising in pitch, "This is insane! Athena, or Ms. Athena? I don't even know what to call you. But please, I want to go home. I want to give my voice back. I want to go back to being Felix's silent best friend. I want to know that one day I will age and die like everybody else. Please just take me back!" She knew she sounded hysterical but was past the point of caring.

"Look around you, Portia," Athena said gently as she waved a milky graceful hand to indicate the gathering of great beings, "the spirits of the evil Sirens are no match for the united efforts of many Gods who even now stand ready to aid you in your battle against them."

"But I don't want to be in a battle!" She turned to Leucosia. "Leucosia, tell them, please. I just want to be normal. A normal kid, worrying about chemistry tests and pimples and colleges. I mean, my God—oops, sorry, I keep doing that—am I still even going to go to college?!"

Athena stepped in further, fielding the question with a wisdom that was uniquely hers.

"It would be odd indeed if you did not feel great anger,

young Portia. For the life that you thought was yours is no longer. Now you must learn to accept your immortality and your powers—though these traits of the Gods are both a blessing and a curse. It will take much time for you to accept this new life, but one day, my sweet Portia, you will. You will not only accept who you are, but you will embrace it."

The supreme calm in the Goddess's voice slowly enveloped the young Siren. Portia started to come down from the hysteria as she allowed Athena's words entry into her weary mind. She could feel her pulse slowing, her breath growing steadier as the Goddess of counsel continued to speak.

"There will be time for you to learn. But now we must figure out ways in which you can strengthen your own powers so that you will not fall prey to any forces of evil."

Nodding her consent to Athena, Portia felt like she had been sedated. The Goddess of Wisdom's voice was like an opiate for the nerves. Portia's mind suddenly cleared, making room for whatever suggestions this bizarre gathering of entities had to offer.

"OK," she surrendered, "tell me what needs to be done."

For many hours the Gods conferred, each one offering up a unique perspective on the situation. They compiled a laundry list of vocal feats that they wanted Portia to practice with her new voice—a divine homework curriculum. Ares added some exercises in psychological warfare while Morpheus offered some tricks of the trade to help Portia come out of a dream as soon as she felt it going awry.

Overwhelmed and exhausted, Portia assured them all that she would do her best to tackle the list, but first she needed some sleep. Athena had spread a purple velvet blanket over the grass.

"Lie down, my dear. You've certainly had enough for one night."

Portia followed Athena's advice and took refuge on the blanket. Her last thought before sleeping was that the blanket must surely have been cut from the same cloth as Dionysus's robe.

I wonder where I can find a few yards of this fabric...

And within moments, she fell into a deep and dreamless sleep.

Soon after, Ares gently lifted the slumbering Portia onto the winged back of Leucosia.

"When the time comes, Leucosia, we will be ready to do battle with you," said the great God of War.

"I thank you all," responded the aged Siren, her wings beginning to flutter. "I must admit that what frightens me the most is not knowing when that time will be..."

With this final concern planted in the minds of the Gods, Leucosia flew into the timeless sky, a sleeping Portia nestled firmly between her giant wings.

Chapter 21

Max could not stop thinking about her. He had tried calling a million times after the babysitting date went sour. Over and over he played out the night in his head, wondering what he had done to elicit such a bizarre response from Portia.

He looked down at his hand. The wound had begun to scab, forming tiny keloids on his flesh. It was 3:45 in the morning, and he considered calling or texting her once more but decided the better of it. She obviously needed some time to cool down from whatever it was that had spooked her.

He turned over, hoping beyond all hope to get in an hour or two of sleep before he had to get up for school. His mind was infested with thoughts of her. Her beauty, her smell, her voice. He couldn't focus on anything else. He kept looking at his clock, knowing that every minute that passed meant one less minute of sleep.

On the other hand, every minute that passed also brought him closer to seeing her again.

Jesus Christ, man—get a hold of yourself! You'd think you never met a girl before.

But despite his self-recrimination, he knew it was hopeless. There was something about this girl. She was like a rampant, incurable virus.

Forcing himself to focus on something mundane—the dreaded chemistry periodic table—he finally drifted off to sleep. But thoughts of her muscled their way right into the unguarded landscape of his dreams. There she was at a water's edge, her silken hair glistening in the sunlight as she carelessly hummed a tune.

Max was flying above the waters in the clutches of an

unfamiliar winged creature when suddenly, without warning, he was plunged into the wavy waters below. He began swimming to the shoreline. But with every stroke, the sea widened and the current grew stronger.

He could see her so clearly, her fiery blue eyes, the tiny freckle she had right above the left corner of her mouth. Why couldn't he reach her?

The waves were furious, slapping him hard, pushing him under the foamy waters.

"Portia!" he managed to scream out.

Suddenly she looked up and spotted him. She was immediately up on her feet, walking closer to the water.

A profound relief came over him, knowing that Portia would surely save him. She raised her slender arms, perching herself to dive in, but instead she just shrugged her shoulders questioningly, her voice carrying strong.

"What would be the point, Max? I'd only kill you when you got here."

And then she began to laugh. She laughed so hard that she cried. Silver tears streamed down her flawless cheeks as she watched Max struggle to find his breath above the water.

The sound of Portia Griffin's laughter was the last thing he heard before he was completely submerged in the blackened waters of the sea.

Max was gasping for air when his eyes flew open, and he was once again above water.

What the hell was that about?

It was 5:00 a.m.—time to accept that a solid hour or two of rest was not in the cards for him that night.

Throwing on some sweats and sneakers, he decided to go for a run. The duck pond was calling to him, a favored destination for all Ridgewood runners. When he got there, Max was relieved to find that it was still pretty empty, given the early hour. About to start his third lap around, he sensed someone fast on his heels.

"Hey," Max offered a concise greeting. He was in his groove and didn't want to lose his momentum.

"Hey," the other runner responded. The blonde corkscrews of the stranger's hair, on the longer side of masculine, bounced and bobbed in the sunlight. He was not at all breathless or sweaty, despite the effort he was exerting to keep up with Max's fast pace. Everything about the guy seemed eerily perfect, save for an impressive scar on his left cheek.

Lengthening his stride, Max hoped to outrun the stranger. The last thing he felt like doing now was making conversation. As he stepped it up, though, the stranger kept up with him, effortlessly cruising into a faster gear.

"Sure beats a treadmill, huh?" His voice did not hold the faintest hint of a tremor, though he was pounding the pavement. Hard.

"Uh-huh." Max picked up his pace even more, but the hint went unnoticed.

"I think they say three times around is a mile, right?"

"Actually, four." Max delivered a curt and uninviting response as he tried kicking his pace up one more notch.

"So things with Portia didn't go too well last night, huh?"

The running came to a screeching halt.

"Who the hell are you?" Max asked, his breath sporadic, sweat dripping off his forehead.

The stranger looked up at him. His eyes held a translucence, which Max found unnerving. His chin was angular, the muscles of his jaw flexing involuntarily with the words that he spoke.

"I'm just a guy who knows a few things."

"Well, I'm just a guy out for a run. So why don't you back the hell off, man?" He started running again.

"She's going to destroy you, you know."

Max stopped again and turned around. The men stood barely an inch apart.

"What are you talking about? Why don't you mind your own bloody business?!"

The stranger smiled, Max's hostility bouncing right off of

him like a ricochet. "Listen to me, Max—"

"—How the hell do you know my name?" Max seethed.

"I told you. I know things. For example, I know that Portia gave you that wound on your hand." He pointed to the bloody rainbows. "I know that thoughts of her are consuming you in epidemic proportions. I know that soon there will be nothing you will be able to refuse her. You will never be able to rid yourself of thoughts of her."

The stranger bent over and tightened one of his shoelaces.

"I'll give you this, though," he continued, "you're no accident. The powers that be chose well. You'll show some resistance."

The runner bent over and adjusted his other shoelace, savoring the pregnant pause in the conversation.

"But don't you see, Max? That makes for an even better kill. You might think you've been sent here to play out some fairy-tale love story. You might think that your mother's disappearance was just another sad chapter in the many inexplicable sad chapters of your life. But I think not. I think your story is far more intriguing. I think that you were sent here so that her first kill would be completely irresistible."

Max was riveted by every word that came out of the ranting stranger's mouth.

"But don't you worry. Just when you can't take it anymore, can't stand not being with her for even a minute, can't stand not hearing her speak to you for even a millisecond, just then will she choose to destroy you. You will welcome death at that point, because it will be your only true escape from Portia Griffin."

All the while the stranger was speaking, he smiled offhandedly, as if he was talking to Max about the weather.

"Best of luck to you, Max Hunter."

"Who the hell are you?" Max demanded.

With a twinkle in his cellophane eyes, the man said, "I'm just a guy out for a run."

With that, he sprinted ahead of Max and vanished into the distant abyss.

Chapter 22

Hermes's whiskers felt foreign, but not unwelcome, as they brushed Portia's cheeks. She forced her eyes open, invariably welcoming a gush of memories. Memories of the night before, spent in a way that couldn't have actually been real.

Could it have?

Leucosia was standing over a steaming mug of coffee, kneading her shoulders with a gentle fist, when Portia walked in carrying the plump feline.

"I think he likes me," she announced, setting Hermes down in front of a bowl of food. "How's your back? Does it hurt?"

"Oh, don't worry about me, Portia. I've been resilient for a long time. The question is, how are you? Ready to face the day, despite our busy night?"

"Hah! 'Busy' is a nice euphemism, Leucosia. I would've gone with 'surreal' or 'insane,' but 'busy'? Come on."

"Well, at least you've got your wit this morning."

"Yeah, well I don't think my wit is going to be able to explain to Max that your deranged sisters have wormed their way into my subconscious. My wit is not going to help me accept that last night I actually encountered Gods. GODS, Leucosia! And I sang for them—we sang for them. I do have to admit we sounded pretty good, by the way.

"Maybe my wit will help me think of something clever to say to Charlotte to explain to her why I needed her to cover for me last night. And perhaps it will help me explain to my mom and dad why I failed the chem quiz that I will have to take today because even though Charlotte and I were supposed to be studying last night, I was actually too busy sipping ambrosia from a golden goblet to even glance at the periodic tables!"

The two women stared at each other, each assessing the truths that had just spilled out of Portia's mouth. What was there to say? The facts were the facts.

"About that chemistry quiz," offered Leucosia feebly, "maybe I could pull a few strings…"

But when she got to school that morning, Portia was made brutally aware of the fact that chemistry was the least of her concerns. Her whiteboard was filled to overflowing, all of the messages authored by boys. Many with whom she had never so much as exchanged a single voiceless word.

"Hey, Portia, saw u at the café. U were awesome! Wanna hang out after school?" The message was signed Daniel Becker, a senior with a prominent position on the football team— quarterback, was it?

"Portia, can't stop thinking about you since the café— Call me, Caleb." Caleb Samuels?! She erased it quickly before Charlotte could see.

"Wanna hang?" The brevity of this note was totally in keeping with everything Portia had heard about William Marks. Big on looks, small on personality.

She read through all the notes dismissively, searching for the only one that really mattered to her. Finally, scrawled into the bottom corner, she found it.

"Whoa, Miss Popular. U think you'll have time for me today? Text me. Pls."

Max had signed his name "Max H."

As if I wouldn't know?

She took out her phone instantly.

"Music room? Lunchtime?" Her fingers were shaky.

"It's a date. Let's hope it ends better than our last one."

She was mortified by the reference to last night's disaster.

Was that just last night?

She didn't have time to respond to his text, though, as three junior boys approached.

"Hey there, Portia," the tallest one said. She had no idea what his name was and was mildly disconcerted by the familiarity with which he said hers.

She nodded in acknowledgement and turned back to her locker to get out her books for first period. The male posse moved in closer.

"Portia, how about singing us a tune?" one of the other guys said.

"Yeah, Portia," said the third musketeer, "you were hot at the café the other night. Give us a little sumpin' sumpin' to kick off our day."

"Uh, not this morning, fellas. I've gotta focus on my chem quiz."

"Come on, just a quick jam…"

She was about to walk away, but in a flash she changed her mind. Why not? Why not give them a little solo performance? An odd feeling came over her, a yearning to prove herself, her powers.

"Ok, fine. So who can give me a beat? Something along the "Bust A Move" lines?"

The boys looked at each other, not believing their luck. The tallest one brought his hands to his mouth and started beatboxing the Young MC classic.

Portia closed her eyes, adjusting to the beat and hinging at her hips, enjoying the sudden attention of her suitors. One of the boys called out a provocative "*Bust It,*" prompting her to begin:

> *This here's a jam for RPA boys,*
> *From a Goddess who now can make noise.*
> *Used to be about maintaining my poise,*
> *Now about treating y'all like play toys.*
> *OK, fellas, time to get jealous,*
> *Not a one of you can make me feel zealous.*
> *You want a piece of me like a slice of pie,*
> *Well, you'll have to skip dessert, kiss me good-bye.*

She felt good. Better than good. She felt high as a kite as

the words fell out of her mouth with the ease of reciting the alphabet. The crowd around her grew.

> *Café was flowin', then fists were throwin',*
> *Until I grabbed the mic and minds started blowin'.*
> *So cat's outta the bag, and my jig is up,*
> *And now you're begging me to refill your cup.*
> *Best friend ditched me, and hottie kissed me,*
> *And everything around me now is a mystery.*
> *So give it up now for this private show,*
> *Now step aside, fellas, and let me go…*

The boys offered a weak rendition of the chorus, their voices and articulation paling in comparison to Portia's as she began to saunter away. But the crowd drew in closer, demanding more.

Their insistence was irritating at first but then as the drug of their desire began to course through her veins, Portia couldn't help but give in.

> *Homer told it, then he sold it,*
> *His story so messed up it makes you say 'hold it.'*
> *Women with six heads, Giants with one eye?*
> *Odysseus was one helluva guy!*
> *Then you switch classes, put on new glasses,*
> *Another subject that appeals to the masses,*
> *But just because you left it, don't be fooled,*
> *Keep asking yourself how this world gets ruled.*
>
> *Gods are planning, mortals scanning,*
> *Entrances and exits they are all manning.*
> *Athena'll call you in for a calming chat,*
> *Stay away from Ares—OH, I heard that!*
> *But we'll be ready, holdin' steady,*
> *As long as my voice ain't makin' me heady.*
> *And now I've gotta go, nothin' left to prove,*
> *So outta my way while I bust a move…*

Portia pushed through the crowd of students who stood, their mouths agape, wondering at the mythological turn her rap had taken. She strolled off, a suggestive swing in her hips, past Luke and Lance, who had been standing on the periphery admiring her performance.

"Christ, Portia, where the hell did that come from?" Lance questioned her.

"Just giving the people what they want," she offered, still basking in the glow of the boys' attentions.

Charlotte and Jacqueline had also appeared on the scene.

"Portia, you are like honey for ze bees this morning." For some reason Jacqueline's accent was suddenly very irritating.

"Yeah," Charlotte added, "you better be careful or the guys are going to be throwing pebbles at your window tonight."

"And what—would that make you jealous?" Portia smirked.

Visibly wounded, Charlotte paused for a moment of disbelief, before turning on her heel, walking briskly in the other direction.

Portia was as shocked as anyone at her own callousness. It was like some über-bitch had suddenly usurped her power of speech.

"Wait, I'm sorry, Charlotte," she called out. "I didn't mean that. I have no idea where that came from…" But her words just littered the hallway, which started to empty with the sound of the first bell.

As the morning wore on, Portia was continually assaulted by greetings from her male schoolmates, making it impossible for her to focus on any of her classes. Worse yet was her own inability to gauge how she would react to each encounter. Sometimes she felt thrilled with the attention, but other times she could see something in the boys' eyes, something feral that scared her.

Before lunch, she decided to consult Leucosia about her new "celebrity status."

When she walked into the nurse's office, there was a very tall blonde girl sitting on the gurney, a thermometer lazily hanging out of her mouth. Portia nodded a casual greeting and shot Leucosia a desperate look.

The thermometer beeped, and Leucosia glanced at it.

"OK, Danielle. You don't have any fever. Why don't you go back to class and if you still have a headache later, come back and see me again."

Danielle looked disappointed as Leucosia shuttled her out of the office.

"That girl is such a hypochondriac—oops, probably shouldn't have said that, confidentiality and all that. By the way, I spoke to your chemistry teacher and told him you had been to visit me with a bad head cold. He agreed to postpone your quiz until you were feeling better."

With all the commotion of the day, Portia had completely forgotten about the looming chemistry quiz. Although grateful that she wouldn't have to suffer through it today, she still didn't feel any less overwhelmed.

"What's the matter? I would have expected at least a smile for getting you out of the quiz—"

"I'm getting an obscene amount of attention from the boys," Portia interrupted. "And I gotta admit, I'm kind of into some of it."

Leucosia flinched slightly as Portia described her rendition of "Bust A Move."

"…Boys who never even knew that I existed are suddenly all over me. It's like they've never seen a girl before or something…"

Leucosia sat her down. "Look, Portia, the other night at the café, you showed these boys something the likes of which they have never seen or even imagined. The impact your voice has already had on anyone who heard it that night is immeasurable. In their eyes, you are already a Goddess. Your physical beauty has increased to them. You even have an aroma about you. And your voice, just the memory of your voice, is enough to send any male into a tailspin."

Leucosia pulled a hand mirror out of her desk drawer, handing it to Portia, who took it reluctantly, knowing that Parthenope and/or Ligeia might be staring back at her. Holding it up tentatively, she examined her reflection and was relieved to see her normal self. But even she had to admit that she was looking pretty good, her skin more lustrous and the blue of her eyes more chromatic than ever.

"No. This isn't me." Her voice was barely above a whisper, but still she could hear the loveliness it held. "The real me is gone…" She forced the mirror back at Leucosia.

"You are not gone, Portia. You will never be gone." Portia looked up and Leucosia sat down next to her, holding the mirror back up so that both of their reflections appeared. Their combined beauty was breathtaking.

"Oh, but I pray to the Gods that you remain grounded, for so easy will it be for you to control those who now beg your attentions. I fear that the day will come when your beauty will lead you down a path of evildoing. I hope that at that moment you remain wise, for then the destruction of mortals will seem to you sweeter than the finest ambrosia."

"Whoa, Leucosia—we're not at Mount Olympus. You don't need to speak to me like that."

The green of Leucosia's eyes suddenly turned stormy gray.

"What? What's happening?" Portia was suddenly alarmed at the unmistakable sense of dread that had fallen over her mentor.

"Surely, Portia, we are now in the presence of a God, for no other force would have guided my language unto the style to which I was born. My arms and legs even now feel the prickle that alerts me that there is a God among us who does not wish to make his or her presence known."

"Leucosia, you have to stop speaking like that—it's freaking me out."

Leucosia did try a few times then, but her efforts were in vain. Everything she said sounded Homeric.

And dire.

The hair on the back of Portia's neck stood on end.

"You mean your sisters are here? At RPA?!"

"Indeed, at least their spirits are here. I fear that they have become ever more powerful, for why else would I be thus feeling the prickle of the Gods? We must not allow them to know our fear," she said, though her voice lacked the confidence that Portia wished it would have had. "If they perceive our fear, it will only fuel their powers. You must go about your day as usual. I beseech you, though, keep your eyes wide open. Do not tarry alone, not even for a moment. I will now reach out to the Gods for counsel, praying all the while for your safety."

If Portia was not terrified beyond all measure, she would actually have laughed at the ridiculousness of the situation. How was she supposed to go hang out with Max now, acting like everything was totally normal?

They are just spirits. They are just spirits. She repeated the mantra to herself as she headed out into the hallway. *They can't really harm me. They are just spi—*

But just as Portia was settling herself into the comfort of these words, she felt an unwelcome prickle travel down her own arms and legs like a slithering snake.

Max was in the music room as promised, his fingers floating lazily over the black and white keys of the baby grand. She watched him through the window of the door, his eyes closed, lost in his own world, his fingers dancing over the keys:

> *I've seen blue in ocean tides,*
> *Have tasted blueberries sweet,*
> *Sang the blues as moods I ride,*
> *Blue flames have licked my feet.*
>
> *Then blue I saw inside your eyes,*
> *My world now monochrome.*
> *It's all gray—the sea, the skies.*
> *In black and white I roam…*

He stopped for a moment, taking a pencil to the sheet music that rested on the shelf of the instrument. Suddenly he noticed Portia and motioned for her to come in.

"Hey, there. Where's your posse of male suitors?" There was a bite to his words.

"I don't know if I would exactly say suitors. More like some kind of testosterone overdrive in the air or something." Portia attempted to make light of her new celebrity status.

He moved over on the bench, and she sat down next to him, immediately noticing the scabs on his hand, crusty and three-dimensional. She ran her finger over them gently.

"Let's not talk about it now, OK?" His words were music to her ears.

"OK, that works for me." She glanced up at the sheet music. "So that was pretty lighthearted stuff you were working on, huh?" She took a chance with the jab and luckily he let out a smile.

"Yeah, I decided to explore the lighter side of our relationship today. It was between that and 'Every guy in school's got a thing for my girl.' "

Portia tried to change the topic. "You know, I play a little—"

"Are you kidding? How come you never told me?"

"Well, it's been a really long time. When I was younger, my parents thought that since I couldn't speak, maybe the piano would be a good way for me to 'vocalize.' I think they saw that Holly Hunter movie, *The Piano*, a few too many times. I took lessons for about two years, and I wasn't bad—I think that's when my Ella obsession started. I loved playing jazz and since I couldn't scat with my mouth, I let the keys do it for me.

"But one day I just got so angry that this *thing*, this instrument built by man's hands, was able to make sounds and I wasn't—so I just stopped. Oh my God, you wouldn't believe how I used to take out my anger on that poor piano! I started doing things like heaping my book bag on top of it to scratch the veneer and messing with the pedals so that their footing was totally off. One day I even encouraged Felix to help me glue the keys together." Portia smiled at the memory of her and Felix creeping into the living room with a paintbrush and a big bottle of Elmer's. "Luckily the glue was washable—I spent about two days getting every last bit of it out with a wet toothbrush."

Max let out a hearty laugh.

"Yeah, yeah—it all sounds so funny now, but I gotta tell you that piano was my nemesis. Finally Helena—I mean, my mom—donated it to the Ridgewood Retirement Home. She couldn't stand to see the instrument take any more abuse." Portia looked up into Max's eyes. He was hanging on her every word. She wondered if it was because her story was truly riveting or just that her voice was irresistible.

"So come on," he encouraged her. "Let's see what you got."

"Um—no, thanks. I think I'll pass."

Max wasn't going to give up so easily, though. "Come on, it's just me."

"Yeah, just you, who can play, like, every instrument under the sun."

"Well, I haven't fully mastered the harp yet." He grinned. "Come on—I know you can sing like nobody's business. I'll chime in. Please?"

How could she say no to those eyelashes?

"Ok, fine. But if I suck, I'm stopping right away."

"Deal." He scooted over a few inches to give Portia more room.

She remembered the way he had cracked his knuckles that night when he sang her to sleep and perfectly mimicked the motion. The crack was louder than she had anticipated.

"Wow, I guess I am really rusty."

But as Portia's fingertips touched the keys, she was amazed to find that she wasn't rusty at all. In fact, she was shocked at the fluidity of her own fingers, her memory of the chords, the natural feel of the pedals beneath her foot. She closed her eyes, allowing herself to enjoy the music. She played a few melancholy bars before her fingers started cruising the keys on an autopilot, eking out every bit of sultriness that the voice of a piano could possibly hold.

Is there no end to these Siren superpowers?

To her surprise her fingers were replaying the exact melody Max had been singing before she walked in. He stared at her.

"What are you, like some kind of a savant?"

"I don't know where this is coming from," she lied. "I guess I really liked what you were working on."

"Yeah? Well, baby, there's a lot more where that came from."

"OK, so give me another verse," she commanded as her fingers scaled the keys. They might as well have been suddenly relocated to a smoky bar in Casablanca for the sudden change in the climate of the room. The air had grown hazy with the promise of love. Of touch.

"Um, OK," he faltered for a minute. It was nice to see him have to second-guess himself for once. But he recovered quickly:

> *"I was warned 'bout girls like you,*
> *Once in, there's no way out,*
> *But until now, I had no clue*
> *What they were talkin' about.*
> *And now you sit here, skin so smooth,*
> *it's beggin' for my touch—"*

Portia had begun to harmonize with him, and Max looked slightly disoriented at the sound of her voice. She decided to pick up where he had stopped:

> *"Don't know that I'd say 'beggin',*
> *But thank you very much…*
> *I too was warned to guard my heart*
> *'gainst smoothies like you.*
> *I see the way you look at me,*
> *It's like you're looking through…"*

Max emitted a smooth falsetto as a backup to her words. They were engaged in a kind of vocal foreplay, his voice the satin to her lace. The gauzy way the lyrics fell from his mouth reminded her of the gentle way in which he kissed. In that moment, Portia understood the kind of ecstasy that had been produced by the sound of a voice. In this moment, he seemed just as much a Siren as she was and so she continued:

> *"Warnings are for cowards,*
> *And I'm ready to play.*
> *Take you out of monochrome,*
> *No longer the gray…"*

He murmured the harmony offhandedly now, completely

trapped in her voice.

And then a crash.

She pounded the keys with her fists, interrupting the melody. *What the hell?*

Max looked at her in surprise and shook his head, motioning her to keep playing despite the minor trip-up.

But she couldn't unball her fists. Her fingers curled around themselves, despite how hard she tried to straighten them.

Just keep playing…

She tried knuckling the keys, hoping to ward off the inclination.

But then more pounding. With each slam of the keys she could feel the evil spiraling its way through her limbs.

Get out of me!

But she just pounded on the keys again.

Max tried thwarting her fists with his hands. "Portia, come on—what are you doing?"

It was too late. She tried thinking back to the homework list that the Gods had given her just last night. Was there any clue in it on how to exorcise these demonic inclinations from her body? But there was no time for clue searching. She couldn't stop her fists from pummeling the keys, releasing angry bursts of noise in every direction.

"Stop it!" he urged.

She wanted to. She really did. But her fists only gained speed.

And then she started to laugh.

Shut up!

"It's not funny, Portia! What the hell are you doing? Stop!"

But she kept laughing and laughing, her feet slamming on the pedals, her hands hammering the keys.

And then it was gone. Just as quickly as it had started.

Max stared at her, her short breaths filling the air around them.

There was nothing to say. Nothing that could even remotely explain her behavior.

So she got up.

And ran.

Portia thought about heading back to Leucosia's office but was suddenly faced with an unavoidable reality. What happens when Leucosia isn't just a few rooms away?

Instead she sprinted toward the library stacks, the most remote place she could think of, taking refuge in the far corner bathroom. But no matter how isolated she was, there was no escaping the presence of the immortals and the intensifying prickle on her limbs.

Where are you? Where the hell are you?

As she neared the bathroom mirror, the prickling grew hotter, burning her skin, itching and sizzling.

All right. All right, you want a piece of me?

She took a deep breath and boldly looked into the glass.

Evil Portia was waiting for her, smiling, chomping at the bit.

She leveled her eyes with her loathsome twin and felt a sudden rise in her own posture. Clearing her throat, she stood taut:

"OK, OK…

> *So you are mythological,*
> *Your planning diabolical.*
> *You think you're agonistical,*
> *Your death will be statistical!"*

The reflection smiled offhandedly, welcoming the verbal battle and coming back effortlessly with:

> *"You try to be angelical,*
> *Never anticlerical.*
> *In fact you are panoptical,*
> *You're not quite so monastical…"*

Portia's anger was further fueled. She was not about to be outdone by Leucosia's perverse sisters.

> *"You think you're mystagogical,*
> *Will guide me psychological.*

My voice is phylacterical,
I laugh at you hysterical."

Evil Portia grinned back and offered:

"I see you are quite skeptical,
Think I can't keep up metrical.
My powers oratorical
Are not just allegorical."

Portia pushed up her sleeves. Her voice gained volume. Her rage picked up momentum, causing her to realize that until now her anger had only been set to a low simmer.

"Of words I am alchemical,
A master alphabetical.
I blend my sounds harmonical
Until they are volcanical.

They fight pugilistical,
They're backed polytheistical,
They bounce and jump gymnastical,
My range—it is fantastical!"

Her reflection started to answer, but Portia raised her voice even louder, stepping in closer to the mirror and grabbing the edges of the sink.

"And it's not pedagogical,
It's purely biological.
My words apopthegmatical,
My sayings are so radical."

The verses ricocheted like bullets off the metal doors and cinderblock walls, spurring her on.

"My voice it is magnetical,
Beyond the hypothetical.
It's more than polytechnical,
A traffic-stopping spectacle."

The mirror began to quake with every word she flung at it. Evil Portia had stopped smiling somewhere during the last verse.

> *"I am no longer ethical,*
> *No need to be mimetical.*
> *My questions not rhetorical,*
> *Don't care for the historical."*

Portia was entirely engrossed in her verse, each word a blade stabbing away at the creature that was trying to control her.

> ***"I'm blessed organoligical,***
> ***My powers are robotical.***
> ***I am your diametrical,***
> ***You're no longer majestical!***
>
> ***We started antiphonical,***
> ***You thought your words demonical.***
> ***But my verse exorcistical—***
> ***The real Portia is mystical!"***

With the final boom of her voice, the mirror shattered, spitting shards of glass into the air. A sharp pebble flew past Portia's neck, grazing it and bringing forth a droplet of blood. But she was too caught up in her victory to care.

I did it, you miserable monsters! I beat you!

When she looked back at the spot where only loose remnants of the mirror still hung, Portia wasn't sure what she expected to see. Anything from blankness to a shattered image of her hypersexual self would have done.

Instead what she got was a blonde man with ice blue eyes and a moon-shaped scar looming large on his face.

"Who are you?!"

But in an instant, he was gone.

The room was empty but for an oatmeal-colored moth flying out of the bathroom's small rectangular window.

Chapter 23

Proteus was blessed with visions of the future, excepting only matters of the heart. But because of his mischievous ways, the God would not reveal to Ares his visions for battles yet to come. As Ares prevailed upon him, Proteus became a lion, a serpent, a leopard. And then a soaring eagle, who flew away, leaving Ares to wonder at the warfare that lay ahead.

The Great God of War thus plunged unprepared into a bloody battle in which he watched two of his sons die upon the sword.

Ares was forever changed by the death of his sons. Often when the moon did shine as a mere crescent in the night sky was Ares reminded of the arc he had carved into the cheek of the evil shape-shifter who did not forewarn him that of the loss of his kin. He had never again beheld Proteus since that day.

But as he did charge into one battle after the next, Ares thought of all his foes as none other than the evil Proteus, often carving his signature scar into their faces before taking their lives.

After many years, Ares gave up on avenging the death of his sons, assuming that Proteus must have met his own demise.

Until the day that Leucosia brought him tidings of a scar-faced shape-shifter who was surely aiding her sisters in their plot.

Now nothing would stand in the way of his revenge.

Yet Ares wondered at the connection between Proteus and Leucosia's sisters. Upon considering the matter, he believed that nothing other than love would have spurred Proteus on these many years. Especially the love of a Siren, whose voice could captivate like no other.

Thus Ares had no choice but to reach out to his old lover, the Goddess of all Love, Aphrodite. When Ares arrived in the waters of Cypress to appeal to Aphrodite, he was not surprised to see that her beauty was as magical as ever. Were it not for the serious nature of his visit, he would have fallen in love with her all over again.

"What brings you here today, Ares?" The Goddess sprang forth from the water around the island, revealing her beautiful breasts, her milky skin.

"Aphrodite, long has it been since the death of my precious sons Chariton and Hesperos. But now do I have a chance to avenge them…"

Ares cried tears that had not been shed for centuries, his impassioned plea reaching the generous heart of Aphrodite. And so the Goddess of Passion revealed to Ares the story of the love that did once blossom between Ligeia and Proteus.

And then, because Ares had a way of softening her heart, Aphrodite added an as yet unknown element to the story.

"He visits her in Hades every year on the anniversary of her death, weeping tears for all to see…"

Of particular interest was this melancholy behavior to Ares, knowing that proper timing was half the battle.

When the God of War returned to Mount Olympus, he took out the silver machine that had been bestowed upon him as a gift from the beautiful Siren Leucosia. At first Ares had thought the machine to be a frivolous item, though the mortals seemed wholly dependent on the "computer." But alas, after he had learned to navigate his way around the vast seas of the Internet, he came to appreciate the MacBook, using it at least once every day.

Now he desired to send an urgent message to Leucosia. He opened the machine and typed in the e-mail address of the Siren, leucosia@syrinx.god.

> Dearest Leucosia,
>
> I thank you again for this miraculous gift, which enables me to offer you tidings with the mere press of a button. Aphrodite has offered me some valuable insight into the behavior of the dreaded Shape-shifter Proteus, who was indeed the lover of your sister Ligeia. I believe that the best time to attack will be on the very anniversary of your sisters' death.
>
> I must warn you, Leucosia, that though I desire nothing more than to avenge my sons, the defeat of a shape-shifter is no easy feat. Proteus must be paralyzed before he is to be killed.
>
> You may wonder just how this paralysis will befall the

evil God. I propose that only through the powers of the young Siren Portia can the shape-shifter be prevented from altering his form. For though your own voice is as pure as the heavens themselves, the sound of a virgin Siren's voice is beyond compare. Therefore it is with great urgency that I beseech you to prevail upon your charge to keep at her assignments and sharpen her great tool.

The power is within her, Leucosia. She simply needs to procure it.

I remain your faithful God of War,
Ares

Ares clicked on the icon that read "Send" and then decided to seek out Dionysus.

He really needed a drink.

Chapter 24

Dean was sleeping again, though miraculously he had regained consciousness during the night. The doctors were optimistic that the brain damage was not as severe as they had originally suspected. Especially since his first question was whether or not he had totaled the new bike.

Felix sat at his cousin's bedside, enjoying the solitude. He had sent everyone home to shower and rest, assuring his family that he could man the ship for a few hours. Looking down at his cousin, tubes snaking in and out of him, he couldn't help but wish that Portia was there with him. Seeing Dean like this had forced him to gain some perspective. After all, it wasn't life or death with her—even though her performance had felt like a deadly blow.

But now he had to deal with the realities of the situation. And the truth was, her new voice should make no difference to him since he couldn't hear her anyway. A true friend would just be happy for her. And that is all he was. Her friend. If he was ever going to move on, he needed to accept once and for all that he and Portia were just friends.

Right?

"Stop looking so morbid," Dean had garnered all his strength to sign the words to his pensive cousin. The boy's hands were still slow to follow the instructions of his brain—but at least they followed, which was more than could be said for his legs.

Felix attempted a weak smile but couldn't hide his worry, "Hey, you're up. Thank God. I was worried that you slipped back into a—well, never mind."

"No—just tired." He spoke the words now that Felix was looking at him. "These must be some serious drugs they have me on…could be addictive." He attempted a weak smile, which Felix didn't return.

"Listen, Dean-o, you gotta get out of here. Do you hear me? You gotta stay focused on walking out of here."

"I don't know, man. That's feeling like a whole lot of pressure." His cousin looked aged and defeated.

"Yeah, well, pressure never seemed to bother you when you were riding the crest of like a forty-foot wave or boarding out of bounds with ski patrol after you."

His cousin smiled, reaching his hands down to his inert legs.

"Anyway, let's change the subject," Felix suggested. "That girl, Meadow, was here this morning—what a name—I think she's hot for you…"

Felix waited for a response while Dean seemed to be sorting out his thoughts. "Felix, why are you still here?"

"What? What do you mean?"

"I mean, I wasn't sleeping the whole time, man. Just too tired to open my eyes…I heard everything you said. About Portia. So why are you still here?"

"You must have been dreaming, Dean-o…Why wouldn't I be here?"

"It wasn't a dream. I *heard* you. You gotta be more careful, you know. Just because you are deaf, you can't assume that every drugged-up potential paraplegic is also. I know what you admitted to me. *You* know what you admitted to me." Dean had lifted his head to enunciate his words but then let it fall back to the pillow.

Felix raised the head of the bed with the button so that his cousin wouldn't have to strain himself.

"Thanks, that's better. Shit, I can't even keep my head up."

Felix didn't answer—couldn't answer. What could he say to his cousin when everything was still so uncertain?

"Hey, listen up, dumbass," Dean decided to break the silence on his own, weakly signing the words he was speaking, "I'm gonna make you a deal, OK?"

Felix inched closer, relieved that his cousin was swearing again. Dean was famous for his toilet mouth.

"OK, I'm listening, well, lip reading…and, by the way, you could use some mouthwash."

Dean ignored the dig. "You go back and get her, and I will walk out of here on my own two feet." He followed up the verbal contract with a weak smile, but Felix recognized the fear in his cousin's eyes.

"I think you might be getting the raw end here, buddy." Felix signed back. He couldn't bear to speak the words aloud. The doctors had cautioned the family to be encouraging but not to offer any false hope.

"With that mug? I don't think so. I'll probably be running a marathon before she even gives you the time of day."

They laughed.

The Fein boys who shared the same birthday, a passion for sports, a love of spicy food, an obsession with *Harry Potter*, an insistence that Coca-Cola could only be drunk from a glass bottle—they laughed.

If they hadn't laughed, they would have cried.

And laughing just seemed far preferable.

Portia sat on her bed and stared at her "homework." How she wished she had the simple threat of a calculus test looming over her. Instead she was struggling through the calligraphed list, written with a quill no less, that had her figuring new methods of vocal manipulation in her every waking moment. Upon reviewing it, she still wasn't sure how any of the exercises would have helped out in the music room a few days ago, but since then she had to admit that the training had come in handy…

Erase a Memory: Well, she could certainly cross that one off the list. She thought back on how easy it had been to convince Max that they had never even been to the music room, let alone shared in a romantic duet. The guilt she felt at deceiving him paled in comparison to the shame brought on by her fitful behavior at the piano. At least her powers were able to help out in some way.

Beg Forgiveness Where Forgiveness is Undeserved:
Check. Her first instinct here had been Felix, but since he was still away, not to mention the fact that he wouldn't have been able to hear her anyway, she turned instead to Charlotte. Her friend had proved a tough nut to crack after Portia had accused her in front of everybody of being jealous. She wouldn't meet Portia's eyes and continued to chip away at her nail polish while Portia apologized over and over again. Finally Portia took a chance with "CHARLOTTE, YOU WILL FORGIVE ME." An awkward moment had ensued, and then Charlotte broke out into a smile and asked Portia if she wanted to see the new Ryan Gosling movie that night. Portia was relieved at having been forgiven but vowed to herself to try to be more careful in front of Charlotte in the future.

Infuse Love and Passion into a Moment: She preferred not to think of that one for fear that she might throw up. She had wracked her brain for a way to do this without landing in dangerous territory. Then, when she was helping Helena prepare dinner one night, she remembered the book *Like Water for Chocolate* and sang corny love songs with her mother while they sliced and diced. By the time her parents were finished with the succulent meal, Portia literally had to tell them to "get a room" and, to her sheer horror, they did, leaving her to clean up the aphrodisiacal leftovers. Eeww…

Learn to Calm Yourself with Voice Alone: This one was a work in progress. When Leucosia had told her that her distorted reflection was actually a shape-shifter who was aiding and abetting her sisters, she would have done anything to have mastered this skill. The conversation had been so out of the realm of reality that she had half expected Professor Dumbledore to walk in and toss her an expelliarmus charm.

"So this guy can change into anything he wants—"

"Anything living," Leucosia had interrupted matter-of-factly. "He can't transform into an inanimate object."

"Oh—well, that makes me feel a lot better then." She couldn't help her sarcasm, which incidentally was also a skill listed in her homework. ***Ease Up on the Sarcasm!*** But she suspected that Leucosia had just snuck that one in there self servingly.

"Portia, Ares has been after Proteus for as long as I can remember. He will surely help us defeat him. We just have to have patience."

That was one thing that no amount of homework could help her acquire.

"Yeah, well, about that. Can you explain to me why exactly we have to wait three whole weeks to execute a plan? I'm already starting to have less time in between the, um, bad moments."

Leucosia had then explained all of the various reasons why the anniversary of her sisters' death would be the optimal date to attack. "Until then, Portia, you must remember that my sisters cannot truly control you—they can only influence you. They lost the powers of their Sirenhood at the very moment they lost their lives…"

None of it had helped to calm her. And though she tried speaking aloud to herself, singing, and even yogic chanting, she still could not calm herself with her voice alone.

She knew that there was one thing that could calm her. Had always calmed her. But Felix had kept their communication to a minimum while he was with Dean.

She knew she was being selfish, that her problems paled to Dean Fein's, who might never walk again. But still she checked her phone and e-mail constantly for signs of her elusive best friend. And then finally, late one night, he had texted her.

"Am boarding plane in a few. I'm coming home to straighten things out. Hope you're up for it."

She was a little confused by the comment. Why wouldn't she be up for having her best friend back? Up for resuming some semblance of normalcy? Of course she was up for it.

"Of course I am :)"

"Good," Felix had written back.

Portia was so relieved that he didn't bring up the voice thing that she just sent him an XO to conclude the text exchange.

Looking back at the homework list, she had to admit that though she had not used her voice, just knowing Felix was coming back had brought her an immeasurable dose of calm.

Chapter 25

Felix and Wendy snuck in a quick Starbucks the next morning before school.

"Why'd you take the red-eye last night? Dad wouldn't have cared if you missed another day of school." She eyed him suspiciously.

"What?"

"Did you use more of that gel I left you?" She reached out to touch his hair. "You did! What the hell, Felix? Trying to look good for Gabrielle Parker or something?"

Felix busied himself by sprinkling some cinnamon onto his latte, prompting Wendy to practically shove her signing hands up in his face.

"What are you not telling me?"

He was forced to stop fussing with the condiments and look at his sister full-on.

"Is it Gabrielle? I mean, I didn't peg her to be 'the one' for you, Felix, but if she is and you came back to—"

But Felix was shaking his head. "It's not Gabrielle, Wen. Stop, OK? There's nothing going on."

But she would not be deterred. "Wait a second. Hold up, here. Is it Portia?"

At the mention of her name, Felix went back for the mocha powder.

"Felix, you never add mocha. Look at me."

He turned toward her, unable to mask his guilt.

"I don't believe it—it is Portia! Of course it is. You took the red-eye back for her. Are you, like, finally going to declare your love to her or something? Not that it needs declaration. I mean, we all kind of knew it all along."

"I don't think this is skim," Felix tried dodging this inquisition. "Does this look like a skim latte to you?"

"Felix, I'm talking to you!"

"And I can't hear you—remember?"

She grabbed the collar of his shirt with her fists, having to stretch to her tippy toes to reach it.

"Read my lips, Felix—"

"What? No new taxes? So now you're running for President?"

Wendy's face reddened with anger, and finally Felix put his cup down and eased her hands off his collar.

"OK, Wen, you got me. I'm gonna do it. I'm gonna get me the girl."

"What do you mean? What made you decide? Well, except that I've been telling you for years that you guys were literally born to be together…"

"I don't know," he pilfered a couple of extra Splendas, preferring his coffee to taste like a milkshake. "Something Dean-o said, maybe. Or just seeing him like that. Or maybe that it's just time, you know? I mean, I'm not looking too bad these days, right? Especially with all that hair crap you've been shoving my way—"

Wendy looped her arm through his when they had finally finished doctoring up their drinks. As they headed out of Starbucks, latte and frappuccino in hand, she wasn't even sure why she bothered saying, "Gabrielle Parker's gonna be crushed."

Even if her brother had not been deaf, he was way past hearing the obvious.

But forasmuch confidence as he felt with Wendy, Felix was not quite so sure of himself a half hour later when he returned to RPA and found that the entire male population of the school was suffering from "Portia Fever."

He had assumed he'd just find her hanging around their lockers—most likely in the company of Max Hunter, for whom he had already prepared a dignified apology for everything that happened at the café. Instead a small throng of boys was waiting for a chance to scribble something on Portia's overcrowded whiteboard. And this throng actually included some guys on the football team, a species of human that Portia would never have deigned to befriend.

Would she?

He spotted Charlotte on the periphery, an equal measure of confusion on her face. In the week and a half he had been away, Felix had to admit that Charlotte had really begun to morph. Her face was no longer camouflaged by harsh streaks of makeup, and she was actually wearing an RPA button-down shirt rather than her trademark turtleneck. She looked like she had even put on some much-needed weight, and Felix had to admit that Portia's neighbor was actually, well, pretty.

"Hi, Charlotte, how's it going?"

She responded with a tilt of her head in the direction of Portia's locker.

"I guess you didn't hear about the new RPA rage while you were in Canada, huh? How's your cousin, by the way?"

"He's doing OK, thanks. What rage?"

"I don't know. It's like ever since that night Portia sang at the café—oh, sorry…"

"It's OK, Charlotte. I was there. I saw what happened."

"Right, so…anyway, I don't know. Something is going on with her. I mean, sometimes she complains to us about feeling suffocated by all the boys, but other times you can tell she loves every minute of it." Charlotte looked a bit uncomfortable at ratting out her friend. Felix put a reassuring arm on her shoulder. "Don't worry, I'm sure it's nothing."

When she finally did show up, Portia approached Felix, ignoring all the other boys and offering him a running hug. He welcomed the embrace with notable enthusiasm, determined to start laying the groundwork immediately for the turn he hoped their friendship could now take.

"Where's Max?" He couldn't believe those were the first words that spilled out of his mouth and quickly followed them up with, "I wanted to apologize to him for the other night."

An oddness settled on the moment suddenly, a nonchalance on Portia's part that left Felix slightly uncomfortable.

"Oh, he doesn't like to come around when all the guys show up in the morning. He usually waits for them to clear out."

Felix decided, against his better judgment, to delve.

"What do you mean, *when* they show up?" He signed out the letters to the definitive word. "Is this some kind of new daily routine for you? Show up to school and have to ward off a group of guys before first period?" He tried sounding indifferent, but something about the way she was so matter-of-fact about the situation was unnerving. "I mean, Daniel Becker?" he continued, not able to control himself. "Come on, Portia, you don't even know what a quarterback is—"

And then he caught a flash of something in her eyes that left him cold. What was it? Arrogance? Presumption?

"All that matters, Felix, is that Daniel Becker knows who I am…"

No, it wasn't just arrogance. It was blatant narcissism.

He spotted the light on the bell and excused himself to class, grateful that they weren't in first period together. Something about her felt different. He needed some time to figure out what it was.

Later that afternoon Felix's confusion was stretched further when Portia told him that she got an "A" on her makeup chem quiz, even though she had left half of it blank.

"I just kind of told Mr. Rooney that it would sure be nice if I could just get an A. And that's all it took. He gave me an 'A.' They should add that to my homework list—'get teachers to give you perfect grades…'"

"Who's 'they'? What homework list?"

But just as suddenly as she had divulged this bizarre tidbit, she begged off to the nurse's office, claiming a headache.

He had spotted Max in the hallway a few minutes later, and

though he really wasn't in the mood to make nice, considering how differently this day was going than how he had expected, he approached the guy, who still bore some scrapes from Felix's angry fists.

"Hey."

"Hey, how's your cousin?" Max asked. He wasn't doing the overenunciating thing this time, which Felix appreciated. In fact, Felix couldn't help but notice that Max looked slightly dejected.

"Listen, man, I want to apologize for the other night—"

"Don't bother. It was bound to happen, right, mate? I'm just not sure why we're all trying to win the same prize. I mean, I guess, I get you and me. But all these guys?"

"Yeah, what the hell is going on with that? She's never—" But just then Felix was startled out of his thought by a kiss on his cheek. He turned to see Gabrielle.

"H-i, b-a-b-e." She signed out the letters with fingers whose nails were painted a joyous shade of pink. She was so clearly proud of having mastered the sign language alphabet.

Felix smiled at the simplicity of her.

"Hey, Gabs, you know Max, right?"

"Of course," she answered, oblivious to the fact that maybe she shouldn't have interrupted the boys who had just recently tried to kill each other. "I'm glad you guys made up. Now maybe we can double date, right? I mean, Max, Portia is your girlfriend, right?"

Max hesitated. "Yes, Gabrielle, she is." He started to walk away and then turned around and added a meek "I think."

Felix never got a chance to talk to Portia that day and the next morning when he got to school, he found her standing against her locker, locked in conversation with Daniel Becker. All the hair flipping and eyelash batting that they had so often made fun of were suddenly part of her own repertoire. Coupled with the distastefully short hemline of her skirt, he couldn't help but wonder just what the hell had gotten into her.

"So tell me what exactly the quarterback does…" Reading her lips, he would have sworn he misinterpreted.

When Max entered the picture, he threw a disapproving glance her way but then just continued on to his own locker. Portia flashed him a sardonic grin and, rather than putting the brakes on, she actually moved in closer to Becker. Flirting shamelessly.

Felix actually felt bad for Max. "Hey, dude," he made his way over to his nemesis. "Did you guys have a fight last night or something?"

"No, I have no idea what the hell is going on. Everything has been going great with us." And then remembering who he was talking to, "Um, you know, things are pretty good."

Not exactly soothing words for Felix to have to take in, but he had brought it up after all.

"Why don't you say something to her?"

"That's the weird thing," Max looked up helplessly. Felix registered, not without a degree of satisfaction, that he was a good two or three inches taller than him. "I want to go over there and beat the shit out of that Becker kid. I know I can take him. But I literally can't move. It's like I'm paralyzed."

Felix was underwhelmed by Max's lack of bravado. Why the hell was everybody pussyfooting around Portia like this all of a sudden? He decided to take matters into his own hands.

"Portia, can I talk to you for a second?" he grabbed her by the hand and pulled her out of Daniel Becker's clutches.

"What the hell is going on with you, Portia? You're acting like a tramp."

"A 'tramp'? Is that the best you can come up with, Felix?" she challenged him.

"I was trying to be delicate. Didn't you see Max standing right there? You know I'm not the biggest fan of the guy, but come on."

In response, Portia did something that Felix interpreted as laughing.

"Max is a big boy, Felix. I mean, come on—world traveler, mother disappeared, father locked up in a loony bin. I think his skin is thick enough to handle a few games d'amour."

Felix could not believe what was coming out of her mouth. It was like a demon had taken her over. He was about to tell her just that when suddenly Ms. Leucosia, the school nurse, of all people, interrupted their conversation.

"Portia, can I see you in my office, please?"

"Now, Leucosia?" He was surprised at Portia's familiarity with the nurse. He, too, had known her for years, but he would never have dreamt of dropping the "Ms." in front of her name.

"Yes, right now."

"Sorry, Felix." Portia said. "I'm just in such high demand." She walked off in the direction of the nurse's office. Felix noticed that her gait had transformed from light and sporty to seductive and deliberate.

He looked around and found a thousand pairs of male eyes noticing the exact same thing.

As they walked to her office, Leucosia noticed every male head turn to get a good look at Portia. Things were worse than she had feared. There was a spring in Portia's step that she hadn't seen before, a swing of the hips that was less than subtle.

As they approached her office, the young Siren started to come down from the high. She quickly pulled her hair into a messy ponytail and tugged her skirt down a little.

Leucosia closed the door to her office and instructed Portia to sit down.

Now.

"Portia, things are not looking good…The way you've been acting—like a burlesque performer—well, it seems my sisters have already wormed their way under your skin."

Portia jumped up and started pacing nervously. "I can't control it, Leucosia. Part of me wishes I could just fade back into the woodwork. But the other part of me feels like I'm on fire. Like, in a good way. And then it's like my mouth has its own motor, and I don't have the key to shut it off. I mean, the look on Max's face before, when I was flirting with what's-his-name, should have broken my heart into a million pieces. Instead, it—it thrilled me. Why didn't he say anything? Try to stop me?"

Leucosia sat her back down. "You must stop pacing—you're making me dizzy. Max doesn't say anything to you, Portia, because he is afraid to upset you. He is so smitten with you that the thought of losing you is like losing his ability to breathe. He would literally let you walk all over him right now."

And then Leucosia saw it. The evil. Portia revealed a smile, just for an instant, that bore an uncanny resemblance to the ones her sisters would flash after their killing sprees. Just as quickly, it was gone.

"What?" Portia asked. "You look like you just saw a ghost, Leucosia."

"I believe I did." The always-composed Leucosia was visibly shaken.

"Leucosia, you're freaking me out. Come on, think. You must have some other tricks up your sleeve that can help smooth out these 'mood swings' of mine."

But Leucosia was tapped out. After seeing the evil in her charge's face, she felt an overwhelming fatigue the likes of which she had not felt since the days when she had to trail her sisters on their killing sprees.

"I'm afraid my sleeves are empty, Portia."

"Well, then, I don't have a choice. I think I'm going to tell Felix." The words tumbled out of her mouth, landing with a solid dismount. Clearly she had rehearsed this declaration and was determined to see it realized.

The announcement shook Leucosia out of her stupor.

"No, Portia. You can't. You just can't."

"Why not? What's the worst that can happen?"

"Um, he'll think you're insane and might try to have you committed!"

"No, Felix wouldn't do that to me."

Leucosia sat down in her desk chair and wearily massaged the tight muscles of her neck. She was running on reserve power, feeling every year of her infinite age.

"Leucosia, listen to me. Felix might be able to help me

over the next couple of weeks—you know, keep me in check. He's the only one who's immune to my voice, right? I just…I need him right now. And now that he's back from Canada, he's definitely noticed that something is off with me. I feel like every day since the café is just pushing us further apart, and I can't let that happen. I need him…"

Portia's tone had become desperate, a hint of silver clouding her tear ducts.

"Perhaps I can persuade Zeus to allow this one transgression, Portia. It is not customary for immortals to identify themselves as such. But I suppose I understand your need for a true friend right now. I mean, other than me—I guess our age difference does prove a bit of an obstacle. But I urge you to be selective in what you reveal. We don't want Felix to try anything heroic that might put him in the way of further harm."

"What do you mean 'further harm'?"

"No, I meant harm—any harm. I'm just weary, Portia. Now, tell me, how exactly do you plan on revealing yourself?"

Leucosia hoped that the young Siren had a plan, because sure as Hades, for once, she did not…

The next day Portia found it especially grueling to suffer through Mr. Morrison's class. Another sleepless night had passed with her rehearsing the many different ways she could try to convince Felix of who—make that what—she really was. Now she sat in the Homeric elective feeling like Plato taking Philosophy 101. If anything, she could be teaching Mr. Morrison a thing or two.

When she walked into class that day, the word "Hades" was scrawled out in big letters on the blackboard, sending an instant shiver down her spine.

This oughta be interesting.

She took a seat next to Felix. Max had opted to sit in the back, keeping his distance from her after she had made some callous remarks to him that morning about his music not going anywhere now that he had dropped out of Performing Arts.

She shuddered at the memory and was actually happy to see him take a stance against her cruelty. She turned to look at him, but he stared her down, shaming her into looking away first.

"So today we are going to speak about the underworld…" began the teacher. "The Halls of Hades have always confused me a bit—"

Yeah, you and every other God.

"…Who can tell me why Odysseus set out for Hades in the first place?"

Zachary Wilson's hand shot up in the air.

Does he actually have an intelligent thought in his head?

"Circe told him that he needed to get a prophecy from that blind prophet Tiresias."

"Yes, very good, Mr. Wilson. I've always wondered about Tiresias. It seems odd to me that Homer depicted the dead prophet as still retaining his powers to see the future, yet all the other spirits Homer saw were essentially just sad and useless."

Portia's ears suddenly perked up. How could she never have thought of this? When she had read *The Odyssey*, she had been so caught up in the emotion of Odysseus seeing his own mother in Hades that she had barely paid attention to the Tiresias part. Now she felt like she was on the precipice of discovering a monumental piece of the puzzle. She raised her hand.

"Does it ever say anywhere why Tiresias was blind? I mean, was he born that way?"

Mr. Morrison sat on his desk. "That is an excellent, if somewhat off-topic question, Ms. Griffin. There are several theories bandied about that would explain the prophet's blindness. My favorite one is that, no, indeed he was not born blind, and then one day he spied on Athena, who was bathing naked…"

A few snickers emerged from the less mature students in the class.

"Anyway, they say that the Goddess was so embarrassed that she actually blinded the prophet irreversibly. Pretty harsh, don't you think? Maybe they pitied him down in Hades, and that's why he was able to keep his prophetic powers even after his death."

The teacher got up and picked up his book. "Now, if you'll turn to page eighty-eight—"

"Holy shit—that's it!"

The whole class turned to look at Portia, including Felix, who was shocked to see Ellen Chadwicke signing out the expletive.

"Ms. Griffin, did you have something to add?"

"Yes…um, I mean, sorry. The cursing, it turns out, isn't really in my control. Are you saying that Tiresias was still able to see the future even though he was dead because the Gods of the underworld pitied him?"

"Yes, that is one theory…but, again, quite off topic. Now, back to page eighty—"

"Um, sorry, sorry Mr. Morrison. Can I be excused?" She got up to leave before he answered. "On second thought, I don't need your permission."

The words shot out of her mouth without any prompting from her brain. It was a terrifying proof that her newly formed hypothesis was undoubtedly correct.

When Portia got to Leucosia's office, there was one of those tacky signs on the door with a clock indicating that the nurse wouldn't be back for an hour. She couldn't wait that long. She had to test her theory now.

Charlotte had Poetry Slam now—she knew because they had rehearsed her poem last night. She was incredibly nervous about performing it in front of the class. It was called 'Name Change' and it revealed her neighbor's conflicting feelings on whether or not she should change her surname back to her original father's or if she should keep Trotter so that she'd:

"remember the pain, remember the blame, and always, always, add fuel to the flame…"

When Portia peered into the classroom, her heart went out to Charlotte, who was standing in the front of the room, baring her soul for all to see. She detected a tremor in Charlotte's hands—she had also been nervous yesterday when she had read aloud for Portia.

I might as well test my theory now…

She opened the door to the classroom a crack and closed her eyes, bringing back the lines of Charlotte's poem from yesterday's trial run.

Suddenly Charlotte's posture rose up and her voice traveled down a path of steady amplification:

> **"You say it's just a name,**
> **And to you it's all the same,**
> **Your fortune, your fame,**
> **In mine there's so much shame…"**

Charlotte's eyes registered shock at her own sudden fortified stage presence. Portia noticed the trembling in her hands slow down, and she could have sworn Charlotte grew in height while she delivered the end of the poem.

> **"But truth is, it's part of me,**
> **My own identity,**
> **So brand it in and burn it.**
> **Charlotte's my name—so learn it."**

Charlotte looked into the eyes of her classmates, who were riveted by her poem.

> **"I swear to God I've earned it…"**

The class erupted into wild applause, which seemed to further shock the typically stage-terrified Charlotte.

"Um, excuse me," Portia interrupted the applause. "Would you mind excusing Charlotte Trotter for the rest of class?"

The clapping stalled as the class looked up to see who had the audacity to interrupt this moment.

"Portia, I'm in the middle of something." Charlotte flushed red with embarrassment.

Portia looked at the teacher. "Allow me to rephrase—you *will* excuse Charlotte for the rest of class."

The girls were headed down the hall in a flash.

"Portia, what the hell was that about? You know I love that class."
They were safely tucked away in the stacks bathroom, where
Portia noted that the mirror above the sink had been replaced.

Tread lightly…tread lightly…

"Yes, I'm sorry about that, Charlotte. But I have a sort
of emergency."

"What emergency? What are you talking about?"

"Charlotte, listen, I have to confess—I spied on your slam.
I was, um, worried cuz you seemed so nervous yesterday. You
sounded great! How'd you feel while you were reading it?"

Charlotte softened a bit at Portia's inquiry. "You're right, I
was so nervous last night. And then today, I started out nervous,
but then, like, all of a sudden it was actually pretty amazing…I
just stopped being scared. But I kind of feel guilty. Like I stole
something. It felt like it wasn't really me speaking the words—
only it was me. I think. But I'm not sure why you had to call me
out of class about that right now. You've been acting so weird
lately…" She let the words trail off.

"Yes, I know I have, Charlotte, and please let me get this
out while I'm still lucid—I don't know how much time I have.
Although I have a feeling that this room is a safe zone for
me now."

Charlotte stared at her in utter confusion.

"Anyway, I had this idea in class before, and I wanted
to test it out. It's kind of like a ventriloquist thing, only you
were the dummy."

"Look, Portia," Charlotte actually looked a little panicked,
"I owe you my life. Not to mention what a great friend you have
been, but—"

> *"Amazing Grace, how sweet the sound…*
> *That saved a wretch like me…*
> *I once was lost but now am found…*
> *Was blind, but now I see…"*

When the solo was over, Charlotte was breathing hard.
"Jesus Christ. What the hell was that? Did I just sing that?"

Portia was both terrified and delighted at her new discovery.

"Sort of. I mean, actually, it was me singing through you. The same with the poem. I delivered the words through you, but you felt them, right? I mean, I saw your eyes well up—I know you were feeling it… and just now you felt the high of the music, right? Of the voice?"

"Are you kidding?" Charlotte said, almost giddy. "You should dime bag it and sell it—whatever *it* was."

"So it's not my subconscious. Well, I mean, it is, but Parthenope and Ligeia—they never fully lost their powers. They're speaking through me. That's why I have no control over some of the things that come out of my mouth."

She forgot that Charlotte was there, theorizing aloud, exploring all the possible angles.

"It all comes down to everyone's need for a mother's love, I guess. I mean, these evil witches—they are actually pitied down under. It's unbelievable. That's why their spirits are so mobile. That's why Morpheus can't keep them out of my dreams. And that's why they're not just spirits. They have powers—like Tiresias. Oh God, oh God. This is not good. Where the hell is Leucosia? This is not good."

Charlotte had started to inch toward the door, the fear more apparent in her eyes. "Portia, you're freaking me out. I think I should get back to class…"

And then Portia remembered her promise to Leucosia—Felix would be the only one that she would reveal herself to.

And so she did the only thing she could think to do:

Erase a Memory.

After guiltily erasing Charlotte's memory, Portia went to see if Leucosia was back, but the nurse didn't return at all that day. And once Portia had confirmed that indeed Parthenope and Ligeia were not quite as "powerless" as she had hoped, her anxiety was mounting at an exponential rate.

Learn to Calm Yourself with Voice Alone.

She tried. She really did. But she couldn't go it alone.

She needed someone, and Charlotte was definitely out of the question. Max was pretty much off the table, too, considering how maliciously she had been toying with him all day.

There was no avoiding it.

She approached Felix right before last period. "Hey—do you think you can come over after school today? There's something I need to talk to you about." It was still so strange to speak to him aloud, so she signed out the request.

"I don't know…I think I have a literary journal meeting…" She was continually amazed at his ability to imbue his words with sarcasm even though he couldn't actually hear them.

"Felix, I'm not kidding. I need you."

"Since when? Besides, I have plans to study with Gabrielle—"

"Cancel them," she ordered out loud.

He stood motionless for a second, and she wondered if maybe the voice had penetrated the barrier between them.

"Why the hell should I cancel? Because you happen to have some time for me this afternoon?"

OK, so the voice was not going to work. Instead she went for brutal honesty.

"Felix, don't you want to know why I've been acting so, um, fickle lately?"

"Fickle? I would have gone with bitchy. Maybe ruthless. But fickle?" She definitely had his attention now. "Does this all have to do with Max? Cause I gotta say, I'm not missing a date with Gabrielle for that…" His voice lowered steadily, though, and she could sense his resolve dwindling.

"It does have to do with Max, Felix, but not in the way you think. In fact, you'll be happy to know that a part of me actually wants to kill Max."

"Yeah, by the way, I'm not really digging your sense of humor too much lately, either."

If only I was kidding…

But she persisted, flashing him her best puppy eyes.

"OK, I'll reschedule Gabrielle. I guess I can hop a ride with my parents when they come to pick your folks up for dinner.

You better not be wasting my—"

But she was already walking away. She needed to try to make amends with Max before the day was out.

She found him at his locker, angrily flinging a few books into his knapsack. Taking in a deep breath, she approached him cautiously.

"Hey," she said humbly.

He slammed his locker shut.

"What do you want, Portia?" His voice was a serrated blade, each jagged tooth cutting her to the quick.

"I, um, just wanted to apologize for my behavior today— you know, all those nasty comments I made about your music. I'm not sure what came over me. You know I would never intentionally try to hurt you."

He slung his bag over his shoulder.

"Actually, Portia, I don't know that. You seemed pretty hell-bent on mocking me all day. Am I some kind of toy for you? Is our relationship some sort of game? Cuz I gotta tell you, I'm done playing. I deserve better."

Portia was aghast at his boldness. His ability to stand up to her went against everything Leucosia had told her.

"I'm sorry, Max. I really am. I hope you can forgive me."

Beg Forgiveness Where Forgiveness is Undeserved…

"Whatever, let's talk later, Portia. I'm exhausted from my trip yesterday."

Portia had completely forgotten that Max had had to make another emergency visit to see his father. What was it this time? She couldn't remember what he had told her.

Reading the blank expression on her face, Max resentfully volunteered, "Don't you remember I told you there was a staffing issue? My dad's regular nurse seems to have vanished into thin air. They replaced her with this new young nurse, Khloe, but my dad's having trouble getting used to her."

She was relieved that he was opening up to her.

"How so?"

"I don't know. It's just that he's been imagining more and more that my mom has been there visiting him. He claims that this nurse keeps telling him that she knows where my mom actually is, and that it would be impossible for her to be visiting. Obviously he's hallucinating all of it."

"Jesus, that sounds pretty bad. Are they trying new meds?"

"Yeah, well, that's the problem. He didn't used to be hallucinatory—just depressed. The doctors don't really know why he's suddenly seeing things—seeing her. He's getting so much worse."

Now would be a wonderful time to laugh at him, Portia!

Drown Out Their Voices with Your Own.

She had not yet tackled this assignment but now seemed an opportune moment.

She tried to speak forcefully. "MAX, I'M SO SORRY THAT YOU'RE IN SO MUCH PAIN. I CAN'T IMAGINE SEEING MY PARENTS THAT WAY."

"Thanks, Portia. But I don't exactly need it broadcast to the whole school."

Now he's being flip with you? No good deed goes unpunished. And neither should he…

"Stop!" Obviously she was going to need to work on the drowning out thing.

"I should stop? Everything you've said to me today has been offensive, and I should stop?"

"Max, I wasn't talking to you. I'm sorry." She felt the evil churning inside her. She had only moments before she was going to lose it entirely.

Infuse Love and Passion into a Moment.

She leaned over and placed a gentle kiss on Max's cheek, allowing her fingers to linger in his hair.

"I care, Max. I know you can't believe it, but I care."

He accepted the kiss gracefully and excused himself.

"I gotta go clear my head," and with that, he stormed off in the direction of the music room.

Portia once again marveled at his strength. At yet another moment when he hadn't succumbed to her power.

It makes for a better kill!

She needed to revisit that damn homework list…

Chapter 26

Felix's recent growth spurt was especially evident when he and Portia settled themselves into the hammock, where they had so often enjoyed each other's company. That was before the tension. When it was easy between them. Now she adjusted herself to accommodate his long arms and huge hands, which were cupped behind his head. Her toes ended at the top of his calves.

"Just how tall are you now, Felix?" she signed to him as she tried to muscle her way into a comfortable position. She looked up into the canopy of treetops, the familiar dialogue of the birds calming her nerves.

"I think I hit about six three last month." Clearly he was pleased with his own imposing size. "So what's going on with you, Portia? This whole emergency meeting?"

Portia reversed her position in the hammock so that that they were toe-to-toe, or at least toe-to-calf. She needed to see him, to gauge his reaction.

"So what did you think of Morrison's class today?" She spoke the words aloud, and he skillfully read her lips.

"Why are you trying to change the topic? I canceled a date for this, remember?"

"Yes, Felix, I remember—you only mentioned it like a thousand times. Gabrielle Parker? Really?"

He shot her a look of warning, and she backed off. Now wasn't the time. She had more important fish to fry at the moment.

"Anyway, I'm not changing the topic. Believe it or not, Morrison's class…well, it is actually the topic—"

Felix sat up and took Portia's hands in his. His skin felt

warm, his hands safe. "Portia, where did you go?" There was no sarcasm now.

"What?"

"Where did you go? I feel like since the beginning of school, you've been wandering off. Like every day you are further and further away from me. From us. I mean, there was an 'us' once, wasn't there?"

Her heart shattered. She needed to make him understand.

"Yes, Felix, there was…is…always will be an 'us.' But something has changed, and you are the only person who I can talk to about it. Literally. And I had to get a dispensation from Zeus just for telling you."

He dropped her hands. "You're not right. Something's not right with you."

"No, something is not right—that's what I'm trying to tell you. Listen to me, Felix."

Her voice had risen, lost on his deaf ears. But her desperation must have shown in her face because he evened his eyes with hers, offering her the stage. She wasn't sure how to begin and tried to take her cue from the night with Leucosia in the alley behind the café.

"Do you remember when I once told you about how birds have syrinxes instead of larynxes?"

"Yeah, so?"

"Well, did you know that Sirens also have syrinxes, and that's part of what makes them able to sing so beautifully?"

"No, I don't think Morrison ever said that. Was that in your research paper? The one you, um," he let out a dramatic cough, "got a 'B-' on?" Clearly he enjoyed the jab. He had gotten an A- on his Cyclops research.

Yeah, well, your paper wasn't intercepted by a three-thousand-year-old Siren…

She plunged ahead. "Sometimes the development of the syrinx has to follow the pace of the Siren's maturation into womanhood, which could cause, like, a lack of voice for a long time." She tightened her posture a bit more and continued, despite the look of confusion on his face. "Anyway, once the syrinx is fully formed, everything falls into place, and the sound that is produced by the combination of the syrinx and the larynx is, well, superhuman."

Portia couldn't believe how ridiculous she sounded.

"OK," said a confused Felix. "Why the sudden Siren anatomy lesson?"

"Felix, the reason I couldn't speak or make any sound for the first sixteen years of my life is because my syrinx was slow to develop."

"Wait, what? Why would you think you have a syrinx?"

She braced herself as she dropped the dreaded bomb.

"Because, Felix, I'm a Siren."

He stared at her, speechless, and then began to laugh so hard that he threatened to tip over the hammock.

"I'm not kidding, Felix. Stop laughing and hear me out."

There was a despair in her eyes that made him take pity on her. "OK, I'm all ears."

She couldn't even manage a smile at the irony of his remark.

"Have you ever noticed, Felix, that Ms. Leucosia hasn't aged one bit since we've known her? I mean, in all the years that we've been at RPA, that woman has remained as flawless as she was the first time you brought me into her office, right? Always with those two pinned-up braids? That perfect skin?"

"OK, I'll give you that. Maybe she's had Botox or something," he conceded.

"No, Felix. Not Botox. The reason she has remained the same is because she is one of the original Sirens. You know, like, from *The Odyssey.*"

He grew suddenly very serious, knitting his eyebrows in that way he reserved for the most somber moments. "OK, Portia, now you listen to me. What I'm about to say is being said out of love." He hesitated for a second, seemingly afraid to upset her. "I really have been worried about you—all your mood swings and, like, split personality stuff. So I did some Googling, and I read that schizophrenia is likely to come on in women who are eighteen to twenty-five. I think it might be hitting you a little early. And I kind of feel like you know something is really wrong, too, or else why would you be spending so much time in Ms. Leucosia's office?"

He had stopped the hammock from swinging with his leg. His brow relaxed slightly once he offered her his official diagnosis.

"No, Felix. Not schizophrenia. That is not why I've been spending so much time with Leucosia. Listen to me! Leucosia used to have two sisters, Parthenope and Ligeia." Her fingers stumbled over the spelling of the names as she clearly enunciated each one. "They were the evil ones—the ones that used to call in the sailors and kill them. One day Leucosia fell in love with a mortal man—a guy named Nereus—and her sisters killed him right in front of her eyes. They didn't know that she was pregnant at the time—with a daughter, Melina."

She was nothing if not impassioned as she spun the implausible tale.

"Wow, you've really been doing your mythology homework. Where'd you come up with all of these names?" Doubt edged his voice, along with a frustrating dose of patronization.

Ignoring him, she continued. "Remember the Goddess Athena in *The Odyssey*? You know, the one they always describe as clear-eyed and pale-armed?"

Felix did something between a shake and a nod of his head.

"Well, Athena convinced Leucosia to leave the island where she lived with her sisters so that she could raise Melina, a demigod, in peace. Unfortunately, Melina did not inherit either the immortality or the Siren gene. She did marry and have children, though, with a very nice mortal named Nikolas. They had a few daughters. Again, none of them hit the immortality jackpot."

Portia was growing breathless as Felix continued to do the shake-nod thing.

"Anyway, on her deathbed, Melina made her mother—Leucosia, that is—swear that she would stay alive until the next Siren was born so that she could prevent her from becoming power-hungry and evil like her sisters."

She paused to take a breath, allowing Felix a moment to digest the story. He fixed her with an uncomprehending stare.

"Felix, why do you think the boys are suddenly fawning

all over me? I mean, it's not like I became this ravishing beauty overnight."

"Um—yeah, actually you did," he responded. "Well, not overnight, I guess. I think it was once you got the braces off… God, that metal mouth was not working for you, Portia—"

"It's the voice, Felix! It can do anything." The look of doubt on his face forced Portia to play her last card. She braced herself and told him about the Trotter debacle.

"…When I saw what was going on, it was like some crazy force overtook me. I started quaking and all of a sudden my voice just, like, emerged. Before I knew it, Mr. Trotter was following me, following my voice out to the well. You should have seen the look in his eyes, Felix—I was willing him to climb in, and there was nothing he could do about it. Charlotte and her mom pulled him out—I'm still not sure why. As far as I'm concerned, they'd have been better off with that guy dead. But anyway, in case you were ever wondering why Charlotte and I suddenly became such good friends, well, now you know."

Felix stood up and began pacing around the hammock.

"Portia, what the hell are you talking about? How could you have even dreamt up a story like this? And why would you? I can't believe I'm validating you by even asking!" His pacing was having a dizzying effect on her. "I mean, do you realize how insane this all is? I've known you forever. And now you're telling me that you are actually some kind of God—"

"Goddess," she corrected him.

"Goddess," he corrected himself, "who can manipulate people with her voice?"

"Everyone except you, Felix." She signed out the letters of his name tenderly.

He stopped in his tracks and stared at her as panic visibly cloaked him.

Portia stood up and took Felix's hands in her own. She held them up to her face and pleaded with him.

"Please, Felix, I need you to believe me."

She leaned her cheeks into his fingers. Tears were streaming down her face, baffling him further with their silver hue. He brushed them away with the pad of his thumb, which stained silver from the gesture.

After a long moment, he pulled her into the warmness of his arms. "Don't cry, Portia. We'll get you through this. Whatever this is. I just need time to process everything you just told me. I don't know what to say. Please, don't cry. Don't cry. I'm not saying I don't believe you. I just, um, I need some time."

"I don't have time, Felix. I need your help now." She stepped away to sign out the words, too choked up to speak. She wanted so much to tell him about the upcoming battle, but with the way this conversation was going, she just couldn't push her luck. He already had her chalked up as a lunatic.

"Portia, I need time. I need time." He repeated the words over and over, as if trying to convince himself as well. He brushed his fingers through her hair. She could feel the tremor in them as he moved away any strays that had fallen on her face. "God, I miss you so much, Portia. I just…" There was nothing else to say.

He leaned over and kissed her on the forehead. The gesture seemed so natural, a reflexive show of the affection they had always shared for each other. Taking comfort in the kiss, Portia closed her eyes, blocking out a world that had become impossible to deal with.

He moved away then, and when she opened her eyes again, it was to see Felix running away, his long legs carrying him as fast they possibly could.

"Where have you been, Leucosia?!" Portia was in her room and had been e-mailing the absent Siren for the past hour. When her iChat ringer finally sounded off, she assumed it was Felix, doubtlessly wanting to tell her that he had decided that she was totally nuts and he couldn't really be her friend anymore, but instead Leucosia's face popped up on the screen.

"You video chat?"

"Yes, Portia—they don't age discriminate at the Genius Bar,

I've already told you that. In fact, I've actually been devising new ways to blend technology with the powers of my voice—but we can get to that another time."

"Where have you been, Leucosia?" she repeated. "I have a million things to tell you."

Leucosia looked weary. "There was another situation surrounding Scylla. Something is definitely amiss there, but I'm just too overwhelmed to figure out what it is."

Portia didn't really care about what was happening with the six-headed freak of nature and wasted no time interrupting and telling Leucosia of her terrifying epiphany. The blood drained out of Leucosia's face as she told her about the Tiresias discovery and how she had tested her theory with Charlotte.

"You threw your voice?"

"Oh, is that what you call it? I was thinking of it as like an advanced form of ventriloquism—"

"I cannot believe you actually threw your voice. Voice throwing is usually reserved for Sirens with a lot more experience. I don't think I was able to throw my voice until I was around three hundred years old. That's why we didn't even bother putting it on your homework list. I mean, just the other day, after my one-to-one at the Apple store, I figured out how to throw my voice into Siri. Boy, was I proud of that. And I'm proud of you, too. Proud, but still worried. I mean, if your skills are so innately advanced, how are we to ensure that my sisters don't prey on your expertise for their own purposes?"

"Thanks for pointing that out, Leucosia," Portia offered sarcastically. "I guess it wasn't terrifying enough for me to discover that your sisters are still wielding true powers from beyond the grave. Anyway, I was so freaked out that I actually bit the bullet and told Felix."

"Oh. How did that go?" Hermes was blocking Leucosia from the screen, purring like an engine.

"He ran away. I mean, he listened to everything, but I don't know—it was so frustrating that I couldn't convince him with my voice. I mean, you yourself just said that voice throwing is an advanced skill. Isn't there an advanced skill for getting deaf people to hear your voice?"

Leucosia looked away, and Portia detected a trace of guilt in the Goddess's eyes.

"Hey, it's not your fault, Leucosia. I mean, if there's no trick, there's no trick. Anyway, he ran and I haven't heard from him since. He probably ran straight into the perfectly sculpted arms of Gabrielle Parker."

"Oh, come now, Portia. Pettiness does not become you." She seemed distracted, typing and looking away from the camera while Hermes kept obstructing the view.

"Yeah? Well, at least Felix doesn't suspect that Gabrielle might be a paranoid schizophrenic. Leucosia, are you even listening to me?"

Leucosia continued typing. When she was done, she turned back to Portia. "I'm sorry, I was just Googling a bit more about Tiresias. Athena really did get a little carried away there—I think at the time she was going through a bad body image thing. I guess I can understand if he was pitied in the afterlife. But my sisters?! How can anyone pity them? I have some digging to do, Portia, and you have had an exhausting day. Why don't you try to find something fun to do from your homework list before bed?"

"Fun? Are you kidding me?"

But Leucosia had vanished from the screen, and Portia figured that she might as well unroll the parchment that she kept in her night table drawer.

Induce Growth of a Flower before Your Very Eyes.

That certainly wasn't screaming "fun" to her.

Stop the Rain from Falling upon You and Yours.

Intriguing…but when she looked outside, it was a perfectly clear night.

Command Respect, Aretha Style.

Now that sounded like fun.

Dionysus must have put that one in there.

She hopped out of bed, grabbed a hairbrush, and started to sing an earth-shattering and cathartic rendition of the Queen of Soul's best-known song.

She must have been louder than she thought because

halfway through her parents barged into her room and joined in on her impromptu performance. At first she was a bit put off by their guest appearance—I mean, who wants to see their mother screaming out "R-E-S-P-E-C-T" while their father is doing something that's sort of a half shimmy, half seizure?

But after a few minutes of singing and dancing around with them, Portia gave into the sheer joy of the moment, basking in the love of her parents, allowing herself to feel once more like a child.

She had a feeling that this moment would officially mark the end of what was, despite its impediments, a very happy childhood.

Chapter 27

The morning after Portia tried to convince him that she was a Siren, Felix awoke and wondered if he had dreamt the whole thing. But as he went about his morning routine, he couldn't stop mentally interlocking the pieces that fit her story so well. The way the other boys had suddenly started falling all over themselves every time she walked by. The way Max admitted to him just the other morning that he was powerless to stop her from flirting with Daniel Becker. And all the time, he, *deaf him*, was able to see the situation objectively.

He was not relishing going to school that day, especially after having totally bailed on Gabrielle last night, even for a late-night video chat. But he had missed enough school while he was with Dean, and frankly he was worried about Portia. She had been so convinced of her own story, so convincing.

He couldn't help but notice how easy it was for him to slip right back into the "thinking only of Portia" mode. Maybe now that they had reopened their lines of communication, things could go back to normal with them. Maybe even progress past normal.

But with barely one foot through the door at RPA, 'normal' was nowhere to be found.

The area around Felix and Portia's lockers was littered with boys. Some were waiting for a turn to write on her message board. Others seemed to be just waiting. The air was charged with a blend of testosterone and desperation, the combination of which Felix actually found nauseating.

A tap on his shoulder interrupted Felix's assessment of the situation, and he turned around to see Jacqueline and Charlotte. On the periphery, he caught Gabrielle shooting him a nasty look and storming off. But he just couldn't muster caring at the moment.

"What the hell is going on here? Ce n'est pas possible!" questioned the French girl.

Felix liked Jacqueline but had had to spend a great deal of time acclimating himself to reading her multilingual lips.

"Your guess is as good as mine." He hoped he sounded believable. If Portia really was going nuts, then the situation needed to be treated delicately, without the addition of unsolicited judgments and idle gossip.

"She's not even here yet," Charlotte chimed in, "and they're already lining up. I just don't get it."

What's to get? he thought to himself. *Her research paper went to her head and now she's convinced herself that she's a Siren and has probably been flirting relentlessly with like every one of these guys…*

The threesome turned back toward the bizarre scene. Daniel Becker must have arrived super early, as he held the first spot just in front of the locker. Right behind him, Felix was disappointed to see that Luke and Lance had muscled their way in for a prime location. The twins had a glazed look in their eyes and weren't even talking to one another. It was the first time Felix had ever seen them maintain a modicum of silence. Zachary Wilson's head popped out of the crowd, and the rest of the boys just kind of blended into each other, a messy sea of suitors, all vying for a dose of Portia Griffin.

When she finally sauntered in, ear buds dangling from her ears, Felix noted an arrogance about her. There was an exaggerated sway in her hips, a haughtiness that sent shivers down his spine.

He wondered if lithium would end up being the prescribed drug as his heart wrenched at the sight of her.

"Hi, boys," she purred as she navigated the crowded path toward her locker.

The boys began clamoring for her attention, a hungry pack of dogs competing for a raw steak. Trying to speak above one another, they inched in closer, each one trying to outwit the other.

A slow grin came to Portia's lips as Felix followed her gaze to the approaching Max Hunter.

"Whoa, ease up there, fellas." Felix read Max's lips, sensing that the guy was feeling a greater unease than he was letting on.

Portia pushed her way through the throng of boys.

"Hi, Max." She fingered the collar of his shirt, flaunting crimson painted nails. "I was just thinking about you—I guess it's this song that reminded me of you. Remember when I admitted to you I was an Ella Fitzgerald fan? Did you know there's actually a site where people post their own songs that they've written posthumously just for Ella? Kind of like 'Ella Fitzgerald Fan Fiction.'"

Felix had trouble making out the word "posthumously," but still he was only too aware that something was very off.

"Well, this one really got me," Portia continued, her eyes bright and dewy, "so I decided to make my own recording of it. Wanna know what it's called?" she taunted.

Max took the bait. "Sure."

"You Can Take It Slow, Baby," Portia said, revealing a magnificent mischievous smile.

"I beg your pardon." He looked around to find that everyone was observing their interaction.

"You know, as in the best kind of all-nighter. It actually reminded me a bit of a Cole Porter track—you know, all that hidden subtext. Maybe they should add this one to the RPA musical…" Portia pulled the headphones out of the iPod and turned the volume all the way up. The halls of RPA were suddenly draped in the velvet of her recorded voice.

> *"You can sing out slow, baby,*
> *You can start at the top,*
> *But once you sing down low, baby,*
> *I'm gonna beg you not to stop…"*

Portia couldn't resist the urge to join in. She began harmonizing to her own voice, edging in closer to Max.

> *"You'll reach octaves high, baby,*
> *Notes you never thought you'd get,*

> *And when you can't go on, baby,*
> *I will make it a duet..."*

Her voice completely surpassed the legendary Ella's, mesmerizing all who were present. Felix didn't have to actually hear the sound that was coming out of Portia's mouth to know that she had sparked a car chase that would undoubtedly result in someone crashing. He glimpsed Luke and Lance elbowing each other aggressively to gain a better vantage point. In fact, all the boys were trying to elbow their way in for a better view.

She's actually playing the role. She is so convinced that she is actually fooling them all...

Meanwhile the swagger in Portia's hips grew more exaggerated as her eyes became a lusty storm of sapphires. Max was practically foaming at the mouth.

> *"...And when the record's done, baby,*
> *We'll just play it again..."*

The left hook to Lance's face was completely unanticipated. Luke landed the punch right onto his brother's nose, and the twins fell to the floor, wrestling furiously, punching and kicking. Felix ran over to try to break up the fight.

But everyone else was ignoring the brawling brothers, refusing to be even momentarily distracted from Portia's performance.

> *"...'cause if you think we should stop, Baby,*
> *I say, 'No, I'll tell you when...' "*

Daniel Becker was suddenly on the floor, wrestling it out with the O'Reillys, screaming out some kind of expletive and declaring that he had dibs. Felix had to do something to break the spell. A split-second opportunity arose for him to shoulder his way in closer to Portia, the ringmaster of this circus gone awry.

"Snap out of it, Portia!" he screamed, simultaneously signing at her, his hands right up in her face.

"Portia," he spelled her name out with superhuman speed, having formed his fingers around the familiar letters a million times before. "Please stop. You're out of control."

Portia danced in closer to Felix, throwing him a challenging look.

> "—*Cuz you can take it slow, baby,*
> *You can sing and croon,*
> *And when you hit those notes, baby,*
> *You can watch me swoon…*"

"It won't work on me, Portia. I'm not interested. Where are you? Where is *my* Portia?"

His words were the magic clap of the hypnotist. She stopped singing, her head practically doing a three sixty, taking in the chaos around her.

In earnest, she signed to Felix, "Please get me out of here."

Felix shot Max a final look of pity before grabbing Portia's hand and heading for the door.

"OK, so let's say for one crazy moment that you are actually what you say you are," he signed when they were finally settled on the top bleacher at the football field, "then what's with all the Jekyll and Hyde stuff? Wouldn't you just be, like, Goddess-like all the time?"

And so in a torrent of emotion, Portia signed out the entire harrowing tale of how Ligeia, Parthenope, and Proteus were trying to take her over in order to take revenge on Leucosia. She had to respell the names for Felix several times before he finally got them right. When she told him of Proteus's shape-shifting abilities, he began to laugh as he had done the day before. But she remained steadfast, and his laughter disappeared just as quickly as it had come. He didn't offer any reaction after that, reserving all of his questions for the end.

When Portia was finished unloading all the details, she was completely spent. The only thing she had omitted from her recap was the plan to take Proteus down on the anniversary of Ligeia's death, afraid that Felix would try to thwart or, worse yet, aid her efforts. This was her battle—well, hers and Leucosia's—and she certainly wasn't going to put Felix in harm's way by getting him involved.

"So are you gonna abandon me now that you know just how much of a freak I am?" She delivered the question jokingly, but inside she was quaking with fear.

They sat in silence for a prolonged moment until finally he reached for her hand.

"You've always been a freak, Portia," he teased her playfully, "a bird-loving, book-reading, soccer-playing, music-obsessed, silent—but now vocal—freak."

She had to admit, he did have her number.

"But you're *my* freak," he continued. "And I'm not going anywhere. I promise. I'm not saying that I'm ready to jump on the whole Siren vs. Shape-shifter bandwagon, but I will try to help you through whatever it is you're going through."

Flooded with relief that Leucosia was no longer her sole ally, Portia pulled him in for a hug.

She tipped her forehead gently against his and they sat for a minute, feeling each other's warmth, the sweetness of each other's breath. A slight drizzle interrupted the moment, forcing them to draw apart and start gathering their things together.

Glancing at his watch, Felix couldn't believe that they had already missed first period.

"Shit, we better go."

But she wasn't ready to face everyone yet. "You go—I need a few minutes to pull myself together."

"You sure?"

"Yeah, go ahead. I'll be in soon."

He grabbed his bag and gave her hair an awkward tousle before heading off. As she watched him approach the school, Portia felt a sense of peace that she had not felt for weeks. At least he would try to be there for her. To understand.

The rain had started streaming down, and suddenly she remembered something from her homework list:

Stop the Rain from Falling upon You and Yours.

Closing her eyes, she tilted her head to the sky and sang.

She sang for Felix, who could never know the glory of her voice. Who would never know how much she loved and respected him. Who couldn't see how beautiful he truly was to her.

She sang because she couldn't protect him from the heartache and the confusion, but at least she could protect him from the rain…

Max avoided Portia for the rest of that morning, seething about the way she had made such a spectacle out of herself. She had become a field of land mines that he was tired of navigating.

So why the hell was he?

When Felix had finally dragged her away that morning, Max was mercifully released from the spell of her song. He had stormed off into the men's room, where he proceeded to kick in the door to one of the stalls with such force that it immediately came off its hinges.

"Hey, Max, what gives?" It was Mr. Woods, his music teacher.

"Oh, hey, sorry. I'm just blowing off some steam. I'll fix it…" Max tried fidgeting with the door hinges but they weren't salvageable. "Well, I'll make sure it gets fixed, Mr. Woods, don't worry."

"You wanna talk about it?"

"No, I don't want to bloody well talk about it!"

The teacher took a crack at fixing the door himself, but the task proved too challenging for him, too. "It's that girl, right? That one I've seen you in the music room with? I've heard through the grapevine that she's become quite forward with the boys."

Max was surprised that his music teacher had his finger on the pulse of the social drama at RPA.

"Yeah, her name is Portia and she's like this…like this disease or something. It's like I know she likes me, but then these moods come over her where she starts throwing herself at other guys. Right in front of me! And I want to dump her. I do. But I can't. I literally cannot. I don't think I could live without her at this point."

"Probably not." The certainty with which his teacher spoke to the matter was annoying but before he could protest, "Hey, Max, why don't you try playing fire with fire?"

Max looked up, wondering at his teacher's strategy.

"What do you mean?"

"Well, have you ever noticed the upright in the far left corner of the dining hall? It's actually pretty close to where the sophomores sit."

An idea began to gel in Max's head. "Mr. Woods, I do believe you have something of the devil in you."

"You should only know, Max." The teacher shuffled the boy into the hallway. When he was alone, Proteus looked into the mirror and traced his finger along the raised arc on his blue-eyed face.

Max waited until the dining hall was filled to capacity. Bypassing his usual table without even a curt greeting, he wondered if Portia even caught the snub. At this point, he didn't care. He was on a mission.

Sitting down at the Story & Clark, he noted that the instrument was not nearly as high-end as the Steinway in the music room, but it would do well enough. A couple of quick chords confirmed it—he was on his game.

Rolling up his sleeves, the veins in his arms flexed excitedly, intuiting that they were about to get a good workout.

He banged a spoon on a glass tip jar that someone must have set on top of the piano as a joke. "Excuse me, excuse me, please." The din in the room settled down—it wasn't everyday that the students were treated to a lunchtime performance. "I don't know if all of you know me—I'm Max. I'm a sophomore here at RPA, recently transferred. Anyway, I wrote this song the other day for my girlfriend, Portia Griffin. At least, I think she's my girlfriend. But lately, not so sure, you know how it goes. Anyway, I thought I'd share it with all of you, if that's OK."

Max took the continued silence in the room as a go-ahead. "All right, well here goes…"

He did the exaggerated knuckle thing and flashed his dimples to the crowd.

> *"Without games there'd be no music,*
> *Without love there'd be no song.*
> *But, babe, the way you play your games*
> *Is to the right of wrong."*

Portia's eyes ignited with fury as Max exposed her new persona to the entire RPA student body.

> *"You think my heart is made of clay,*
> *Well, yours is made of stone.*
> *You think your notes groundbreaking,*
> *But I hear monotone.*
>
> *So check the scoreboard, Baby.*
> *I'm Home and you are Guest.*
> *I think you'll be surprised to see*
> *You're no longer the best…"*

It wasn't just the public airing that had Portia unhinged. It was the sharing of him. How dare he try to charm anyone but her? He was hers after all. Wasn't he? She was seething. But still, she had to admit, the song was damn good…

> *"Your wits so sharp, you never thought*
> *I'd prove a worthy match.*
> *Your fingers stroke me tenderly,*
> *And then go on to scratch."*

She looked around her table, expecting to gain sympathy from her friends. Instead they were blatantly ignoring her. Charlotte was engrossed in the song and Jacqueline was carelessly doodling hearts in her notebook. Luke and Lance were saying something to each other about that kid "having brass balls," and Felix just shrugged at her.

Her fury was rising.

"You want to snake your venom in,
Then be the antidote.
You wrap your arms around my neck,
then you're a noose around my throat…"

His voice was so smooth. Portia couldn't decide if she wanted to throw herself at him or cut him down entirely.

"…So you better check that scoreboard, P,
I'm Home and you are Guest.
I think you'll find after this song,
You're no longer the best…"

He finished with a flourish and bowed to the applauding crowd. When he met Portia's furious gaze, he let out a smug grin.

And it didn't take a lip reader to make out the three words he threw her way before sauntering out of the dining hall.

"Game on, Baby."

"Wow, that was some performance today—I mean Max's. Well yours, too, I guess, but…" Charlotte left the sentence unfinished as she took the seat next to Portia on the bus, something she hadn't been so quick to do since the onset of Portia's raging mood swings.

"Yeah—I guess I deserved it, though," Portia said humbly. "Right?" Her voice broke a little, a precursor to tears.

"Look, Portia. I wish I could say no. Or that he was being harsh. But you've been treating Max like shit. You've kind of been treating everyone like shit. And the thing is, I know that that's not who you are. It's like *Invasion of the Body Snatchers* or something. Do you think maybe you should go talk to someone?"

Oh, but I did. I talked to Zeus and Ares and Athena…

"You thinking Vitamin P, Charlotte? Zoloft, maybe? I think Felix is thinking the same thing. Meds aren't going to help—I promise you."

"How do you know, Portia?" Charlotte moved in a bit

closer, lowering her voice. "My mom started Prozac, and it's been working wonders—"

"With all due respect, Charlotte, my situation isn't even remotely similar to yours or your mom's. Or to anyone's, for that matter."

Charlotte looked like she might slap Portia, who did feel ridiculous claiming the lion's share of problems here. But, as ever, Charlotte extended Portia a patience that even she didn't think she deserved anymore.

"I'm not sure what your 'situation' is, Portia, because you've become so secretive." Her tone was not accusing, just curious. "I thought *I* was a good secret keeper, but you've turned it into, like, an art form…"

A silence hung in the air, Charlotte's face expectant. Portia wished she could fill the void with a plausible explanation for her behavior, but the silence remained.

"Well, anyway, Portia, even if you're acting bitchy beyond reason, I'll just convince myself that you're having really bad PMS or something. But I'm here for you—you know that, right?"

Portia nodded, afraid that if she spoke she would end up bawling.

"Anyway," Charlotte continued, relieved to have her little awkward speech out of the way, "we all have our crosses to bear, right? Like this stupid Newark thing." A flash of pride danced across her face.

"What are you talking about? What Newark thing?" Portia was happy to divert the topic.

With a slight blush, Charlotte admitted, "Well, I, um, was awarded this, like, state prize for that poem I read to you the other night." She clearly still had no recollection of her encounter with Portia in the stacks bathroom the following day. "And there's a poetry slam in Newark in a couple of weeks, and I'm supposed to read it out loud to like a million people."

Portia was bursting with pride for her friend, astounded by Charlotte's courage, her honesty. It was so inspiring to see Charlotte muddle her way through the mess of her life. "That's amazing! Why didn't you tell me?"

"I didn't tell anyone. I'm too scared. I don't know how I'm going to get through it."

"Oh, I think you'll do just fine, Charlotte. In fact, I'm one hundred percent sure you will." Portia gave Charlotte's hand a quick squeeze along with a reassuring smile.

She did trust that Charlotte had it in her to kick some ass at the poetry slam. But she would sure as hell be there just in case. Portia looked out the window as the bus plodded along, mentally patting herself on the back for achieving voice throwing in under three generations.

Chapter 28

Hermes arched his back, executing the perfect cat pose, a favorite of Leucosia's yoga asanas. She scratched the silken cat under his chin, allowing him to settle his flat face on her shoulder. She could feel the vibration of his purring and marveled to herself how easy it was to please a feline.

Opening her MacBook, the Goddess couldn't help but smile when she remembered first suggesting to Zeus that they get Wi-Fi at Mount Olympus. The assembled deities had looked at her like she was trying to stage some kind of technological coup. She was persistent, though, bringing her laptop with her one day and showing them all how easy it was to navigate this thing called the Internet. Within weeks, her fellow immortals had e-mail addresses and were setting up websites, birthing an entire divine virtual underworld.

Scrolling through her e-mails, she tried losing herself in the diesel engine that was Hermes's special language, but she just couldn't relax. In fact, Leucosia couldn't remember the last time she had actually experienced a true moment of relaxation.

Her sisters' control over Portia was growing stronger by the minute. And the sudden regressions in her own speech were becoming more frequent, a sure indicator that Proteus was indeed only a stone's throw away. From the way Portia described Max's musical tongue lashing of her, Leucosia suspected that the mischievous shape-shifter was no doubt encouraging Max's boldness. Surely in all their time together, Ligeia would have explained to Proteus that the more a mortal tries to resist a Siren, the stronger her desire to destroy him will become.

Now that Max was showing Portia some true gumption, Leucosia worried that the young Siren's desires would get the best of her sooner rather than later. And where was that gumption coming from? She wondered at Max's ability to stand up to Portia, even if Proteus was egging him on. The last time she had seen a mortal show true signs of resistance was with her dear Nereus. Taking comfort in the similarity between Max and Nereus, Leucosia was at least assured that her charge had fallen for a true gentleman.

Hermes rolled over for a tummy tickle. He and Leucosia danced their special dance, her scratching his tummy, him deigning to lift all fours into the air with the haughtiness that only a cat can possess. Scrolling through her e-mails, she was intrigued to find one from Dionysus, who enjoyed the apt e-mail address, *Dionysus@oenophile.god*.

> *"Dearest Leucosia,*
>
> *I hope that this electronical mail finds you in good tidings. I must admit that often do I venture off into this wonderful interweb. Even I have learned a thing or two from winenthusiast.com. I dare say that the Napa Valley has been blessed with the most delectable grapes…"*

Leucosia adored Dionysus but couldn't help feeling impatient as she read through his verbose description of his latest Cabernet discovery and the new set of stemless wine glasses, which were gifted to him by Ares. About two paragraphs into the e-mail, the Siren was finally stunned back into reality.

> *"But as you know, Leucosia, my domain reaches beyond only the hedonistic. I know we often avoid the topic of Madness, as your sisters were so obviously consumed by the worst kind. But something has come to my attention, which could have been procured by chance but also could be more than just a coincidence.*
>
> *A strange disappearance occurred recently at the Havenhurst Institute. A nurse who for many years did work at the Institute, attending to those encumbered by all forms of madness, did recently vanish. She was replaced instantly by a perfect candidate who was at the ready. You might dismiss this as idle news, but is it not intriguing that one of the patients of this nurse is none other than the father of Max Hunter?"*

Leucosia went stiff at the sight of Max's name.

> *"Am I correct in bringing this matter to your attention?*
> *Please advise if you'd like me to delve further.*
> *Ever yours,*
> *Dionysus"*

Dionysus's words further enervated the exhausted Leucosia. How far did this plot stretch? Were her sisters preying not only on the innocent Max Hunter but on his poor ailing father as well?

She considered her options, but her overworked mind couldn't see any of them through to the end. The thought of launching a whole new investigation was altogether paralyzing.

> *"Dear Dionysus,*
> *Ever am I grateful for your e-mail, which I do consider to be of the utmost importance. I beg you, as you are privy to the world of those who have been stricken by madness, would you pursue this matter?*
> *Indeed, if my sisters and Proteus are trying to weave a web that extends far past the confines of Ridgewood, I must know of it.*
> *Many thanks and ever yours,*
> *Leucosia"*

Within five minutes, she received a surprisingly brief response from the great God.

> *"Dearest Leucosia,*
> *NP.*
> *Dion"*

She admired his brevity of speech and wondered just how much time he had actually been spending on the "interweb" learning about pop culture and the like. She felt a relief that he would be looking into the matter for her, alleviating her of yet another burden.

What she never suspected was that Dionysus had sampled a magnum of his new favorite Cabernet before responding to her e-mail, which he then deleted, never to be remembered again...

Chapter 29

Jonah and Ryan were fighting at top volume over who was going to pick out the one bedtime story promised to them by their big cousin. Of all the nights for his aunt and uncle to go out. Max wasn't sure he was going to make it through this babysitting session without losing his mind.

The day with Portia had been particularly harrowing. Every time he tried to engage her in conversation, she would throw a spiteful laugh his way and saunter off. And despite all of his attempts to think about something, anything else, he couldn't process a single thought that was not monopolized by her.

"I have an idea," he raised his voice above the screaming of the boys. "I think *Percy Jackson and the Lightning Thief* is On Demand. How 'bout we watch that and I'll go make us some popcorn with, like, a sickening amount of butter?"

The boys looked at each other, not believing their luck.

"And Buncha Crunch?" they practically asked in unison.

"Don't push it, boys." Max navigated the buttons on the remote and bought the movie, settling his cousins into their parents' bed.

When he got downstairs, he took out his aunt's biggest pot and drizzled its bottom with peanut oil. His mom had always opted to make popcorn this way, insisting that it tasted better from a pot than from a microwave. He melted some butter over it, allowing the smell to envelop him and bring him back in time.

Smells were often the trigger for his memories of her. An unexpected whiff of the Coco Chanel she always wore. The smell of hazelnut coffee freshly brewed (milk, no sugar). The mouthwatering aroma of General Tso's chicken from the Chinese takeout.

When he got back upstairs, the boys were contentedly snuggled in their parents' bed, engrossed in the mythological thriller. Max handed them the bowl of popcorn, along with a careful warning not to make a mess. They immediately shushed him, afraid of missing a single critical moment. Envying their ability to get lost in the land of make-believe, Max remembered when names like Poseidon and Zeus used to intrigue him, too. As a child he had loved all of that mythological stuff and was even enjoying *The Odyssey* as an adolescent. But it all just seemed so removed from the realities of his life right now.

And what exactly were the realities of his life right now?

He plopped down on the chaise to ponder the question. He had a girlfriend. Well, at least that's how he liked to think of Portia, who had been avoiding him ever since he had taken a chance by singing to her in the dining hall. At this point, he had grown accustomed to her blowing hot and cold. But lately she was just blowing cold.

And he missed the heat.

Over and over again he had wracked his brain, trying to figure out why she was toying with him.

When he had first met her, he would never have pegged Portia as a diva. In fact, in the beginning, he had been drawn to her for what he thought was a rare maturity. Either because of, or in spite of, her handicap, voiceless Portia had seemed so disinterested in typical high school antics and drama.

Why couldn't he just move on? He knew he wasn't a bad-looking guy. Plenty of girls had shown interest in him. Even his father's new nurse, Khloe, who was undeniably beautiful, albeit maybe a little old for him, had flirted with him the last time he was in New York. But even then, all he could talk about was Portia. Though she didn't seem to mind hearing all about it.

Khloe had lent him a sympathetic ear in the hospital cafeteria, encouraging him to tell her anything and everything about his troubled girlfriend relationship. She listened attentively while he poured out detail after agonizing detail about Portia's mood swings, her violent behavior, and her constant taunting of him. At the end of the conversation, she gave him a pep talk, reminding him to show some gumption. Her words had really imbued him with confidence, her voice soothing his worries.

He had felt so much better after their exchange, stronger and ready to face Portia and her moods. But by the time he had gotten back to Ridgewood, he was checking his phone every five seconds to see if she had texted him.

Jonah and Ryan were arguing with each other about who would be a greater success at Camp Half Blood.

"What do you think, Max?" Ryan looked up at his cousin beseechingly. "Me or Jonah at Half Blood?"

Max was no fool. He knew that the only diplomatic response was to declare a draw.

"I think you'd both make great demigods, guys."

"That's lame, Max." Jonah was stuffing another fistful of popcorn into his mouth. "Hey, though, you know who would make the best demigod of all?"

Max couldn't wait to hear this one. He was sure that his little cousins were about to pay him some major homage.

"Portia!"

He was completely startled by the sudden mention of her name.

"What makes you think that, Jonah?"

"Because, Max, Portia can do magic."

Max stared at his little cousin in amazement. Had he been so obvious in his obsession with Portia that even Ryan and Jonah had caught the bug?

"Yes, little dude, she certainly can…"

He flipped open his laptop and once again tried inviting the elusive Portia Griffin in for an iChat.

As the numbness settled upon him, Alan Hunter glanced bleary-eyed at the IV sending the potent drug through his veins. Reclining deeply into the La-Z-Boy, he couldn't recall his psych meds ever being this strong.

The redheaded nurse took his vitals and scrawled a few

notes into his chart.

"So how are we today, Mr. Hunter?" she asked, her voice enveloping him like a silk stocking.

"Better. Now that she was here. Much better." His tongue felt thick and sluggish as he formed his lazy lips around the words.

She sat down on the edge of his bed. "Who are you talking about, Mr. Hunter?"

"Norah. She was here just a few minutes ago."

The nurse let out a huff. "How many times are we going to go through this, Mr. Hunter? She wasn't here. There is absolutely no way your wife could have been here."

"Why do you keep saying that? How do you know?"

"Because I know. And one day you will, too."

She started to sound distant as the effect of the drugs grew stronger.

"Would you like me to continue reading to you?" she questioned.

"I'm telling you, she was sitting right where you are now. She was asking me all about Max, wondering when he was coming in next. She told me that I should encourage him to keep going out with his girlfriend—I think her name is Portia."

Suddenly he had the nurse's full attention. She put down the worn-out copy of *The Odyssey* that she had been reading to him and moved a little closer.

"She told you about Portia?"

Alan offered a slow nod.

"What else did she tell you about her?"

"She said that Max's girlfriend is giving him a hard time, but that he should stick with her because it will all be worth it in the end."

The nurse plugged him for more information, slowing down the drugs, so that he'd be lucid enough to tell her everything.

"Before she left, she said she didn't know when she'd get to see me again, but that it would all be over soon. What did Norah mean 'it would all be over soon'?" His voice grew confused and panicked. "Why can't she stay? Why the hell can't she just stay?!"

His words were garbled, his voice stricken with grief.

Khloe gleaned a few more details about these mysterious visits from him before speeding up the drugs again, calming his tears.

And then, just in case the drugs weren't enough, **Erase a Memory**...

Portia was tired. Really tired.

The opposing forces within her body were battling it out on a moment-to-moment basis. And, as the day of the great attack against Proteus and the sisters neared, she couldn't help but feel that the evil force was winning out.

Her dreams were perhaps the most inviting forum for her unstable emotions. Anytime she drifted off, her mind was poisoned with twisted images of her perverse self, taunting groups of boys and men, lifting them up into her hands and crushing their bones. While sleep was still upon her, she felt invigorated by the pain she was inflicting. But when she awoke, she was flooded with guilt and tried consoling herself with the knowledge that the evil was way beyond her control. In the end, though, that realization proved more terrifying than comforting.

Worse yet were the destructive thoughts that were a constant barrage while she was awake. What might start out as an innocent conversation with an unsuspecting male classmate had Portia fantasizing within seconds about what it would feel like to bring the boy to his knees and have him beg for his life to be spared. Though cognitively she knew that she had to put the kibosh on these obscene thoughts, her savage instincts were slowly getting the best of her.

She considered ditching school entirely, but her mom and dad would never tolerate truancy. She would have to suffer through it, hoping beyond all hope that she would not be the cause of irreparable destruction.

These were the thoughts preoccupying her when she found Max waiting at her locker on a Wednesday morning.

"Hey. I'm not going to be able to study French tonight—I have to go back to New York after school today. I got a call from my dad's nurse yesterday saying that he was really agitated."

Mock him. Laugh at him! Portia tried desperately to ignore the evil voices in her head. She had still not figured out a way to silence them.

"What do you think set him off?" she managed.

"I don't know. She said she was in the middle of reading to him—funny, she likes to read him *The Odyssey*—and that all of a sudden he just started 'flipping out.' Strange choice of words, actually, for a professional, but she's young, I guess."

Portia could feel her internal tug-of-war gaining momentum. She tried to stay focused.

"Do you want me to go with you?" She didn't even think about it before the words came tumbling out of her mouth.

Max was shocked by the offer. Niceties were so rarely offered by her lately.

"Thanks, but I think my dad would be embarrassed for anyone to meet him this way. Besides I need someone to take good notes for me while I'm gone."

Why don't you tell him how hopeless his situation is? Explain to him that his father would be better off dead. Portia's mouth was watering as the voice persisted. Her only hope of not ruining the moment was to get away. Fast.

"When will you be back?" she gushed quickly.

"It depends, I guess." He reached out and allowed the back of his hand to graze her cheek. "I'm hoping I'll only have to be gone a day. I guess I'll have to gauge the situation once I get there."

A grotesque image of Max's bloodied, lifeless body suddenly flashed in her mind. She tried blinking it away, but she could smell his blood, taste it even.

With a quick peck on his cheek, she started to make a hasty exit. "Well, text me—"

"Whoa, where are you going?" his hand gripped her arm.

When Portia turned back to him, there was nothing at all friendly about her smile.

She yanked her arm out of his grip, ignoring the shock on his face. "You think you can control me? Tell me where and when to go? You got it backward, Max. I control you."

She moved in closer to him and rather than telling her to go screw herself, Max reached his hand around her waist and pulled her in even closer.

"Poor Max. See what you'll be missing while you're in New York?" she purred as his hands traveled up the smoothness of her legs. "Go tend to your father. Go see what good you can do. But know this: getting over a woman you have loved is impossible—"

A grip from behind interrupted Portia. She turned around to see Felix, staring at her wide-eyed.

"You need to come with me now," Felix signed.

To Max he said, "And you—get your hands off her. Can't you see she's not right? She's—um—confused…"

The spell broken, Max flushed with anger. "Yeah? Well, we're all bloody confused." He gave Felix a shove to the chest. "You wanna stick around to help through her 'confusion,' go ahead. I'm out. No more games for me. I've got enough shit to deal with."

Felix ignored the shove. He actually felt bad for the guy. He had heard through the grapevine what a hard time Max was having with his father. The last thing he needed was to be at the mercy of some ruthless bitch whose favorite game was "How far can I push Max Hunter before he attempts to rape me?"

"You're right, and you should go take care of all that other stuff. Seriously, dude, go…"

To everyone's horror, most of all her own, Portia started laughing at all the drama.

"Shut up, Portia." Felix admonished her. He turned back to Max. "Get out of here, Max. Go. Now!"

Max started backing away, his eyes holding a curious blend of pride and defeat.

Felix pushed Portia in the direction of Leucosia's office, ignoring the light that was now flashing on the school bell.

It was one of those rare moments when he was grateful

that he was deaf. He couldn't have stomached the laughter that continued to flow out of Portia's mouth.

"I never saw anything like it," Felix was speaking and signing to Leucosia, a shell-shocked Portia sitting upright on the gurney, staring off into space. "He was practically ripping her skirt off—right there in the hallway!"

Leucosia took a moment to let Felix's story settle in. She found herself thinking out loud, "There's something about that Hunter boy. Something that ties him to her so viscerally, even after everything she has put him through."

"Yeah, the guy's in love with her," Felix pointed out.

"With all due respect," ventured Leucosia, "so are you, Felix."

Portia was still staring off into space, oblivious to the conversation.

"Maybe I am," Felix defended himself. "Maybe that's why I haven't totally checked out yet. I mean, I must be crazy to even try to buy into all the insane stuff that Portia has said to me. I mean, Ms. Leucosia, she actually thinks that she, that you both are Sirens. Why aren't you getting her any help? Shouldn't you be telling her parents? They're a close family—they'll get her help."

Leucosia held his eyes unflinchingly.

"I mean, don't you think she needs help?"

"She does need help, Felix. But not the kind you think." As she spoke the words to him, she felt the same frustration that Portia described at not being able to convince him of things with her voice alone. But then again, she had no right to expect the poor boy to overcome his deafness.

How could she convince him? She was out of options. She couldn't just call in a random student to vocally manipulate, as she had promised Zeus that she would not involve any more innocent mortals in this obscene turning of events. And sprouting her wings right now would probably destroy everything in her tiny office. She would have to rely on some good old-fashioned wisdom.

"Felix, I have watched you and Portia grow together for years," she signed and spoke aloud. "I have rarely seen, especially between a boy and a girl, such a complete and honest friendship. Can't you just focus on that right now? What you have had all these years? Let it carry you, at least for a while. I beg of you."

"You 'beg of me'? Sounds like you've bought into the whole story, too, Ms. Leucosia."

"Every story has many sides, Felix. Let's just say that I'm coming at it from a different angle than you."

"Sides, angles, whatever. I'll do the best I can, but I'm coming at it from the 'normal' angle—"

"No, Felix. Like I said before, the 'love' angle. That's your angle." She detected a note of defeat wash over his face and knew that she had driven home her point, despite not being able to manipulate him with her voice.

And with that, she handed him a note and sent him back to class.

He accepted the exit opportunity as willingly as Leucosia's declaration that he was indeed in love with Portia Griffin.

Portia dozed lightly, her thoughts and dreams a combination of Felix and Leucosia's voices, which she could hear on the periphery. But there was something else. Something Max had said before kept muscling its way into her thoughts, preventing her from falling into the deep sleep that she so desperately craved.

…*Funny, she likes to read him* The Odyssey…

And then in a flash it gelled. Her lids flew open and she bolted upright.

"Proteus has been visiting Max's father."

It came out slightly mumbled, and Leucosia asked her to repeat herself.

"PROTEUS HAS BEEN VISITING MAX'S FATHER!"

"What? How do you know?" Leucosia asked.

But Portia didn't even hear her. "That's why he keeps

thinking that his wife has been there. He's been transforming himself into Norah Hunter and visiting him. Oh my God. Everyone thinks he's hallucinating. They're pumping him full of drugs. We have to tell Max. His father's not crazy. We have to tell him!"

"Portia, please calm down," Leucosia urged.

"Leucosia, I'm sure of it! But why? Why would Proteus be visiting Max's father?"

Portia stared at Leucosia, awaiting the wise response her mentor would surely have at the ready.

"I e-mailed Dionysus. He was supposed to get back to me. He never did."

"Well, e-mail him again, Leucosia. This isn't a joke."

Leucosia wasn't smiling. "No, it isn't. I'm afraid that this isn't the first time Dionysus has let his propensity for alcohol interfere with his Godly responsibilities. I swear that God really does need an intervention."

"Leucosia, please, stay focused…"

"Yes, sorry. Portia, you must promise me that you won't tell Max anything. It's enough that Felix already knows. I have an idea of how to find out what is going on over at Havenhurst. In the meantime, please excuse me so that I can write to Dionysus to tell him how utterly disappointed I am in him. Perhaps I'll send him a link to the twelve steps…"

Chapter 30

The blood in Athena's veins was threatening to boil over. She still could not believe what Leucosia had revealed to her about Tiresias.

Pitied? Pitied?

When the now-dead prophet had happened upon her in the river, he had not been satisfied with a mere glimpse of her naked form. He had actually thrust himself upon her, wanting to have his way with her. Had it not been for the chance arrival of Aphrodite to tell her that they were being summoned by Zeus, Tiresias surely would have stolen Athena's virtue. The wise Goddess had been so ashamed by the scandalous event that she had never spoken of it to anyone.

Instead she had blinded him.

Over the years, Tiresias had come begging for her forgiveness, claiming that he had gone mad at the sight of her naked beauty. Even if she would have taken pity on him, though, the blindness was irreversible, as often such curses are.

"You should be thankful that ever are you able to still see the future, Tiresias…" and with that she had thought that Tiresias's name would never be spoken to her again.

But now Leucosia had requested that she visit the prophet in Hades, begging a vision that would explain Proteus's intentions.

If it weren't for the fact that she loved her friend Leucosia as a sister, she would have flat out refused. Instead she was now burning a mixture of Boca burgers and soy chicken, hoping that the Gods of Hades would accept the Vegan sacrifice—slaughtering a sheep was so five centuries ago—and allow her to conjure Tiresias's spirit.

"Who summons me so with a sacrifice so foreign that all

who inhabit the underworld are guessing at its origin?"

"I see you are still blind, Tiresias. But I suppose that has no bearing on your sense of smell. It is I, Athena—"

"Athena?" His spirit was fuzzy, fluid. "Why have you come? Have you thus figured a way to restore my vision, though I am now but a mere spirit?"

Athena marveled at how foolish Tiresias was. "I have told you, Tiresias, there is nothing I can do to bring back your sight. I have come instead to seek a favor—"

The spirit of the God swirled around her. "A favor? Why should I grant you a favor after the way you have ruined me?"

She had been anticipating this question. "Because Tiresias, until now I have never told another God or mortal of the way you attacked me those many years ago. If you do not cooperate with me now, I will surely tell all who will listen. I will tarnish your name forever and no longer will the Gods of Hades pity your blind soul. They will banish you to Tartarus forever."

The spirit stilled his motion. "All right, Athena. You have my ear. What is it you would like to know?"

Chapter 31

As she continued to heave into the toilet, all Portia could think of was how thankful she was to have her own bathroom. The last thing she needed was for her parents to start insisting that she go to the doctor. She herself was shocked at the physical manifestations of her internal battle. Frequent dizzy spells, fevers, chills, and vomiting—all symptoms of the malignant disease that was metastasizing inside of her at record speed.

The symptoms had definitely grown worse after her last conversation with Leucosia.

"So Athena basically found out that Proteus has indeed been visiting Alan Hunter. His purpose in doing so is to ensure that the father will convince his son to keep on dating you, despite whatever differences you may be having. The last thing they want is for Max to suddenly decide he's had it with you—especially now that they've come so far. You have to admire the cunning of the shape-shifter, Portia."

"Admire? I don't have to admire shit, Leucosia. Sorry—the curse word was them, not me; this voice throwing is a nightmare. We have to tell Max—"

Leucosia infused her voice with authority—she still had a few years up on Portia, and she needed her charge to know that.

"Portia, you will not tell Max anything. We are days away from our battle against Proteus. When we destroy him, this business with Alan Hunter will stop, and it will be as if it never happened. You will not tell Max, Portia."

After a prolonged silence, Portia looked back in defeat.

"So this is what it feels like, huh? When I tell people what to do or, in this case, what not to do, and they have no choice but to listen? I don't like it, Leucosia. But I'm too sick to fight…"

And so she had let it go for the moment. But repressing the secret that Max's father was not hallucinatory had only made her condition worse.

She wished she could just stay at home tethered to her bed, resisting all the malevolent temptations that were calling to her. That fear of a doctor unearthing her secret, though, forced her to keep going to school.

Leucosia's office had become a safe haven for Portia, and somehow she had trained herself to head straight there when she felt the evil coming. Or, if Felix was around, which he was quite often, he would guide Portia to the nurse's office at the first sign of her "unusual" behavior.

Felix persisted in his half-hearted pursuit of Gabrielle Parker, which had prompted even more inexcusable behavior from Portia's evil self.

"Gabrielle, do you really think you're a worthy competitor for me? Do you really think you are as good for him as I am?" She had cornered the innocent girl in the gym locker room, imbuing her voice with the most menacing tone she could muster. Gabrielle had grabbed her stuff and bolted.

When Portia thought back to the exchange, she was further sickened by the idea that she wasn't actually sure if that was the sisters' voice or her own. As she tried to separate out her own thoughts from the ones that were being hurled into her mind, that was the only one whose source remained a mystery.

Am I actually jealous of that brainless cheerleader? She has nothing up on me...

Portia knew that as the days wore on, her physical beauty was intensifying. The boys were relentless in their pursuit of her, and the girls had started avoiding her at every cost. She didn't blame them. She had become that stereotypical character, usually reserved for the set of *Pretty Little Liars*, not the halls of RPA.

Yet there were moments when the disdain of her female classmates actually nurtured the seeds within her. She thrived on their jealousy and the cold looks that even Charlotte and Jacqueline had begun to throw her way.

And then there was Max.

When she thought of how she had been treating him, she had moments of deep shame, which were then quickly overtaken by a sexual desire that she thought was only reserved for books about men who were fifty shades of something or other.

Portia had always been so quick to judge people who developed addictions. Whatever their poison—drugs, alcohol, sex—she had trouble sympathizing with those who opted for a life of debauchery. But now, as every ounce of her tingled at the thought of Max—seducing him, toying with him, and ultimately destroying him—she saw how easy it could be to fall prey to an addiction.

She retched into the toilet again as an image of Max with a deep red gash in his throat popped into her mind. She wondered if the vomiting was her way of trying to expel the thoughts, the forces from her weary body. But no matter how much she retched, she was still consumed.

Distracted by the vomiting, she didn't even hear her mother knock on her door. She heaved into the toilet again and collapsed back onto floor, her body wracked with spasms.

"Portia, oh my God, what's the matter?"

Through her watery eyes she made out Helena's worried face leaning over her, the back of her hand swiping her forehead to feel for a fever.

"It's nothing, Mom." But her words were croaky and breathless.

"That's it. I'm calling Dr. Loring and making an appointment for you first thing in the morning. Do you think you can even hold out that long?"

Portia opened her mouth to try to placate her mother, but her gag reflex kicked in and once again she was hunched over the toilet.

"Oh, baby. What's going on with you?" Helena was wringing out a washcloth and mopping Portia's brow. Admittedly her mother's touch felt so welcome. She was tired of fighting this battle all on her own and would have loved nothing more than to surrender herself to some much-needed TLC.

Easing her into bed, Helena tucked her daughter in securely, adding a second blanket. Her words were soothing as Portia let go of some of the tension that had been filling her every nerve.

"I'm gonna go call Daddy and tell him that he needs to cut his trip short."

"No, Mom—don't." She was barely able to instill that Siren edge into her words, her powers weakening by the minute. But she couldn't let Helena ask her father to come back now. She had been so relieved when her dad had announced that he was scouting out some new properties out West and would have to be away for a few weeks. Things had been so uncomfortable with Joshua lately anyway. Portia felt bad for him, for any father who had to contend with the evolution of 'Daddy's Little Girl' into 'No Longer Daddy's Anything.' Portia wondered if his sudden interest in properties out West might even have been sparked by her intolerable adolescence.

Whatever the case, the less she had to involve her parents the better.

"Ok, fine," Helena was wringing out a washcloth with water and alcohol, "but only if you promise you'll go to the doctor tomorrow and," she added, mopping Portia's brow with the cool cloth, "I'm sleeping on your futon tonight."

Portia started to protest, but her strength had ebbed away entirely.

"You might want to call or iChat or whatever it is you do with Felix or Charlotte and tell them you won't be in in the morning."

Helena dimmed Portia's light and hurried out of the room to get her cell phone.

With a surge of panic, Portia signed on to iChat and was relieved when Leucosia accepted the chat right away.

"Oh, dear God, Portia, you look terrible! Well, I mean, you look beautiful, but terrible nonetheless. What's going on?"

"I'm sick, Leucosia. This thing has literally been making me sick. I was trying to hide it from my mother, but she just walked in on me vomiting, and now she's insisting on taking me to the doctor tomorrow. What am I gonna do? I don't know if I'll have the power to talk my way out of things—do you understand? My powers are slipping as I become more…more infested…"

Portia would have cried, but she was so devoid of energy that even the shedding of tears seemed an overwhelming prospect.

"It's going to be OK, Portia," Leucosia continued to stroke Hermes calmly, a pensive look on her flawless face.

"Leucosia, did you hear me? The jig is up! Tomorrow I'm probably going to be totally busted. They're gonna see that I am some kind of superhuman freak, and I won't be able to, like, erase the doctor's memory with my voice because my voice is starting to crap out on me. There's nothing 'OK' about this whole situation!"

"Portia, please calm down. It's all going to be all right. I'll figure something out. Right now I just need you to get some rest. If you strain yourself like this, then of course your powers are going to be compromised. You must remember—you are and always will be a powerful Siren." Leucosia was doing the 'you-have-no-choice-but-to–believe-what-I'm-telling-you' thing, and Portia welcomed every word like a dose from a morphine drip. "We have only three days until we take down my sisters and Proteus, and I need you to be in top form. Do you understand, Portia? So much of this is riding on you."

Portia could feel the bile rising in her throat again as Leucosia alluded to her upcoming responsibilities. She couldn't handle having anything "riding" on her right now.

"What do you mean, Leucosia? I thought this was a group effort. I thought Ares was the main player here."

"Listen to me, dear." She infused her velvety voice with a further dose of calm. "Ares wrote to me the other day to explain that the only way to take down a shape-shifter is to paralyze him first."

Portia swatted away the beads of sweat that were stinging her eyes. "Yeah? And how exactly is that supposed to happen?"

"You will make it happen, Portia."

Portia began laughing, which quickly segued into another round of vomiting. Luckily Helena had placed a garbage can next to her bed.

"Oh dear," Leucosia said squeamishly, "that does indeed look bad. I am so sorry for you, dearest Portia. You must remember, though, that there is nothing as powerful as the voice of the virginal Siren. The power is within you to paralyze Proteus—to paralyze anyone."

Portia stared blankly at the screen. What could she even say? Right now there was nothing within her but bile.

"We will make it through this, Portia," Leucosia continued. "Please do not despair. Now I must go and make some arrangements. Listen, I want you to promise me that after we sign off you are going to lock away your worries and get some sleep. If your mother wants to take care of you for a night, let her—you deserve it. You need to get well, Portia. OK?"

Portia had already begun to drift off.

The last thing she remembered was Helena shutting her laptop off before she was carried off into her demon-infested sleep.

Chapter 32

The familiar surroundings of Dr. Loring's waiting room would normally have put Portia at ease. The pediatrician had been treating her since she was a baby. He still had the same old-fashioned black and white View-Master, which showed a tattered film as the crank was manually turned. Portia had never tired of watching the silent movie of the boy having a pie-in-face fight with his friends.

Back then a visit to Dr. Loring's office meant fleshing out a new theory about her silence. Now they would be fleshing out a theory to explain her voice.

Portia looked over at a young brother and sister taking turns with the View-Master. As one peered into the window of the aged copper machine, the other turned the crank to keep the movie going. She envied the siblings their normal life.

"Portia Griffin." Gladys called her name, a thick file in hand.

Portia reached out and gave her mom's hand a quick squeeze. She had already told her at home that she was too old for Helena to come into the exam room.

"Is it true?" Gladys asked as they walked toward the exam room, "Um, true that you can talk now?"

"It sure is," Portia offered. Her tone made it clear that further questions were not welcome.

The nurse smiled at her as she ushered her into the small room "That's wonderful, Portia. Really wonderful."

When she sat down on the exam table, Portia tried to keep her panic at bay. She was taking calming breaths and trying to conjure peaceful images until out of nowhere an all-too-familiar prickle attacked her limbs.

Holy shit, he's here. They're here.

She got up and opened the door, ready to bolt, and ran right into the solid figure of Dr. Loring entering the room.

"Whoa, Portia, where are you headed?" The doctor's heavy jowls shook when he spoke.

"Um, I thought I was going to puke again."

Dr. Loring led her back to the exam table. "Well, those certainly wouldn't have been the first words I would have chosen to hear with your new voice, but I have to say it is wonderful to hear you at all."

Despite his bulldoggish looks, there was something reassuring about the pediatrician, and Portia tried to relax a bit, though the prickle persisted.

"So what's ailing you today?" he asked as he gently felt the glands in her throat.

Ailing?

"Well, my mom kind of forced me to come." She paused briefly, measuring the force with which she spoke her words. "I've had some kind of, like, virus the past few days."

"Oh, yeah? What kind of virus?"

Portia tried to make light of her symptoms.

"Well, I've had an upset stomach. Maybe some chills off and on."

And definitely a prickling right now. Where are you, Proteus?

The doctor expertly tapped on her back and took out his otoscope. Portia felt a knot in her stomach at the sight of the instrument.

"Do you think your symptoms could have been brought on by nerves?" the doctor asked, shining the light into her ears. He stopped short in front of Portia, waiting for her response.

"What do you mean?" She was distracted by the prickling, her eyes darting everywhere to find the elusive shape-shifter.

"Well, it's not every teenager that is scheduled to go up against an evil God and his spiritual sidekicks."

She almost fell off the gurney.

"How did you know? Who are you?" The words came gushing out, a mixture of shock and fear.

Suddenly the husky build of the doctor melted before her

very eyes and transformed into the delicate frame of a woman. Portia's immediate instinct was to run. And then she recognized the face of the deity before her.

"Athena?"

"Yes, Portia. It is I, Athena. Did you not know that I, too, can alter my shape?"

Portia thought back to when Athena had stood in for Mr. Morrison in class. "Actually, I did know that—I just forgot. What are you doing here?"

Athena reached out a tentative hand toward Portia. "You look weary, my child."

Her words released a floodgate of tears. Portia cried hard, the silver tears streaming down her face as she thought about just how weary she actually was.

Athena comforted her, offering her soothing words, assuring her that everything would be OK. When the young Siren's tears were spent, Athena waited patiently for the many questions she was sure Portia would have.

"Where is Dr. Loring?" came the first inquiry.

The Goddess crossed the room to a closet door, which she opened to reveal the slumped form of Dr. Loring sleeping soundly.

"What is it you kids say? I, um, slipped the good doctor a mickey. Some lotus flower petals will erase any memory he might have of meeting me." Athena bent over and tried to straighten out the doctor's compressed spine. "Portia, Leucosia called upon me yesterday because she knows that I do care for her greatly, which means I care for you as well."

"Thanks, Athena. And thank you for helping out with that whole Tiresias thing. I'm sure that couldn't have been fun for you."

"Let us not speak of it." A faint blush spread through her milky cheeks. "I know, of course, that a madness has been consuming you and is stretching further and further out of your control. Leucosia thought I might be able to offer you a—um— prep talk?"

"Pep talk," Portia corrected.

"Yes, a pep talk. She fears that because you have been unwell, you have not been able to tackle some of the more challenging assignments given to you by the Gods."

"Like what, Athena? What is possibly going to help me stand up to Proteus and the sisters? Making a flower grow? Stopping the rain? It's pointless—it's all pointless!"

Athena sat down. "Portia, there was one assignment on the list—**Go Beyond Your Voice**. Did you get to that one yet?"

Portia was at the end of her rope. "No, Athena, in between sparring with a shape-shifter in the mirror, trying to control the vile words that the sisters are throwing through my mouth, and vomiting up the contents of my stomach, I haven't actually been able to get to that one yet. Go beyond my voice? Hell, I'm not anywhere near my voice, let alone ready to go beyond it."

"Portia—"

But Portia was only getting started.

"Go beyond my voice? Do you realize that I might die in the next few days? Or worse, kill someone? Kill Max? What will my parents do? My friends?"

She got up and started pacing around the small room. "Look, Athena, I'm sure Leucosia has explained to you just how sick I've been these past few days, these past few weeks. I want to be strong for you, I do. I just don't know if it's in me. And I don't even know what exactly 'it' is. I mean, what is it exactly that I am bringing to this battle that is so incredibly valuable?"

Dr. Loring let out a snort from the closet.

"Portia, listen to me. I know you have suffered much pain since discovering that you are a Goddess. But you must also think of the powers you have acquired. Think of the way you put an end to Harold Trotter's abuse. The way you mesmerized Max's little cousins—"

"Jeez—is there anything you guys don't know about?"

Athena sat Portia down again, trying to soothe her like she did that day on the mountaintop. "Let's get back to the assignments for a moment. Tell me what you have had success with."

Portia told Athena about erasing Max's memory, sending her parents into an amorous frenzy, and stopping the rain from falling on Felix. When she mentioned the voice throwing, Athena was visibly impressed.

"Oh—and then there was the R-E-S-P-E-C-T performance—".

"Yes," Athena smiled, "Dionysus is a huge Aretha fan."

"I figured," Portia was starting to relax a little bit. "Last week I attempted to **Control the Flow of Water** by singing over the bathtub. But I had already added bubble bath, so I couldn't really tell if the water was following my voice. I have to be honest, Athena, when I saw that last line on the list, **Go Beyond Your Voice**, I kind of dismissed it. I thought that it was like saying 'You go girl!'—I never attempted it. I don't even know what it means."

Athena placed a comforting hand on Portia's shoulder.

"Portia, if I could explain it to you, even achieve it for you, I would. But going beyond your voice requires you to search deep within yourself. You have the powers to defeat your demons, Portia—you just need to believe that you do."

Portia was about to launch into a million more questions when Athena pulled a flower from the pocket of her lab coat and began gently plucking the velvety petals into a mortar that rested on the doctor's counter. She took the pestle and slowly began crushing the petals, turning them into a paste.

"Portia, our meeting must end now, for I do not wish to worry your mother. You must believe me when I tell you that you have barely just scratched the surface of your powers."

Before Portia could say another word, Athena morphed back into the ruddy Dr. Loring. She poked her head out the door and called out for Gladys.

"Please tell Mrs. Griffin that it is just a mild flu, and that with some rest it should go away in a day or two."

When she closed the door again, she said, "OK, off you go, Portia. May you find only favor in the eyes of the Gods."

A dumbfounded Portia rose up and began making her way out of the exam room. As she did, she saw Athena gently feeding the mashed up lotus flowers into Dr. Loring's sleeping lips.

Chapter 33

Portia stood outside Max's door. She could hear him alternate between tapping on and strumming his guitar. She was moved by how solemn and sophisticated his sounds were—more so than any sixteen-year-old should be producing. But what should she expect? Beautiful music is always inspired by the trials of love, isn't it?

> *"…And it's a cold, cold place*
> *way deep down in your soul,*
> *And I just can't stay away,*
> *I've lost control.*
>
> *But I know this love will lead me somewhere warm…*
> *And so I ride the storm."*

He strummed out the last chord angrily, and she gently knocked on his door and pushed it open, reluctant to interrupt him.

"Are you really here?" Her heart broke at the desperation in his voice.

"Yeah, I'm really here. Am I interrupting anything?"

She hoped any hostility Max felt for her would vanish the instant he heard her voice, which she kept gentle. Calm.

"No, no. I was just working on some tunes. It's so good to see you. I texted you this morning to find out why you weren't in school, but you never texted me back."

Portia let the implied question as to her whereabouts that morning float into oblivion. She fingered a few random trinkets that lined the shelf above Max's desk, stopping at a beautiful letter opener with a carved mother-of-pearl handle. She held it up questioningly.

"My dad thought my mom might write to us. I think I've mentioned that he's old-school—I mean, who the hell uses a letter opener anymore?"

She crossed the room to his bed and sat beside him. While she felt strong from the visit with Athena, she needed to focus on what she came here to say. She wanted to be sure that she tied up all her loose ends before the big day arrived.

He seemed strong, too, right now. Perhaps the Gods were granting them a moment's peace. The calm before the storm.

Gently Portia eased Max back as she laid her head down on his chest. She could feel the acceleration of his heartbeat at her every touch. She curled in close to him, inhaling his scent and willing the world away.

Patiently Max stroked her hair, her cheek.

"Max, I wanted to try to explain a few things to you before I get too out of control."

His body released a slight tremor when she spoke.

"What do you mean?"

She curled her legs closer into his cautiously, hoping that she wasn't pressing her advantage.

"Max, I, um, have been going through some changes lately. And I just wanted you to know, in case anything happens to me over the next couple of days, that I think you're amazing, and I'm sorry if I've hurt you in any way."

Max tipped her face toward his.

"What do you mean 'in case anything happens to you'?" The worry in his voice was so sincere, driving yet one more nail into the coffin of her impending doom.

"Let's just say that I've gotten mixed up with some people that I wish I wouldn't have, and I can feel them gaining on me."

Max sat up and combed his hands through his hair nervously.

"Is that why you've been acting so…moody? Because you've gotten messed up with some bad people? Why don't you let me help you, Portia? Or go to the police or something? You sound pretty resigned to letting these 'people' get the best of you."

His voice had risen with anger and fear. Portia was afraid

that he would draw the attention of his aunt and uncle or, even worse, the kids. She pulled him back down to her, bringing his face within an inch of her own.

"Max, I'm trying to work it out. Believe me, I'm not resigned to anything. I'm just…tired. I need you to know, though, that when I'm not with you, I'm missing you just as much as I imagine you are missing me. I think about you all the time and wish things didn't have to be so complicated."

"So why do they? I don't get it, Portia. If you have feelings for me, why can't we be together? Why does everything have to be such a battle for you?"

At his use of the word "battle," Portia started to cry. She prayed that her tears would run clear. But it wouldn't have mattered if they were fuchsia. Max was so intent on kissing them away, his own eyes closed as he touched his lips to her eyelids, her cheeks, down to her mouth.

At the touch of his lips, Portia forgot altogether why she had made this visit in the first place. She surrendered herself to the moment, planting her hands firmly in Max's mess of brown hair and drawing him in further.

He pulled away after a minute. "Portia, you know how I feel, right? Despite all of it, I am ridiculously, helplessly, and most definitely in love with you."

She wanted so much to tell Max that she loved him, too. At least she was pretty sure she did. But her mouth just wouldn't form the words, not while her whole life hung in the balance. Not to mention that even now, even while Max's trembling hands caressed her, somewhere in the deep recesses of her mind she couldn't shake the image of Felix's face.

Forcing any intrusive thoughts from her head, Portia told herself that she was entitled to this one moment. Hadn't she been through enough? Hadn't they both been through enough? She pulled Max's face back to hers and kissed him fiercely, her lips delivering all the messages that she couldn't bring herself to say aloud.

His hands traveled the path of her body, and she allowed him to pass his fingertips over her shirt, eliciting an earnest moan from her.

She could feel his heart pounding, and she kissed his Adam's apple as it traveled wildly up and down his throat.

Stepping outside of herself, Portia took a moment to measure the situation. There was a distinct possibility that she might be dead before the end of the week. Did she really want to go out not knowing what all the fuss was about?

She had always imagined that she would save herself. If not for her husband, then at least for that college boyfriend who had been hanging around for a year or two. But right here, right now, that prospect seemed entirely out of her reach. Maybe *this* was her moment.

Enter the voice of reason. You're sixteen! You're not even remotely old enough to take this kind of a step. Haven't you learned anything from all those talks with Helena? You're too young!

As her internal debate raged on, Portia suddenly felt Max pull away. He held his head in his hands while he tried to steady his breath.

"Let's not do anything we might regret, Portia."

The feeling of relief that flooded her confirmed that she was definitely not ready. But what was holding *him* back?

The question hung in the air as she tried to read him.

"Don't get me wrong. It's all I think about. But you've got this, like, sense of doom about you, and I don't want you to do this just because you want to cross it off your bucket list, you know?" He turned back around to look at her. "There is nothing I want more in the world right now than to be with you. But I just don't want it to be like this."

She was impressed by his clarity, and her brain told her that he was one hundred percent right. But her body was having trouble following suit.

"You're right," she offered reluctantly. "I know that this isn't so major for you—I'm sure you've been with other girls, but it's a big thing for me—"

"Portia, I promise you, this is major for me, too. The way I feel about you is major. This," he drew her hand up to his heart.

"this is major."

Portia smiled weakly. She leaned over and kissed his cheek. "You are a gentleman, Max."

"I try." He rested his head back down on the pillow, and Portia eased her head back onto his waiting shoulder.

That's when she felt it.

Like a bolt of lightning, the evil shocked her. A giant billboard flashed in her mind of Max, prostrate on his knees before her, bleeding and begging. The evil was stronger than ever. As if the devil himself was perched on her shoulder, shooting poisonous darts into her mind.

"Max, I gotta go." She sat upright and made her way hurriedly to the door.

Don't go, Portia. Why not stay and have a little fun?

Portia closed her eyes. It was like an amplifier had been installed in her head.

"What's the matter?"

She couldn't help but let her gaze travel over to the letter opener.

Go ahead. Pick it up. The thrill is indescribable.

She needed to get out of there before she did anything she regretted.

"Nothing. I just have to go."

It was threatening to choke her.

"Portia—wait!" Max started after her as she ran out his door.

Before she ran down the stairs, she turned around and stole a glance at him.

She hoped it wouldn't be her last.

Chapter 34

Felix wondered how long he had to wait after knocking before entering Portia's room. Based on Leucosia's e-mail, he didn't want to give it too much time.

"Deaf boy coming in!" he said aloud as he pushed open her door. "Hope you're decent. If not, don't worry—I have a lot of sisters…"

He stopped in his tracks as soon as he saw Portia lying corpse-like in her bed. She didn't seem to register his entrance, her eyes remaining fixed on the far wall of the room.

Dropping to his knees beside her bed, Felix reached his hand out to touch her forehead. Though her pallor was almost as blue as her eyes, her skin was hot to his touch.

Smoothing her hair off of her face, he tried to get her to focus her attention on him.

"Portia, can you hear me? Jesus Christ, Portia, can you even hear me?"

After an eternity, she reoriented and looked into his eyes.

"Portia, I'm here. Leucosia told me it was bad, but I didn't realize it was this bad."

She brought her hands up to sign.

"It's getting worse every minute."

"What, Portia? What's getting worse? Why are you so sick?"

She wished she could explain to him that what had started out as an invasion of her dreams had morphed into a full-on takeover of her body and soul as the big battle grew nearer. But she couldn't. She had sworn to herself that she wouldn't. And what would be the point anyway? Felix wouldn't be able to help her. No one would.

Instead she focused all of her energy on sliding over a few

inches, not believing how much effort the simple movement required. Felix settled in alongside her, and she rested her head on his shoulder, bringing her hands up once more before she drifted off to sleep.

"I'm scared, Felix. Hold me."

And he did.

When Portia was sleeping soundly, Felix eased her out of his arms and went downstairs to check in with Helena.

"How's she doing?" Helena didn't give him a chance to answer, speaking and signing nervously, "I definitely thought we were on the upswing after seeing the doctor. But this morning she started relapsing."

"She seems better—I think she's just tired," Felix responded casually, grabbing an apple from a bowl on the counter. "I know from my sisters that teenage girls need a lot of beauty rest." He hoped the light remark would stave off Helena's worries. But for good measure, he flashed her his most charming smile, which thankfully did the trick, eliciting hers in return.

"I have to show a house in about an hour, Felix. I was going to cancel my appointment, but do you think you can hang around with her since she's feeling a little better?"

"No problem, Helena. I got it."

She sized him up. "Felix, I think you grew a foot since I last saw you. You've become a man overnight."

"Not quite overnight." He handed her her bag and started leading her toward the door. "Feel free to stay out as long as you need to. Maybe I'll order us a pizza or something for lunch."

"OK, thanks again, sweetie." She gave his shoulder a quick squeeze and headed out the door.

The minute she was gone Felix planted himself at the desktop computer in the kitchen. In an instant, Leucosia's worried face popped up.

"How is she?"

"She's really sick, Ms. Leucosia." No matter how many times

Leucosia had told Felix to drop the "Ms.," he just couldn't bring himself to do it. "I swear to God, she looks like she's dying."

Leucosia's face crumpled with fear.

"Felix, listen to me. She is not dying. She is not going to die. She just needs a dose of normal, do you understand? To keep the demons at bay. Can you do that, Felix?"

"Sure, I can do normal," there was a hint of rage in his voice, "normal is all I do, actually. I wish I understood what the hell was going on here—why everything is so 'not-normal.' I mean, you guys have already told me some pretty insane stuff, so why can't you just come clean with this? I don't think it would be possible for me to think that you are both any crazier than I already do, you know?"

"I can't, Felix. I need you to be safe."

"What do you mean safe? Who's not safe?! Ms. Leucosia, who's not safe?"

But the nurse just shook her head. "Normal, Felix. Just give her normal." And with that, her face disappeared from the screen.

He darted back up the stairs and was relieved that Portia at least seemed to be awake now, although the stillness of her body made it hard to tell.

"I got your mom out of the house. How are you holding up?" He sat down next to her and felt her forehead again. She was still burning up.

"The same," she signed, "but not worse."

"OK, OK, that's a good sign. You think you could manage a bath? It might help break the fever."

Portia had to admit that the thought of a bath was tempting. But the bathroom door seemed to be a thousand miles away.

"I'll help you, don't worry. And I promise to be a gentleman."

Felix got up and headed for the bathroom. While he tempered the water, Portia managed to sit herself up. She allowed a moment for the lightheadedness to pass and then attempted to swing her feet over the side of the bed. She had one firmly planted on the rug when he came back out.

"Whoa, wait a second. Here, put one arm around my neck."

He scooped her up and carried her over to the bathroom. She gave him a weak smile when she smelled the lavender.

"You put in bubble bath?" she asked him. Her voice was stronger than before. Not that he could hear it anyway.

"Only the best for you. I'm gonna set you on the ledge of the tub and turn around while you get undressed, OK?"

His command of the situation was such a welcome relief. Portia peeled off her clothes, damp from sweat and eased herself into the tub. The bubbles felt like silk against her burning skin.

Felix slunk down to the floor and, true to his word, sat with his back toward her. Conversing with him this way was obviously not going to work. When Portia was certain that she was well blanketed by the foamy bubbles, she splashed some water at him, and he turned to face her.

She extended her hands above the water.

"Talk to me, Felix."

To his credit, Felix rose above the awkwardness of the situation with tremendous grace. He took Portia on a welcome walk down memory lane, recounting the time when they had challenged each other to a gummy candy contest. Anything from Fruit Roll-Ups to Sour Patch Kids qualified, and they both ate so much that at the end they proceeded to vomit all over Helena's brand-new rug. "Rainbow vomit" was what they called it—a concoction they referenced for years.

He reminded her of the time they were lying in the hammock, and Portia was going on about something to do with birds when suddenly a huge droplet of bird poop landed on her sleeve, sending her into absolute hysterics. From there he segued into the time when he had fallen asleep on the couch, and Wendy and Kate had convinced Portia to team up with them and give him a makeover. They had even managed to paint his nails before he woke up.

With every story Portia felt her strength ooze back. Thinking back on a time when she was normal—voiceless, maybe, but still normal—was truly medicinal. She marveled to think that her biggest worry used to be what prank she and Felix would pull next. Or how early they could get to the bookstore to get the next *Harry Potter*.

Felix kept talking, intermittently signing when he grew unsure of his voice, comforting Portia with his words, sheltering her with his stories. As her fever subsided, she added some hot water to the tub, inhaling the steam floating off the top of the water. The time with Felix was so natural, so easy.

Without thinking, she raised her hands and signed, "Felix, you know I love you, right?"

He turned to look at her, making sure his eyes were leveled with hers, though the temptation to let them travel was hard to resist.

"I know you will."

She wasn't sure what to say. For all she knew, by this time tomorrow, she could be dead. How could she leave Felix behind? Felix, who had been so patient with her. Felix, who remained by her side her even while she had become more and more infected by the evil.

He relieved her of the burden of having to find the right words by standing up, holding up a giant bath towel for her, and closing his eyes. Portia climbed out of the tub and allowed him to wrap her up in the soft towel. She was feeling much steadier on her feet and signed to him that she was OK to get herself dressed.

"I'm feeling much better. Why don't I meet you downstairs, and we'll have something to eat?"

"Yeah, OK. I'll meet you downstairs." Before he let go of her, though, he wrapped his arms around her waist from behind, nuzzling his face into the side of her neck. She leaned back into the safety of him.

But after a moment, he gently pushed her away and, without a backward glance, headed for the stairs.

Part Four

Battle

Chapter 35

On the morning of the fated day, Portia woke up feeling surprisingly normal. The sun was illuminating her room, lending it a pleasant warmth. Watching dust particles float in the beam of the sunlight, she smiled to herself when she recalled the lazy Saturday she had passed with Felix the day before.

This isn't so bad. She curled deeper under her covers. *Maybe I was worked up for nothing.*

The sunlight continued to pour into her room, forcing her to move her pillow over to avoid its glare.

She tried to recall exactly what Leucosia had told her to do that morning.

"Sit tight and wait for me to come get you. Whatever you do, Portia," she had warned, "do not leave the house."

Piece of cake. She was feeling cocky now, except for the damn sunlight, which seemed to be following her across the bed. *What time was it anyway?*

A look over at her bedside clock revealed that it was only 5:30.

Morning light should barely have broken.

Oh, shit.

She made to reach for her computer—she needed Leucosia. Now. But though her mind said, "your laptop is six inches away from you," her arms mocked her.

Oh my God—I'm Harold Trotter! I can't control my own movements! They want me to walk over to the light. I will not walk over to that light. I will not climb into the well.

And then she heard the laughter. Surely everyone heard it. It was the only sound on earth, wasn't it?

"Good morning, Portia." The voices spoke in unison. The

light flashed brighter at the sound, a lightning bolt cracking her in half. Unwittingly Portia swung her legs over the bed.

When her feet touched the ground, she spotted her cell phone lying on the floor.

Portia, you are a Goddess, too. Pick up that cell phone.

She tried curling her toes around the iPhone, but her feet were just as useless as her hands.

"Do you really think there is any way you're not going to come to us, young Portia?" The voices had broken apart, and she wasn't sure which one of them was speaking to her. "You must not resist. Your story has already been written. Come to us now."

The voice was so seductive. She knew she shouldn't follow it, knew that death was now in the cards, although for whom she could not be sure.

They started laughing again, surly giggles that bounced off every crevice of her room. If only she could hold her ground.

But then they started to sing.

And so came the beginning of the end:

> *"In Hades there are songs we sing,*
> *Songs the spirits know.*
> *Some are sad, of truth they ring,*
> *Some of love do glow.*
>
> *But when we are alone at night,*
> *Our voices join as one,*
> *Welcoming the bloody fight,*
> *Which now we know we've won…"*

Portia's feet started taking her toward the window. Toward the sound that was the only sound in the universe. Half of her knew the danger, but the other half wondered how she had ever drawn breath before hearing them? Why had she bothered existing before now?

> *"Tartarus has open doors,*
> *ever now inviting,*

But first my lover evens scores,
Taking wrongs and righting…"

Portia could only assume that Ligeia was the lead vocalist for this verse, referencing Proteus, his determination to exact revenge upon Leucosia. She picked up her pace as the light shimmered through the silk of her window shades.

"Knowing not the fruit I bore,
For she was mine alone.
Knowing not that Scylla swore
To offer her a home…"

She trailed the voice mindlessly, surrendering herself bit by bit.

Once again they sang in unison:

"…And now your former life abated,
The winds are blowing strong.
You cannot know how long we've waited
To hear your blessed song…"

Portia reached the window, her breath coming fast and sharp. Slowly she raised her hands to the shade, the same hands that had told Felix yesterday that she loved him. The same hands that had caressed Max's beautiful face. The same hands that had once been held lovingly by her parents.

Easing back the drape, she readied herself for whatever was out there.

"I am a Goddess, too. I am a Goddess, too." She repeated the words aloud.

When the curtain was drawn back completely, the light was blinding. Portia closed her eyes momentarily in order to acclimate to the fiery beam. When she reopened them, she was standing face-to-face with the giant winged creature that had haunted her many dreams.

"I'm not afraid of you." Her words were tiny.

The blended form of Ligeia and Parthenope was both beautiful and grotesque. The whiteness of their outer feathers was staggering, but underneath the surface, Portia detected a layer of down that was graying and matted. With each blink the creature took, a murky film muddied its eyes and then evaporated into the air, revealing a haunting shade of green.

Once more Portia attempted a weak "I'm not afraid of you."

"Well, naturally. There is nothing to fear, Portia. We are here only for your betterment, to show you a world of pleasure that you never could have imagined."

Beholding the creature while it spoke only intensified the effect of its voice. The evil disease that had been building in her these past weeks calcified instantly. She could feel the thick tumors of evil multiplying and filling up her veins.

She was playing in the big leagues now.

"Now, be a dear and go prepare yourself. Have you given any thought yet to what you would wear today, the day of your rebirth?" The giant batted its wings, giving off a faint aroma of stale lavender. When it spoke, its mouth divided in two so that each of the sisters could put in her two cents.

Their voice reverberated in places within her that she didn't even know existed. She was inclined to drop to her knees and worship the giant creature.

"Hurry up, dear. Max is waiting."

If the pleasure of his destruction came even remotely close to hearing the creature utter Max's name, then Portia couldn't waste another moment.

She threw on a white tank, which hinted scandalously at the black bra she was wearing underneath. It was a look Helena particularly hated, one that Portia had always avoided. Until now. A painted-on pair of denim shorts and the Frye boots she kept buried in her closet finished off the look.

Moving things along, Portia rubbed some scented oil over her legs until their bronze tone was glistening. With each preparation, her appetite for whatever events lay ahead was further whetted. She applied heavy strokes of black liner to her eyelids and then filled in her lips with the darkest shade of lipstick she had.

She could smell Max. Taste him.

Any resolve she had had to resist the sisters was forgotten as her head filled with images of Max begging her to spare his life. The anticipation was too much to bear as she inserted giant hoops into her ears.

She was bathing in a river of his blood. Dancing in a claret waterfall.

She admired her reflection in the same mirror that had witnessed her evolution these past months. What a fool she had been on the first day of school—her greatest sense of accomplishment coming from the fact that her braces had finally been removed. How could she have ever taken pleasure in anything so mundane?

Portia tiptoed down the stairs, taking care not to wake her mother. Why should she involve Helena in this? It would just delay her in reaching Max.

As she inched her way toward the back door of the house, she was momentarily paralyzed by the worst pain yet between her shoulders. The winged creature laughed at the sight of her wincing.

The laughter drove her on, and Portia emerged into the cool morning air. The promise the day held in store gave way to her absolute euphoria. She smiled up at the creature, supplicating herself, hoping that her appearance met favor in its eyes.

The pain pierced her back again with greater force.

Their laughter grew louder as the pains started coming one on top of the other, stretching her skin apart, choking her vertebrae.

Falling to her knees, Portia stopped breathing as the agony between her shoulders radiated its way down her spine. She was certain she was going to die. Breathing through this would simply not be possible. Grateful that at least the last sound she would hear would be the laughter of Parthenope and Ligeia, she tried desperately to gasp some air.

"Stand up, Portia! Where is your backbone?!" Parthenope laughed at her own wit.

"Portia, you mustn't disappoint us," said Ligeia. "For it is on this one day alone, the very anniversary of our death, that we have the strength for this journey. Now breathe through the pain!"

Portia wanted to do as the voices commanded her, but she felt as though her back was being cut open with a rusty handsaw. She managed a small breath, but still the world was receding from her.

"Portia, think of Max. Max is waiting for you."

The sound of Max's name forced her to gulp a bubble of air. Slowly she straightened herself out and started pushing through the pain. The stretching, the tearing—it was inconceivable. And then, just when she didn't think she could take one more stab, she felt the wings emerge from her back. As they moved through her skin, she could feel the cool silkiness of the feathers, their tips soaked with the blood of her own flesh.

The pain receded enough to allow her own laughter to bellow forth as the wings carried her up to meet the spirits of the sisters. She was weightless, euphoric, high on the drug of her own powers.

"What say you, dearest Portia, who ever now has wings to rival even the greatest of the Gods?" The sisters were equally as delighted with the young Siren's metamorphosis.

"I say," Portia flapped her new wings boastfully, "what the hell are we waiting for…"

Leucosia could not believe that she was brewing her father a cup of tea at 6:00 a.m. on what was perhaps the most important day of her interminable life.

Out of respect, she would never have refused the visit from Achelous, who had knocked on her door just as the sun was making its way into the sky. When she had felt the prickle on her skin informing her that another God was about, she had assumed Athena was coming to give her some last-minute words of wisdom, but instead opened the door to the worried face of her father.

"I've come to wish you great fortune on this day, my sweet

Leucosia," he said as she ushered him into the house. "For much have I heard from the Gods about your endeavors to defeat the great shape-shifting Proteus."

Leucosia tried making light of what was indeed a dire situation.

"Many are the Gods, Father, who will aid us in the defeat of Proteus. You mustn't worry. For what is the power of one God when upon him comes the wrath of so many?"

Achelous was old indeed. But with his age had come great wisdom.

"Leucosia, do not spare me the truth about the battle upon which you now embark. For I have heard that the spirits of your evil sisters have been growing ever stronger in their efforts to control Portia."

Leucosia should have known that her father would have been privy to the gossip mill of the Gods. Her anxiety mounted as she noted the time. She had promised Portia she'd be there first thing in the morning, but how could she not appease the fears of her father, who had already lost two daughters?

"Father, your wisdom is boundless. Of course you are aware of my tiresome struggle with Proteus and my sisters. But you must take comfort in knowing that Portia is ready to battle the evil forces that are upon her, as are we all."

The deep lines of Achelous's face relaxed noticeably with the confident words his daughter offered him.

"Shall we partake in a cup of tea before you embark on your mission, Leto? It will help to calm your nerves and hopefully mine as well." Tea had always been the River God's drug of choice.

Minding the time, Leucosia hurriedly set about brewing her father a cup of tea. She took out her silver tea set and started rummaging through her refrigerator for some fresh mint.

"Come, dear child, sit beside me. It is but early to partake in breakfast fare."

"Yes, I know, father, I was just looking for some mint."

"We don't need mint, Leto. Come sit."

The hairs on Leucosia's neck stood on end. Her father

never drank his tea without mint.

"Father," she ventured, "remember when we were little, and you visited us on the island, surprising us with a litter of puppies?"

Achelous released a hearty chuckle. "Yes, my dear. Ever did you and your sisters love animals."

Parthenope had always been terrified of dogs.

Leucosia brought the tea set over to the coffee table. She lifted the silver teapot, positioning it over the tiny cup and saucer, then suddenly splashed the boiling contents into the face of the stranger who was in her home.

"WHO ARE YOU? WHO HAS SENT YOU?"

The stranger cried out in pain as the burning waters dripped from his face. In an instant, the figure of Achelous transformed into the God that bore the crescent moon scar.

"You are clever, I'll grant you that." He hissed his words. "What gave it away? I even used your nickname. Was it the mint? I had a feeling I should have just kept my mouth shut. But my mission has been accomplished. For even now does your precious Portia fly with her own wings to carry out her destiny."

Total panic set in as Leucosia grabbed for the fire iron, the closest thing she could get her hands on. It was of no use, though. Proteus was already flaunting his spotted butterfly wings, flying up to the ceiling and circling her playfully.

She couldn't waste a minute. Any efforts made by her to destroy Proteus on her own would most certainly be futile and she needed to get over to Max Hunter's house immediately.

As Leucosia ran out of her house, her own wings emerged and she was on her way in an instant. She wondered for a moment what Proteus's next move would be when suddenly she felt the back draft of a flying eagle soaring way above her.

Max had been waiting for this day all along—the day when he would go mad. These things usually run in the family. Still, he just couldn't believe how real it all seemed.

She had arrived at his window just moments before, rousing him from his sleep. He had assumed she had climbed up the trellis, but when he opened the window, she was suspended in the air.

By wings.

That moment marked Max's official descent into the insanity that had claimed his father.

He locked his eyes shut and screamed, begging it, her, to stop.

At the sound of his hysteria, Portia told Max in no uncertain terms to shut up. The sound of her voice immobilized him and brought about his immediate silence. All he could do was strengthen his grip on her back, one arm looped fiercely around her neck as they continued to soar higher and higher, the flapping of her wings causing him to choke on the air.

He wished he had a bottle of pills to swallow just as his father had. How else would he be able to escape the trappings of his own mind? The madness had already killed him in so many ways, hadn't it? It must have been him all along, imagining Portia's mood swings, demonizing her for reasons of his own mental instability. And the mysterious jogger whose face kept reappearing to him in his dreams? All part of the inevitable breakdown.

Afraid to utter a sound, he wondered at the path his insanity had taken. Why Portia? What was motivating him to project this twisted image onto her? And why would he be hallucinating the grotesque hellion that trailed behind them?

He wanted to scream again but was afraid they would come to get him. The men in the white coats. And so he had no choice but to ride it out. Literally. If he let go of her, he would surely fall into the abyss, real or imagined. He clenched his eyes shut again as they continued to soar through the air.

As they progressed further into their journey, the creature that followed behind was singing in a foreign language. Greek, maybe? Portia's wings seemed to be flapping in time to its song, spurred on by its voice, until suddenly the creature stopped.

"It is with great sadness that we must leave you now,

Portia." Max almost fell off for how abruptly she stopped midair. "For the powers of mere spirits are no match for the gathering of Gods that await you at Mount Olympus. Unto the halls of Hades shall we return now, waiting to hear tidings of your success from Proteus."

With the departure of the apparition, Max hoped that the hallucination was drawing to an end.

But Portia wasn't letting him out of her clutches so fast.

"Don't worry for me. You've done your job. I assure you I can take it from here." Her voice was just as glorious as theirs.

Portia swooped away from the melded creature, boasting the trophy of the helpless mortal between her silken wings.

Max closed his eyes, allowing the insanity to further invade him. It would have to end eventually.

Wouldn't it?

Chapter 36

The fact that her wings guided her straight to the peak at Mount Olympus did not surprise Portia in the slightest. It was like she had a built-in navigation system, which only added to her sense of omnipotence. Fully focused on the task at hand, the only mild distraction along the way was Max's whimpering.

During her flight, any remnants of the Portia Griffin that had once been intimidated by the sophisticated Max Hunter had turned to dust. Now the fear seeping through Max's pores into her own actually fueled her strength. When they reached the mountain peak, Portia was almost disappointed at having to end the exhilarating flight. But she knew that the events about to take place would prove far more exciting. Bringing them down for a landing into the brush of a field adjacent to the mountain peak, Max rolled off of her back and onto the ground.

He looked up at Portia, his usually rich skin tone now a sickly shade of white. His eyes were bulging with fear and stained from tears.

"Who are you? What the hell is going on?" He stumbled over the words.

"Oh come on, Max. Don't you know by now?"

"No, Portia. I don't know anything anymore. Well, except for that I'm as bloody messed up as my father. I mean, I'm hallucinating all of this, right?"

Portia laughed.

"Max, you aren't hallucinating. And guess what? Neither was your father—but more about that later." She laughed. "I assure you that everything you are feeling right now is absolutely real. The fear, the draw, the desire to please me. It is all real, Max. And it is about to get realer."

Max dropped to his knees.

"Portia, let me go. Please take me back home. You'll never have to see me again. I'll go back to New York, I promise." His voice broke with intermittent sobs. "Please, Portia…"

The wry laughter that emanated from Portia's lips as she heard Max's pleas could not even be classified as human. She watched him shudder at the sound of it.

"Poor, poor Max. The gorgeous prodigy from New York blessed with musical genius. Mother and father lost to him. It's all just so dramatic. But, hey, remember that song you were working on when I came over the other day? How did it go again?

>*"Well, it's a cold, cold place*
>*Way deep down in your soul.*
>*But I just can't stay away,*
>*I've lost all control."*

She executed a perfect rendition of the tune Max had been working on, though she had only heard it once.

>*"But I know it will lead me somewhere warm,*
>*And so I ride the storm…"*

"Well, guess what, Max?" Portia approached him slowly. "You're in the eye of that storm right now."

From her front pocket, she took out the letter opener that she had pilfered from his desk, touching its tip to Max's cheek, drawing it down to the hollow of his neck.

"Hey, Max, do you know what a griffin is?"

Max couldn't speak, afraid that any move he made would force the blade into his skin.

"Well, I'll tell you. It's a mythological creature—half eagle, half lion. King of the beasts and king of the birds. I think that's an appropriate surname for me, don't you?"

Max nodded ever so slightly.

"Before I could talk I used to spend endless hours lying around outside in the hammock, memorizing different birdcalls. I used to imagine what the call of the griffin might have sounded like. Would it be a short chirp, a loud roar, or a longer melodious song? Shall I show you what I thought it would sound like?"

Max tried shaking his head no but found that instead he was nodding emphatically.

Placing the opener back in her pocket for the moment, Portia raised both of her beautiful arms into the air. Her face pointed at the sky, she released a sound from her throat that was so sonorous Max could have sworn he felt the earth shake beneath them. The call was delicate and vulgar all at once. Euphoric and mournful at the same time.

At the sound of the extraordinary call, something emerged from the fog.

"Ahhh. Look who's here. How nice of you all to join us." Portia inched her way over to the Gods who had walked onto the scene. "Allow me to make some introductions. Max Hunter, this is Athena, the great Goddess of Wisdom; Ares, the great God of War; and Dionysus, the great God of Wine. Oh, and Madness. I believe he knows your father," she added viciously. "Great Gods," she pointed to the prostrate figure quivering on the ground, "this is Max Hunter."

The Gods exchanged a knowing look with each other. Except for Max's whimpering, a heavy silence fell over the odd grouping.

Athena was the first to speak.

"Portia, was that you who made that wondrous call only a moment ago? The sound was ever glorious."

Portia grinned widely, baring all of her teeth. "I see why they call you the Goddess of Wisdom, Athena. Flattery is a wonderful form of distraction. But I won't be sidetracked. Not today. There's been a change of plans, folks. Instead of us teaming up today to destroy Proteus, I have something else in store for your viewing pleasure."

She took out the letter opener and with lightning speed flew over to Max, grabbing his arm and making a deep slash in the palm of his hand. A river of blood flowed forth from the pad of his skin as he let out an agonizing cry.

As if nothing had happened at all, Portia continued what she was saying.

"I am going to kill Max Hunter before your very eyes."

She grabbed his other hand and slashed that palm as well. The Gods moved to stop her but found that they were rooted to their spots, unable to approach the voice that was keeping them at bay.

"I'm sure you are all wondering why I would want to do such a thing. Well, here it is. I am here today to prove that among the Gods, there is none as powerful as the Siren."

Max stared at her blankly, stains growing on his sweatpants where he tried applying pressure to the geysers of blood that were his hands.

"Oh, come on, Max, surely you knew. Weren't you paying attention in Mr. Morrison's class? The Siren exists to symbolize the absolute power that women have over men. Their seduction is impossible to resist."

Max continued to stare at her in shock.

"Lest you all think that I am a novice at this, allow me to reassure you that my skills are honed. Maybe you shouldn't have given me that homework list after all."

With that she walked over to a tiny tuft of buds sprouting in the grass.

> *"Mary, Mary quite contrary,*
> *How does your garden grow?*
> *With silver bells and cockle shells,*
> *And a Siren who's ready to blow…"*

The words just fell out of her mouth effortlessly. Before anyone could say anything, the tiny crop ballooned into a thicket of cherry blossom trees in full bloom.

Athena shot Ares and Dionysus a look of fear.

Portia's wings emerged again, and she flew around the trees she had created. She flapped her plumes, white as the driven snow, and started circling the group of Gods as well.

"So let us be clear—I have been reborn. I am now Portia Griffin, destroyer of men, indestructible among Gods."

Portia sounded off another round of griffin calls, the haunting noise reverberating for miles around. Though still paralyzed by the Goddess's voice, Athena did manage to convey a message to Ares and Dionysus in a hushed tone.

"Leucosia has ever now texted me that she is on her way. She begged us to stall Portia, for there is something she must acquire before she comes to join us. You must work with me to stave off the murderous appetite of the young Siren."

Dionysus then interrupted Portia's griffin mimicking frenzy.

"Portia, do you not think that a moment such as this is worthy of the finest wines of the Gods? I recall your young self refusing the goblet when last you visited Mount Olympus, but surely now that you are a woman with great powers of seduction, a celebration of your rebirth is called for."

The words of Dionysus found favor with the frenzied Portia, and she ordered him to go fetch some wine while she protected her prey.

Athena was thankful for the extra time and hoped to Zeus and all who are mighty that Leucosia was on her way.

After Proteus sidetracked her, Leucosia's knee-jerk reaction was to fly straight to Mount Olympus. The only flaw in that plan, however, was, well, that there was no plan. What was she going to do when she got there? She never imagined how powerful Parthenope and Ligeia would prove to be today. How could she have underestimated the situation so grossly?

I'm too old for this, she told herself. *Maybe I am fighting a losing battle. Look at me. Now I'm on my way to the home of a perfectly innocent boy to try to involve him in a situation that is nothing short of abysmal.*

Her wings slowed momentarily as she second-guessed her decision to suck Felix into the dangerous confrontation.

Suddenly her phone vibrated. Dionysus had texted her.

"I have been able to buy some time by offering the young muse some wine. Shall I lace it with the petals of the lotus flower?"

The offer was so tempting. If Portia consumed the lotus flowers, then she might forget what it is that is motivating her.

But it was a big "if." Most Gods were able to resist the powers of the memory-erasing plant. What if Portia just became even angrier that they had tried to trick her?

Also, if the flowers did work their magic, what then? When would the struggle end? Eventually Proteus and her sisters would get hold of her again, and this whole laborious process would begin all over.

Frankly she just didn't have any fight left in her.

"No, Dionysus. Please just offer her the mildest wine—remember she is but a child. We must see this thing through to the end today, or it will never be over."

Once again she sped up her wings and decided that no matter the consequences, her only hope of saving Max was to involve Felix. She would have to bear the wrath of Zeus—she'd borne worse.

A great relief flooded her when she saw the Fein home looming directly beneath her. Coming in for a subtle landing in the backyard, Leucosia took a moment to collect herself before knocking on the door.

Kate Fein answered the door, registering a slight look of surprise at seeing the school nurse at their door at 9:30 a.m. on a Sunday.

"Miss Leucosia, hey. Did you need to see my dad about something?"

It took Leucosia a minute to remember that James Fein was technically her boss.

"Oh, no dear, thank you though. I was actually wondering if I could see Felix for a moment. I was doing some extra paperwork this morning, and I realized that I had forgotten to administer a new hearing test to him this year. I had a bit of a nasty letter about it from the Board of Ed and thought that maybe he could come with me now so that I could just tick it off my list."

Leucosia prayed that her story sounded plausible.

"Sure, I'll go get him. Do you want to come in?"

"Oh no, thank you dear, I've left the car running." Damn. Why did she have to say that? What if Kate actually looked for her car?

Leucosia quickly stepped into the house and shut the door behind her.

"Well, maybe just for a bit to warm my feet while I wait. There's a bit of a chill in the air today."

"I know," responded Kate as she started up the stairs to get her brother, "preview to winter, I guess…"

While Kate was upstairs, Leucosia took in the charming interior of Felix Fein's house. There were family pictures everywhere, and his mother obviously had an affinity for French provincial decor. She found it endearing and felt an even greater pang of guilt at involving the boy in this mess.

Within moments, Felix came racing down the stairs, a look of fear plastered on his face.

He signed quickly, "What's going on? Is she OK?"

"I need you to come with me," Leucosia signed back.

"OK, let's go."

Leucosia took in the thin T-shirt Felix was wearing.

"You might want to take a sweatshirt."

"I said let's go, Leucosia," he commanded, hurrying out the door. It was the first time he had ever dropped the "Ms."

"Where's your car?" Leucosia was having trouble keeping up with Felix's long legged strides. She had never really noticed just how tall the boy had recently become.

"Around the back," she signed guiltily.

Felix hurried around to the back of the house, wondering where exactly she meant.

"No, Leucosia. I asked where your car was?" he repeated, gesturing to the vast and empty backyard.

"Felix," the Goddess signed, "you definitely want to help Portia, right?"

"Oh, man, I don't like where this is heading."

Without further warning, Leucosia brought forth her enormous wings, causing Felix to reel backward onto the ground.

"No way. Are you kidding me? There is no way you just sprouted a pair of wings."

She took Felix's hands in her own, hoping to assuage his

fears with her touch, especially since she couldn't calm him with her voice.

"It's the only way we can even hope to get there on time. Felix, please. She's going to kill Max."

He rose back up cautiously, circling Leucosia, surveying the situation.

"So it's all true. All the stuff you guys told me. What did you leave out? What's happening now?"

"Felix, there is no time to waste. I will reveal everything to you on our journey. Now we must go!"

"I can't believe it's true. This stuff doesn't really happen."

"Now, Felix. There is no time to waste."

He stared at her incredulously. "But I'm like a thousand times bigger than you," he said, circling her, gently touching the wings. "How exactly is this supposed to work?"

Without answering him, Leucosia knelt down before him. When he had his hands clenched firmly about her neck, she took flight as if she bore nothing on her back but the weight of a mere feather.

Chapter 37

The alcohol that Dionysus procured for Portia only added to the Siren's malevolence.

A repertoire of songs began to spill from her painted mouth, showing off her vocals and reminding all who were present just who was running this show. Everything from the score of *Les Misérables* to the latest Black Eyed Peas seemed worthy of airtime to Portia in her moment of glory. With each note she sang, she became more deranged, the evil burrowing its way deeper and deeper inside her.

"Don't you fret, Monsieur Marius—or was it Marsyas?…" The *Les Mis* line sounded so menacing as it danced across her lips.

Max was writhing in pain, giant beads of sweat spilling off his forehead, their salt landing on the wounds of his hands, stinging his raw skin.

"What are we waiting for, Portia? Why don't you just get it over with already?" He hadn't planned on goading her, but his agony clouded his judgment.

Dionysus tried distracting Portia from the boy's provocative question by offering her a refill.

"No, thank you, Dionysus. As much as I would love to indulge, I must keep my wits about me."

She flew over to Max and circled him wildly. When she landed, she sauntered up to him and kissed him hard on the lips. She was delighted that he returned the kiss with equal fervor. Everything the sisters had promised her had been true.

"In answer to your question, Max, we are waiting for the arrival of Leucosia. Oh, you probably know her as Ms. Leucosia. Did you know that she is also a Siren? You should hear her sing. It's unbelievable. The problem is, she doesn't know just how much fun the other side is. I think it would add immeasurably to my pleasure if she actually witnessed me killing you. In the meantime, though, I can definitely give you more of a taste of what's coming."

Portia landed the tip of her boot right into Max's upper back, causing him to double over in renewed pain.

After this new assault, Portia delighted in watching Ares willing himself over to her in vain.

"Ares, I'm so sorry," she offered acerbically. "I know this was supposed to be a glorious day for you. That sword must be burning a hole in your, um, robe. I would relieve you of it, but I think my arsenal is complete—"

"Please, Portia," Max was begging, "why are you doing this to me?"

The redundancy of his questions was really starting to get on her nerves. She chose to ignore him and jumped up on a rock, facing them all.

"Hey, this one goes out to Dionysus:

> *Ninety-nine goblets of wine on the wall,*
> *Ninety-nine goblets of wine…"*

Portia held up her own golden goblet, toasting the gathering to which she now held court.

> *"…If one breaks,*
> *Let's raise the stakes,*
> *Ninety-eight goblets of wine on the wall…"*

She started dancing suggestively, imbuing the air with even more sexuality. There was nothing—not one word, not one lyric, not one poetic verse—to which she could not offer the magic of her voice.

Max tried—they all tried—turning their faces away from the frenzied Siren. It was like passing an accident on the road, though: vile to behold, yet too fascinating not to look. And so she continued her performance, the debauchery growing worse by the second. She had just started a perverse rendition of "Killing me Softly":

"I'm killing you softly with my song," she laughed, "killing you softly, won't be long—"

"Portia, what are you doing?" The voice emerged from the fog, followed by Felix Fein and Leucosia. Though she was knee-deep in her performance, Portia was jolted at the sound of his voice.

"What the hell are you doing here, Felix? Get out of here! This has nothing to do with you." But her tone had immediately lost some of its edge.

Just then a giant winged eagle swooped down and landed on the rock that was Portia's stage. The eagle morphed into the form of the young man who had accosted Max on the running track and in his bedroom. It was the same man Portia had seen in the shattered mirror.

"Portia Griffin, I don't believe we have been formally introduced. I am Proteus, son of Poseidon. I have come at the will of my great love, Ligeia, to witness the carnage that is about to occur so that I may present my beloved with the ultimate proof that justice has been done."

Portia extended a hand to Proteus.

"Portia, look at me." Felix's voice was strong. But Portia ignored him, making idle chatter with Proteus.

When she introduced him to Max, the shape-shifter said, "Yes—we've met before. And I've visited your father many times, Max. Of course, he always mistook me for your mother, but then again, can you blame him?"

The God suddenly morphed into the form of Norah Hunter. Max tried inching nearer to the mirage of his mother but recoiled when once again it was Proteus he was looking at.

"LOOK AT ME, PORTIA!"

Reluctantly the Goddess turned her head and leveled her gaze with Felix's. There was a slight glimmer of shame in the pools of her eyes.

"Felix, I said this has nothing to do with you. Leucosia never should have brought you here." Her posture slumped slightly when she addressed him. "I'm past the point of no return," she signed silently.

Felix approached her slowly, amazing all who were gathered by his ability to resist her.

"Portia, you don't have to do this. You CAN'T do this. You can still live a normal life—"

Portia began to laugh. "There is no normal life for me, Felix. I am a freak of nature. I will never age. I will never die. Unless of course I decide to drown myself. I will never know true love—true love of me and not just my voice."

Droplets of liquid silver began to pool in her eyes, and she angrily swatted them away.

"You know that's not true, Portia. You're just too afraid to admit it. I don't know why. I mean, it's some kind of, like, crazy defense mechanism, fear of I don't even know what, that makes it impossible for you, for me to acknowledge that I love you. I *have* loved you and *will* love you always."

Portia's posture slackened even more as Felix continued to traverse the grassy field.

"Portia, of what nonsense does this mortal speak?" interjected Proteus. "He doesn't understand you like I do. He knows not the pleasure of conquering mortals. A God can only feel his true powers when he destroys mortals—especially mortals who have deigned to resist them. And Max had certainly tried to go up against you, has he not?"

With that, Proteus morphed into an exact clone of Max and began mimicking the song from the dining hall…

"…Better check that scoreboard, P…"

Portia inched over to the manufactured Max, laughing at the ludicrousness of it all. She was starting to feel confused. Suddenly nothing seemed real.

Except for Felix's voice. But when she wasn't holding Felix's gaze, it was easier for her to remain focused on what she had come here to do. And so she tried to focus only on the feats of the shape-shifter, amazed at how he replicated himself into Max down to the dimples.

"Of course, Proteus. You're right." The words were certainly not floating out of her mouth with the same ease. It was as if a sudden wind in her throat was trying to blow them back down, to stifle them. But she persisted. "I'm sorry I got distracted." She turned back to the gathering. "Now, without further ado, let's get this show on the road." She flew off the rock over to Max.

Once again she pressed the blade of the letter opener firmly to his throat.

Leucosia tried reasoning with her apprentice, talking her down from the ledge. But no matter how many millennia of Sirenhood she had under her belt, there was no way Leucosia's voice was going to be able to control the virgin Goddess who was about to know her first kill.

A tiny drop of blood from Max's throat fell to the floor, a scarlet reminder of the imminence of his death.

"Portia, wait!" Felix had stopped in his tracks at the sight of the blood. His voice was still resolute, but he was afraid to make any sudden moves. "Listen to me. You know, when I got sick after second grade, I used to watch my mother cry all the time. And then when the virus passed, she kept thanking God, the doctors, anyone who could possibly be thanked. I never saw my mother smile as much as in those two weeks after the doctors said I was out of the woods."

"Where are you headed with this, Felix?" The impatience had returned to Portia's voice. "We all know how this story ends. They never understood what the virus was and why it caused your hearing loss. I've heard it all before." But despite her callousness, Felix persisted.

"When my hearing started to go, she was inconsolable. I used to watch my dad comfort her all the time, catching a few words here and there while I still had some ability to hear. Do you know what one of the last things I ever heard was, Portia?"

Portia looked up at him, her eyes filled with curiosity.

"It was my dad saying to my mom, 'Natalie, everything happens for a reason.' There was something in those words. Even though I was only eight, I just knew. I knew that I had stumbled onto this, like, monumental discovery. Everything happens for a reason."

The blade of the knife began to quiver with the shaking of her hand, revealing the uncertainty Portia was beginning to feel.

"You're that reason, Portia. My reason. The reason I get out of bed every morning. The reason I don't give a shit about cochlear implants and exploratory surgery. The reason I Google bird trivia and even venture into secondhand bookshops. It's all you. Silent you, talking you, I don't care. It's like I told you that day all those years ago—you are my forever."

Portia yanked Max's hair, pulling his head further back. His neck was fully exposed to the blade, his Adam's apple rising and falling, flirting dangerously with the sharp edge. But her confidence was dwindling.

"What's your point, Felix? You don't get it. I might have been good for you all those years, but I'm not that person anymore. Don't you see?"

"Yes, Portia, I see. All I do is see. Hell, if I can't hear, then you can be damn well sure that the least I'm gonna do is see you every chance I get. Really see you. I see you when you're not even there. I relive every moment with you over and over again in my head. Every detail of you. The tilt of your head, the freckle on the back of your shoulder that you probably don't even know you have. Christ, the way you looked yesterday lying in that tub, your cheeks shining from the steam. All I do is see you, Portia. All I do is want you. And it has nothing to do with what you are. I mean, I've never even heard you utter a single goddamned word." He inched closer to her.

"That's the point, Felix. My words are 'God Damned.' They've taken away my ability to control what I say, what I sing. Even what I think—"

"So take it back. Whatever it is you think you've lost, Portia, you can take it back. Now. Before it's too late."

Felix signed out the words as he spoke them, his gestures fluid and calm.

Blinking her tears away, Portia looked hard into the ebony of her best friend's eyes. Her limbs started to grow weak.

"You think I haven't been hurting these past months, Portia? I've been walking around as half of myself, looking to my friends, to Gabrielle to make me whole again. But there's no me without you. You know that, right?"

He continued to approach her as the letter opener quivered threateningly in her hand.

"No, Felix…" She was shaking her head, but her eyes showed traces of defeat.

"You are good, Portia."

They were standing face-to-face.

"My Portia, the Portia I see, is good. Now give me the knife."

He held out his hand.

"GIVE ME THE KNIFE, PORTIA!"

His voice felt suddenly distant, drowned out by an intense ringing in her ears. Portia fell to her knees, dropping the blade and collapsing onto the grass, a wave of nausea flooding over her. Crawling under the shade of the nearest tree, she laid her burning cheek against the cool grass. The last thing she saw before losing consciousness was the distinct spark of hope that had been ignited in Felix's raven eyes.

Chapter 38

When she awoke, Portia saw Ares waving his sword in the determined pursuit of a bat. The bat flew low, scraping the heads of the small gathering of Gods and landing tauntingly on a branch of one of the newly grown cherry blossom trees. The group charged the creature, but just as they were about to secure the bat in their clutches, it flew off once again.

It took Portia a moment to realize that she was witnessing a game of cat and mouse between Proteus and the Gods who were trying to save her. On the periphery, she saw a bare-chested Felix tending to Max, ripping up his T-shirt to make bandages for the many wounds she had inflicted upon him.

What have I done?

She couldn't understand how it had all gone so awry.

"I WILL AVENGE THE DEATH OF MY PRECIOUS SONS!" Ares was screaming as the bat continued to elude him.

How could I have been so weak? Portia sat herself up, leaning against the trunk of the tree. Her limbs felt heavy and the rush to her head took her a minute to shake.

Proteus had flown up to an even higher treetop, transforming back into himself for an instant. Leucosia's wings were out instantly as she charged him.

"You will never defeat one as powerful as me!" The Shapeshifter was clearly enjoying himself.

Just as Leucosia was about to reach him, Proteus became a snake and slithered down the tree. When he hit the ground, he morphed into a grasshopper, hopping tauntingly in front of Dionysus and Athena.

Regaining her bearings, Portia looked over again at Felix and Max.

"It's OK, man. It's all going to be OK…"

She couldn't believe how clear-headed Felix seemed to be, considering the circumstances. She owed it to him to make it all OK. But her mind was so muddled she couldn't think straight. The cries of Max's pain, the soothing words of Felix, Proteus's taunts to his potential captors. The sounds were all ricocheting in her brain like gunfire, making it impossible for her to focus on any one thought.

Also, something Ligeia had said—no, sung—was circling her thoughts. Something that had her feeling even more overwhelmed. What was it?

She scrambled through her memories of the morning while she watched in horror as Dionysus trapped Proteus, the winged moth, into a wine jug. Within seconds, the glass of the jug exploded, sending shards splintering into Dionysus's face. A fierce lion appeared, roaring viciously, baring its teeth, and sending Dionysus cowering behind Ares.

Proteus roared again, the sound so loud that it shook the fruit from some of the treetops. A ruby red apple landed on the grass a few inches from where Portia was lying.

> *Knowing not the fruit I bore,*
> *For she was mine alone…*

A flash of light up in the sky interrupted her thoughts. She looked up and saw the spirits of Parthenope and Ligeia circling above the scene, the sound waves of their laughter rippling for miles. But something about their laughter was different to Portia suddenly. It was that it sounded…it sounded, well, pitiful.

"Proteus," Parthenope began, "Ligeia beseeched me to traverse these many miles so that we may witness your victory with our very eyes. At first I feared for our safety, but now do I see that my sister has not exaggerated your skills as a supreme warrior."

Portia cleared her throat. It was time for some divide and conquer.

"Oh—I thought you guys came back because you wanted to tell Proteus about the daughter Ligeia has hidden from him for all these years."

The commotion came to an immediate halt, Proteus instantly morphing back into his own person.

"Of what nonsense does the Siren speak, Ligeia?"

Portia continued as if the question had been addressed to her. Her strength was slowly returning, refueling her will to emerge the victor.

"Yeah, Proteus. For someone who can shift his shape like nobody's business, it's hard to believe that you never happened upon your own daughter in your travels. Oh, wait, I guess your travels would have had to lead you to Scylla—the one with the six heads. I think she was the one who raised your daughter after Ligeia…you know…" Portia gesticulated the proverbial knife slashing the throat, "offed herself."

Proteus's face crumbled. He looked up at the spirit of his lover, tears clouding his eyes.

"Ligeia, I pray you, tell me this is not so. So many years have I wept for the loss of you. Could I have known the love of a daughter to ease my pain?"

The bird creature's mouth split into two as Ligeia's voice feebly attempted to ease the blow.

"Proteus, you cannot know the hurt that was mine at the hand of my own mother, Terpsichore. It was my will that our daughter know only the true love of a mother…"

Her words floated off into the air as a familiar feeling began washing over Portia. A vibration in her throat, a shortness to her breath, an intense awareness of her every pore.

Proteus's face was filled with rage and hurt. "You had no right, Ligeia. She was but mine to love as well." His voice rose with fury. "SHE WAS BUT MINE TO LOVE AS WELL!" He repeated, screaming.

Watching him unravel, Portia felt even stronger, the vibration in her throat intensifying. The last time she had felt this way was when the school bus had passed Charlotte's house. She knew now that the episode she had had on the bus that day was all part of one grand design. She wasn't sure who exactly the designer was, but that day was destined to unfold the way it did.

She had been forced to call upon her new powers in order to stop Mr. Trotter. And now those same powers would lead her to paralyze Proteus, who was already showing signs of weakness.

Rising up, Portia allowed herself a moment to gain her footing. When she felt firmly planted, she took a few steps in Proteus's direction. He had once again morphed, this time into his favored eagle, and flown into the treetops so that he could confront Ligeia face-to-face.

Bolder with every moment that passed, Portia moved faster, extending a cautious hand to Max's back as she passed him by to reach the others. The vibration in her throat was soothing, infusing her with the confidence she needed to control the moment. Looking up at the treetops, she was a cannon ready to release fire. She stared down the eagle eyes that looked down upon her and opened her glorious mouth.

Go Beyond Your Voice.

> *"You think you are the only one?*
> *To take new form and Gods outrun?*
> *Well I am a Goddess, too,*
> *And now I'm going to outrun you."*

All eyes were upon her immediately as she let out the first lyrics.

> *"An eagle am I with giant wings,*
> *But get this—this eagle sings!*
> *This leopard's spots are made of onyx.*
> *This lion's roar's a boom that's sonic."*

Up in the branches, Proteus had unwittingly transitioned back into his own form, the bulge of his scar highlighted by the shining sun.

> *"You made me think like you I'd be.*
> *But now I have remembered me.*
> *Yes, now I have remembered me…"*

Portia approached the tree and focused all of her energy on Proteus. She was well beyond her voice now. Further than she had ever gone, had ever allowed herself to go. She had never felt this strong.

And as her journey into an unchartered vocal stratosphere continued, Proteus began to register something that she recognized as fear.

> *"I, too, as a snake can slither,*
> *Shedding skin that made me wither.*
> *A peacock now I fan my plumes,*
> *A wisteria with fragrant blooms."*

To his great horror, Proteus started climbing down the tree. He stopped on a branch and closed his eyes, willing himself to transform again, but he was absolutely paralyzed by the voice of the young Siren.

And that voice was beckoning him into the clutches of death.

> *"Ordained the Queen by honeybees,*
> *A forest full of Maple trees.*
> *I am these things and now I'll flaunt it.*
> *Watch as I throw down the gauntlet..."*

Portia's wings emerged as she flew up to the branch where a shaking Proteus was perched. She held her hand out to him, forcing him to reach out to her. As she led him down, branch by gnarled branch, she sang even louder, staring directly into the evil God's eyes.

"Leucosia," spoke Ligeia, "I beg you, do not let Portia take the life of Proteus, who has shown me only kindness. Have you not caused us enough pain, stealing the love of our mother? Lowering yourself to share love with a mere mortal?"

> *"...The sun has now entered my corner.*
> *Your pigment pale, you're quick to mourn her.*
> *And every star that lights night's skies*
> *Is now the sparkle in my eyes..."*

"Ligeia, Parthenope," Leucosia's dazzling smile took on a mischievous glow as she spoke the words she had longed to say for so many years. "Get over it."

She flew up to where Portia was hovering and began circling her protectively.

> *"A meadow I am lush with grass,*
> *No bones or decaying mass.*
> *You've landed on the highest peak,*
> *But I'm the mountain, hear me speak!"*

The song of the Siren was too much for the sisters to bear. They hurried away from the battleground, but there was no escaping Portia's voice.

> *"...Yes, now I have remembered me..."*

Still, as they flew further and further away, even reaching the edges of Hades, the music grew only louder.

> *"A Bonsai now I am serene,*
> *Knowing you'll be off the scene..."*

The sisters had to escape her song. It was excruciating, haunting them, cursing them, mocking them.

> *"No longer will this fear I shoulder.*
> *A pebble once, but now a boulder..."*

There was only one way to escape.

> *"A ladybug who brings good fortune,*
> *Ambrosia sweet, a hefty portion.*
> *A bat I can sleep upside down,*
> *The Mayor of this God-filled town,*
> *Of the ship, I am the prow,*
> *Behold I am a SIREN now..."*

Together Parthenope and Ligeia plunged down into the deepest layer of Hades, begging entry to Tartarus, a place from which they would never again emerge. As the gates to the hellish abyss opened up for them, they felt tremendous relief.

But just as they began to savor the success of their escape, they heard it. There was no mistaking it. It had followed them.

Her voice had followed them. They were surrounded by the song of Portia Griffin, which would now haunt them for an eternity.

Proteus had reached the ground. His instincts told him to run, but the choice was not his to make. Ares approached him slowly, savoring the moment.

"Spare me, Ares. I beg of you. Your sons were weak. It is not my fault that they were lost to you in battle."

Even Athena had run out of patience at this point. She shot Ares a resolute glance.

"…You made me think like you I'd be…"

"ON YOUR KNEES, PROTEUS!"

The great shape-shifter was sobbing, begging for his life to be spared.

"But now I have remembered me."

Ares raised his sword.

"Yes, now I have…"

"THIS IS FOR CHARITON AND HESPEROS!"

"remembered me."

The sword came down with one terrifying swoosh as Proteus's head rolled inches away from his lifeless body.

Chapter 39

A quiet calm rested over the grassy field before everyone sprang into action. Dionysus immediately ran over to Felix and Max to offer them help. He pulled a golden flask from beneath his robe and passed it to both of them. Managing a quick swig first, Felix poured some of the whiskey onto Max's wounds, thankful that he was unable to hear the agonizing screams brought on by the burn of the alcohol. After dousing them well, he encouraged Max to drink some, too. Anything to offer the poor guy some relief.

Ares, in the meantime, gathered up the decapitated remains of Proteus and excused himself. He wanted to bury the body immediately. He sought closure and the obliteration of any reminders of the evil God.

In the meantime, Athena raced over to Leucosia and Portia.

"My dearest sisters, a great victory have you won here today. I pray there will be much time to rejoice. But now, I beg you, tell me how we shall treat the mortals that have witnessed both the horrors and the miracles we have seen here today?"

Leucosia and Portia both slumped to the ground, exhausted and breathless.

Looking over at Felix and Max passing the golden flask between them and Dionysus blotting Max's wounds, Leucosia was the first to speak.

"I fear the only approach is to feed the mortals the lotus flowers." She turned to Portia. "Unless you would like to erase the memory with your voice, Portia. I myself do not have a single song left to sing."

Portia shook her head. "I'm with you, Leucosia. I'm tapped out." But while the lotus flowers were the obvious answer for Max, she wasn't as sure about Felix.

Maybe it was selfish, but Portia needed Felix to remember. Why shouldn't he? He already knew she was a Siren. She had nothing to hide from him. She knew that he would never hold the events of today against her. And how refreshing would it be not to have to hide anything from him? A friendship without secrets, without barriers.

Reading her mind, Athena looked directly at Portia.

"Why don't you give him the choice?"

Portia nodded silently and headed over to Felix and Max. She could hardly look at Max, his wounds pulsing, their blood drawn by her own hand. Keeping a comfortable distance, she motioned for Felix to come over. When he approached, she noted how tired he looked, the darkness underscoring his eyes, making him appear much older than his almost seventeen years. His chest was still bare, except for the smears of Max's blood that spotted it every so often. She reached out to touch his face.

Felix closed his eyes and rested his head heavily on her hand. His skin felt warm to her touch.

When he reopened his eyes, Portia signed to him.

"Felix, I need to ask you something. Let's sit down."

"No," he signed back, "just ask me. What is it?"

"We, um, have decided that it's in Max's best interests not to remember what just happened here. There's a certain flower, you see—"

"The lotus flower?" he spelled out with his hand.

She had forgotten that he, too, was taking the elective on *The Odyssey*. That world seemed a million miles away right now.

"Yes, the lotus flower. Anyway, I thought it should be your choice whether or not you wanted to forget this day. I mean, you might have nightmares or PTSD or something." She attempted a weak smile. "You might come to think of me as a horrible monster…" She dropped her hands to her sides, humbled and vulnerable.

"So Max gets to forget and I get to remember, huh? I had a feeling something like that might happen."

"It doesn't have to be that way, Felix. I just thought you actually might *want* to remember, because, um, because you are my best friend."

He moved in closer to her, wiping away some silvery residue that had fallen to her collarbone. His touch was electric, a bolt of lightning zapping away the words 'best friend,' replacing them with something more alive. More charged. They were a long way away from platonic now, as the back of his hand swept the side of her neck.

"Portia, I would never want to forget anything about you— good or bad." He leaned down and whispered into her ear, "You are so etched in my mind, Portia Griffin, that I don't even think a lotus flower would make a bit of difference. I don't think arsenic would make a difference. You're going to haunt me well beyond the grave. So no lotus flowers for me, OK? Not today." He stood up straight and looked sharply at her. "Not ever."

He walked away then to tend to Max Hunter, the boy who Portia had thought was definitely 'the one.'

But now she was not so sure…

Athena and Leucosia were speaking in hushed tones when Portia reapproached them.

"He doesn't want the flowers." She looked to each of the Goddesses, who seemed suddenly very distracted. "What? What's going on?"

"Portia," Leucosia responded. The calm in her voice did not jibe with the look of concern on Athena's face. "I need you to go somewhere with me. Athena has promised to watch over Felix and Max for a bit. It won't take long. Just something I have to do."

Portia looked over to Athena.

"Go, my sweet child. I will take care of everyone here. Worry not." And then she turned to Leucosia and embraced her fiercely. "You will always be my dearest friend, Leucosia." The clear-eyed Goddess's eyes were even more haunting when they were filled with mist.

Leucosia stood up and brought forth her wings, Portia

following behind, though something about this sudden journey seemed altogether foreboding. Rising up into the air, the two Goddesses plunged into the dense fog that covered the peak of Mount Olympus.

Leucosia took Portia's hand in hers and guided them toward a small reef at the edge of the angry waters that neighbored the mountain. As they landed on the rocky surface, Portia felt a severe panic rise up in her.

"What's going on, Leucosia? Why are we here?"

"I'm so tired, Portia."

"I know, so am I. Let's go home."

"No, Portia. I mean I am *tired*. Tired of it all. I have lived too long with the weight of these wings."

Portia began to tremble. "What are you talking about?"

"I CAN'T DO IT ANYMORE!" the ancient Siren screamed, her voice echoing off the crevices of the mountain range. "I'm done. I can't even bear for a moment to think that Ligeia and Proteus might have a daughter out there somewhere, *do* have a daughter out there somewhere. Who knows what traits she inherited from her parents? I'm too old—too worn out to find out! I have lived so long among Gods and mortals. So many have I buried, so many have I missed. So many have I hurt. Your own Felix I've hurt immeasurably—"

"You haven't hurt anyone, Leucosia. What are you talking about? You've only helped us all." The desperation in Portia's voice was palpable.

"Portia, don't you see? I did it to him. I caused it."

Portia looked back at her mentor, utterly confused.

"The deafness—it was my fault. I needed you to have a friend, an ally who would ride out the storm with you. I met Felix when I followed you to RPA and convinced his father to hire me. Something about him struck me. He had a maturity about him, a wisdom and a kindness beyond his six years. At that point, we had made the decision to slow down your voice until you reached womanhood. I thought that maybe I could forge a special bond between the two of you if he was unable to hear. This way you'd never feel self-conscious around him.

You'd be able to be free and honest."

Portia stared dumbstruck as Leucosia admitted her crime.

"And so at the end of second grade, I called him into my office and injected him with the virus that brought about his deafness. He doesn't remember it because I laced the injection with lotus flowers. I'm sorry, Portia. I'm so sorry. I just couldn't have it all rest on me. I needed you to have somebody other than me!"

The admission came as a terrible blow. How could Leucosia have done this?

"Is it reversible? Can you fix him now?"

"I wish I could. But the same force that prevents me from enabling Dean Fein to walk again and prevents Athena from granting sight back to Tiresias prevents me from restoring Felix's hearing, even though I myself created the damage. Besides, even if I could, I wouldn't. I wouldn't alter one thing about your relationship with Felix. *He* wouldn't alter one thing."

"Leucosia, how could you have done that? You ruined his life!"

"Yes, I did! And I regret it every day. But now he has you. And that seems to be enough for him. I know that doesn't excuse what I did, but please, let me go in peace. Let me die knowing that my crime—"

"Die? Who said anything about dying?" Portia was confused. Desperate. "OK, Leucosia. So maybe you made a bad judgment call, but it's not worth ending your life over. I mean, we all make mistakes, right?"

Leucosia reached out and stroked Portia's silken hair. With the cuff of her sleeve, she cleaned off the remnants of dark lipstick that still coated Portia's lips.

"There, you're already looking back to your normal self."

"I don't know who my normal self is, Leucosia."

"I think you do, Portia. We have all seen today just what a powerful Goddess you are. It was *you* who defeated my sisters and Proteus."

Portia dropped to her knees. "Please, Leucosia. Whatever it is you are thinking of doing, please don't do it. I don't want to be alone."

Leucosia fell to her knees, too, and gazed hard into Portia's eyes.

"You are not alone, Portia. You have wonderful friends and family who cherish and adore you. And there are Gods with whom you haven't even yet been acquainted who will delight in getting to know the new and powerful Siren whose reputation spreads even as we speak."

Realizing her pleas weren't getting her anywhere, Portia began to sob. "I'll reverse the current, Leucosia. I will. You'll keep floating back to shore."

"No, Portia. You won't. Oh, please don't cry, sweet Portia. You must think of me finally being reunited with the spirits of Nereus and Melina. In time you will recognize that this is what is best."

Portia grabbed Leucosia's hands in her own. She was desperate. She couldn't fathom a life where she would have to navigate her way through the twists and turns of immortality without Leucosia's guidance.

"I can't do it, Leucosia. I can't let you go."

A single silver tear slid down Leucosia's cheek. Portia stared at the teardrop and as it fell, the flawlessness of Leucosia's skin began to fade. Within moments, she became unrecognizable, deep wrinkles lining an age-spotted face, her fiery red hair streaked with gray, her eyelids drooping so heavily that the green of her eyes was impossible to make out.

"This is what I am, Portia. Please, you must let me go. This is what I am…"

The aged face of Leucosia was terrifying to behold. Portia had always marveled at the beauty of the Goddess, but now all she could see were the thousands of years that had taken their irreversible toll. How could she ask her to keep going?

"Why did you bring me here? Why didn't you just do it quietly? Without telling me?"

Leucosia's voice was suddenly thick with age. "When my spirit travels into the halls of Hades, dearest Portia, I want it to be blessed. Blessed to enter the Elysian Fields, blessed to command a visit with the spirits of my loved ones. If I had deceived you about my intentions, had not told you of my crime against Felix, I would have been commencing my afterlife with a lie. That is not how I want to go."

Portia wept shamelessly.

"Besides, I had to say good-bye. You have given me such great peace, Portia, and for that I must thank you. You are no less than a daughter to me, and you have made me proud. You have found the goodness that lies deep within you, have traveled beyond your voice and back again."

Leucosia stood up again and brought forth the cumbersome weight of her giant wings, whose feathers now appeared wilted and worn.

"Will you sing to me, Portia? I would like more than anything to hear you sing one last time."

Portia felt sick. How could she possibly rise to the occasion here? She thought of the beautiful school nurse who had followed her from elementary to high school, honing her expertise in checking for lice and dispensing aspirin, all so that she could keep a watchful eye on her charge.

A mental image of Leucosia coming across the webcam, scratching Hermes lovingly under his chin, popped into her mind. The joy they had shared on their first visit to Mount Olympus when together they had created miraculous music.

Portia looked up again at the old withered face of Leucosia. She felt like she was looking at a stranger. She knew then that she had to let her go.

Rising up, Portia conjured her own wings. Their emergence was still painful but nothing like what she had experienced that morning with the sisters. Her own feathers were so lustrous compared to Leucosia's. She suddenly admired the way Leucosia had camouflaged her age all these years.

With a sadness unlike any she had ever known, Portia opened her mouth to sing.

> *"Did I know all those years ago?*
> *A scraped knee and ego bruised,*

A poultice then to ease the blow,
Hurt lovingly diffused…"

The Goddesses took flight, hand in hand. Portia could feel the sudden effort it was taking for Leucosia to gain height, so she exerted extra force to help propel the aged Siren.

"You followed me for many years,
And now you are too old.
We've shared metallic silver tears,
But these ones will be gold."

They were circling the stormy waters beneath them, their molten tears falling into the waves of the sea.

"Upheld promises with patience true,
Oaths sworn in moments dying.
But now these oaths have conquered you,
And loose ends you've been tying…"

Leucosia kissed her charge gently on the forehead before prying her hand out of Portia's grip. Her wings flapped slowly, suspending her in the air just long enough to brush away the new tear that was streaming down Portia's cheek. Without another word, she turned around and began to plunge downward.

"Taught me lessons, quelled my fears,
Your product line's been sold.
We've shared metallic silver tears,
But these ones will be gold…"

Portia raised her voice as loud as she could. She swatted away at her face with fingers that became gilded with the stains of her tears.

"…A final battle you have won,
Victory is yours.
And so you feel your mission's done,
You're off to hallowed shores…"

The Sirens looked at each other one last time before Leucosia's distant form broke the surface of the dark wine waters.

"Please know that for all my years,
When my story's done and told,
They'll remember all my silver tears,
But not these ones of gold…"

Portia then turned to fly away.

"…Only for you, the gold…"

Chapter 40

The auditorium at Newark Academy was filled to capacity. RPA had hired a bus to take its students over so that they could support one of their own in the poetry slam.

Portia looked around the room. Felix was sitting a couple of rows in front of her with Gabrielle Parker. She thought of moving up, but that would defeat the purpose of the distance she had been putting between them since that day on the mountaintop.

She thought about him all the time. The way he had saved her. The way he had touched her neck, breathed beautiful words into her ears. But every memory was clouded by the confession Leucosia had made before she died. And no matter how much she tried to get that cloud to lift, it simply would not.

I'm no good for him. Look at what he's been through already because of me. I can't ask him to be with me through anything else. He deserves a life. Some normal.

These were now the thoughts that governed her actions toward him. And though he was perplexed and disappointed at her behavior, he seemed to have decided not to push the matter. At least for now. Maybe he figured she was too distraught over the loss of Leucosia. Or the harm she had inflicted upon Max.

Max.

He sat next to her, blissfully oblivious to what had befallen him. Portia took his hand and traced her finger over the deep red scar in his palm, the one that he was convinced happened during a running accident.

"So they said that you must have grabbed on hard to the road barrier when you tripped," she had told him. "It really sliced your hands open. They said that the divider gave way, though, and you ended up tumbling down the hill. You only lost consciousness for a few minutes, they think…"

She had offered him the story once he was safely stitched and bandaged—Zeus had taken on that task—and back in the safety of his bed.

He had bought it hook, line, and sinker.

A heavy blonde girl was up on the stage, delivering a powerful poem about the injustices of a world that idealizes the likes of Kate Moss.

Charlotte was up next, and Portia hoped that her friend's confidence had not waned. Portia had been ready to take on the entire task of supernaturally delivering Charlotte's poem, but she had seen a change in her friend these past weeks leading up to the big contest. With each time Charlotte practiced the poem for her, she seemed to acquire another level of fearlessness.

"The bottom line is, Portia," Charlotte had offered the other day, "standing up in a room full of people will probably pale in comparison to some of the stuff he put us through. Even if they hate me."

"They won't hate you, Charlotte. Nobody could ever hate you."

Now Portia hoped her words would prove true and was ready and willing to offer backup in case Charlotte choked.

She scanned the room to see who else had come to show their support. Her own parents sat in the front row with Janie Trotter. She knew Helena and Joshua felt tremendous guilt for never having known about the abuse that was being carried out just an acre away from their own home. Helena and Janie had actually developed a strong bond over these past months.

Jacqueline was sitting a few rows behind her with Luke and Lance. And even Zachary Wilson had made an appearance. Maybe the guy wasn't so bad after all.

The audience applauded the blonde poet who exited the stage. Charlotte walked out next, and though Portia detected a slight tremor in her neighbor's hands, her posture was taut, a look of sheer determination plastered on her face.

A hush fell over the room as Charlotte adjusted the

microphone to accommodate her elfin height. She cleared her throat and Portia straightened up, preparing herself for the worst. But from the first word uttered, Charlotte seemed to have it in the bag:

> *"A fist came, a battle axe,*
> *Upon her. Upon me.*
> *And then another.*
> *And another…"*

Portia beamed with pride at her friend who stood before the judging eyes of her peers, delivering her words with the confidence and vehemence with which she had written them.

Felix turned back toward her. "How's she doing?" he signed out.

Portia responded with a thumbs-up.

> *"And now I'm left with a name.*
> *A name I choose to claim.*
> *A name that holds the pain.*
> *A name that doles out blame."*

Max gave Portia's hand a squeeze as Charlotte continued to belt out her words. She was a quarter of the way through, and with each line uttered, she grew more resolute.

Portia allowed herself to relax a bit. She wouldn't have to throw her voice after all. She took out her phone and started typing out a text to Leucosia:

"She's doing amazing! I'm not even gonna have to—"

And then she remembered. Still, she didn't have the heart to delete Leucosia from her contact list. Seeing her name on her phone made Portia feel like Leucosia was somehow still out there. Somewhere in a world mythological, virtual, supernatural. One day those worlds would inevitably cross over one another, wouldn't they? Even if for the briefest moment? She still had so much to say, so many questions to ask.

> *"Colors can define us.*
> *Mine so often red…"*

Charlotte continued to bare her soul as the audience sat riveted. And then a sudden trip-up:

> *"Mountaintops once lush with green*
> *have witnessed deaths of Gods obscene…"*

What? Why would Charlotte have said that?

And that's when Portia felt it.

A bed of thorns. An acupuncture. A thousand tiny needles piercing her skin all at once.

A prickle unlike any other.

Epilogue

The redhead wasn't really in the mood for poetry. She much preferred the task of gathering information from the unstable Alan Hunter while pumping him full of drugs. Besides, she had spent a grueling night with Scylla trying to quiet the hostage. All of Norah Hunter's screaming about getting back to Max, to Alan, had really given her a migraine. What she really needed was to get home and take some Immitrex.

But how could she have passed up this opportunity? The entire cast of mortal characters that comprised Portia Griffin's life under one roof? It was too much of a gift to miss.

And so she took them all in, one by one. Portia's parents—her own extremely distant cousins. They were, after all, descendants of her Aunt Leucosia's, which would make them cousins how many times removed? Not worth figuring. Especially with the worsening of her headache.

Then there was the Hunter boy, who shared dimples identical to Marsyas's. Why should that have surprised her? The boy had inherited his ancestor's musical genius, so why not a physical attribute or two? Although she wondered if Ligeia's childhood friend had also possessed such disarming good looks.

And the one who might prove to be a problem. Felix Fein. Leucosia had done well to bring about the boy's deafness. She was impressed that her aunt had spotted such exceptional qualities in Felix at such a young age. The deafness would be a stumbling block to her own plans, but she was not all that concerned.

She would figure out a way.

And she would start right now.

As the slight figure of Portia's dear friend Charlotte walked onto the stage, Khloe sat upright.

She had always loved throwing her voice, had been able to do it from a very young age. But this time would be different.

Today it was not just her voice she was throwing but the first punch in a battle that promised to bring a peace that had evaded her for thousands of years.

Glossary of Silent Echo's Gods

A Modern Glossary of *Silent Echo's* Gods and a few ancient mortals. For a more illustrative guide to the Gods, please visit *www.elisafreilich.com* (WARNING - may contain spoilers!)

Achelous – God of the Rivers. With Terpsichore, Goddess of the Dance, he fathered the three Sirens, Parthenope, Ligeia and Leto.

Aphrodite – The Goddess of love.

Ares – The mighty god of War.

Athena – Goddess of Wisdom.

Dionysus – This God of Wine and Madness.

Leto – A Siren and the youngest daughter of Achelous and Terpsichore. Also known by another name.

Ligeia – A Siren, and the middle daughter of Achelous and Terpsichore.

Marsyas – A god blessed with uncanny musical ability.

Melina – The daughter of Leucosia and Nereus, married to a mortal named Nikolas.

Morpheus – The God of Dreams.

Nereus – The mortal captain of the ship held captive by the Sirens.

Odysseus – A mortal sailor who was not lured in by the song of the Sirens as he was tied securely to the mast of his ship when he heard their song.

Parthenope – A Siren, and the oldest of the three daughters of Terpsichore and Achelous.

Polyphemus – A giant Cyclops, and son of Poseidon.

Poseidon – The Great Earth Shaking God.

Proteus – A shapeshifting God, able to see the future in all matters except those clouded by love.

Scylla – A murderous Six Headed Goddess who resided right near the Sirens' favored island.

Terpsichore – Goddess of the Dance. With Achelous, God of the Rivers, Terpsichore gave birth to the three Sirens, Parthenope, Ligeia and Leto.

Themis – A Goddess with clear visions of the future.

Tiresias – A prophet who could see the future, even after his death.

Zeus – King of all the Gods.

Acknowledgments

There are so many people to whom I owe a formidable shout-out. Without the help of family and friends, *Silent Echo* might still be a story continually unfolding in my overcrowded mind rather than one being shared with readers.

David, for someone who is not a bibliophile, you sure could have passed for one during the creation of *Silent Echo*. Thank you for reading all the rounds of editing, listening to all of my ideas (no matter how inane they might have been), and for remaining the man I knew you to be at the mere age of 20. You are, without a doubt, the best decision I ever made.

Marc Frommer, a.k.a. Dad—I miss you and all of your complexities, for without them I don't think I would have stories inside me. And for the gift of words, I thank you. You were and always will remain my all time favorite wordsmith.

Alice Frommer, a.k.a. Mom—you have turned "rising to the occasion" into an art form. Every hysterical phone call, moment of doubt, frustration over rejections was met with words of wisdom that fell out of your mouth with, well, Sirenic ease. Thank you for always being there for me and for believing in me.

Abigail, Charlie and Juliette—thank you for allowing me to talk to your friends about *S.E.* ad nauseam. You are my world and have transformed our home into its own Mt. Olympus, replete with magic, wonder and discovery.

Jessica Regel—there is no better, more patient agent out there. You always had the right words for me, held my hand through so many rounds of editing and taught me the true meaning of showing vs. telling. Thanks for believing in me and in *Silent Echo*.

Mary Cummings and all the folks at Diversion Books.

Thank you all for being patient with the "nuclear reactor" that is me. Your collaborative efforts have come together and produced an elegant and wonderful result. I'm so happy to be taking this ride with you.

Amelia Wilson Ryan—you sure can design a website (and deal with a detail obsessed client)!

Jen and Rachel at Over the River Productions—you are filled with original ideas and are tireless in your efforts. Thank you!

To all my sisters-in-law (Jen, Helen, Stephanie and Phyllis)—use of "in-law" is superfluous. You are my sisters and I appreciate all of your encouragement throughout this process.

Beth, Bonnie, Jill, Yocheved and Shani—Thank you for enduring my constant chatter about SE and for all of your multiple rounds of readings (Shane—it looked great on your night table). You are all wonderful friends who have enriched my life and my creative pursuits in so many ways.

Keenah at Staples—I told you you'd get a shout out! Thanks for all the millions of times you printed out *S.E.* so that I could mark it up with the proverbial red pen. You Rock!

And to Gregory Maguire—taking fiction and spinning off more fiction from it? What a concept! Thanks for your inspiration.

About the Author

Elisa Freilich was born and raised in rural Monsey, New York, where she spent her days reading whatever crossed her path and developing a keen appreciation for the ever-present music in her home—from classical to rock. From the time she could read and write, Elisa would often be found composing poems, song lyrics and satirical newspapers.

Throughout the years, Elisa has retained her devotion to all genres of books and music and was determined to synthesize her passions into one refreshing and original platform. The result is her debut novel, *Silent Echo: A Siren's Tale.*

When Elisa is not writing, her creative outlets still abound. She is fierce with a set of knitting needles, a hot glue gun and any ingredients that can somehow be fashioned into a sinful and highly caloric babka.

Elisa lives in New Jersey with her husband and three children.

For more about Elisa Freilich and the world of *Silent Echo: A Siren's Tale,* please visit *www.elisafreilich.com*

CPSIA information can be obtained at www.ICGtesting.com
Printed in the USA
BVOW04s0633191214

380122BV00001B/9/P